VALHALLA

ABSENT WITHOUT LEAVE

VALHALLA
ABSENT WITHOUT LEAVE

BY

LEE GOLD

www.penmorepress.com

ISBN:13: 978-1-950586-77-6 (Paperback)
ISBN:13: 978-1-950586 76-9 (e-book)

BISAC Subject Headings:
FIC009100 FICTION / Fantasy / Action & Adventure
FIC010000 FICTION / Fairy Tales, Folk Tales, Legends & Mythology
FIC009080 FICTION / Fantasy / Humorous

Cover design: Book Cover Whisperer

Address all correspondence to:

Penmore Press LLC
920 N Javelina Pl
Tucson AZ 85748

Dedication

With thanks to Karen Anderson, Robert Dushay, Kathy Edwards, Barry Gold, Joshua Kronengold, Christina Paige, and Brian Rogers

ACKNOWLEDGEMENTS

Quotations from "The Childish Edda," November, 1960, by Poul Anderson and Ron Ellik are used with permission of the Trigonier Trust. The whole song can be found in *The Filksong Manual*, edited by Bruce Pelz, available as a pdf from Lee Gold. See https://conchord.org/xeno/.

CHAPTER ONE

There aren't any computers in Valhalla, the Hall of the Slain. It's near enough the root and branches that computers could work, but the master of Valhalla wants to keep the residents thinking on-mission, not distracted by video games or email or mailing lists. He doesn't use any computers either. He doesn't need to. He uses the Two Raven System instead.

Memory never smashes or crashes or leaks or eats up anything she's not supposed to. She's faster than lightning, which is after all fairly slow, especially in an atmosphere, and often arrives at her destination days before she left for it. It doesn't confuse her, but she's learned not to bother other people with the details.

Thought doesn't condescend to do anything as slow and clumsy as flying. He dwOms and (by definition) he doesn't need an IO device to do it. (Just as well, given that Jupiter's moons and Zeus's girlfriends aren't in Valhalla's known universe. Neither are you, in case you were wondering.) Thought does what Odin means. Sometimes you'll see him everywhere you look, which is disconcerting till you get used to it, and sometimes you can go ages without seeing him anywhere, which is embarrassing if you like to think you're important, because it means that Odin doesn't care about what you're doing.

The folk who live in Valhalla take it all in their stride. That's because they're heroes, the greatest warriors that the Choosers of the Slain can find in Midgard. The Choosers are Odin's daughters but they can't use his ravens. Instead, they have to get by with just swan cloaks. It's slower but prettier.

There were lots of heroes in the old days, when most humans spent most of their waking hours in Midgard, but that was back when there were more farmers and sailors and fewer engineers and programmers, more heroes and fewer bureaucrats. Nowadays most humans spend all their time in the workaday world, which is too boring to qualify as one of the Nine Worlds.

Heroes are the people whose hearts are high enough to lift them to Midgard, at least for a few minutes every now and then. Even that's enough to make them feel ill at ease in the workaday world, like wanderers who've blundered into the wrong house and can't remember the way out, let alone the way back home.

The Choosers never miss a hero. They watch over a candidate, making sure that nothing trivial goes wrong for him, watching his fighting skills grow and his reputation spread, until finally he's at the height of his glory. Then they cancel his battle luck and fly down like vultures the moment that he dies, seize his soul and bring him to Valhalla. Or maybe they seize *her* soul and bring *her* to Valhalla. The Choosers are interested in all the heroes of Midgard who die gloriously, male and female, young and old. They sneer at the warriors who get a life and a wife and a good job and worry about what their neighbors think of them and end up dying in bed, like a cow lying in a stable strewn with straw.

Anyway, the recruitment plan that had all the heroes headed for Valhalla was in place before the High Worlds War got settled and the hostages came to Asgard. Now the valkyries start by bringing the heroes of Midgard to the Lady, and she takes her pick for her party in Sessrumnir, Sitting Room Hall. She never picks a woman and she never picks a short, bald man. She never picks a man who's not drop-dead handsome. She never picks a man who doesn't have a thing for tall blondes. A big thing.

So now Valhalla only gets the leftover heroes, but they're still pretty good. They may not pack as much beefcake to the pound as the Lady's men, but they're strong and valiant and they have much more interesting ways of passing the time than just sitting quietly in a chair till it's time to go romp in the Lady's bedroom. The Valhallan heroes get to spend the nights feasting and drinking, and then they get to spend the days by going outside in the courtyard and killing each other.

The courtyard of Valhalla lies east of the main building, and it's surrounded by high walls to keep out trespassers. When Ragnarok comes the walls will fall, and the nine armies of Valhalla will march forth, each to its own target world, to fight Odin's enemies and valiantly die. But until Ragnarok comes the courtyard is a wonderful place to play. It's big enough for all the heroes to fight without feeling crowded. Most of the time they fight one-on-one, which is the most exciting form of battle. There's the hot frenzy of combat mixing with the icy chill of pain as you lop off an old friend's head or feel a sword plunging deep into your own heart and see the world around you fade to black.

You might think that killing your friends is poor practice for a fight against your enemies. Especially when your friends are all human, and the enemies you're supposed to be preparing to fight are frost giants and fire giants and hill giants and sea giants, plus trolls and ogres and wolves and snakes and eagles. You'd be right, of course. Just remember that Odin is a master of battle frenzy and deception and panic.

Valhalla: Absent Without Leave

The Valhalla courtyard is a bloody battlefield, but the pain and maiming and death aren't permanent. By sunset, the heroes are all back in Valhalla again, as good as new—no parts missing, wounds perfectly healed, teeth whole and shining, fingernails clean without any blood under them, hair neatly brushed—and that's how they stay till after breakfast when they go back out into the courtyard.

Night is when the heroes gather in Valhalla and feast together. The Choosers are their waitresses. Sometimes the girls wear swan cloaks and sometimes they wear ringmail corsets and sometimes they just wear little bits of wolfskin here and little bits of snakeskin there. They carry platters heaping with sliced meat and pitchers full of strong drink, and they listen as the heroes swap stories and brag about what they'll do tomorrow and tomorrow and tomorrow. You might find that a petty pace from day to day after you've had a century or two of it, but most heroes enjoy it.

Valhalla's one of the biggest buildings in Asgard. It has five hundred and forty doors that lead out to its courtyard; each door is wide enough for eight hundred heroes to march out through it, shoulder to shoulder, heads up, chins squared, off to the battle. The Choosers have been picking up heroes for centuries, but Valhalla still isn't full and neither is Sessrumnir. The Choosers like that, because when the halls are full they'll lose their jobs, and Asgard doesn't have unemployment benefits. You get fired, and the next thing you know you're being married off to a mortal, having babies, and dying of old age.

What bothers the Choosers is that every year there are fewer new heroes. Some people say that's because the Nine Worlds are getting dull and boring and soon it'll be time for Ragnarok, the final fight with the bad guys, the fight that everybody's planning for, the fight when everyone dies. Other people say it's because there's more competition for dead heroes than there used to be. Thought and Memory may know but they're not telling anyone in Valhalla or in Sessrumnir. They only tell their news to Odin, the All-Father, the Slain-Father, who's also known as Flame-Eyed, Deceiver, Evildoer, Master of Fear and Fury, and Much Loved. If you can't trust someone like that, you certainly shouldn't expect to trust anyone who's less powerful.

If you've got a cave of knee-high dark elves, there's always one who's just a little bit taller than the others. If you've got a room full of wise women, there's always one who's just a little bit less clever. And if you've got a hall full of heroes, there's always one who's just a little bit more apt to trip over his own feet.

There's a hero at Valhalla who's usually the first to die in each day's battle. He's the only one there who can read more than his name and a few hundred other words. His full name is Bersi Bookwyrm Beornson, but the other heroes call him Bookwyrm, and most of them try to avoid talking with him.

Then there's Bookwyrm's best friend and door-mate, the guy who starts each day's battle by killing Bookwyrm (because all the other heroes want to start off gloriously by fighting someone challenging). He's Knut Vidarson, Knut Nine-Toes, whose glorious deeds were sung far and wide across most of the northlands one slow winter week, who first found fame fighting a pack of wolves who bit off Knut's left little toe before he killed all of them, or at least that's how the skalds told the story. Knut's been dead for centuries, but he's still so fond of that nickname that he starts every day in Valhalla by drawing his sword and lopping off his left little toe all over again. In the Valhallan courtyard, Knut generally gets killed off after the first dozen but before the end of the first hundred.

Knut Nine-Toes was standing by Valgrind, Slain Gate, the

western door of Valhalla, talking to the wolf who guards it. Valgrind is Valhalla's only door that doesn't lead to the courtyard, the only door that lets you out to see the rest of Asgard. It's where newcomers sign up on the Hero List. The only other person who ever goes through it is Odin, who sometimes drops by Valhalla for dinner. He's the king of the gods and the commander of the Valhallan army, but even his oldest friends would never call him a hero. Of course, his oldest friend is the guy whose son he killed just so he could use the boy's intestines to tie his old friend up tight so he couldn't get away from the venomous snake who.... Everybody knows that story, and I don't want to be boring.

"Slow day," said Knut.

"Slow century," said the wolf. Knut had known the wolf for centuries but he didn't know his name.

Off to the west, the valkyries were dropping their prey in Thunder River, which workaday folk call the Milky Way. Most of the souls got pulled under right away. A few kept their heads above water for a while, but the river was cold and fast, and in a minute or two they got swept downstream to Hel Falls.

"I don't know why the Choosers keep at it," said the wolf. "What's the point of killing all those boys and girls off in their prime? They might as well let them get old and gray and die in bed like cows. It's been a long time since I saw a cow. Of course, Audumla was big enough to last a good long time, but eventually I cracked her last marrow bone and—"

"Look!" yelled Knut. Someone was crawling out of the river. Someone stood up and waved and headed towards them. A woman. There aren't many women in Valhalla. Some of the men in Valhalla don't mind (and that's why they didn't go to the Lady's Sitting Room). Most of the men in Valhalla stand in line and take a number to spend an hour or two with one of the women heroes who likes men. The few, the happy few, the band of sisters.... Never have so few done so much for so many.

But Knut didn't want to share a woman with a hundred other men, even if they were all heroes, and he wasn't interested in the Choosers either. The Choosers are Odin War-Father's daughters, and they have names like Battle Din and War Cry and Rager, War Axe and Battle Spear, Power and Turmoil and Panic. Very few men measure up to their standards in bed.

And now there was a new woman coming up the hill toward Valhalla, and Knut was going to be the first hero she saw. "How do I look?" he asked the wolf.

"You've got blood on your left shoe," the wolf said. "Aside from that, you look fine. How do *I* look?"

Knut rumpled the wolf's ears. "You look fine, too," he said.

Robin Jonson walked up the hill, in between the towering trees with their bright red-gold leaves. She still felt the shock of being dumped naked into ice-cold water, but the sun was warm on her face and back, and the dirt was warm under her bare feet. A flurry of leaves fell, clinging to her wet skin, and then suddenly the leaves were gone and she was wearing soft, comfortable, dry clothing. She stopped and looked down at her new clothes and saw they were the same red-gold as the leaves, a tunic and pants. She shrugged—finding herself here after she'd died was weird enough that nothing should surprise her any more.

She reached up and pulled down a small branch. It broke off in her hand, and she touched the leaves. They felt like leaves, not cloth. Then leaves and branch fell apart into tiny bright fragments and a warm wind blew them away. "I'm sorry," she said to the tree, and then looked up to see a new branch had appeared to replace the one she'd broken. This one had green leaves. She started uphill again, toward the man and the dog and the big stone building.

She felt incredibly wonderful. She wasn't short of breath, and she wasn't dizzy, and she didn't feel like throwing up, and nothing hurt. As she reached the top of the hill, she quickened her pace and felt her breasts flopping gently against her chest. You've got to pay attention. I said she got out of the river naked and then got a tunic and pants. I didn't say anything about a bra and underpants.

Robin stopped and touched her breasts, feeling each one soft and full in her hand, no lumps or tender spots, no scar tissue or scabs. Then she put her right hand up to touch her head, and felt long, cold, dripping hair. She grabbed a hank of it and pulled it around, and there it was in front of her eyes, dark brown and incredibly beautiful.

"Welcome, Robin Grima," called a woman's voice from above. "Here's your death day present."

She looked up and saw a swan flying overhead. It dropped something, and she reached up—that didn't hurt either!—and caught the thing.

It was a white sword scabbard and belt, with a silver hilt sticking out of the scabbard. She'd never seen or touched it before, but she'd known it for years. She tied the belt around her waist and pulled out the sword and looked at the shining blade. She waved the sword around in a circle over her head, waiting for it to say something, but it was silent. That meant that she wasn't in any immediate danger. Or that it wasn't really Grima's sword Frostbite.

She looked up at the sky again, but the swan wasn't there any more. She stuck the sword back in its scabbard and walked over to the massive stone building and its iron-bound door, confronting the tall, smiling, red-haired man and his large, gray, yellow-eyed—that wasn't a dog; it was a wolf!

"Greetings, Hero," said the wolf. "This is the door to

Valhalla. Can you write your name?"

"Yes, of course I—" she started indignantly, and then stopped and whispered, "Valhalla?" She'd read all the Norse myths when she was a child, and she'd studied them when she took a Viking persona, but she'd never expected—

"It means Slain Hall," the man said helpfully. "My name is Knut Vidarson, Knut Nine Toes. The wolf wants you to sign the Hero List as a pledge of loyalty to Odin. Once you've signed, you'll be home."

She looked at the black feather resting in the inkwell and at the.... She touched her fingers to the grayish-white sheet. It was too rough for paper or even for parchment. It was laced with low ridges that formed small diamonds, like a three-dimensional watermark. "What is this stuff?" she asked.

"Bark," said the wolf. Knut winced but didn't say anything. After all, it had just come out that way because they were standing in front of Valgrind where everybody speaks the language of the incoming hero. They wouldn't have to do that any more once Robin signed. After that she'd understand everyone in the Nine Worlds no matter what language they spoke.

"I've been getting a lot of bark lately," Robin said, remembering long, boring hours lying on a bed, watching the taxol made out of yew bark run down the tube and into her arm.

"Not like this you haven't," said the wolf firmly. "This is ash bark from the World Tree."

"I'm in Valhalla, and this is Yggdrasil's bark," Robin said in wonder. She picked up the feather and wrote ROBIN on the bark and looked at the dark red letters of her name. "Is that blood?" she asked, laying the feather down. The wolf was silent, trying to figure out whether to say yes or no or maybe.

"It's Kvasir's blood," said Knut, smiling at her, trying to make a good impression. "Or you could call it poet's mead or Odin's brew." Knut's father had taught him all the old kennings. "Use as much of it as you want, Shieldmaiden. It never runs out."

"Write down your nickname and family name too," said the wolf. "We've already got six Robins."

She gripped the silvery sword hilt, cool and solid and reassuring. She didn't want any of her old nicknames from her schooldays. Not Robin Hoodoo and not Lit Chick and not…. The valkyrie had called her Grima and given her Frostbite. She picked up the feather again and dipped it in the inkwell and wrote "GRIMA JONSON" and hoped that was right. Her father's name was Jacob. Should she have written Jacobsdaughter?

"Welcome home!" said the wolf, except it sounded more like "Velkomin heim!"

And then Robin felt as if she was back in the river, drowning again but this time in information. Valhalla's heroes sign in with a quill feather from Memory's right wing, so they can all access the same database. Six other Robins, and now she knew their faces and their battle strengths and weaknesses. Sixteen Knuts, and the red-haired man facing her was the least and last of them when it came to fighting other heroes in the courtyard. One hundred seventy-two Bersis, but only one Bookwyrm. Six thousand, eight hundred twenty-three other heroes….

"Wait a minute," she said. "Only 6,824 heroes? There are 540 doors to Valhalla and each of them is wide enough for eight hundred heroes."

"We don't march out touching shoulders," Knut Nine Toes said, one language ringing in her ears, another one in her mind. She tried to focus on the one she understood. "We need room to swing our weapons," he said. "That means each door is only wide enough for a shield wall of four hundred of us to walk out with our swords drawn."

"Yes, but—"

"Okay, right now there's only twelve or thirteen heroes per door," Knut said. "When I got here, there were only eight or nine heroes per door."

"When I got here, there weren't any heroes yet at your door," said the wolf. He wasn't looking at Knut or Robin; he was looking up over their heads, at the door beam. Valgrind, Slain Gate, has three guardians. There's the wolf at the door, the boar's head mounted above the door and, sitting on top of the head, the giant eagle: frost white head and body, charred black wings and tail.

The head grunted in what might have been laughter or irritation; Knut couldn't tell, and he didn't think it mattered. The head's name was Saehrimnir, Sea Boar, or at least that's what the cook said. Knut ate chunks of Saehrimnir boiled and roasted and broiled for dinner every night and saw him brought back to the kitchen again as a headless carcass every morning. Knut had been in Valhalla for eleven centuries and he'd never heard Saehrimnir's head say anything, just grunt or squeal or snort.

Sea Boar wasn't really a boar, of course. His skin had dark gray scales like a snake, and his head had a long tusk on each side of its lower jaw. His tusks didn't look like a boar's or a walrus's; they spiraled like a narwhale's horn, but they were striped in blood red and shining gold, not like a narwhale horn's pure white.

The eagle sitting on top of Sea Boar's head couldn't fly because he didn't have any feathers on his wings and tail. He didn't have any eyes in his head, but that didn't mean he couldn't see. He didn't say much, but when he did, the wolf shut up and listened. The eagle's name was Thiazi, and he was a has-been giant, and nobody in Valhalla knew why Odin trusted him to guard Valhalla. Giants are the enemy.

The kenning for eagle is "corpse-gulper" and the kenning for wolf is "corpse-troll." They're both omnivores, and they'll both eat carrion if they can't find anything fresher. But finding fresh meat to eat is never a problem at Valhalla. Saehrimnir's body is huge and tasty; the heroes love its meat and so do the hall guardians, including Saehrimnir's head, even if that does sound disgusting.

"When I got here, Valhalla only had this door," the eagle said. "Then the valkyries built the other doors, sixty of them for each of the Nine Worlds, and Odin started signing up heroes."

"Who decides which door I get assigned to?" asked Robin, thinking about standing around at grammar school recess, waiting to see which team captain was going to pick her. She knew all the heroes now—and they all knew her. They knew that she was a zero level fighter with no training and no experience; they knew that this was the first day she'd ever touched a real sword.

"You get to choose your own door," Knut said. "Bookwyrm and I are at Door Thirteen. You can always try another door if you get tired of our company."

"I'm not superstitious about thirteen," Robin said. "It's bad luck to be superstitious." Usually that got a laugh, but Knut wasn't smiling; he was nodding in agreement. "What world does Door Thirteen—" Then a wave of information swept in, and she knew that the first sixty doors of Valhalla led to Hel. Her right hand fell down to Frostbite's hilt and caressed the smooth firm metal. *"Want to go to Hel, Sword?"* she thought.

"Land of cold and shadows," the sword whispered. *"Rivers flowing with knives. Lady Hel Lokisdaughter, half corpsedark, half living. Yes, Grima! Take me to Hel!"*

The wolf growled softly, but he didn't say anything.

"Door Thirteen sounds like fun," Robin Grima said.

"Come on in," Knut said, "I'll introduce you to Bookwyrm."

"What about the others?" asked Robin, and then said, "Oh," as a new wave of knowledge swept through her from the sea of Memory's database. There weren't any other heroes at Door Thirteen. Not because the heroes of Valhalla were superstitious. Not because Bookwyrm and Knut kept getting killed off early in Valhalla courtyard. Just think of all the millions of fighters who didn't get into Valhalla at all. No, it was because Bookwyrm was a rune writer, a spell caster, and Knut was a skald, a poet. The other heroes weren't comfortable palling around with weird people like that.

True, Odin was the patron of Valhalla *and* the patron of the runes and of spells and songs and poetry, but Odin was weird too. Just having him look at you with his unblinking right eye gave you chills.

Odin drops in on Valhalla to eat dinner at least once a month. The heroes are quiet that night, and there are more leftovers from Saehrimnir than usual, even though Odin takes a huge platter for his two pet wolves, Greedy and Gobbler, and another platter for his ravens, Thought and Memory.

Odin's left eye is bobbing about in Mimir's Fountain, down in Jotunheim. Giantland. Valhalla Doors Two Hundred Forty-One through Three Hundred are set to attack Jotunheim when Ragnarok starts. Their primary mission is to defeat the giants, and their secondary mission is to capture Mimir's Fountain and fish out Odin's eye. The giants know all about it, and they've set up a special task force to guard the fountain. The heroes know all about that, and....

Everybody in the Nine Worlds knows all about Ragnarok, at least everybody who cares enough to do a little research. Everybody knows Odin's plans and Lady Hel's plans and the giants' plans. Everybody knows which people are going to fight each other and who's going to win each fight.

"I still don't understand," Robin said, looking at the wolf and then up above him at the other two Valgrind guardians. "I know I didn't die in bed, but what am I doing here? I'm not a hero."

"They cut you with sharp knives," said Saehrimnir. Knut looked up in surprise at hearing the head speak.

"They poisoned you," said the wolf.

"They burned you," said the eagle. "You didn't beg them to stop. You kept coming back for more."

"Yes," Robin said. "They cut off my breasts, and they gave me chemotherapy, and they gave me radiation treatment. They did that to a lot of women. I had to wait in line to have them do it to me. I had to *pay* to have them do it to me."

"My eyes can see all the Nine Worlds," said the eagle. "I saw you in Midgard when the earthquake shook the hospital, Robin Grima. You got up out of your bed and put on your clothes, and you helped the nurses pull patients out from under fallen machines and crumbling walls. You helped carry injured people outside and then you turned away from safety and went back into danger, again and again, even after the fire started. You didn't give up till the oxygen tank exploded and killed you."

"That's a hero's death," said Knut. "You can learn fighting skills, Robin Grima. You can't learn courage."

"You don't need to learn any fighting skills," Frostbite whispered. *"Not as long as I'm with you, Grima."*

"All right," Robin said. "I won't argue." She set her hand on Valgrind's black iron handle and then looked back at Knut. "How did *you* die?" she asked.

"A war worm bit me," he said.

A worm, Robin wondered. No, wait, she was mixing up

the two languages: the one he was speaking and the one she was hearing in her thoughts. What he'd really said was "A war *snake* bit me" or maybe "a war *dragon*." But what was—

"He's using poetic diction," the wolf said. "He means a sword." There's a good reason most heroes aren't comfortable around poets. It's hard work figuring out just what the poets are talking about.

"I was fighting a duel," Knut said. "The other guy was stronger and more experienced, but I was faster and smarter and younger, and that made us even. We ended up killing each other, but I got to Valhalla and he went to Dead Shore. Let's go have breakfast, Robin. I'm hungry."

Robin pulled the door open. There was a blare of sound like a ram's horn wailing as she and Knut walked inside.

The wolf stayed outside and watched the door shut behind them. "It's going to take her a while to get used to the way we do things here," he told the other guardians.

The leviathan head grunted.

"Or maybe vice versa," the eagle said.

Valhalla's a bright, warm hall. The ceiling is roofed with oak shields with steel bosses that shine like silver stars. The walls are made with ash spears. The floor is paved with red gold that shines like the sunset and is warm as a banked fire. Valhalla doesn't have a hearth or fire trench, but it's still bright enough that you can recognize someone a hundred paces away. The air is clear and sweet, and there isn't any smoke except sometimes a little from the kitchen, and that's full of good smells like fresh-baked bread or roast meat with garlic or apple pie.

There are nine long feasting tables at Valhalla, one for each of the Nine Worlds. There were six thousand, eight hundred and twenty-two heroes altogether sitting at the nine tables, but nobody was crowded. A table gets a little longer when a new hero signs up for it. The heroes all stood up and yelled, "Welcome home, Robin Grima." Then they raised their drinking horns toward her and yelled, "Skoal!" and drank.

A woman in a white cloak of swan feathers brought Robin and Knut a silver basin of warm water to wash their hands. Another offered them linen towels to dry their hands. A third handed Robin a drinking horn. "Drink it down, Shieldmaiden," she said. "It'll bring you good luck."

Robin didn't realize how thirsty she was till she started drinking. Then it tasted cool and refreshing and sweet and incredibly good, and she gulped it down while the heroes beat their weapons against their shields and shouted her name.

When the horn was empty, the valkyrie took it from her and turned it upside down to show it was empty. The heroes cheered one last time, then sat down at their tables and resumed their eating.

Robin turned back to Knut. "What happens now?" she asked.

"We eat breakfast until mid-morning," he said. He led her across the room to the first table, the one with a stone carving of a woman standing at its head: her left side snow white; her right side flame red. They walked down the table to Section 13, marked with the rune Yew (like a downward slanting angular S in the Roman alphabet).

Breakfast in Valhalla is a light meal, at least compared to dinner. There's hot porridge and bread, butter and cheese, apples and nuts, and a dozen different kinds of cold herring, plus cold slices of Saehrimnir, You can eat all you want and never gain weight or even have high cholesterol. Drinking is more complicated. You can drink all the ale and beer and mead you want at breakfast and never get more than a little tipsy, and that goes away the moment you go out to the courtyard to fight. Dinner drink is stronger. Nobody ever gets sick and has to throw up, but you can get falling down, fall asleep with your face in your plate drunk if you keep on drinking long enough in the evening. Then you wake up in the morning without a hangover, hungry for breakfast, with your liver in perfect condition.

Bookwyrm was waiting for them at Section 13, carving runes in the table with his eating knife and coloring them with red sour cream from the platter of pickled herring with beets and cucumber. The table would be healed by dinnertime, just like the heroes. Magic runes are colored with blood: either the spellcaster's blood or the sacrifice's blood. These runes didn't have any magic power; that's why the heroes in Sections 12 and 14 were still sitting there, eating, instead of moving over to somewhere safer.

Robin looked at the table and saw what she knew were runes: a P-like letter, an M-like letter.... She waited for a wave of knowledge but nothing happened. Her hand dropped to her sword hilt. *"I need subtitles, Sword,"* she thought. *"This is your culture, not mine."*

Knut traced the runes one by one with his left little finger and said slowly, "Wynn and Eoch and Lagu is Wel." ("V and E and L is Vel," echoed his voice in Robin's mind.)

"It's your culture too, Grima," Frostbite whispered. *"You're not living in Kansas or California any more. You're not living anywhere any more. Do you still have your dice, or did you lose them when you died? If you don't have your dice, then how can we tell which one of us is on top today?"*

"K and O and M is Kom," said Knut. "She's here, Bookwyrm. Stop writing and greet her."

"Subtitles," Robin Grima thought firmly. *"I'm the one who was cut and poisoned and burned, not you, Sword. I'm the one the river couldn't drown. I'm the one who signed the*

Hero List. I could go outside right now and throw you in the river, and then come back in here again and have an adventure without you."

"*It was just a joke,*" the sword whispered, and she saw "VELKOMINHEIMROBING" appear in Century Gothic under the line of runes and, under that, a third row of letters in Times New Roman that read "Welcome home, Robin G".

Bookwyrm looked up from carving the R of Grima. "The first robin brings the spring with her," Bookwyrm said, "and if you wish on her, your wish will be granted. Make a wish, Knut."

"I wish that you win today's weapon storm," Knut said. Weapon storm is a kenning for battle. So is whirlpool of swords and assembly of chainmail and din of shields. If you google, you can find a webpage with nearly two thousand kennings. It's got over six dozen kennings for battle and less than a dozen kennings for drinking and dancing and food and sex combined, which could be fun if you tried it with the right friends. That shows what Viking poets and their audiences were and weren't interested in. This isn't a Viking poem, in case you haven't noticed.

"That's a wasted wish," Bookwyrm said. "You should have spent it on something useful, Nine Toes, or saved it for a better time. Talk sense or be silent. A glib tongue that goes on chattering sings to its own harm." Those last bits were from the *Havamal*, which is one of the Poetic Eddas. There's a good reason most heroes aren't comfortable around rune readers. They quote Odin's insults to you, and if you object, then you're criticizing Odin, who doesn't have a sense of humor about that sort of thing.

"I never heard about making a wish on the first robin," Robin said. "Some people say if a robin flies into the house it means someone's going to die, but that's just a superstition and it's bad luck to be superstitious."

Bookwyrm laughed at her joke. Then he looked serious and said, "Cattle die, kinfolk die, every man is mortal. Almost everyone here in Valhalla is going to die today, Robin Grima. But that's what happened yesterday too, and here we are again. A good name never dies, and neither does your name on the Hero List." He picked up his knife again and carved an I, pleased at how he'd worked in two more bits from the *Havamal*: "cattle die, kinfolk die, and every man is mortal" and "a good name never dies."

"If someone from Table Thirteen wins today's weapon storm, it won't be like yesterday," Knut said.

"What are the rules?" Robin asked, helping herself to a spoonful of each kind of herring and a couple of rolls.

Knut pushed the basket of red apples over to her. "Eat one every day," he said, "and two if you start feeling tired. They're from Idunn's storehouse, and they'll keep you feeling young and energetic."

"There aren't any rules," Bookwyrm said without looking up from the M he was carving. "Rules are for going to an island with a sword and a shield and fighting a duel with someone else honorable. We're practicing to fight Helfolk. Brother shall strike brother, sharp swordplay and shields clashing. A wind-age, a wolf-age till the world falls in ruins. No one shall show mercy. Backstabbing is fine, and so is fighting a dozen to one, and so is using magic."

"Only he won't do it," said Knut. "He knows how to cut them, read them, stain them, prove them...."

Hold them and fold them, Robin thought, but she assumed they'd never heard of Johnny Cash or "The Gambler," so she didn't say it out loud, just kept eating the apple.

"...evoke them, score them, and send them," Knut said, "but he won't do it. He just lets the sword shakers butcher him." He helped himself to a bowl of steaming hot porridge and a silver spoon and began eating. Back when he was alive, he'd only had wooden or bone spoons, but Odin can afford the best tableware.

Robin finished her apple and started in on the herring.

"It takes too long," said Bookwyrm. He carved an F-like rune that the subtitle said was the last letter of Grima, and looked up at Robin. "By the time I got done cutting the runes and staining them and evoking them, I'd be dead." He dipped his fingers into the sour cream and beets, then ran them across the fresh-carved runes, dyeing them red like the others.

"There are other ways to use magic," said Robin, and drew Frostbite and laid it across the table, where it promptly froze Knut's bowl of steaming hot porridge and turned a pitcher of mead into something stronger with ice chunks floating in it.

"*Will you help my friends, Sword?*" she thought. "*Yes, Robin Grima, I will always help your friends as long as they are fighting for your cause,*" Frostbite whispered.

"Touch your blade to it, Bersi Bookwyrm," she said, "and we'll see what happens."

The Dungeons and Dragons games had started in the cancer support group after a visiting lecturer told the patients that they should try visualizing themselves killing their cancer, and they thought that it would be fun doing it with magic swords and magic spells. Barney's lung cancer had spread to his brain and killed him and George, his golden dragon cleric ("Saint George *is* the dragon!"), but Gregorio's adult acute lymphoblastic leukemia had gone into remission and Blanco, his knight in white armor, dropped out of the game after Gregorio's five year checkup. Malik's prostate cancer was still watchfully waiting after radiation and chemo and estrogen treatments, but it hadn't tried to metastasize in the last four years. Robin's breast cancer kept going into remission and then coming back, but she never gave up; Grima the ninth level Viking fighter never gave up.

They'd found Frostbite in Barney's dungeon when they killed a fire ogre mage, back when Grima was only fourth level and Robin was almost done with her second round of chemo. "Nonstandard Frost sword," the weapon card said. "Name: Frostbite. Ego 12, Intelligence 12. Telepathic communication with wielder but can't speak out loud. Able to dominate wielder below Level 12. Plus three to hit and damage. Plus six to hit and damage against fire creatures. Extraordinary power: Freezes liquids its point touches (but any liquid over a gallon gets a saving throw). The wielder is immune to fire and ice damage. Frostbite can at will have this effect: Any non-magic steel or iron weapon that touches Frostbite's blade for at least 1 round will acquire the same abilities for 1 day."

That last sentence meant she'd kept Frostbite in its scabbard against enemies with metal weapons if she thought the sword might be tempted to trade up, but most of the dungeon monsters Grima faced didn't carry weapons; they had their own special attacks. Glioblasters touched you with their snaky tentacles, causing weakness or blindness or muteness. Carcinumbs were soft, bouncy nerf balls, and anywhere they touched you, you went numb. Boners were skeletons with huge erect penises ("We're all adults here, and this is an R-rated game," Gregorio said) that squirted blood now and then, and every time that happened they'd scream, loud and startling, and their touch was burning pain. Limp-wights were white skeletons too; their kicks could break your leg, and even Cure Serious Wounds would never properly heal it; you'd always limp afterwards. There were lots of cancer monsters in the dungeons. When they read the Web, they weren't just looking for new treatments; they were looking for new dungeon ideas.

"Go ahead," Knut said. "Try it."

Bookwyrm shrugged and drew his sword and put it down on the table, crossing Frostbite. Knut drew his own sword and put it on top.

"All for one, and one for all," said Robin, "just like the Three Musketeers."

"I've never heard of that saga," said Knut. He tried taking another spoonful of porridge, but his spoon was frozen in the bowl. He shrugged and picked up another spoon and helped himself to some herring in sour cream.

"It's a novel by Dumas," said Robin. "I can tell you the story."

"Valhalla doesn't have a library," Bookwyrm said, "but Saga's hall does. Can you read, Robin Grima?"

"I can read English and a little French," Robin said. Then she pointed at the runes he'd carved, "And I can read those too but it might take me longer."

"Then you can read me the saga of the Three Musketeers," said Knut.

The horn blew twice, and some of the heroes got up from the tables. "Soon the fight starts," said Knut. "Do you hold your sword one- or two-handed, Robin Grima? And do you want to wear a bear's shirt?"

"I'm not a berserk," Robin said. "And I mostly hold my sword one-handed." ("*Yes,*" whispered Frostbite.)

"Bare is back without brother behind it," said Bookwyrm. "We ought to discuss the details of that one for all and all for one battle formation."

CHAPTER TWO

The sun was sinking toward the horizon. (Anyone who wants to hear the details of ten hours of fighting should go away and read a Viking saga.) Robin and Knut and Bookwyrm were still going hot, and their swords were still glowing cold.

No, they didn't have shields, and neither had any of the people they'd been fighting. A Norse wooden shield (between a quarter-inch and half an inch thick, never thicker, with an iron stud in the center) might last a few minutes in a formal island duel, but the only way it's useful in a real battle is when a bunch of warriors get together in a formation, and that's not the way heroes usually like to fight. Heroes like the glory of showing off how good they are when they fight single-handed.

They didn't wear armor either, although a few wore helmets. The stronger armor is, the heavier it is, and the more it slows you down and tires you out and makes you thirsty. Some Norse armies went into battle wearing chainmail, but most heroes refuse to wear it in Valhalla. Their armor is their flickering swords.

The tall warrior nicknamed Beewolf dropped his broken

sword and drew his knife. "My bright blade is bitter with blood," he bragged. "Beware of its bite."

"I don't accept alliterative bragging blindly," said Knut.

"False friends can fool and outfox you," agreed Bookwyrm. "Vainly was it spoken, for it avails you naught." He kicked the ribs of the berserk who lay motionless in front of him, his spear parrying Beewolf's knife, while Knut stepped forward to cut off Beewolf's arm and watch the man's gushing blood freeze into red icicles.

The berserk abruptly rose up on his knees, his sword slashing upward. Bookwyrm jumped out of its way and stomped on the berserk's wrist till the sword fell back on the courtyard stones, then started kicking the berserk's head. Knut came over and joined him. There's no point in using a sword on berserks, even a magic sword; steel won't bite them and fire won't burn them and ice won't freeze them. You have to either club them with a fresh-cut branch or strangle them with fresh-cut vines or use your own fists and feet and teeth against theirs.

With Knut and Bookwyrm both busy, that left Robin Grima and Frostbite to take care of the three other heroes still attacking them. One of them took off his helmet and threw it at her. It burst into flames, but she caught it with her left hand and threw it back. It struck the middle man's helmeted head with a clang, and he slumped to the ground, his long braided red hair burning. Frostbite snaked out to sever the third hero's left ankle and then rose delicately to the bare-headed woman's throat and drove through it, so the frozen blood spattered out like red hailstones.

"Who's next?" whispered Frostbite.

"You're bloodthirsty, Sword," Robin Grima thought.

"Only for your enemies' blood," Frostbite whispered.

The burning man rose to his knees and threw a knife. Frostbite slapped it out of the air onto the ground, and Robin

Grima lunged forward to skewer the man's chest. He screamed and dissolved into mist, another phantom. There had been a lot of phantoms to fight this day. Door Thirteen had three hundred ninety-seven phantoms who walked out side by side with Knut and Bersi and Robin, and then tried to kill them. One of Odin's names is Battle-blinder.

The three comrades clustered together, back to back to back, looking out across the courtyard. All the bodies lay still. Better yet, they'd all stopped bleeding.

"Last round," cried a valkyrie watching them from the rooftop.

"That *was* the last round," said Knut. "We're not going to fight one another. Today's weapon storm is over, and we're the winning warriors."

"All for one, and one for all," said Robin.

"The sun is setting," said Bookwyrm. "Praise the day when it ends, and the sword when you've tried it, and the maid who keeps her promise. Praise the fight when it's over. My throat is dry, Chooser. Bring us our drinks."

The valkyrie flew down and handed them each a gold-bound horn of mead.

Robin Grima started to lift it to her lips, then looked at her door-mates and raised it on high the same way they were doing. "To our king and commander, our lord and leader, High One and Hanged One," Knut Nine Toes said.

"Id est Furor," said Bookwyrm. "Fury and Frenzy and Fear, All-Father and Slain-Father."

"To Odin," said Robin Grima and felt the name strong and sweet on her lips. She washed it down with the liquid in her horn, and that was strong and sweet too. "What is this stuff, anyway?" she asked. "I know it's not beer or ale or wine."

"Goat's milk," said Knut. "The eddas say that the Valhalla roof-goat's milk is mead, but I think it tastes more like apple cider."

"Our roof-goat nibbles on the World Tree," Bookwyrm said, "and its bears ash honey and beehives, not apples."

They went back into the hall singing "Gaudeamus Igitur" in three different languages and stood at the head of the tables while the other heroes came up to congratulate them and tried to make polite conversation with Robin Grima Jonson. There wasn't any food on the tables yet. The Valhalla cook understands that after you've been killed, you've got to get a little drunk before you're up to eating meat.

"Jonson," one hero said. "I had a cousin who lived in Ireland named John. Maybe we're related." A second asked where she'd lived and, after she'd explained that she'd grown up in Topeka and gone to school in Los Angeles and that both cities were in Vinland, he asked if they still had much trouble over there with the Skraelings, which meant the Native Americans. A third asked who her godi had been (a godi is a sort of a cross—oops, wrong religion; crosses are Christian—a sort of mixture of priest and politician), and she couldn't remember the name of the hospital chaplain or her district representative in DC or Sacramento. A fourth asked her how she'd come to be nicknamed Grima, the masked woman, and got very confused when she tried explaining first Dungeons and Dragons and then the Lone Ranger. ("Who *was* that masked woman with the silver sword?" the game master's characters used to exclaim after she rescued them, and all the players would laugh.)

Robin Grima kept drinking. The questions got sillier and sillier, but it would be rude to laugh. Everyone here was a hero, and some of them were famous enough that she'd even read their sagas. "I was sick and weak too," Grettir the Strong said, "when I died in my last fight. Did a witch curse you, Robin Grima?"

"Gaudeamus igitur," sang Bookwyrm, starting over again, "juvenes dum sumus." "Therefore let us rejoice while we are young," Robin's mind heard. "Death comes quickly and snatches us up atrociously." (Yes, Bookwyrm was running lines from two different verses together, but it was on purpose. Valhallan heroes don't have to worry about "molestam senectutem," a troublesome old age, so there's no point in singing about it.)

"No," Robin Grima said, "nobody cursed me, and I wasn't an outlaw, just a university student." She was a college freshman the first time the cancer showed up, and covered by student insurance. She was a junior when her first remission ended and the cancer came back. After that, she kept switching majors, kept taking easier and easier classes, so she could keep her student health insurance, because nobody was going to hire her when she wasn't up to working eight hour days more than three weeks out of four.

"The world needs rune readers too," Grettir said, smiling at Knut and Bookwyrm, then heading away before either of them said something he didn't understand.

"I could read and write letters," Ermentrude said proudly. "When the king of England sent me a handsome young Jutlander with a letter asking me to kill him, I tore it up and wrote myself a new letter begging me to marry the messenger." She shook her head sadly. "I'll introduce you to my first husband when we march against Hel. My handsome Amleth was doomed to Nastrond for treacherous murder because he got his uncle drunk and then killed him with his own sword. Even taking blood vengeance for your father isn't enough to excuse something that cowardly." Robin agreed and decided it wouldn't be polite to tell Ermentrude about how Shakespeare had changed Amleth's story.

After a while, the valkyries started bringing platters of food and pitchers of drink out from the kitchen.

"I thought for sure he'd come tonight," Knut said. "A new hero for the first time in years, and she lasts to the end of her very first day of combat in the courtyard, but if he hasn't come by now—"

"They haven't set up his wine table," Bookwyrm said, carefully not saying "Odin" because that might draw the master of Valhalla's attention. "If he's not here by now, then he's not coming. Hail to the one who knows, joy to the one who understands, and delight to those who listen. Let's head off to Saga's library before we're too drunk to find it."

"Do they have food in Saga's library?" Robin asked.

"Food for thought and food for teeth," Bookwyrm said, "and drink enough to wash it all down."

They left the hall still singing. "Bibit hera, bibit herus, bibit miles, bibit clerus," sang Bookwyrm. "Trinkt die Herrin, trinkt der Herr, trinkt der Ritter, trinkt der Pfaffe," sang Knut. "The lord drinks, the lady drinks, the soldier drinks, the cleric drinks," sang Robin.

Outside, the night sky was bright with aurora asgardis, flickering across the heavens like spears of gold, like a rain of blood, like silver icicles. The aurora asgardis are Odin's daughters, the valkyries, dancing in the sky with their shields and swords and spears and swan cloaks. Even when there's a big battle brewing in the mortal world, and the valkyries circle overhead, waiting for heroes to die, there are still hundreds of off-duty valkyries flying over Asgard, so it never gets really dark at night. With all that light pollution, you can still see the moon (unless it's new moon) but you can't see the stars, not even the Pole Star. Astronomers and astrologers try to avoid going to Asgard when they die.

Knut and Bookwyrm and Robin Grima walked across Asgard singing "Five Hundred Forty Doors in the Hall" in three languages, to the tune of "A Hundred Bottles of Beer on the Wall." They sang it as they crossed the plain of Idavoll, passing by gold-roofed Gladsheim and silver-roofed Vingolf. "If Door 327's heroes should meet us and fall, there'd be one door's less heroes to fight when we call," they sang, as they took the path that leads downhill to Saga's hall.

The air got colder with every step Robin Grima took. Saga's hall is built next to a calm shallow river whose cool waters are bright with clusters of ice crystals. The hall's glittering walls look like diamond or crystal or ice or pearl. Robin looked at it and thought of Superman's polar Fortress of Solitude. "I should have brought a cloak," she said, her teeth chattering. "Is Saga's hall colder than this?"

"It's a warm night," Knut said.

"It's her first time here," said Bookwyrm. "Praise her, Nine Toes."

"Don't blame me," Frostbite whispered. *"Immune to fire and ice damage means heat and cold won't kill you. It doesn't mean they won't make you uncomfortable."*

"Robin Grima's repute is rising in glory," Knut said, and Robin felt her face grow warm. Was she blushing? This was like a mild version of the hot flashes that started when chemotherapy sent her into menopause at nineteen. They started in her face and then spread downwards till even her feet were hot and sweaty. But this warmth wasn't uncomfortable; it felt wonderful.

"The Choosers are bragging of their wise choice," Knut chanted. "Her sword imparts power to all blades that touch it. She cut blood runes with it and won every fight. She won brave men's eyes with her grace and her beauty. Her first day at Slain Hall will be sung of forever. All hail, Robin Grima, Valhalla's new hero."

"Thank you," said Robin Grima. "It feels summer warm to me too now."

"The meter limped," Knut said modestly. "There wasn't enough alliteration, and it would sound better with kennings, but you don't like kennings so I'm trying not to use them."

"It's not that I don't like them," Robin said. "I just don't understand them."

"Teach her a new one every day at breakfast," Bookwyrm said. "That's how my father taught me."

"My father taught me a new poem every Odin's Day," Knut said. ("Every Wednesday," Robin heard.) "Then we spent the rest of the week unknotting the poem's kennings. Until my twelfth year came, and my father departed."

"That's when Knut started limping," said Bookwyrm. "Tell her how you got your name, Nine Toes."

"The winter wind blew at our doors and our windows," Knut said. "The wild wolves came walking into our home, dealing death until sated they slumbered. I seized a sword and vowed to take vengeance. One by one I woke them and called out my challenge. 'Wake up!' I shouted. 'This is your death day!' The wolves howled; they ran to my sword blade. When the fighting was finished, I bore only one wound. Their leader's last act was to bite off my toe. That was the day I was nicknamed Knut Nine Toes."

Robin Grima clapped her hands in applause. "That was wonderful, Knut. You may limp, but your story didn't. What's your nickname story, Bookwyrm?"

"Drifa, my wife, burned to death in a fever," he said. "My luck died with her, and I was alone. My enemies gathered, nine men at nightfall. They crept up upon me like craven cowards. They set a fire; I woke up in flames. I ran to my runebooks and looked for an answer. My book learning taught me to bind them and blind them. They were roped by the runes drawn with blood on my body. They saw me transformed to a figure of fire, a dark-hearted dragon breathing bright flames. They trembled in terror and perished in panic. The flames fiercely fed on their treacherous flesh, leaving ashes as black as their hearts and their deeds. My close neighbors and kin of the killings called me Book Dragon in praise of my skill."

Robin applauded again.

"Now tell us how you earned your nickname Grima, masked woman," Knut said.

"I can't tell it as well as you two told yours," Robin said.

"We've had centuries of practice," Knut said. "Tell it as well as you can, and I'll help you turn it into poetry."

They were standing just outside Saga's crystal hall, its bright walls flickering with color under the aurora asgardis. A light snow was falling out of the cloudless sky, but the air was warm on Robin's face and hands, and the soft powder snow under her feet felt warm too, as warm as Knut's praises.

"There were four of us in the cancer therapy support group," Robin said, "and they told us to fantasize ourselves killing our cancer, so we started a roleplaying game. My pretend character was a Viking fighter named Grima. I didn't know Grim meant mask until I went to the library and started rereading the Norse myths. I just thought it meant stern and unrelenting and in a bad mood, which is how I felt when I thought about dying of metastasizing breast cancer."

"Cancer's a bad death," agreed Knut, "hurting and helpless, weak and woebegone, lying in linen like a steer in the stable straw, not fiercely fighting like a weaponed warrior."

"Now tell her how to tell people her story," said Bookwyrm.

"Her body turned traitor," said Knut. "Her breasts harbored bane-flesh. They sharpened their short swords and cut her to cure her, but the bane-flesh was stronger than all her skilled surgeons. They tried every poison but the bane-flesh persisted. Their flames burned her body, but the bane-flesh kept breeding. They told her to dream of destroying its danger. She made up a mask and she named herself Grima, a high-hearted hero who frostbit her foes."

The shining hall door swung open before them.

Robin had expected to see a library full of shelves of books and scrolls. Or maybe a brightly lit feast hall like Valhalla. Instead what she saw was a blizzard of white snow and twinkling silver stars.... She walked inside and put out her hand and caught a star. It turned into a white parchment book whose title page said *Lokasenna*, Loki's Insult Contest. If you haven't read the *Lokasenna*, let me recommend it. It's a lot of fun, just like listening to Ratatosk, the clever squirrel who runs up and down the World Tree with all the latest news. If you want to make sure you haven't missed anything, you should read his blog: http://9www.ratatosk.yg. (No, that's not Yugoslavia. Yg is the code for Yggdrasil, the World Tree; don't bother googling for it unless you've got Nine Worlds Web access.)

"It helps to concentrate," said Bookwyrm. He put out his hand and caught a book and showed it to her and Knut. It said *The Three Musketeers*. He opened it and started reading.

"It always helps to concentrate," whispered Frostbite. *"You can depend upon it, Grima, when a man knows he is to be hanged, it concentrates his mind wonderfully. That's why Odin Gallows-Burden hanged himself on the World Tree when he wanted to take up the runes."*

"You're wrong, Sword," Robin Grima thought. *"I spent eight years knowing I was going to die of cancer, and all I ever learned from it was to focus on the here and now: the textbook I was reading, the test I was taking, the next step of the treatment plan. And, besides, you're quoting Dr. Samuel Johnson, and when he said that he was lying. Johnson knew that Dodd hadn't written all those pleas for mercy: Dodd's last speech at the trial, his sermon before he*

went to jail on "What Shall I Do to be Saved?", his petitions from jail to the lord chancellor and to the king, and even his death day declaration to the sheriff. Dr. Johnson wrote every single one of them, and he never admitted it till after Dodd was executed."

Robin's first major had been English Literature. Her last major was Recreation Studies, and she was the only one in her classes who wasn't on a sports team. She wrote a term paper for one class on upper body exercises after a double mastectomy that the professor said was good enough that she didn't have to take the final, which she appreciated because she was scheduled for radiation that day. That's why she was at the hospital when the earthquake knocked it down, and not at the university where the buildings surfed the seismic waves and stayed intact. Some victories are worse than defeats.

Have you noticed yet that I'm not the conventional omniscient narrator because I've got too much personality? Are you wondering how I came to know all this stuff about Robin Grima Jonson? Are you wondering what my name is? No, I'm not Knut or Bookwyrm or Frostbite or Robin or any of Valhalla's guardians. Yes, you've heard of me, at least if you've been paying attention to what I've told you. For now, just go ahead and wonder. Eventually I'll tell you almost everything.

"Concentrate anyway," whispered Frostbite.

Robin sat down in a comfortable leather armchair and began to reread the *Lokasenna*, not noticing that sometimes she was reading the third line in English and sometimes the second line in transliterated Norse and sometimes the first line in runes, not noticing when she started chanting it aloud. The story started out at the sea king's palace, at an ale feast with enough drink to fill a brewing cauldron the size of the ocean basin.

After a while all the references to ale began making her thirsty, and that reminded her that she hadn't had dinner yet. *"All right, Sword,"* she thought, *"Bookwyrm said they'd have food and drink here. I want a glass of something cold and wet and a menu that's got more choices on it than herring or sea pig. I'm concentrating."*

"Drink joyfully," said the waiter. Robin Grima looked up and saw a goblet of bright gold on the dark wood table in front of her and her door-mates. She raised it to her lips and tasted cool bubbly dry apple cider with a slight sting of alcohol.

"And what would you like for dinner, Hero?" asked the waiter. "Pork chops? Beef pie? Goose? Smoked salmon? Lamb chops? Baked eels?"

"Goose," Robin said, and the hot platter slid down in front of her: half of a cut-up roasted goose surrounded by small baked apples. "Now where do I put my book while—"

"Your hands won't get it dirty," the waiter said. "Is there anything else, Hero?"

"No," she said, and he disappeared into thin air just like a phantom except that nobody had killed him. She picked up her eating knife and stabbed a goose wing and brought it up to her mouth. On her right, Bookwyrm's lips moved as he read his book and dug his spoon into his pie. Knut's right index finger traced a line of runes that were too far away for Robin to read, and he gnawed at the pork chop he held in his left hand. She looked back at the *Lokasenna.*

"I'm missing my hand," Tyr said to Loki,
"but the trade took its toll on your son Fenris too.
The mighty wolf's bound fast, waiting and watching,
till Ragnarok rounds off the fate of the rulers."

"Now Loki's bound fast too," whispered Frostbite, *"forger of evil, waiting till Ragnarok."*

"He wasn't evil at first," Robin thought. *"Just a practical joker."*

"Either way, he's not a safe person to trust—if the Lokasenna's right."

"Odin kept trusting him," Robin thought. *"Who should I trust here, Sword?"*

Frostbite didn't answer.

Robin looked back at the *Lokasenna.*

"You shall not run free," Skadi said to Loki.
"They'll tie you up tight so you cannot escape,
bound with the bowels of your frost-cold son.
I'll set a snake to keep watch upon you,
to thrust its fangs deep into your lying mouth,
dripping a venom so you writhe in torment."

Robin Grima finished the book and the goose and the cider all at once, and then stood up and stretched.

"Time to head home," said Bookwyrm, and Knut put down his book too and put his pork chop bones in one of the bags tied to his belt. The auroras were still dancing across the sky as they walked back home, and Robin taught her friends a song she'd heard at a science fiction fan convention, "The Childish Edda" by Poul Anderson and Ron Ellik, to the tune of "The Ballad of Jesse James." The valkyries flew down low above them to hear Robin singing the strange new lyrics that told the old stories.

"Frigga took a year or so and, except for mistletoe,
Got from everything an oath for Baldur's good.
Evil Loki wished him harm, so he hired Hodur's arm—
And the staff the blind god threw was kissing-wood.

"Tyr vowed Fenris-wolf his hand if he couldn't break
  the band
That All-Father's wisdom made both light and hefty;
Lupine muscles strained away, but the magic held its
  sway—
And until the end of Time they called Tyr 'Lefty.'

"Yggdrasil, where Nine Worlds flash is a noble piece of
  ash
That shelters Norns and Gods and all that crew;
There's a dragon gnaws the base of an eagle's resting
  place
And four harts, a goat and squirrel complete the zoo."

A rumble of thunder came from a nearby hall.

"That used to be Red Thor's hall," Knut said, "but he doesn't live there any more. He went to Jotunheim one day, but afterwards, when he was trying to get back to Asgard, he had a quarrel with an old ferryman called Harbard, who turned out to be Odin in disguise."

"Harbard Odin told Thor that his mother Jord had died," said Knut.

"Jord means earth," Bookwyrm said.

"But if Thor's mother is Mother Earth, how can she die?" said Robin, confused. "The land can't die!"

"Jord isn't Mother Earth," said Bookwyrm. "She's just a hill giant."

"Odin was teasing him," Knut said. "It was a senna, an insult contest. Odin and Loki loved insulting each other, and Odin was trying to get Thor to learn the game."

"'Odin takes the noble hearts who fall in the fight, and Thor takes the race of thralls,'" said Bookwyrm, quoting the *Harbardsljoth*, Harbard's Poem.

The hall flashed suddenly bright, lighting up the landscape into color and dazzliing their eyes, then went dark again as thunder rolled and the ground shook under their feet. (Like a house shaking when there's a sonic boom, Robin thought.) Knut made the sign of Thor's Hammer.

"And Thor got so angry at Odin's insults that he took his wife and children away from Asgard and swore he wouldn't come back till Ragnarok," said Bookwyrm.

"When I went to the great temple at Uppsala," Knut said, "they had statues of Thor and Odin and Frey, but Thor's statue stood in the center."

"The great temple was for the people's sacrifices," Bookwyrm said. "Farmers begged Thor to save them from famine, and traders begged him to send them good sailing weather. I was a farmer and a trader, and I know it's a thrall's life. When you're on your own land, you work for your fields and your animals, and when you're abroad you work for your ship and your silver chest. The prophecies don't say that Thor's hallfolk will fight at Ragnarok."

Robin went back to "The Childish Edda."

"When Thor went out to fish, he quickly got his wish
And he hauled Jormungandr from the bay;
But Hymir cut the cable, and Thor was only able
To brag about "the one that got away."

"When Thor called on the Giants, they didn't show
defiance,
But they soon got rid of him and of his hammer.
For the sea he could not swallow, and old Grandmaw beat
him hollow,
And the house-pet caused an awful katzenjammer."

The others joined in on the chorus. Then Robin asked,

"Where did Thor build his new home?" And then, when no one answered, "Which of the Nine Worlds did he move to?"

"No one's seen him since he left Asgard," Knut said, "but the common folk still prayed to him back when I was alive. Maybe he moved to Midgard. Maybe he moved farther away. Was there lightning in your home in Vinland, Robin Grima?"

"We called it electricity," Robin said, "and nobody prayed to Red Thor."

"He has other names," Knut said.

"Go back to the song," Bookwyrm said. "A couple more verses should bring us back home to Valhalla."

"Each god's apple every day kept the doctor far away
Till a Giant kidnapped Idunn from their halls.
Loki fetched home Bragi's bride with her health-food
    store beside,
Plus a char-broiled eagle underneath the walls.

"Odin said to Mim, 'I think I would sort of like a drink.'
Mim said, 'That will cost you your left eye;
For you've come so very late to the well at Wisdom's Gate
And the set-up prices after hours are high.'"

They sang a last chorus and went back through the wide doors into Valhalla. A few heroes were still eating and drinking and a few more lay asleep on their benches, but most of the benches were empty—and turned over on their sides, lifting up the golden floor beneath them to disclose stairs that led down to a dim lower floor.

"The bed closets are down there," Knut said, "unless you want to sleep on a bench."

"There are small bed closets for people who want privacy," Bookwyrm said, "and larger ones for people who want company."

"I'm used to sleeping alone," Robin said, a little nervously. She'd tried sex a couple of times with Barney, but she was dry because of the menopause, and they couldn't figure out how much lubricant to use. Too little, and it was like sandpaper, and the friction hurt both of them; too much, and there wasn't enough friction to get him excited, or at least that's what he said. Maybe it was because she didn't have breasts any more. Maybe it was because he was too tired from his own chemo. Maybe it was because they didn't love each other. They decided to give up trying for a while, and then a couple of months later, he died.

They walked downstairs and she got her first look at a bed closet. The floor was knee-high and cushioned by a soft feather mattress covered with blood-red silk sheets with a pile of pillows at one end, but it was less than five feet long, because the Norse slept sitting up. Robin told herself that she could sleep in an airplane seat or a bus seat, and she could sleep here too.

She took off her sword and tucked it behind the pillows, got into bed and closed her eyes, relaxed fully for the first time in eight long years, and fell fast asleep.

****

Knut Nine Toes woke up early and looked around, but Robin Grima's and Bookwyrm's bed closets were still closed. He sat on the side of his bed and drew his sword and cut off his left little toe. Then he got dressed and limped upstairs, carrying his bag of pork chop bones. He went outside Valgrind and greeted the wolf and threw the bones on the ground for him. He'd have brought breadcrumbs to scatter for the birds too, like a good fairy tale hero, except that there aren't any birds in Asgard. Not for long. Sometimes a bird flies in from one of the other worlds. A white swan or dove might fly in from Light Elfland. A nightingale or mockingbird might fly in from Vanaheim. And sometimes a happy little bluebird might fly beyond the rainbow—also known as Bifrost Bridge—up from Midgard. But none of those birds lasts very long in Asgard; the valkyries catch them and eat them.

The wolf daintily nibbled all the meat from the pork chops and then chewed up the bones for their marrow. He licked the bag clean, and then he licked Knut's fingers clean too. "Any luck with the new woman?" he asked.

"Not yet, but I think she's worth waiting for."

"Ratatosk says you're not the only one who thinks that," the wolf said. "He came by last night and told me his list, and I knew a few names he was missing—including yours—but I didn't tell him."

"She said she's used to sleeping alone," Knut said, "but I think she likes me." Then he went back inside Valhalla and found Robin Grima, with a drinking horn in her hand, talking to Beewolf, who sat at Table Five, Section One, Door 241, assigned to fight in Jotunheim.

"So Grendel wasn't really a troll?" Robin was asking.

"Just a big ugly berserk," said Beewolf, "and the nicors were just walruses, and the fire-breathing dragon was just an outlaw band who'd picked up some Greek fire when they were working in Byzantium. You can't always trust poets, Robin Grima."

"What about Grendel's mother?"

"The woman in his cave? Her hair was still dark, and her face wasn't wrinkled. Maybe he was her son. Maybe he was her lover. She wasn't ugly, but she was definitely berserk. And human."

A horn blew for breakfast, and the valkyries brought in platters of food and pitchers of drink. Robin walked over to her table section and inspected the platters and bowls. "Don't they ever change the menu?" she asked.

"Not since I came here," said Knut, "and that was the year King Harald started combing his hair." He meant Harald Halfdanson who vowed not to cut or comb his hair till he was king over all of Norway. He was called Harald Tanglehair for ten years, and then he was called King Harald Finehair.

"Glasir Grove didn't have a single green leaf in it till you picked an old branch," Frostbite whispered to Robin. *"You can change things."*

Robin walked over to a valkyrie. "I want eggs for breakfast today," she said. "Soft-boiled, for three minutes."

"Go back to your table, Hero; they're already there."

Robin knew that was magic, but she didn't realize just how magical it was. There aren't any egg timers in Valhalla, and the Asgard folk reckon time in eighths of a day, each one three hours long, not in minutes.

Robin went back to Table Thirteen and found a bowl of soft-boiled eggs. Knut was holding an egg in his left hand and salting each spoonful before eating it. She sat down next to him and took a hot roll and cut it open and broke an egg into it. Knut passed her the salt shaker (which arrived in Valhalla a few decades after it was invented in Midgard, around the start of the twentieth century), and she shook it briskly, then passed it back to him. One of the few good things about chemo was that it lowered her blood pressure so she could have all the high sodium foods she loved. One of the many bad things about chemo was that even if she managed to score enough marijuana to keep her food down, she still didn't feel hungry two weeks out of four. Of course, that sort of diet will give you a good figure, but Robin had stopped appreciating how she looked in the mirror after she'd lost her breasts. *Maybe tomorrow,* she thought, *I'll ask a valkyrie for dill pickles and lox and bagels.*

"Your kenning for today is wolf-wine," Knut said. "That means blood."

Valhalla: Absent Without Leave

The horn blew three times, and Door Thirteen swung open, and the four hundred heroes—three real, 397 phantoms—walked out into the courtyard. Robin stood there, holding Frostbite, waiting for the phantoms to attack the way they had yesterday, but this time, they just walked forward and formed a battle line in front of her and her friends. *"A shield wall,"* whispered Frostbite, *"to defend their door."* And then, as the phantoms bent their line to encircle Grima and her friends, *"No, it's a shield wall fortress to defend their leaders."*

No, the phantoms didn't have shields on their left arms; their weapons were their shields, and "shield wall" was a kenning.

There were seven rows of Door Thirteen phantoms around them to protect them from the other doors, but the other heroes were attacking them fiercely, throwing spears and boulders. "Why aren't there any archers?" Robin Grima asked.

"They're all in Yewdales with Ullur," Knut said. "The prophecies say Ull's archers will fight on our side at Ragnarok, along with the Lady's men and the rest of our allies."

Eventually, there was only one a double-line of phantoms left to protect them. "Charge!" yelled Bookwyrm, and they ran forward, the phantoms stepping aside to let them pass and then running after them to defend their backs.

A couple of hours later—I already told you I don't do battle details—the sun was high and hot in the heavens, and there were only half a dozen heroes left in Valhalla's courtyard.

Knut and Bookwyrm and Robin Grima stood back to back to back.

"Last round," called a valkyrie.

Bookwyrm picked up a severed head and threw it at an

opponent, then took advantage of the woman's flinching to cut off her head. Knut parried a blow by cutting off his opponent's wrist. The blood froze into splinters. Knut charged forward and pierced the man's heart, which pumped a spurt of red icicles and then froze in death. Robin Grima swung Frostbite two-handed against an enemy, breaking the woman's sword and slashing her throat, which gushed a stream of red hailstones.

"And that's that for today," said Knut. "Now what do we do?"

"Find out what our new friend fights like on her own," said Bookwyrm. "Take off your magic sword, Robin Grima, and pick up one that nobody's using any more."

Robin spent the afternoon doing sword drills. It was hot and sweaty and tiring but educational. She hadn't realized how much of the fighting Frostbite had been handling till she had to do it all on her own.

When the sun finally set, she tied on her scabbard again. *"You've been helping me too much, Sword,"* she said. *"I want to learn to do this stuff on my own."*

"You chose your target," the sword whispered. *"I just helped out your attack now and then. And your defense."*

"Stop helping me so much, or I'll find myself another sword."

"I'll let you make your own mistakes here in Valhalla," it whispered. *"But when you're facing a true foe and fighting for survival...."*

"When that happens, you can help me as much as you want, and I won't fight you."

"I won't fight you then either, Hero. I'll fight for you against your enemies as long as you keep me at your side."

That night they stayed in Valhalla. After dinner, they went off to a side room where Robin Grima could practice some more—while looking at herself in the wall mirror. It reminded her of ballet class. After a couple of hours, they said she'd worked long enough for the day and showed her the bathroom.

No, I don't mean a room with a toilet. Valhalla heroes metabolize their food completely without any waste products so they don't need toilets or toilet paper. They also don't get heartburn or gas or acid reflux. The women don't menstruate or get pregnant, and the men don't produce sperm; once you're dead, you can't start a new life. But a dead hero can still appreciate a hot sweat bath, followed by swimming across an ice-cold pool, and then relaxing in a toasty warm bathtub while sipping a mug of hot cider or cool beer. There's always a bathroom free at Valhalla, whether it's for one person or a dozen door-mates or a thousand tablemates, and they never run out of hot water or drinks. Nothing but the best for Odin's heroes.

One thing more, the bathroom towels in Valhalla are always clean and dry and fluffy and warm, just as the sheets and pillowcases in the bed closets are always clean and unwrinkled and the feast hall never has any crumbs on the floor, let alone bones, and except when the heroes are eating, the plates and drinking glasses and tableware are always spotless. Valhalla doesn't have any dishwashers or housekeeping staff, but it's always clean and tidy. This may be a greater miracle than restoring dead and maimed heroes to perfect health and life every day at sunset.

Robin had had hydrotherapy every week for a year. Some doctors think it enhances the immune system against cancer. Some think it can stop hot flashes from chemo-induced menopause. Robin's insurance didn't cover it, and after a while Robin's income wouldn't cover it either, so she stopped. But the hydrotherapy spa she went to had the water temperature set at a hundred degrees Fahrenheit. The Valhalla sweat bath was a lot hotter .

"We'll be just next door," Bookwyrm reminded her. "Knock twice if you get lonely and want company, and we'll come in and join you." He thumped the wall once to show her. Then he and Knut Nine Toes left her there alone.

Robin Grima laid her hand on Frostbite's hilt. *Should I take you along with me, Sword?*

"Only if you think you're in danger of dying from heat prostration," he whispered.

Robin laughed and walked into the sweat bath.

CHAPTER THREE

The next morning, Robin Grima's third day in Valhalla, her breakfast kenning was "scabbard dragon." It meant sword. *"Do you like hearing yourself praised, Sword?"* she asked it later.

"Yes," he answered. *"I like hearing myself praised by someone who sincerely appreciates me."*

"I'm sorry if I was rude yesterday," she thought. *"I just wanted to get better at this stuff, be more of an equal partner. I need you a lot, Sword. I appreciate you a lot."* Then the horn blew twice, and they went to stand in front of Door Thirteen.

"Anything else you'd like to learn today, Robin Grima?" Bookwyrm asked.

"What happens when you die here in Valhalla?" she asked. "Is it like falling asleep, and then you wake up and it's sunset?"

The door swung open, and Knut drew his sword. "I'll show you," he said and stabbed her through the heart.

*****

"I hope you didn't mind," Knut said nervously as he helped Robin stand up again and made sure her feet were steady on the frost-covered ground. "I thought you'd want to get it over as fast as possible. I hope it didn't hurt too much."

"It hurt," Robin said, touching her fingers to her chest, underneath her left breast. "It hurt horribly, but it doesn't hurt any more." She drew a deep breath. The air was biting cold in her lungs, but at least there wasn't a wind. "Why didn't you just tell—"

"My word oar was locked," said Knut. "My poet's ship—"

"You haven't taught her those kennings yet," said Bookwyrm. Robin looked through the mist and saw him sitting on the ground a few feet away from her. He rubbed the back of his head, reassuring himself that it was intact once again. Having your head get cut off and sent bouncing along the ground is more of a shock than being stabbed in the heart, though only the heroes of Valhalla are really in a position to make the comparison.

"My tongue couldn't tell you," Knut said, "and my lips were locked up. This place is secret, Odin's secret. We can't talk about it where outsiders could hear us."

Overhead, there was a long, harsh, scratchy sound, a raven calling, and a wave of knowledge swept over Robin. They were in Blind Hall, where nobody could see them, where they could practice fighting against their true enemies. This cold, misty land was a simulation of Hel, the place she and her door-mates were assigned to fight when Ragnarok started.

Odin lets me come into Blind Hall and look around whenever I want to, because he knows I won't ever tell anyone about it. Please note that I'm not claiming Odin trusts me. Odin doesn't trust anybody. Blind Hall is woven out of runes and songs, darkness and silence, legends and lies, nightmares and nonsense. It's impossible to describe it to anyone who's never been there, at least not to anyone who'll believe you. The only reason I can tell you about Blind Hall is that we all agree that this is fiction so there's no chance you'll believe me. The other only reason I can tell you about Blind Hall is that it's not the same nowadays as it used to be. There's a third only reason too, but I'm keeping that one to myself. I'm keeping *all* of the third reasons to myself.

"I'm sorry," Knut said. "You asked what it was like, and you had to come here someday, and we couldn't stay outside forever, and—"

"It's all right," Robin Grima told him. *"Sword, did you know about this?"*

"Yes," whispered the sword, *"but I couldn't tell you. I swore an oath to keep Odin's secrets."*

"Hail, Odin," a man's voice called. "Giver of Victory, Lord of Valhalla." A few other voices took up the chant but not many. Valhalla's heroes are selected for bravery and loyalty and intelligence in battle; piety is fourth place or lower.

A grey wolf walked out of the mist. He didn't look friendly.

"He's not a real Hel-wolf," whispered Frostbite, *"just another phantom. Everybody here is phantoms except for the other heroes and Odin. Is it all right for me to tell you things like that, or do you want me to keep you in the dark?"*

"Tell me everything you think I need to know." Robin Grima stepped forward, her mind remembering yesterday's lessons, her arms and legs remembering two days of fighting the bravest heroes of Midgard. *"By now I should be at least a second level fighter."*

The phantom wolf opened his mouth and howled, louder and louder. His eyes were red flames, and so were his teeth, and his mouth dripped blood. He was getting bigger; his mouth was getting larger. His lower jaw touched the ground and his upper jaw was as high as Robin's head.

She stepped forward and stabbed Frostbite into his throat and down to his heart. "One die extra damage against fire creatures and one die less damage against ice creatures," the sword's card had said. Which one was this?

"Both," whispered the sword. *"But I could still kill it with one blow even if it were real, not just a phantom."*

"Behind you, Grima!" yelled Knut.

She pulled the sword free from the wolf and whirled around and saw a walking corpse with long gray hair. Its hands were reaching toward her neck, fingers spread out to strangle her. She swung her sword at it again and again, until it finally stopped moving.

After that was a large white snake whose head came up to her waist and that tried to push its cold way up in between her legs and into her, and then another walking corpse, this one a man with a sword, and then....

And then it was over. The mists were gone, and the night stars were shining bright overhead, and a loud voice called, "Hail, heroes. You've won once again. Come here, Robin Grima, and let me congratulate you on your victories."

She looked up and saw a tall bearded man, wrapped in a dark blue cloak, holding a golden spear. She'd always imagined Odin as old, wrinkled-faced and white-bearded, but this man was young, hair not quite brown, not quite gold, the color of polished bronze. One of his eye sockets was empty; the other was dark blue. He was smiling at her. A black raven sat on each of his shoulders.

She walked up toward him, and the heroes drew aside from her path and hit their swords across their shields in rhythmic applause, in time with each of her steps. It was like going up to get your diploma. It was like the triumphant march at the end of *Star Wars*.

Then she was only a step away from him, and he reached out and hugged her briefly, warmly. Like Father after she got her high school diploma. But then she'd gone to the party, and when she got home she'd found the police waiting because there'd been an accident and Father and Mother were both dead. Like Dr. Schmidt when he told her that she was in full remission, only it didn't last: the cancer came back a year later.

Odin stepped back. She looked around, because that was one of the things she'd learned here, but nothing was sneaking up on her.

"Welcome to Asgard," Odin said. "I'm proud to have you here with me. But even if you hadn't been strong enough to make it to Valhalla, you'd still never have gone to Hel. Your home would be in Fensalir, Fen House, with my wife Frigga. You'd be spinning and weaving and feasting and dancing there with the other wise and honorable virgins."

"I'm not a virgin," Robin said.

"You never fell in love," he said, "and you never got married. I could take you to my bed tonight and change that for you, Robin, but I have other plans for you, and I think you'll like them better. I want you to free my allies and fight my enemies, You don't have all your powers yet, Grima. There are things you need to learn that Valhalla won't teach you fast enough. Do you trust me, Robin Grima?"

"I'm living in Valhalla to fight for you," she said, which wasn't quite an answer, but then she wasn't quite sure how she felt, and at least it was the truth.

"Look over there, and you'll see a fire like the one we kindled to burn the Lady when she first came to Asgard. She went through it three times, and each time she came out stronger and more beautiful, just like burning gold to refine it. Walk your way through the fire ordeal, my hero, and you'll get the rest of your power."

"I'm supposed to be immune to fire as long as I hold Frostbite," she said. "At least if it still works the way it did back when we were roleplaying.”

“Go walk through the gold-path fire and find out,” Odin said. Then he disappeared, and there was only her and the bonfire.

“*Should I take you off, Sword?*”

“*Only if you don't want my company,*” the sword whispered. “*But the ordeal will make me stronger too.*”

“*That's good,*” she said. “*As long as you're on my side.*”

She walked toward the fire, wondering whether she'd still have her hair when she came out, remembering the months after her hair fell out when she put glue on her bald head and then sprinkled sequins on it.

Third degree burns all over your body hurt a lot more than dying with a sword in your heart. They even hurt worse than waking up after surgery when the anesthesia had worn off and the morphine drip was just starting. Robin hadn't liked being burned when the oxygen tank exploded in the hospital, but that only lasted a few seconds; she didn't like doing it all over again in Blind Hall, especially when the pain went on and on.

After a while she couldn't see any more because her eyes had burnt out. John Hersey wrote that some of the people who looked up at the Hiroshima fireball had their eyes burn out. Robin used to think about that when she lay on the clinic table getting her rads. She'd never expected it to happen to her. Especially not after she'd already died.

She kept walking anyway, glad that her legs hadn't burnt off so she didn't have to roll, hoping she was walking straight ahead, hoping that the fire wasn't going to go on forever.

“*At least there aren't any dogs outside,*” the sword whispered. “*Dogs like eating cooked meat.*”

“*There are wolves.*”

“*The only real wolves here are Odin's, and they only eat what he feeds them, and Odin has other plans for you. Loki once found dogs eating the half-cooked heart of Angurboda, the Jotunheim midwife. The other hill giants burned her to death when they found out she was a witch. Hill giants don't like magic. Loki drove the giants away, and swallowed the rest of Angurboda's heart for safekeeping, even though it was bitter. He used to say he was simple and kind-hearted before he met Angurboda. A little later, he found himself pregnant with Fenris Wolf and Lady Hel and Orm Midgard Serpent. You wouldn't like having dogs or wolves eat you, Robin Grima. Trust me."*

And then the air was cool on her face, and she rubbed the soot out of her eyes, and she could see again.

"Is that enough, Sword, or should I do it twice more? The rules said I was going to be immune to fire damage, not just regenerate from it. "

"I don't know, Robin. I don't know everything. I can't do the same things for you here that I did for Grima in the game. It's your decision, Robin Grima."

She turned around and walked back toward the brightness, the heat, the pain. *"I want to be strong and beautiful,"* she thought. *"I want all my power."*

It hurt worse the second time. She opened her mouth and started to chant the poem Knut had written about her. "Grima's repute is rising in glory." The flames poured down her mouth and burnt out her tongue. Then they fingered their way down her throat and into her lungs so she couldn't breathe.

She crawled out of the fire on her hands and knees. Her hair was all burnt away, and so were her fingernails and toenails, and so were her teeth.

"Sword, are you all right?"

"I was safe in my scabbard."

"Next time I'll draw you and wave you around in the fire so you can enjoy it, too."

She turned around and faced the fire again. "Third time pays for all," she said out loud, wondering whether she was really going to do it again. She drew Frostbite and saw its silver blade glint red in the light of the flames. *"This time neither of us will be safe, Sword."*

"One for all, and all for one," whispered the sword, and she walked back into the flames again, holding it out in front of her.

This time the fire wasn't hot and the flames didn't hurt her. All that happened was that her flesh burned away, starting with her fingers that held Frostbite's hilt, till finally she was just a skeleton. Like the ones Grima had fought in the D&D games. Like the one Robin had seen in her x-rays. *"Are you all right, Sword?"*

"Yes, Hero." Frostbite's blade was flame-red now from tip to hilt, but her bone fingers still held it tight.

At the height of the flames, at the heart of the fire, her flesh started to grow back again. She stood there and looked in the mirror of the shimmering golden flames and saw her body restored to her: golden-tanned and lovely. She felt the warmth rising inside her with the friendly flames, starting between her legs where the Hel-snake had tried to force its way, where Barney had hurt her because she was too dry, but now it didn't hurt any more, nothing hurt, and the warmth spread tingles down to her toes and up to her palms till she tasted its sweetness on her lips and heard her sword singing to her wordlessly: sweet and clear and loving.

She walked out of the fire, still smiling, and turned back again and saw the fire was gone, and there was only a golden mirror. She went up close and touched its cold surface, then stepped back and looked at her reflection. Her hair was still dark brown, but now it had red-gold highlights. Her brown eyes had gold glints too. But those were just minor details. The real change was harder to define, but—

"This morning you were a beautiful girl," the sword whispered. *"Now you're a beautiful woman."*

"Don't be sexist, Sword."

"I can't help it. I'm a phallic symbol. Just look at me."

She did. He had changed too. *"Do you want a new name, Sword?"*

His blade was bright gold, its edge and tip blazing with red fire. He laughed at her question and dimmed back to his old cool moonlight silver. *"Let's keep any changes our secret,"* he whispered.

"I know what happened to me in there. What happened to you, Sword?"

"There are eavesdroppers everywhere, Robin Grima. Draw a magic circle around us to keep them out, and I'll tell you what happened to me."

She drew the circle with Frostbite's point and saw the ground turn white at his touch.

Afterwards (No, I'm not going to tell you the sword's secret. I couldn't hear it. Yes, I found out about it later. I'll tell you about it later, too. After the sword gets broken.) Robin went back to Valhalla and had a long soak in the bathroom and then ate dinner. It was the same as the night before, the same as it is every night: Saehrimnir steaks and Saehrimnir bacon and Saehrimnir sausage, Saehrimnir boiled with cabbage and Saehrimnir fried with onion rings and Saehrimnir baked with a beer marinade, and another two dozen Saehrimnir recipes. There were side dishes of green peas and turnips and rhubarb and Vinland vegetables like potatoes and tomatoes and maize, and there was bread and flat bread, cheese and butter and a dozen kinds of jam and a dozen kinds of pie. There were pitchers of buttermilk and apple juice, beer and cider and ale. Robin wasn't tired of it yet but she thought she might be in another year, let alone another century.

CHAPTER FOUR

The next morning, Robin Grima's breakfast kenning was "battle board" which means shield. Later on, Door Thirteen swung open, and Knut killed Bookwyrm and Robin killed Knut, but that meant she didn't have anyone to guard her back, and the phantoms sneaked behind her and backstabbed her. A few minutes later, Robin and Knut and Bookwyrm were all standing in Blind Hall, and a gray wolf leapt out of the fog and tore Robin's throat out.

"I promised I wouldn't help you," the sword whispered, *"but if you'll take my advice—"*

"Fight on, Robin Grima!" yelled Knut. "You don't need a throat to hold your sword."

"That was supposed to be my line," the sword whispered.

Robin Grima tried to yell something cheerful and brave back at Knut, but she found that she couldn't say anything. You can't talk without a throat to carry air to your mouth. Yes, you can't breathe without a throat, but that doesn't matter: the heroes of Valhalla are dead; they don't need to breathe.

Robin Grima killed a couple of wolves—she wasn't sure if

either of them was the one who'd wounded her; there was too much fog—and then killed a huge snake that was coiling around her leg and trying to break it.

"A snake that big means we're getting near Dead Shore," Bookwyrm said. "Look out for murderers, Robin Grima."

They fought their way downhill. Robin kept getting stabbed in the back until finally she learned to sense enemies coming up behind her. Her right thumb and forefinger got cut off, but Frostbite's hilt held fast to her hand. They went past the World Tree but didn't waste their time carving their names in the trunk; they were too busy fighting the Dead Shore murderers. Worse yet, waiting ahead of them was the giant dragon Nidhog, who spends her days and nights gnawing the lowest root of the World Tree, sucking its sap, not worrying that she's going to kill the tree. When that happens, Hel and all the other worlds will fall away from each other and away from the Sun and Moon and stars and be lost in the darkness.

"We'll come back for Nidhog some other day," Knut said. "Robin Grima, when you're in better voice, you can challenge Nidhog to a duel."

"Don't waste your time," cried a red squirrel, up above them on the trunk of the World Tree. "Nidering Hog's just a cowardly pig. You won't win any honor in killing her. The giants would roast her for dinner but they can't decide how to eat her. She's too big for one bite and too small for two. The eagle at the top of the World Tree could tear her apart with one talon behind its back but he doesn't like the way she smells."

The three heroes turned away without answering cute little Ratatosk (Robin didn't have a choice; she wouldn't be able to speak till sunset) and finally made it down to Hel River. Robin looked around but there wasn't a bridge or a ferryboat.

Hel River is full of bitter cold water and colder ice and little knives sharp enough to cut off your eyelids or nose or fingers as they flow by, but it's the only water in Hel outside of Hel's Hall, and its shores were lined with the thirsty evil folk of Dead Shore trying to drink from it. It was red with blood from their faces and hands, and there were little bits of their fingers and lips and tongues and noses floating in it.

"Touch my tip to the river," Frostbite whispered, *"and you won't have to ford it. You can walk across on the ice."*

"Maybe next time," Robin Grima thought back, and she stepped into the cold water.

By the time the heroes had gone through the river, they'd met enough sharp knives that they were all limping, not just Knut Nine Toes.

Before them rose Hel's Hall, made out of boulders of white hail mortared together with red blood. A crowd of Lady Hel's guests were standing outside. One of them came up to Bookwyrm, a woman with long golden hair, her thin shape wrapped in a white sheet. "Take a good look," he told Robin Grima. "It's what my wife Drifa looked like when she died from the fever. It's what she'll look like when Heimdall's horn summons us to march against Hel. Try to look for her at Ragnarok; try not to hurt her."

Robin couldn't speak but she nodded in agreement. She looked around to see if Barney was there, but she didn't see him. She didn't see any of the people she'd met in the hospital's cancer clinic over the years.

Bersi Bookwyrm fingered through the bags that hung from his belt and began digging out food that he must have put away at breakfast this morning and at dinner last night: bread rolls and cheese, slices of Saehrimnir, boiled eggs and apples. Knut and Robin stood next to him, beating back the other phantoms so Drifa's likeness could eat her fill.

"Shield wall!" someone yelled, and the heroes began to

form into ranks. Bookwyrm kissed the phantom goodbye and took his place in line. A rust-red cock stood up on Hel's Hall roof and started crowing, and a huge gray dog got up from where he'd been lying next to Hel's Hall door and stretched, his legs getting longer and longer, till he was as tall as the hall. His tail wagged happily, but his ears were back and he was growling.

"That's Garm Hel-hound," said Bookwyrm. "He and Lord Tyr will kill each other at Ragnarok."

Suddenly Garm leapt forward and seized Bookwyrm between his teeth and lay down again, chewing the man, spitting out cracked bones. They could hear Bookwyrm screaming inside the dog's mouth.

"Try not to let it happen to you, Grima," whispered Frostbite. *"I don't think you'd enjoy being chewed up like that."*

"Charge!" someone shouted, and the Valhallan shield wall rushed forward. There were hundreds of heroes, but the door widened to let them all in. Hel's Hall is never too full not to have room for more guests. You could kill everyone in the Nine Worlds and everyone in the workaday world too, and Hel's Hall could swallow them all down and still be hungry.

Inside, Hel's Hall was bright with jewels and warm with firelight. There was a huge table, spread with white bone china platters and ruby red glasses and bright gold knives and spoons. An ash-blond man sat in a throne at the far end of the table, his hair shining brighter than the gold or the fire. A black-haired man sat in a throne at the near end of the table. Both of them were chained to their chairs by ropes of bright stars at elbows and feet to show they were in death's dominion. They both had the same face. Neither of them was eating or drinking from the platters of food and pitchers of drink set before them. The fair-haired man was weeping; the dark-haired man was dry-faced because he didn't have any eyes to cry with. His eye sockets were charred; the eyelids missing.

"*Danger,*" whispered Frostbite.

A tall woman towered over Robin Grima, her left side a white skeleton of ice, her right side a red skeleton of flames, both hands holding a black sword that came crashing down ice cold, splitting Grima's skull, turning her universe into a wasteland of darkness and cold and infinite pain.

*****

Then Robin was lying at her ease in swirling warm water, feeling gentle hands touching her, lifting her up into the warm air, placing her on a soft warm surface. "You don't have to remember all that awful stuff if you don't want to," said a woman's quiet voice.

"I don't want to forget it," said Robin Grima, and then realized that she had her voice back; she had her throat back. She opened her eyes and saw a gold-haired girl, a red-haired woman, a silver-haired woman. They were all smiling at her. Robin reached for her sword hilt—it was good to have all her fingers again. *"Sword, do you see them too?"*

"Yes, Hero. They're the Norns, the real Norns, not phantoms in Blind Hall. This is their well in Asgard, by the World Tree's highest root. Be polite to them."

The Norns are the only people in the Nine Worlds who are more powerful than Odin. They weave the threads of people's lives into the history of the past and the reality of the present and the prophecies of the future. If they decide to kill you, then you're dead. Or if they like you, they can call in Saga and tell her your story, and then you'll be famous throughout the Nine Worlds. Maybe even the people in the workaday world will remember your name for a while.

Urd is the oldest Norn. She's also the most beautiful and the most intelligent and the most interesting to talk to at parties, and I like to think of her as my best friend. Odin would give his left eye to know what Urd knows. In fact, he did. And Urd's the one who asked me to write down this story. I didn't ask her why; I just said, "Yes, ma'am" and went to Saga's hall and started writing, stopping now and then to do research. It's calm and quiet here. Once I'd have thought that was boring, but after hanging around with Robin Grima I appreciate calm and quiet a lot more than I used to.

"Your memories are very glaring," redhead Verdandi told Robin Grima. She twisted the heddle, separating the two layers of warp threads, so Urd could push someone's life-thread in between them. "We could leave them out in the sunshine for a while and let them get bleached, so they wouldn't hurt so much."

"I appreciate your kindness," Robin Grima said, "but I don't want to forget anything."

"I told you so," said the silver-haired Norn. "After all, she went through the fire three times, and she'll go through more saltwater than that before she's done." She looked back down at the bright image in the crystal that lay in her lap.

That was Skuld, the youngest Norn, if you haven't been paying attention. Urd's the gold-haired one who looks like a child even if she was born first. Reality isn't always intuitively obvious.

"We like happy endings," said Verdandi.

"We wish we had more of them," Skuld said. She clicked Close/Save and the image disappeared from her crystal.

"That's why we want you to promise to do us a favor," said sweet little Urd, who's been around since before Ginungagap, the primal mass-energy of the Nine Worlds.

"It depends," said Robin, remembering what happened to Pwyll in the *Mabinogion* when he made a promise without thinking once, let alone twice. "I've got obligations to my friends and to my sword."

"You told Odin you'd fight for him," whispered the sword.

"And I've made a promise to Odin too," Robin said.

"We value your honor even more than you do," said the redhead.

"We won't ask you to do anything to lessen it," said the gold-haired girl.

"We need Tyr's right hand," said silver-haired Skuld. (The Norse say SK where Germans say SH: skipper and shipper, skirt and shirt, skuld and should. Most translators say the youngest Norn's name means "Need," but that's misleading; it really means "Should.")

"You don't have to do it right away," they all said in chorus. "Just bring it to us if you ever get hold of it."

"Sword, what do I do?"

"You make your own decisions, Hero. That's what you said you wanted, isn't it?"

"If I ever get hold of Tyr's right hand," said Robin Grima, "I'll bring it to you unless that conflicts with my obligations to Odin and my friends and my sword—and as long as it doesn't mean doing something dishonorable."

"We accept your promise," said Urd, and Verdandi tied a knot in Robin's life-thread, and Skuld did something on her laptop, and it was done and nobody could undo it. The Norns' position on the World Tree gives them root privilege.

"Don't worry, pretty hero," cried a red squirrel, up above them on the trunk of the World Tree. "Tyr's right hand is safe with Fenris Wolf, and that's where it's going to stay. Tyr will have to go down to Hel and fight Garm Hel-hound one-handed, and the two of them will kill each other. That's what the prophecies say."

"That's what the prophecies say," the Norns repeated.

Then everything went black, and the next thing she knew, Robin Grima was lying on the warm hard stones of Valhalla courtyard, and the sunset horn was blowing three times. Time to come alive and get up and go into the hall.

"Tell me what you remember," whispered the sword.

"The door phantoms killed me, and sent me to Blind Hall...." She stopped in surprise. *"I can talk to you about it!"*

"We're not talking out loud, so nobody can hear us."

That was true. Heimdall can hear the grass grow in the fields and the wool grow on sheep's backs, but even Heimdall can't hear people's thoughts. I'm good at research, but I'm no Heimdall. I didn't find out what they were thinking till Urd gave me the pass to the restricted section of Saga's library, and by that time the details were declassified all the way down to Top Secret, Eyes Only.

"A wolf tore my throat out," Robin Grima thought. *"We crossed Dead Shore's river, and the daggers cut me. Bookwyrm introduced me to his wife, and then Garm Hel-hound ate him. We went into Hel's Hall, and I saw Baldur and Hodur sitting at her table. And I saw Hel, and Hel killed me. It hurt."*

"The first time you see her is always the worst," the sword whispered. *"You'll do better next time."*

"Bath and then dinner, or dinner and then bath?" asked Knut Nine Toes, offering a hand to Robin Grima.

"Maybe she'd rather go to her bed closet and rest for a while," said Bookwyrm. "After all, she's still getting used to how we do things in Valhalla."

"I'm still getting used to being killed," Robin thought. She opened her mouth to tell Bookwyrm he'd really gotten chewed up today, but the words couldn't get past the Blind Hall security system. "Bath first," she said eventually, "but this time I don't want to be alone. Bare is back without brother behind it."

"I'm hungry," said Bookwyrm. "I'll see you two at the dinner table."

*****

Robin and Knut scrubbed each other's backs in the steam bath. "My father's house had a spring almost this hot next to it," Knut said. "That's where I was when the outlaws came, so they didn't see me."

"Outlaws? I thought you said wolves?"

"Wolves on two feet, serpents with swords, outlaws." Knut Nine Toes shrugged. "What's the difference? The only thing that mattered to me was that I had to wait till they fell asleep, and by then they'd killed my father and older brothers and raped my mother and then killed her too. I was only a boy, but I killed them all, even the one who cut off my toe. Six years later, I found out that one of them had a brother. Arnulf the Angry kept visiting my farm till he found a reason to challenge me to a duel. I was eighteen then, and he was thirty."

Only eighteen, Robin thought, from the mature perspective of twenty-five.

"Some of my neighbors bet on me," Knut said, "but more bet on him. We killed each other, so everybody lost except my mother's sister's son, who got my farm. Going to Hel and killing Arnulf and his brother and the rest of the outlaws all over again is one of the reasons I'm looking forward to Ragnarok."

"My parents were killed in a traffic accident," Robin said. "One of my high school schoolmates didn't make it to graduation ceremonies to pick up his diploma because he was too busy getting drunk. He went out to get some more beer and ran into my parents." That was a pun, but Knut didn't appreciate it because he wasn't hearing it in English. "He broke his neck and can't move his arms and legs. All he'll do for the rest of his life is just lie there in a nursing home. If I wanted vengeance on him, that would be enough. What I wanted was my parents back. Are they here somewhere?"

"It depends," Knut said. "Were they heroes? Did they believe in heroes? If not, then their lives probably stopped when they died because they didn't believe that people can conquer death. Did they believe in any of the Aesir and Vanir? If not, then they went somewhere that's not on the World Tree."

Robin thought of her father asking why she bothered to read books that weren't class assignments, of her mother asking why she wanted to record all those sci-fi shows and movies. She thought of how her mother made her take ballet lessons, and how her father told her to never buy cheap clothing because it wasn't name brand, and how they both told her not to waste her time writing adventure game software, and of how thrilled they both were when she got her university admission and scholarship, and how their graduation present to her was a set of summer lessons at the public golf course. "It'll make it easier for you to mix with the other students," Father told her, "the ones who don't need scholarships to go there." She'd sold the golf lessons on E-Bay the day after they died.

"They're not here then," she said and jumped into the cold pool and swam across to the other side with her face underwater so there was a reason for her eyes to be wet.

Afterwards, she and Knut shared a horn of ale, and then he took a hot fluffy towel and helped her dry off. "First the back, and then the front. Tell me if you want me to stop. I won't do anything you don't want. I'm not an outlaw. You have beautiful breasts, Robin Grima. The kenning for breasts is heart's hall pillars."

"What's the kenning for this?" she asked, pointing to a place lower down.

"Warrior spear's cup, woman heart's entry, birth door." He knelt down and kissed it. She was trembling and put her hands on his warm shoulders to steady them.

They threw their wet towels into the bathtub and spread dry towels across the warm floor, and she wasn't too dry or too wet, and he wasn't too stiff or too floppy, and they were both just the right size, and they set each other on fire (metaphorically speaking). And then it was over.

"That was wonderful," Knut said. "You're wonderful." Then he walked over to where he'd gotten undressed and put his clothes back on. Robin got back into the bathtub's bubbling warm water and sipped another horn of ale and told herself to be realistic: even in Valhalla you shouldn't expect to see shooting stars and hearts and flowers and to hear violin music when you have sex. It had felt good, and that ought to be enough. Knut was a nice guy, and that ought to be enough.

Knut walked out of the bathroom without coming back to kiss Robin goodbye, without turning back to tell her he loved her. Maybe that was good manners back where he came from, back when he came from. He'd said she was wonderful, and that ought to be enough. She hadn't told him anything, just held him tight and held her breath tight until it was over, and then smiled at him, kissed him, ran her fingers along his arms and felt his muscles under his warm smooth skin.

She wondered if she loved him. She wondered how she was ever going to tell if she loved him without being able to call up a girlfriend and talk about it, without bringing him home to meet her parents and going to his home to meet his parents, without seeing shooting stars and hearts and flowers and hearing violin music. She thought about chatting about Knut with Ermentrude or one of the other Valhallan women, but they wouldn't understand what he looked like to someone from the 21st century.

Eventually she got out of the bathtub and dried herself off and got dressed, and put on her sword.

"I'm not jealous," whispered Frostbite. *"He's too dull to be jealous of."*

"Dull is a lot better than razor-sharp when it comes to sex," Robin told him, shivering at the thought of Frostbite going up between her legs—freezing her like an anesthetic, cutting her like a surgeon's scalpel. It would be even worse than getting raped by a Hel snake.

*****

That night, Knut and Robin went downstairs to the bed closets. She wondered if he was going to suggest sharing a large bed closet, but he just said, "Good night, treasure tree of sea fire." Robin wondered what it meant, but he was walking away, his arm over Bookwyrm's shoulder. (It means "beautiful woman of gold" or maybe "valuable treasured woman".) Knut and Bookwyrm were going to sleep together that night because they both knew that Bookwyrm always had nightmares after getting chewed up by Garm Hel-hound, and things would go better if Knut was there to wake him before the dreams got too bad.

"Good night, sweet hero," Robin whispered, not sure if Knut was near enough to hear it, not sure if she wanted him to hear it. She kicked off her shoes and got into the bed closet and closed the door.

A bed closet is smaller than a twin size bed and bigger than a coffin, with nothing in it besides the bed. Robin wriggled out of her clothes and folded them under her pillows. (Most of the rest of the heroes slept in their clothes. Some spread them out over their blankets. When they woke up, their clothes weren't wrinkled; it's part of Valhalla's magic housekeeping service.)

She looked dubiously at Frostbite. The first night she'd slept with him behind her pillows, and she was so exhausted she'd slept like the dead. When she'd tried it again the second night she wasn't as tired and the pillow felt lumpy. The third night she'd put him at the foot of her bed, but her feet kept hitting him. *"What am I going to do with you, Sword?"*

"Keep me at your side," he whispered, *"and I won't be too dull or too sharp for you."* So she put him in between the sheets, by her sword arm, and spent the night dreaming of fighting. *"Harder! Faster!"* the sword screamed. *"Again and again! Yes, yes, YES!"*

Robin woke up with the calm and self-confidence that come of knowing you've killed everybody who annoys you, her hand on her sword hilt.

*****

The next morning, when Knut got up, he picked up his sword, set the blade to his left little toe, and then stopped and thought about Robin Grima and what he wanted her to think about him. He put his sword back in its scabbard without cutting anything, and walked, without limping, up the stairs to the feast hall. There were already pitchers of apple juice and bowls of apples set out for early risers.

He picked up an apple, then went out through Valgrind to gaze at the morning sky. It looked the same as always: bright blue and cloudless, the Sun's golden chariot rising in the East. He remembered the songs that said that when Ragnarok came, a wolf would swallow the Sun and another wolf would swallow the Moon.

"I need a new nickname," he told the door's wolf guardian. "I'm going to have ten toes from now on."

"Knut Ten Toes?" suggested the wolf. "Nobody's taken that one yet."

"Too commonplace," Knut said.

"Knut Arnulfsbane? Knut the Skald? Knut Kenning Canny?"

"If you told me your name, I could call myself your friend," Knut said.

The charred eagle laughed, and Saehrimnir's head snorted.

"My name stays my secret," said the wolf, "but you can call yourself Valwolf Friend if you want to."

The eagle and Saehrimnir's head were silent, but a raven cawed overhead. Memory was up there, making sure that Odin knew all about it.

"I'd be honored," said Knut.

"I'll give you your nickname present later on," said the wolf. That's Viking etiquette: if you formally nickname someone, then you owe them a gift, the same way you ought to give a gift to a relative's or neighbor's baby when it's old enough to grow teeth. Letting a friend give you a nickname isn't quite as close as swearing foster brotherhood (when you walk under a raised piece of turf together and cut your hands and press them together, sharing the same blood and swearing to protect each other's honor) but it was closer than Knut felt to anyone else at Valhalla.

Knut Valwolf Friend thanked the Valwolf, then gave him the apple core and scratched him behind the ears and let the wolf lick his face with special attention to the nose and ears. Then he signed the Hero List with his new name and went back inside to eat breakfast with his oldest friend and his new woman. She'd come to him as a virgin. Odin had said so, and the Seducer and the Fulfiller of Desire and the Thruster could be depended on to tell the truth about that sort of thing.

Speaking of Viking etiquette....

Knut couldn't ask a woman who'd come to him as a virgin to tell him the terms of her marriage contract. That was something he was supposed to negotiate with her father. But he couldn't bring betrothal gifts to Robin Grima's father unless he could find him, and Robin Grima said the man wasn't anywhere in the Nine Worlds. Of course, maybe she was wrong. Or maybe she had some other kinsmen somewhere in the Nine Worlds. He'd have to find out.

Robin Grima was a Valhalla hero, Knut's social equal, so he couldn't give her a gold ring or some other piece of jewelry and take her as his concubine; that sort of ceremony was only for slaves or freed slaves. They could take a bath together—a lot of door-mates did, and nobody thought anything about it. They could even have sex in the bath together privately as secret lovers, but he wasn't going to share a bed closet with her, because once word got out that she was sexually available the other heroes who liked women would be lining up, trying to seduce her. If they failed, then they'd annoy her, and Knut didn't want that to happen. If they succeeded, that would be worse.

He couldn't write her love poetry or even use the word "love" to her, not even when nobody else was listening, because that would be disrespectful, as if she were just a concubine instead of someone he wanted to marry, just as soon as he could figure out how to arrange a marriage contract. Writing love poetry to a woman you weren't betrothed or married to was legally the same as slander, and could be cited as justification for killing you or outlawing you.

Maybe someday, if he fought well enough, Odin would offer him a reward for his faithful service, and he could ask Odin for Robin Grima's hand in marriage, because Odin was the All-Father, the Slain Father, and so legally the father of every hero in Valhalla.

Even then he wasn't sure what they could do for a wedding ceremony. Normal weddings involved invoking Thor Redbeard's hammer or Lord Frey's horn, but he couldn't do that in Valhalla; it might make Odin jealous.

Maybe they could invoke Lady Frigga, Odin's wife, goddess of marriage. He'd have to ask the Valwolf if he'd ever seen a wedding in Valhalla. He wondered what sort of wedding oaths Robin Grima would consider binding and what sort of dowry she'd bring to the marriage and what sort of settlement she'd want from him.

Right now, what really mattered was his new name and the obligations it brought with it. Knut had always thought of his wolf friend as one of the Valgrind guardians. He hadn't realized that the wolf called himself the Valwolf, the Slain Wolf. One of the challenges in Asgard is figuring out who's alive and who's dead. The fact that Odin sacrificed himself to himself, nine days hanging on the World Tree, shaking in the wind, a spear through his heart, doesn't help simplify this. It did help Odin get the runes but that's another story.

Valhalla's cook kills Saehrimnir the Sea Boar every morning and cuts him up and cooks him and serves him to the heroes every night. How can Saehrimnir be alive in the kitchen every morning as a headless body? Good question. How come you didn't ask it back when I told you how his bodiless head was alive and talking on top of the door to Valhalla? The answer is that the head and the body are still connected, and as long as one of them stays untouched, the other won't die, at least not permanently. The head doesn't scream in pain when the cook starts whacking pieces off the body; it just grunts a little now and then. Saehrimnir's had centuries to get used to having his body cut up and boiled.

Thiazi the giant got all burned up a long time ago when he put on his eagle skin and flew into Asgard, looking for a goddess who'd spent a few hours in his bed and then run home and taken her magic apples back with her. Now Thiazi's eyes are up in the sky as two shining stars and the rest of him is sitting on top of the Valgrind door with his feathers burned off, and he can still see through his eyes. Life in Asgard isn't simple, and neither is death.

Knut wondered who'd killed his wolf friend and whether the wolf was planning on taking vengeance for it someday and whether he'd ask Knut to help him. He hadn't read the *Mabinogion* (which is Welsh, not Norse), but he'd heard enough sagas and eddas to know that it's not a good idea to promise someone a favor without specifying what you're supposed to do if you owe someone else a conflicting obligation. *I'd rather not get involved in a blood feud that started before I was born*, Knut decided.

"What's my kenning today?" Robin Grima asked Knut when he sat down at the table.

"It's 'child of Fenris'," he said. "That means 'wolf'. The Valgrind wolf guardian is the Valwolf, and my new nickname is Valwolf Friend."

"I've heard of Fenris," Robin Grima said.

"Maybe we'll introduce him to you someday," said Bookwyrm. "He lives here in Asgard, on Heather Island."

CHAPTER FIVE

That day in Blind Hall, Door Thirteen's heroes played hooky from Hel and went off to visit the other eight worlds. They didn't have a tour guide, but Knut and Bookwyrm chanted the relevant bits from the eddas.

They visited Niflheim where the air was a lot warmer than in Hel, but the fog was so dense you could barely see your hand in front of your face. Robin Grima's hair glowed through the mist like a fire, until a gray-furred Nifl wolf sprang howling out of the fog and tore out a mouthful of her hair before Bookwyrm cut him down. After that Knut took off his shirt and gave it to Robin to cloak her hair so it wouldn't attract attention.

They walked downhill through the fog to a frozen river where a silver star shone brightly on the masthead of a skeleton longship. At first Robin thought there were humans and dwarves climbing up and down its sides, hammering in nails and yelling to one another, too busy and too loud to notice her and her table-mates. Then she realized that the river was wider than she'd thought and the longship was bigger: it was about a mile long, and the big workers were giants and the small ones were humans.

"That's *Naglfar*," Bookwyrm said. ("*Wraith Ferry*," the words rang in Robin Grima's mind.) "The sea giant Hymir's workmen are building it. Its beams and planks are murderers' bones, and its nails are oathbreakers' fingernails and its ropes are slanderers' tongues. When Ragnarok comes, the ice from Hel will melt, and this river will flood, and the ship will float up to Asgard. When it passes Jotunheim, the giants will board it and Hymir will lead them to fight us on the plains of Vigrond."

Some of the folk working on *Naglfar* didn't have right arms. Robin saw one of the giants sawing off his right arm at the elbow. He chewed off the flesh and then pinned the bones up against the ship beams with a knee and nailed them on carefully. A man dressed in gray stood on the masthead, under the shining star, yelling orders down at the workmen, his voice even louder than the hammering. "More bones!" he called, and giants came out of the fog carrying bundles of white bones and dropped them by the ship.

"Is that Hymir?" Robin asked.

"No," said Bookwyrm. "Hymir lives by Jotunheim's ocean, and he can't go to a world like Niflheim where there isn't an ocean. We don't know the name of the *Naglfar*'s captain. The prophecies don't say everything."

"The prophecies just say that when Ragnarok comes, everybody will fight and everybody will die," Robin Grima said bitterly.

"Well," said Knut, "at least that way nobody's in a hurry for it to come."

They visited Muspelheim where the air was smoke and the sky was bright with blazing comets, and the fire giants played catch with flaming meteors. The Muspel wolves were as red as the flames, except that their teeth were shining white and their eyes were light-blue like the flames of burning brandy.

There was a ship waiting there too, but this one was on fire: red pillars of flames rising hundreds of feet up into the sky like masts, black clouds of smoke clinging to the flame pillars like sails.

"We don't know its name," said Bookwyrm, "but its captain is Black Surt and his sword is made of a fire that can burn down the World Tree." Robin thought of nuclear bombs and shivered.

"All except for the root by Mimir's Fountain," said Knut. "It's protected by Odin's eye."

After that, they climbed up the World Tree ("You're deserting your post!" yelled the squirrel. "I'll tell Odin you're running away.") until they got to the middle level.

They visited Jotunheim, Giantland, where the sky was bright with stars and the ground was covered with ice and tall white shapes towered above them, most of them silent and motionless, a few tramping loudly across the land.

"The short ones are trolls," Bookwyrm said, "and the medium ones are frost giants, and the tall ones are hill giants." The short ones were as tall as humans, and the medium ones were as tall as telephone poles, and the tall ones were as tall as full-grown trees.

They heard the wolves howling, but it was hard to spot them; they were white as the ice, and their only color was their yellow eyes and gold teeth. "Sometimes you'll see the trolls riding wolves," Knut said. "One of the kennings for 'wolf' is 'troll woman's mount.'"

They circled Mimir's Fountain, and Bookwyrm recited the story of how Odin traded his eye there for a drink of wisdom, and Knut recited the story of how Heimdall kept his horn there and would go down to get it when he saw Ragnarok starting.

They went down to the seashore and walked past a towering building of ice blocks that glowed blue-white as if they had starlight trapped inside them. A giantess with nine heads came out a door and knelt down on the sand and drank till the ocean waves ran away from her, then staggered back inside again. "Hymir's mother," said Knut.

"Hymir's wife is prettier," Bookwyrm said, "and their children take after her: Tyr Fenrisfeeder and Gerd Freyswife."

They visited Dark Elfland where the air was noisy with the hammers of the smiths and smoky with their forge fires. The wolves were black too, and their teeth were red flames and their eyes glowed like red embers.

"The dark elves forged the Lady's necklace and Father Odin's spear," said Knut.

"And Thor's hammer and Frey's ship and Sif's hair," said Robin Grima. "I know some of the stories."

A hundred dark elves chased them, trying to cut off Robin Grima's hair, till the Valhallans ran into a band of heroes from Table Five and joined forces with them and killed their enemies.

They visited Midgard where the highest technology was steel swords and axe blades, and those were no good against most of the enemies they found there. The land was full of berserks and werewolves, witches and rune writers. Every grove hid a bear or a wolf or a boar. Every cave hid a troll; every grave mound hid a draug, guarding the treasure he'd been buried with. The ocean was full of more draugs with seaweed tangled around their arms and legs. They'd stay trapped in the water till they'd each drowned someone else to take their place. And around the ocean stretched the

Midgard Serpent, the monster who holds the worlds together.

"That's Orm Lokison," said Bookwyrm. "When Ragnarok comes, he and Thor will kill each other."

They walked up the rainbow bridge of Bifrost and went east to Light Elfland where everything was silver, even the sun, and the stars shone in the daytime. There were silver snakes in the trees, but they coiled around the eggs in their nests and sang as sweetly as the birds. There were silver wolves hiding in the shadows, but if you stayed very still, they came up shyly and licked your fingers. If you knelt down, they'd lick your face, and then for as long as your eyelids were wet you could see that the trees bore fruit shining like pearls and diamonds.

"Lord Frey rules here," said Bookwyrm. "He's one of the Vanir, but his wife is a fair woman he found on the seashore of Jotunheim, Gerd Hymirsdaughter. When Ragnarok comes, the prophecies say he'll ride out to fight Black Surt from Muspelheim and he'll die because all he has is a stag's antler against Surt's fire sword."

"I don't see any elves," Robin Grima said, looking around, "and I don't hear any hammering."

"The light elves aren't blacksmiths," Bookwyrm said. "They weave words and they herd plants."

"It's just as well we haven't met any," Knut said. "They're the fairest folk and the foxiest. Their songs are sweet and their tongues can tangle your thoughts."

"The rashest wished wish is a witless witch's riches," a sweet voice called from the shadows. "Say it three times running, not walking, not stumbling, and we'll honor your cunning and pardon your grumbling."

Bookwyrm put his finger to his lips, and they walked on silently.

They went west to Vanaheim where the daytime sky was bright with sunset-gold clouds and the grainfields grew fresh-baked bread and the chickens laid boiled eggs. The cows gave milk from one teat and butter from a second and cheese from a third and sour cream from a fourth. The trees held buds and flowers and fruit all at the same time, and sometimes more: a peach tree with baked peach pies, a yew tree with bows ready for plucking, grapevines whose berries were ripe with wine, and treasure trees with gold branches and silver leaves. The silent wolves were the size of mice, and gold-eyed cats hunted them.

The woods were full of singing birds, and the rivers ran over beds of shining jewels, and the ocean waves were bright with rainbow-colored fishes that leapt into the air higher than the white cloud-like sails of the ships that went from harbor to harbor.

And then finally they went to Asgard.

"Why is it here in Blind Hall?" Robin asked.

"We have enemies here too," Bookwyrm said, and he led them to a dark red lake the color of dried blood. In its center an island the color of fresh blood. A huge black wolf stood there, his feet fettered together and chained to the rocks, his head stretched up to growl at the noonday Sun.

"That's Fenris Lokison," Bookwyrm said, "brother to the Midgard Serpent and to Lady Hel."

"When Ragnarok comes, Fenris will kill Odin," Knut Valwolf Friend said.

"But until Ragnarok comes, Fenris can't leave the island," Frostbite whispered.

"I remember that much," Robin Grima told him. *"The fetter's name is Gleipnir and it's made out of women's beards and the sound of cats' feet and other impossible*

things. And I remember that the real Fenris—not this phantom—swallowed Tyr's right hand, and that the Norns want me to bring it to them."

"The eddas say that Loki is in a cave near the foot of Rainbow Bridge," Bookwyrm said. "He's bound to the rocks with his son's intestines. His wife sits there by him, with a bowl over his face, catching the poison that drips down from the snake that makes its home in the ceiling. Sometimes his wife turns aside to empty her bowl, and the venom falls in Loki's mouth, and he trembles in pain, and that's what causes earthquakes."

"That's not all true," whispered Frostbite. *"Don't trust the eddas, Robin Grima. They're truths and lies and half-truths and half-lies, all woven together."*

"Bound with his son's intestines," Robin repeated. "Which son did they cut up to get them? Fenris or the Midgard Serpent?"

"The Aesir took Loki's two sons by his Asgard wife, Sigyn," Knut said. "Their names were Vali and Narvi, Slayer and Binder."

Those weren't really their names, of course. Not even Loki Wyrmtongue would name his little babies Slayer and Binder. Those are the names the Aesir gave them afterwards. The children were originally named Kalinn and Kari, Frost and Wind, odd names for the children if you think that Loki is the god of fire, but of course he isn't. Why would a god of fire give birth to a wolf and a sea serpent and a girl who's half-corpse? Yes, "logi" is flame, but "lokka" means allure and entice and seduce, and "lopt" (another the name the Trickster keeps up his sleeve when it's not sweet on his tongue) means air and sky, which helps explain how he got Odin's favorite valkyrie daughter to marry him.

"The gods changed Vali the Slayer into a wolf," Bookwyrm said, "and he fell hungrily on his brother Narvi the Binder and tore him apart. Then the gods took Narvi's intestines and used them to tie Loki to the rocks. That's what the Prose Edda says."

The Prose Edda never explains why the gods had to bind Loki with the guts of his son. Some people say it's because it takes guts to do something that dangerous. Some say it's because Loki always had a soft spot for his children.

"Was their mother already dead?" Robin asked, "Or did they have to kill her, too?"

"Their mother is Sigyn the valkyrie," said Bookwyrm.

"The white-armed woman who sits loyally by Loki," said Knut. "She's still alive. Only one valkyrie's ever died, the one who married Siegfried's foster brother."

"Loyally!" yelled Robin. "Why didn't she try to protect her sons? Why doesn't she try to free her husband if she's so loyal to him? Why doesn't she get another damn bowl, so she can empty one bowl while she's holding the other one over her husband's face?"

"That's what the eddas say she does," Bookwyrm said.

"And I never thought to doubt them," Knut said. "It's going to be good having you here with us, asking questions."

A raven cawed overhead. They couldn't tell if it was Thought or Memory.

And then the sunset horn was blowing, and they weren't in Blind Hall any more; they were back in the Valhalla courtyard.

"Let's go have a bath, and then have dinner," Bookwyrm suggested.

"*I want to see Bifrost Bridge at sunset,*" Frostbite whispered. "*Should we go look for dice, Grima, so we can see which of us rolls higher and gets to decide what you'll do tonight?*"

"My sword wants to watch the sun set by the rainbow

bridge," Robin Grima told her door-mates. "And so do I." She wondered if there were any dice in Valhalla or if she'd have to make her own if she wanted to teach the Valhallans how to play Dungeons and Dragons. A wave of knowledge swept over her, and she knew that the Vikings gambled with six-sided dice, but not with 20-sided dice. She wasn't sure if she was up to carving icosahedrons and numbering them one through ten twice so she could roll for percentages.

"Don't try to do it yourself," Frostbite whispered. *"Go to Dark Elfland. They'll love the idea of all the different kinds of dice. Just make them swear that the dice will roll fairly."*

"I vote for watching the sun set at Bifrost," said Knut. "That's two out of three."

"Three out of four," whispered Frostbite.

Bookwyrm shrugged and led the way.

Bifrost (that's "Biv Rost," not "By Frost," if you want to say it correctly) only has three colors if you believe the Prose Edda: red, yellow, and blue, but Robin saw orange and green and violet in it anyway. She stood at the edge of Asgard and looked over the wall at the rainbow bridge; and then, thousands of miles away, at Midgard's lakes and forests, mountains and glaciers; and the encircling ocean, while the setting sun colored the clouds of both worlds red and gold and purple.

Nearby them stood the blue and white walls of a castle, its high tower bright with the sunset colors. "That's Heimdall's home," said Bookwyrm, "Sky Mountain. He sits there day and night, watching and listening for the first signs of Ragnarok. When it starts, he'll mount his horse and ride down to Jotunheim and get his horn out of Mimir's Fountain and blow it to tell Asgard that our enemies are coming."

"Why doesn't he keep his horn right here in his castle?" Robin asked. "And if he can get his horn out of Mimir's Fountain without any risk, why doesn't he get Odin's eye out while he's at it?"

"Heimdall's the son of the sea giant Aegir's nine daughters," Bookwyrm said. "He can go where he wants to in Jotunheim because he's pledged not to fight any giants. When Ragnarok comes, he'll fight Loki, and they'll kill each other in the ocean."

"He can hear us talking about him," said Knut.

"Heimdall can hear everybody and everything," said Bookwyrm. "He never sleeps, and he never stops listening. He can hear the swans swimming in the sky and the grass growing in the ground and the sea flowing over drowned men's bones. He can hear the frost and the hill giants plotting in Jotunheim and the fire giants plotting in Muspelheim. He can hear Fenris howling and the Midgard Serpent hissing and Lady Hel giving orders to her servants. He's not going to concern himself with three heroes from Valhalla."

"How many other people in the High Worlds have ties to Jotunheim?" Robin Grima asked.

"Lord Tyr was born in Jotunheim's Ocean," said Knut. "He's the son of Hymir, the sea giant, but Odin adopted Tyr as his foster son, and Tyr lives here in Asgard. The prophecies say he'll fight Garm Hel-hound at Ragnarok."

"Lord Njord was born in Vanaheim," said Bookwyrm, "but he came to Asgard as a hostage so the Vanir would stop fighting the Aesir. He left his old wife who's also his sister behind there. The Vanir like that sort of marriage, but the Aesir think it's immoral." Robin remembered that some of the Ptolomaic Pharaohs had married their sisters too.

"After he got here, he took a new wife who's a giantess, Skadi Thiazisdaughter. The eddas said they spend one week at his home on the seacoast of Asgard and one week at her home in the mountains of Jotunheim. She doesn't like Asgard because the valkyries' swans sing too loudly, and he doesn't like the mountains because the wolves howl too loudly."

"Loki used to live in Asgard," whispered Frostbite, *"and he's the son of Laufey the Leaf Lady of Vanaheim and Farbatti the Ship Beater, the giant ferryman who used to carry people to the concealed place, the cellar, the ninth world, the place for souls that no other world wants. It didn't use to have a ruler until Odin gave the world to Hel Lokisdaughter and killed Farbatti. And Loki is Odin's foster brother and used to be his best friend."*

"Lord Frey Njordson was born in Vanaheim," said Knut. "He was a baby when he came here, and when he grew up he moved to Light Elfland, and his golden wife is the sea giant Hymir's daughter, Tyr's sister."

"Odin's mother was a Jotunheim giantess, and so was Thor Odinson's, and so was Vidar Odinson's," said Bookwyrm. "There's a lot of blood ties between Asgard and Jotunheim when you go back far enough."

"In the beginning," said a quiet voice behind them, "the Aesir and the Giants were kinsmen and allies, and the Vanir were the enemies."

Robin Grima whirled around, Frostbite in her right hand.

The man was as white as a cloud except that his hair and his eyes and his teeth were gold. (At first she thought he was smiling at her. Then she realized he was baring his teeth at her.) His curling horns were as white as sea-foam. (No, I don't mean he was wearing a horned helmet. Viking warriors didn't wear those. Some priests wore horned helmets when they were offering blood sacrifices to Lord Frey, even though he only has two horns: one in his scabbard and another one lower down, between his legs.) The white man's horns sprouted from his forehead and curled around the sides of his face like a ram's horns, but Robin didn't realize that. The only sheep she'd ever seen were in zoos.

The white man was as tall as a tree and growing taller, like an ocean wave ready to catch you up into its heart, away from the air and the sunlight, and pull you deep into the water or sweep you forward onto the sand.

Robin thrust the silver blade back into its sheath and fell to her knees and her mouth said, "I'm sorry, Lord Heimdall. I just got to Valhalla this week, and I wanted to see Sky Mountain, and I should have realized that I was safe here under your protection. Please forgive me for having drawn steel in your presence."

Robin wondered what she was going to say and do next, but that turned out to be all. Her sword whispered, *"You're back in charge now, Hero—until the next time I notice you're about to get yourself killed."*

The white man wasn't looking at her any more but his lips were still drawn back. "I concern myself with everybody and everything," he said, his bright gold eyes fixed on Bookwyrm, "including three heroes who don't stay home in Valhalla." Bookwyrm fell to his knees and bowed his head, and the white man grew shorter, only head and shoulders taller than Knut.

"Your concern honors us, Lord Heimdall," Knut whispered, trying to sound humble, hoping that Heimdall would believe that he was terrified and that Robin Grima and Bookwyrm wouldn't.

"We're always concerned about you," Heimdall said, turning to stare at Knut with his bright gold eyes. "After all, you Midgard folk are our children."

Knut looked down at his feet and tried to convince himself he was bowing his head out of respect, not fear.

"We grew you from trees," Heimdall said, "and we shaped you to look like us, and we taught your great-grandparents how to make children and how to suck eggs, how to manage a household and how to write runes, how to kill animals and how to kill men. Don't be afraid, Odin's heroes. You're just as safe here with me at the sky's edge as you are at home in Valhalla. But be careful when you walk in between my hall and Odin's; there are too many Vanir in Asgard these days. In the beginning the giants and Aesir remembered that they were kinsmen and they fought together to protect their worlds against the Vanir perverts." His voice dropped into a chant, like Knut or Bookwyrm saying a poem. "They marry their sisters and have children by them. Their young men bend down to let a man ride them hard. Their loveliest lady turned her human lover into a hog, and she lay with him without caring what form he took. She spent three long nights letting the dark elves hammer her in exchange for a gold chain."

Some of you liberals may have just gotten offended at what you thought was Heimdall's homophobia. It wasn't as simple as that. The ancient Norse—and the giants and the Aesir—didn't see anything wrong with a man getting his kicks by penetrating another man's anus, so you shouldn't really call them homophobic. No, what offended them was a man offering up his own anus to someone else's penis, because they thought that there were only two ways to have sex and men were supposed to be the aggressors. Claiming that a man was a willing passive sexual partner was fighting words. It was as bad as saying that a man bore children and breastfed them, or that he turned into a woman once every nine days, or that he was castrated, or that he was a coward. You could get outlawed for saying slanderous things like that, and then when you died you'd end up on Hel's Dead Shore with the murderers.

Now that the liberals and conservatives are both equally offended, I'll go on with the story.

Heimdall went back to the rhythm of normal speech. "You may be the Valwolf's friend, Knut, but the Vanir wouldn't mind getting closer than that to Valgrind's guardians if they thought it would let them get into Valhalla and seduce Odin's warriors. Lady Freya already takes half of Midgard's heroes but she'd love to get her hands on all of them."

"The Vanir won't seduce us, Lord Heimdall," said Knut. "We serve Slain-Father Odin, Spear Master, Battle—"

"Odin and the Giants used to be allies," Heimdall repeated. "We fought a long war together against the Vanir witchfolk, till finally the Aesir grew tired of fighting and made peace and exchanged hostages. Now the Aesir who went to Vanaheim are both dead, and the Vanir who came to Asgard are still living here as honored guests."

"He twists the truth even better than Ratatosk the Squirrel," whispered Frostbite, which is quite a compliment if you look at it properly.

"I'm not going to tell him so," thought Robin Grima.

"Good," whispered Frostbite. *"Watch your tongue, Hero. You're not in Blind Hall any more. If Heimdall kills you here in Asgard, you might stay dead."*

"You're our children," Heimdall repeated. "Come inside, Robin Grima and Knut Valwolf Friend and Bersi Bookwyrm, and I'll show you the view from Sky Mountain."

Heimdall didn't take them to his feasting hall. Instead he led them to a tower where spiral stairs swept them up like an escalator (which didn't bother Robin but had Knut and Bookwyrm clinging white-knuckled to the moving handrail) and the tall window slits let them look out and see when they were level with the swan-cloaked valkyries and when they were level with the clouds and when they were level with the moon and the stars.

"Odin and his brothers made the stars out of sparks of fire from Muspelheim," Heimdall said. "His brothers were Hoenir the Well-Intentioned and Mimir the Wise. Odin sent them to the Vanir as hostages, and the Vanir killed them. They cut out Hoenir's heart and cut off Mimir's head and sent them back to Odin. The Slain Father kept Hoenir's heart with him, but he sent Mimir's head to Jotunheim for safekeeping, along with his own left eye. Look down there," he said, pointing through a window, as the stairway obligingly stopped.

The three heroes looked down, and found that the windows could tell what you were looking at and magnified it. They looked across Asgard and saw Valhalla and Saga's hall and Fenris Lokison. They looked across Light Elfland and saw the elves at their merrymaking. They looked across Vanaheim and saw the grainfields and orchards, the trees and the vines, the birds and animals, but the halls were empty and dusty.

"Where are the Vanir?" Robin Grima asked.

"They dug themselves burrows and crept into them," Heimdall said. "They think they can stay down there until Ragnarok and then come up and take over the Nine Worlds."

They looked farther down and saw the World Tree's middle root, the one in Jotunheim, watered by a sparkling fountain. A dozen giants stood in a circle around it, like mountains encircling a valley lake. They were supposed to be guarding it; but what they were really doing was staring at their laptops. Frost giants love to look at fire giant pornography, and vice versa: opposites attract. The giants could have used their root privilege the same way the Norns did (well, at a slightly lower level of course), but they weren't bright enough to do stuff like that.

"Mimir's Fountain," muttered Bookwyrm.

"Mimir the Wise," said Heimdall. "All the giants in Jotunheim came to the World Tree to welcome his head. We swore we'd take vengeance on the Vanir for his death. The only other person in Asgard who ever drank from Mimir's

Fountain is Odin, my foster father, and he had to give up an eye to do it."

After that the stairway started going up again, this time so fast that even Robin Grima felt safer holding onto the handrail. And less than an hour later the heroes stood at the top of the tower looking down at the Nine Worlds. The air blew clear and cool against their faces. They looked up and saw a giant white eagle perched on the top of the World Tree, slowly beating its wings.

"Lazybones," yelled a red squirrel, sitting on a branch below them. "You're too fat to fly. Nidhog will gulp you down and spit out your feathers, and Hel will make herself a new mattress out of them."

"Have some mead," said Heimdall, and held out an ivory drinking horn to Robin. She drank the strong sweet mead and felt the tower swaying beneath her feet, then passed it to Bookwyrm, who took a swallow and passed it to Knut, who held it to his lips and ran his tongue across the rim and then gave it back to Heimdall still almost full. Heimdall held it up high and drank, and then turned the horn over to show that he'd emptied it.

"I heard Robin Grima chanting the *Lokasenna* in Saga's hall," Heimdall said. "Those events happened at a party in Aegirstead, where I grew up. Aegir always made all his guests welcome. Not just giants and the Aesir, but also the Vanir perverts. We even welcomed Loki Wyrmtongue until he called Grandfather Aegir a coward. I've sworn to kill Loki for that insult when Ragnarok comes."

"Heimdall loathes Loki because he can't hear him," whispered Frostbite. *"That's because Loki went through the fire ordeal."*

"Loki is everyone's enemy," said Knut, glad to hear Heimdall say something he could agree with.

"Loki killed Baldur the Beautiful," said Bookwyrm.

"Everyone wept at Baldur Odinson's death, even the giants. Only one person stayed dry-eyed, a frost giantess who said her name was Thokk," (*"Who said her name was Thanks,"* Frostbite translated in Robin's mind,) "but everyone knows Thokk was really Loki Laufeyson, Father of Falsehoods, Mother of Monsters."

"I know all the giants," said Heimdall, "and there's no giant named Thokk, and never was. I keep watch on the Nine Worlds so Loki won't get free till Ragnarok starts. I'll blow my horn then and warn the Aesir, but when the giants come here, what Father Odin and his kinfolk ought to do is to get out of our way and let us kill the treacherous Vanir. Tell your friend the Valwolf that, Knut. Tell him the best thing that Valhalla's guardians can do at Ragnarok is to only let the Table One heroes out to fight Hel and the Table Eight heroes out to fight the Vanir, and that they ought to keep the rest of the heroes safely inside the hall so they won't interfere with the giants when they come to cleanse Asgard." Heimdall turned away from them and walked down the tower stairs, which were still moving up, walking downstairs like white water rushing downhill over boulders.

Bookwyrm walked slowly deosil (you probably think of that as clockwise, but Bookwyrm had never seen a clock; he thought of it as sun-wise) around the landing at the top of the World Tree.

"Don't fall," cried the red squirrel. "It's a long drop, and you'd get thirsty before you hit bottom."

Knut and Robin just stood there looking down at Asgard, no bigger than a chessboard below them, till finally the stairway stopped moving upwards. Robin walked onto the highest step, and it started spiraling down. Knut stepped down after her and then walked down two more steps so he could stand in front of her just in case something tried to attack her. Bookwyrm followed them, facing backwards so he could be sure that nobody would attack them from behind.

When they finally got back to the ground floor, they didn't see Heimdall anywhere and they didn't look for him. They left Sky Mountain, and they shut the door behind them, and they walked back to Valhalla.

Robin Grima's hair shone as bright as a bonfire under the night sky.

"You're not singing tonight," said a valkyrie, swooping down past them.

"That's true," said Knut.

"'Those who are silent seldom make mistakes,'" said Bookwyrm, quoting Odin's advice from the eddas.

Robin Grima didn't say anything out loud. *"Sword, was that what you wanted me to see at Rainbow Bridge?"* she asked silently.

"It went better than I expected," Frostbite whispered.

"I liked Odin. I thought I'd like Heimdall."

"I thought you would too. I'm glad you don't."

*****

"Can Heimdall hear us inside Valhalla?" Robin asked her sword, as she bit a mouthful of roast Saehrimnir off her eating knife (An eating knife has a dull point at its end that you can use to spear a chunk of meat that you've cut off a roast. Anything smaller gets put in your mouth with a spoon. It's fast and easy and it keeps your fingers clean, which is all you can ask of eating utensils.)

"Heimdall can hear everywhere in all of the Nine Worlds," Frostbite whispered, *"and that includes inside Valhalla. But he can't hear or see what goes on inside Blind Hall. Loki and Hodur helped Odin make it, and Heimdall is deaf and blind to all that goes on there."*

"Do the eddas say why the Vanir killed Odin's brothers?" asked Robin, and helped herself to a spoonful of baked apple.

"They found that Hoenir wasn't willing to give advice without Mimir at his side," Bookwyrm said, "so they decided that Odin gave them his brothers because they weren't worth keeping and that meant that they'd been insulted."

"There's a story," said Knut, "that says that Odin didn't get on well with his brothers after he came back from a trip to Midgard and found that they'd seduced his wife."

"There's a story," whispered Frostbite, "that Odin asked the Vanir to kill his brothers for him after he found they'd raped his wife. I heard it from Loki, and he said he heard it from Odin. Maybe it's true."

"Your hair is dirty from the courtyard dust, Robin Grima," Knut said. "Do you want to wash it by yourself this time, or would you like me to help you again?"

"Yes," Robin said, "I'd like you to help me." *"And I don't care if Heimdall heard me say that,"* she thought.

"Heimdall can't spy on you," Frostbite whispered, "any more than he can hear Lady Freya and Loki. You've walked through the fire ordeal, Robin Grima, and Heimdall can't hear you or see you or anyone near you. Go ahead and take a bath with Knut, Robin. Heimdall won't notice, and I'll try not to criticize his inadequate performance."

"Thank you for saving my life today, Sword. Now shut up, or I'll put you at the foot of my bed tonight, and maybe I'll leave you there tomorrow morning."

"No," Frostbite whispered, "please don't put me aside, Robin Grima. I need you. Without you holding me, I'm nothing."

"Then stop being so snippy," she said. "You're a sword, not a pair of scissors."

"Scissors are a woman's sword. That's one kenning

you'll learn from me first." But Frostbite didn't say anything else to her that night, not even when she got into her bed closet, and put the scabbard between her arms and snuggled back into the pillows, holding it tight.

That night, Robin Grima dreamt that she opened Valgrind to go speak to the Valwolf, but Thunder River was out there, waiting for her, cold and fierce, dragging her down into its dark depths, sweeping her downstream toward the Hel Falls, till she drew her sword and stabbed it, and it froze under her feet, thrusting her back into the air and sunlight again.

She held Frostbite up to her face and kissed his cold blade and said, "Thank you, Sword. I couldn't have done it without you."

"If you're really grateful," he whispered, *"break me in two when the right time comes."*

*****

That night, Knut Valwolf Friend dreamed of a beautiful long-haired girl who led him past Heimdall's castle and across Rainbow Bridge down to Midgard, where a smiling couple waited for them in the sunset twilight: a red-haired man with bright gold eyes, a fair-haired woman with sky-blue eyes.

"These are my father and mother," she said.

She stood in the shadows, and Knut couldn't see her face clearly. He told himself that her voice sounded like Robin Grima's.

"Welcome, Hero," the man said. "A wind told me good things about you, and I think I'd like seeing you as part of our family. What can you offer as my daughter's bride price?"

Knut held out his empty hands. "I don't have anything," he said, "except what Odin has given me: my sword and my seat at his table. I can't offer anything."

"You've got things that Odin never gave you," the man replied. "You've got your name and your learning and your honor. Will you give them to me and go without them in exchange for my daughter?"

"NO!" Knut screamed, and woke up with the scream still echoing in his ears.

CHAPTER SIX

In the morning, Robin got dressed, strapped on her sword belt, touched the cool silver hilt and asked, *"Are you still angry with me?"*

"I was never angry with you," Frostbite whispered. *"Where are we going today?"*

"Outside," Robin thought.

She walked up the stairs to the feast hall and past the tables spread with breakfast and out through Valgrind. A valkyrie dropped a hero into the river and flew away without bothering to watch as he floundered about in the swift-flowing water and got pulled under. Knut was sitting on the grass, feeding the Valwolf an apple core.

Robin sat down next to him. "Would you introduce us?" she asked.

"He can't," the wolf said, "and I won't. It's not time yet. And besides, I already know your names, which is more than Knut or you know."

"That's almost as knotted as a riddle," said Knut, "but I know how to untie it. I know Robin Grima Jonson's name, Valwolf, but I only know your nickname and I only know her sword Frostbite's nickname. Robin, this is my friend, the Valwolf. He already knows your names, and someday we'll all know his name too."

"He didn't introduce me," whispered Frostbite, *"just you. I wonder if that means he knows that the Valwolf and I don't need introducing."*

"You'll know everything when it's time to know it," said the Valwolf. "When Loki is free and Fenris is free and Baldur is free, then I'll be free to tell you my name, Knut."

"That won't happen till Ragnarok starts," said Knut, disappointedly. "We'll have to wait for centuries, and then we won't have much time to talk."

"Do we have to wait for centuries for our enemies to start the fight?" asked Robin. "Why can't we take the initiative and attack them?"

"We're the Good Guys," whispered Frostbite. *"Loki told me so. The Good Guys aren't supposed to start the battle that'll destroy the entire universe."*

"It's not honorable to attack someone by surprise," said Knut, very shocked. "Only murderers do that sort of thing, Robin Grima. It would dishonor Valhalla and Odin."

"And it wouldn't help change how things end," said the Valwolf. "The prophecies say that Odin will die and so will all his Valhallans."

"A wolf will swallow the sun and a wolf will swallow the moon," said Knut, quoting the eddas. "Then Hel's ice will melt, and the enemy ships will sail against us, and Heimdall will blow his horn, and Ragnarok will start, and the World Tree will shake, and the Nine Worlds will fall, and when it's over, we'll all be dead. I can wait patiently for centuries till that happens."

"You're dead already," Robin said, standing up. "So am I. So is everybody in Valhalla. I don't want to wait patiently for centuries and then march off to the big fight knowing I'm going to get killed there and not accomplish anything. I don't want to shake the World Tree and destroy the universe. I want to win!"

"Nonconformist!" yelled the red squirrel. "Troublemaker! Outside agitator! Treehugger!"

"They'll kill you," cried the eagle.

"He's right!" yelled the squirrel. "If the giants and Helfolk don't kill you, then Odin will kill you for breaking faith with him and disobeying his orders."

"They'll eat you," said Saehrimnir's head.

"I don't care what they do," said Robin Grima, staring up at the Valgrind guardians. "I want to win."

"You won't get experience points," whispered Frostbite. *"You won't go up levels. This isn't a game any more."*

"You can't do it alone," said the Valwolf.

Knut stood up and pulled Valgrind open and walked back inside Valhalla.

"I'll tell Odin!" screamed the squirrel. "I'll tell Hel! I'll tell the Norns—"

The Valwolf leapt up high into the air, over Valhalla's roof (and the roof-goat bleated in terror and ran to the far side of the roof) and into the branches of the World Tree, and then leapt down again, holding a squirming squirrel in his mouth, and brought him to Robin Grima.

"Let me go!" the squirrel screamed. "Let me go, and I swear I'll go with you and help you."

"And not tell anyone else about us," said Robin Grima.

"Yes, yes, I swear that too," the squirrel said. "I swear by the Sun and the World Tree. I swear by everything. Just don't let him eat me." The Valwolf spat him out on the grass, and poor little Ratatosk stared up at Robin Grima. "Please protect me," the squirrel cried piteously. "You don't want to kill me. I'm too beautiful to die. I'm too clever to die. I've been everywhere in the Nine Worlds, and I know everybody important. I'll obey you, and I'll help you, and I'll keep all your secrets. I swear it. May Thor's hammer kill me if I break my word, and may the giants eat me."

"That's a binding oath," whispered Frostbite.

"All right," said Robin Grima. "Welcome to the party, Ratatosk."

"I was never really afraid," I said. Oops, *Ratatosk* said. He stood up bravely, looking up at Robin Grima's big sharp sword and the Valwolf's big sharp teeth, his bright red fur as beautiful as the rising sun. "This will be a glorious adventure," he said. "The poets and saga tellers will never forget it, and I'm proud to be a part of it."

"I'm proud to have your company," said Robin.

Knut came back through Valgrind with his sword and a sack full of dried food. Beside him, Bookwyrm was carrying his own sword.

"One for all, and all for one," Knut said.

Robin Grima drew Frostbite, and her two friends touched their swords to it, borrowing its strength for the rest of the day.

"I'm coming too," said the Valwolf. He looked at Robin Grima. They were all looking at her, and he asked, "Where are we going?"

Robin looked up at the empty sunrise sky: no clouds, no valkyries, no ravens. Apparently Odin didn't care what was happening. *If I had dice,* she thought, *I'd roll them and see what world was highest.*

"Use your brain, Hero," whispered Frostbite, *"and we won't need any dice luck."*

"First, we'll go to Hel and kill Nidhog," Robin Grima said. "If she stops eating its Hel-root, then the World Tree will be stronger."

"She eats like a pig," said Ratatosk, "and her teeth are as sharp as your swords."

"Let's go," said Robin, remembering wading through Hel River in Blind Hall, remembering the sharp knives and cold water. "You can show us the way down to Hel, Ratatosk."

The squirrel ran a few hundred feet along Valhalla's western wall, away from the door and its guardians, and then scurried up the stone wall onto the roof and leapt back up onto the World Tree. The Valwolf leapt up after it. Knut looked up the stone wall. Then he started to climb, jamming fingers and toes into the crevices between the stones. Robin and Bookwyrm followed his example.

The World Tree overhung the roof of Valhalla, some of its leaves brushing lightly across Robin's face. Knut walked over to the roof-goat and patted her till she calmed down, then reached gently out to squeeze her teats so the warm mead squirted into his cupped left hand. "Say your brag, Robin Grima," he said. "Where are you going to lead us, and what is our mission?"

"I'm going to go through the Nine Worlds and change things so Valhalla wins," Robin Grima said. "And I'm going to get hold of Tyr's right hand."

Knut lifted his hand up and she drank a sip of the strong, sweet liquor.

"I'm going to follow her, and I swear I'll never betray her," said Bookwyrm and took a sip too.

"And so will I," said Knut, and took his own sip, then wiped his hands on the goat's soft hair.

After that they climbed up into the World Tree and joined the Valwolf, and then headed toward the central trunk of the great ash tree. On the way, they passed by the well of the Norns, but they didn't stop to chat. Below them, the Norns didn't look up from the tapestry they were weaving. Robin Grima peeked down and for a moment saw *Naglfar*, the bone ship, surrounded by the icefields of Niflheim. Then the shape disappeared and all she could see was white cloth.

The squirrel ran briskly across the branch and then, headfirst, down the great trunk. The humans followed him downwards more slowly, with Robin wishing she'd been able to pick up some rope before heading off. One of the worst drawbacks of Asgard is that there aren't any shopping malls. Valhalla doesn't even have telephones or internet terminals so people can order from catalogues.

Since they didn't have any climbing gear, the heroes had to descend the tree by kneeling down and grasping a branch with their hands and then letting themselves down, dangling in the air and reaching out their toes to the next branch below. Sometimes they just let go and fell till they hit something and tried to hold onto it. No, they couldn't hug the trunk and shinny down it. I don't carry a tape measure, but the World Tree's probably a thousand feet around. Or maybe it's five hundred feet. Whatever it is, it's too thick for even most hill giants to wrap their arms around it, let alone humans.

The Valwolf waited till they'd all gotten safely down to the next branch and then leapt lightly down to join them, barely shaking the branch when he landed, as if a wind bore him up.

"You're all so slow!" whimpered Ratatosk. "We'll be all day getting down to Midgard at this rate. I'm going to go check my email. Call out when you get below the Bifrost Bridge." He darted off down the trunk.

"What's email?" asked Bookwyrm.

Robin started to answer three times, and each time stopped in mid-sentence because Bookwyrm and Knut didn't want to know what electricity was or what the Internet was, and anyway she didn't really know enough to tell them about those things. "Magic written messages people send each other, and that they watch on a magic glass window," she said at last, and the two warriors nodded, completely satisfied.

She went back to thinking about the things she wished she had with her, the ones she'd bought for Grima on her first dungeon expedition. Fifty feet of rope and some pitons to anchor the rope into the tree. A bow and arrows and throwing knives and flasks of oil that she could burn in a lantern or that she could light and throw to burn enemies. Sacks for food and loot, and skins for water and wine, and a week of food rations. A lantern. A quarterstaff for hiking up and down steep slopes or for poking things from a safe distance or even for using to fight. A holy symbol to scare off vampires. Grima had carried a carving of Thor's Hammer and a Christian cross, even though Grima wasn't a Christian and Robin wasn't either any more. The last time she'd gone to church was for her mother's and father's funeral, and having cancer hadn't changed her mind. She hadn't really believed in the Norse gods either, but she'd prayed to Odin now and then, asking him to give her good dice rolls for Grima. Now she just wished Odin would send her some rope. And maybe a cleric with Cure Serious Wounds.

In case you were wondering, if Robin had kept on going to church, she wouldn't have ended up in the Nine Worlds. People only come here if they believe more in the Norse myths than any other religion. That's why Valhalla didn't get Richard the Lion-Hearted and Robin Hood and Joan of Arc and General Patton.

About half an hour later, they came to the rope. It was light brown except for where it was dark red, and it was about as thick as Robin's thumb, woven of braided strands and tied in an elaborate knot of three triangles.

"Val-knut," said Bookwyrm. ("*Knot of the slain*," translated Frostbite.)

"My namesake," said Knut. (Knut is Norse for "knot"—and the name of a mighty Norse king who ruled Denmark and Norway and England but knew that the ocean tide was even stronger. Norse historians call him Knut Swegenson, and English historians call him Canute the Great. He wasn't related to Knut Valwolf Friend.)

The Valwolf sniffed the rope. "Odin's blood," he said.

"'Wounded I hung on a wind-swept gallows,'" chanted Bookwyrm. "'For nine long nights, pierced by a spear, pledged to Odin; offered, myself to myself.'"

"We can go a lot faster with rope," Robin Grima said, and reached out to untie it. The knot fell apart at her touch, but she caught the rope before it fell.

"Let's see how long it is," said Knut and wrapped it around and around his left arm from the fingers to the elbow. "Two hundred ells," he said at last. (A Norse ell is about twenty inches—a little less than half an English ell—so that's 333 feet, half the Christian Number of the Beast. It's probably a coincidence.)

"If the rope Odin got hanged with is still here, what happened to the spear that wounded him?" asked Robin, reaching out to touch a long-dried blood drop.

"He kept the spear," said Bookwyrm, and Robin remembered the golden spear and Odin's warm, friendly smile.

They tied the rope around their waists, about a third of it between each of them, and climbed down the trunk one by one to the next branch, and then did it again, and the Valwolf kept up with them, never losing his balance as he jumped from branch to branch.

Fifteen minutes or so later they found themselves looking up at the underside of Asgard. It was sky blue, with white clouds here and there. Robin thought it looked like an IMAX screen.

"Men call it Heaven," said Bookwyrm, "and the Aesir call it the Height. The Vanir call it The Wind Weaver, and Frey's elves call it the Fair Roof. The Giants call it the Up-World and the dwarves call it The Dripping Hall, because they only go out when it's raining."

"That's from the Ballad of Alvis the wise dark elf," said Knut. "It ends up with the sun rising and turning him into stone."

"The sunlight turned him into gold," Ratatosk said, abruptly popping out of a hole in the trunk. Not a small hole either, even though it wasn't as big as a Valhallan door. "His friends came out after sunset and took him back to their forge. Odin's spear is made out of Alvis's wise head. and Sif Thorswife's hair is made from Alvis's beard."

"Are you done checking your email?" asked Knut.

"For a while," said Ratatosk. He stepped to the side of his hole and gestured invitingly. "Come on in and take a look." The entry hole was big enough for three humans and a wolf to come in without crowding each other and without having to duck their heads. They left the rope just inside and looked around my beautiful home, bright with the light of a dozen plasma monitors, most of them set up to use the Roman alphabet, though the Nine Worlds weather forecast was in runes.

"'Midgard will be hot and muggy,'" read Bookwyrm, "'with thunderstorms in mid-afternoon. Jotunheim will be cold and clear with gusts of cold winds in the mid-afternoon. Hel will be cold and clear.' We'd better hurry down the World Tree so we can be in Hel before the storms start."

Robin was looking at a monitor with messages from the Bifrost Boffers discussion group. It's a lot of fun as long as you don't take the insults too seriously and as long as you kill a message thread the moment people start mentioning how King Olaf took an oath to massacre anyone in the Orkneys who refused to get baptized. We call that Godwin's First Law, and it's named after Earl Godwin, who helped start the Boffers back in the eleventh century, when it ran on carrier pigeons and valkyries instead of the Net. I didn't tell Robin about that because then I'd have had to tell Knut and Bookwyrm about the modern Godwin's Law that's named after Mike Godwin, and that says that if you keep up a discussion long enough, someone's bound to compare the people on the other side to Hitler and the Nazis, and after that most intelligent people won't bother going on with the discussion. Instead I read the most recent Boffer message.

Third Day of Grain Cutting Month, Odin's Day, 10:15 AM

Heimdall wrote: Odin ought to keep his eye on his Valhallans, not let them run around Asgard without a shepherd.

Ratatosk commented: Odin can't afford to do that. He doesn't have an eye to spare. If you're getting lonely for a shepherd, Old Ram, maybe you should pick up one in Midgard. Do you prefer human shepherds or dogs?

Skuld commented: People with good taste prefer humans to wolves and wolves to dogs and dogs to squirrels.

Knut was tracing another monitor's message with his right index finger: "DEARLY BELOVED," it started, 'JUST CLICK ON THIS MESSAGE, AND WE CAN—" and then it disappeared from the screen as the spam filter finished analyzing the message, tracing it back to its source in Dark Elfland, and alerting the other dark elves there so they could tie up the spammer and throw him outside for the wolves to eat or the sunlight to turn to gold.

The next message in the queue popped up on the screen.

"For sale CHEAP: MAGIC SWORD. Never misses, never rusts, cuts through iron and stone. But wait: there's more! It's cursed! It has to kill a man every time it's drawn, and it'll kill the wielder if nobody else is available. Buy it for yourself if you feel lucky. Buy it for your enemy if you don't."

The Valwolf sat in the entrance, on top of the pile of rope, looking down at the middle worlds.

Robin had been looking at a monitor with a message analyzing the current geopolitical situation, but she resolutely stopped. "Don't read any more," she cried out, "or you'll get trapped in the flow and next time you look up it'll be sunset. We're heading for Hel!"

Reluctantly the others turned away from the monitors and headed outside, pausing only to rope themselves up again.

"Where did you get that rope?" Ratatosk asked.

"We found it hanging around," said Robin.

"It used to be Odin's," said Bookwyrm, "but he's not depending on it anymore.

"Do you have any fault to find with it?" asked the Valwolf.

"Who, me?" said Ratatosk. "No, of course not. No fault. Not at all." He ran past them and scampered down the trunk, and the humans followed as fast as they could, the Valwolf always at their backs.

Now the branches were covered with dark green leaves and dotted with clusters of purple flowers. Robin brought her nose close to one cluster, but couldn't smell any fragrance. (The ash tree is wind-pollinated, so its flowers don't need to attract insects.)

Now and then they heard bees buzzing. *"Don't chase them away from the honey, and they won't sting you,"* whispered Frostbite. Sometimes they avoided a branch with a beehive in it. Eventually Robin Grima noticed that the bees weren't feeding on the flowers but on sap flows along the trunk and branches. *"Ash honey,"* whispered Frostbite. *"Leave it alone, and it'll turn into mead."*

"We can help ourselves to dessert as we travel," said Bookwyrm, dipping his finger into the ash honey and licking it off. Robin did the same and enjoyed the dark, sweet flavor. Knut scooped up a palmful for himself and then another for the Valwolf.

The farther down they went, the more the trunk slanted away from Bifrost, till finally they couldn't see the rainbow bridge any more. The air got colder, and after a while there weren't any more flowers, just black winter buds. Finally they found themselves only a few hundred feet over the icy mountain range that divides Midgard from Jotunheim. Below them, a pack of wolves leapt at a huge elk with broken antlers.

"Where's Mimir's Fountain?" asked Bookwyrm.

Nobody answered, unless you counted the howling of the wolves below. One of the wolves tore out the elk's throat, and a gush of red blood spouted up into the air.

"Do you know any illusion spells?" Knut asked.

"Just one," said Bookwyrm, "and making myself look like a dragon wouldn't help us here."

"I can't do any spells," said the Valwolf.

Robin shook her head. "I've played at casting spells," she

said, "but it was never real, just pretend."

"You're in the Nine Worlds now," said Bookwyrm. "Try again. Try Truesight."

"Truesight," Robin said, waving her hands in front of her, like a stage magician. "Dispel illusion. Detect illusion." She looked up and down and all around, but everything still looked the same.

"Even Thor and Loki couldn't see through the illusions of Utgard's king," Knut said. "but then they weren't skalds or rune readers, and we are. Where's Mimir's Fountain?" he asked. The wolves howled louder, and the elk's blood rose higher and higher, splashing up against the trunk of the World Tree and dyeing the pale wood red.

"Where's Mimir's Fountain?" asked the Valwolf, and Robin and Ratatosk joined in the chorus. That was the third time, and third time's the charm sometimes—or in this case, the way you break the charm.

The elk screamed loudly, the wolves howled, the air turned freezing cold, and the red blood turned into driving red sleet, pounding against them, sharp and cold against their faces and hands and feet.

"Don't close your eyes!" yelled Bookwyrm.

Robin put her spread fingers over her eyes, trying to keep out the sleet but still look down at—

Abruptly the wolves and elk disappeared. There was a jet of red water spurting up from a white pillar and falling back into a red pool surrounded by stone boulders and chunks of dirty black ice that looked almost like—

One of the boulders moved. It dipped a horn into the pool and raised it up again to its lips. It drank its fill and then turned its attention back to its laptop and reached out a dirty cold wet finger to touch the button that would restart the fire giantess video.

"Frost giants," said Bookwyrm. "Guarding the fountain."

"I thought they'd be standing up around it," Knut said, "like sentries. I didn't think they'd be lying down around it, guzzling it."

"Any chance we could sneak in there and take a drink?" Robin asked her sword.

"If you drink from Mimir's Fountain, then you'll see the same future that he did," whispered Frostbite. *"Do you want to know all the prophecies, Robin Grima, or do you want to change them?"*

Robin Grima stared in silent wonder at the scene, then shook her head. "The weather prediction said Jotunheim would have gusts of strong cold winds in mid-afternoon," she finally said. "We're on our way to Hel. Don't get distracted." They circled around the World Tree to the far side of the trunk and kept heading down, wriggling through the hole in the ground where the massive trunk pierced through the surface of the world.

The underside of Jotunheim was dark gray, with black clouds here and there. Beneath them lay the lands of Hel and Niflheim, darker yet, with Svartalfheim a dark shadow in the distance. Robin Grima's hair shone like firelight, lighting their way as they lowered themselves from branch to branch. The leaves were yellow-gold from cold. The blood on their rope—Odin's blood—sparkled like red diamonds. The Valwolf's yellow eyes glinted with gold highlights. Frostbite's hilt was silver starlight. Everything else in sight was shades of gray, plus lots of black.

Halfway down to Hel, Ratatosk wanted to check his email again. This time the entrance was narrower and lower. They had to come in one at a time, and Knut had to duck his head. Inside, the room was pleasantly warm, which was more than could be said of the outside, and Ratatosk offered them cups of hot mulled apple cider with optional apple brandy to keep off the cold. The monitor said it was 2:30 PM.

"When's sunset?" asked Bookwyrm.

Ratatosk hit a few keys and the monitor showed sunset as 9 PM in Midgard and 3 PM in Hel and Niflheim and 12:01 PM on the ocean near Jotunheim.

"The sunset horn will sound in the Valhalla courtyard," whispered Frostbite, *"but it won't sound here. Be careful, Hero."*

I brought out napkins and plates for my guests, and gave them a lunch of bread and nuts and honey, and more of my cider. Knut added an apple that he'd brought along from Valhalla. The Valwolf turned up his nose at everything but the honey and apples. I read a couple of dozen messages and wrote a couple of replies and caught up on the news. It didn't mention our expedition.

Robin sat down in front of a keyboard and tried to log in to her old email account but got an error message: "Probability Not Found." She did manage to find the memorial page for the university hospital, with pictures of what it looked like after the earthquake and fire, a list of victims, a hanging in effigy page for the contractor who hadn't followed the blueprints and hadn't built in compliance with the state and city codes, and even a couple of messages from people she'd rescued. All the web pages were labeled "Read Only" and the Reply buttons didn't work when she tried clicking them.

Then they talked over their plans for the fight. Ratatosk would insult Nidhog and get her angry. Then Bookwyrm would use illusion to look like a dragon and challenge her to a fight. Knut and the Valwolf would keep off the Helfolk. Robin Grima and Frostbite would rush in and kill Nidhog.

Robin drew Frostbite, and her two friends touched their swords to it, so their weapons would share its powers.

"I forgot to tell you a kenning this morning, because we

didn't eat breakfast together," Knut told Robin. "The kenning for sun is the glory of the light elves."

Then they went back outside into the twilight darkness and started down again. Each branch down, the air was colder. It started snowing, and the branches got slippery. Odin's rope stayed dry. It always has, I've noticed, even during the spring rains. For centuries I used to wonder each time I passed it why Odin left it there on the World Tree instead of taking it back home after he'd gotten the runes. When I gave up on that one, I wondered why nobody else had taken it. Loki could have done some very interesting things with a rope with Odin's blood on it. So could the dark elves. After a while I tried untying it myself, but the moment I took hold of it, my fur all stood up on end and my ears started ringing, so I decided to leave it alone, and go do something else more interesting.

Thought and Memory may not have been flying circles around Robin Grima and her friends, but Odin obviously had plans for them.

CHAPTER SEVEN

After the fight....

I said that I wasn't going to do details of fighting. It's obvious that Nidhog didn't kill them all or this would be a much shorter book. And besides, fights are boring unless you're the one doing the fighting, and I was too clever to risk my own beautiful neck, so—

Yes, Lady Urd, I'll tell all the important details. Please don't be angry. Please don't touch my life-thread.

The sky over Hel was dark gray, and you could only see a few feet in front of your nose, but the World Tree's gray-white bark shone like moonlight and its leaves and flowers glowed like embers—if you believe in green and purple embers. Silhouetted against the light was the monstrous bulk of Nidhog Grayback, Striker in the Dark, lying at the foot of the trunk. The closer I got, the better I saw her, and the worse she looked. Her head lay on the ground, and underneath it something was whimpering. That was good: the more noise, the better.

Knut made sure that Robin Grima's hair was covered up.

It turned out that he'd picked up three of my napkins after eating my food. My good linen napkins! When I mentioned politely that I hadn't made him a gift of them, he promised to return them to me after the adventure was over. Of course that still meant I was going to have to wash the stains out, not to mention having them rewoven if they got cut up by weapons or teeth. Saga can afford that sort of thing when heroes drop by to eat at her hall; Odin pays her bills. But there's a reason that most of us don't invite heroes to drop by whenever they're in the neighborhood.

I sat on a branch of the World Tree that was too light to bear Nidhog's weight, and looked down at the huge dragon. "It's a good thing you don't have fingers or toes," I yelled. "You're too stupid to count them. Someday Thor is going to get tired of killing giants and have the dark elves mend all the chains that Fenris broke and bring them down here to tie you up, but they won't fit. You're so fat you can't fit into a size extra-extra-large collar any more. But that doesn't mean you're safe. Loki's daughter will be here in a minute or two, and she's got a sword big enough to kill you." As I yelled my insults and threats, Robin and Knut and Bookwyrm and the Valwolf dropped down from the World Tree's lowest branch and disappeared into the darkness.

Nidhog let go of the woman whose blood she'd been sucking and raised her head up to get a better look at me. Her long black wings stayed furled against her dark gray body. I wasn't afraid that she'd fly up and attack me. Her wings would let her glide across Dead Shore so she could pick up her prey, but they weren't any good for hovering in the air.

She didn't need light to look at me; she could see my warm flesh in the dark. No, she wasn't using any high tech gadgets. She saw me with the infrared-sensing pits between her eyes and her nostrils; a lot of snakes have them and so do a lot of dragons. I had to keep her distracted so she wouldn't turn around and see the Valhallans.

The woman that Nidhog had dropped was slowly crawling away, across the dark frozen land and back into Hel River. She wouldn't be here so close to Dead Shore unless she was a murderess or some other evildoer, but getting away from Nidhog when she had the chance did show she was more sensible than we were.

Robin Grima lay down on the icy ground and began to creep toward Nidhog. The Valwolf laid back his ears and bared his teeth, but silently followed Knut and Bookwyrm to the far side of the World Tree. I stayed on my branch, safely above them.

"Slanderer! Lying little troublemaker!" Nidhog yelled, a cloud of white smoke billowing out from her nostrils with every word she spoke. "I swore truce with Lady Hel when she first came here."

"She's had a lot of time to change her mind since then," I yelled back. "You must have a few brains in that big fat head of yours. Try to use them. If Lady Hel breaks her oath, who's going to punish her? What can the Aesir do to her that they haven't already done? Do you expect a Lokisdaughter to be loyal to her allies? Do you think her father taught her to be sincere and not play tricks on people?"

"I'll bite her big sword into pieces," screamed Nidhog, "and I'll do the same to her, the faithless bitch. I'll bite her left side and her right side apart! I'll bite off her hands! I'll bite off her—"

"Do you have time to fight me first?" asked the other dragon who suddenly appeared in front of Nidhog, his hot breath smelling like burning parchment, his eyes black as ink, his red-gold scales glowing like the summer sun's first sunrise after months of cold dark winter, his voice just the same as Bookwyrm's.

After that the plan began to break down. Plans don't usually last very long.

"Rune magic!" scoffed Nidhog. "Go back to Odin, lying little rune mage, and tell him that even an illiterate old dragon can see through his schemes."

"You're right," said Bookwyrm, letting the dragon illusion fall and drawing his sword. "I'm a rune mage. Do you have time to fight me, old worm, or are you only brave enough to fight people who died of old age and sickness?"

Nidhog opened her mouth, each of her four fangs as long as a sword, a row of incisors behind them, and behind them a row of short molars each almost half as wide as a man's hand. Yes, I know that snakes don't have molars; dragons are different. Some of them just dig their fangs into their prey to suck blood, but a lot of them like to crack the bones so they can suck the marrow, too. Nidhog was one of that sort. She was also hot-blooded. Her blood simmered through her veins and boiled through her arteries, and no, I'm not being metaphorical. Think about the alternative: a cold-blooded creature living down in the frozen wastes of Hel. It wouldn't spend its time gnawing the World Tree's roots or tormenting dead people; it'd be too busy sleeping.

"Fight!" screamed Ratatosk.

Nidhog bent down and seized Bookwyrm's sword between her molars and shook it furiously to and fro, but she didn't like the cold taste of Frostbite's magic so she let it go and watched the sword and man fly off. "That was fun," she said. "Who's next?"

Robin Grima stood up and drew Frostbite, the cold silver point reaching up to touch Nidhog's throat. "I'm next," she said. "I've come here to defend the World Tree. This is no game, Nidhog. Fight me, or die!"

Frostbite opened up a cascade of icicles at the dragon's throat. The Valwolf leapt up on her back and bit through where the spine would have been if a dragon had a spine, tearing his way to her heart and ripping it open. After half a minute, when they realized that none of the Dead Shore folk were coming to the dragon's defense, Knut and Bookwyrm joined in the fight, first cutting off the creature's flailing wings, then slashing at whatever seemed handiest. And Nidhog fought back, biting her attackers' weapons and flesh.

Nidhog weighed over a ton, and at the usual rate of an ounce of blood per pound of flesh that meant Nidhog had over two thousand ounces of blood, over fifteen gallons. By the time the fight was done, there was dragon blood everywhere, steaming warm in the cold air. The World Tree was splashed with it, and so was the land all around the tree's lowest root.

Bookwyrm stripped off his clothing and began rolling around in the blood. "Fafnir's blood made Siegfried weapon-proof!" he yelled to the others.

That's true; I was there to watch that fight, and I remember. Fafnir's blood also healed the wounds Siegfried got in the fight, the same way that Nidhog's blood was healing Bookwyrm's wounds, the ones he hadn't noticed yet and now never would: one on the left side of his neck and another on his right wrist, where Nidhog's fangs had driven deep to inject her poison and suck out his blood.

"Siegfried was weapon-proof everywhere except on his back where a leaf stuck and gave him a weak spot," yelled Bookwyrm. The Valwolf laid down and rolled in the blood. Knut took off his clothing and did the same, not noticing how the blood healed the wound on the inside of his right elbow, just a little away from where the nurse inserts the needle when she draws blood for tests.

"Let's see if it really works," said Robin Grima, drawing her eating knife and slashing at her right arm where her skin was red and warm with dragon blood. The knife didn't go in.

"Is rolling around naked in dragon blood a good idea, Sword?" Robin thought.

"It won't keep you from being poisoned or burnt or drowned," Frostbite whispered, *"but it's still probably a good idea. Just don't get overconfident."*

"What about you?" she asked her sword. *"Should I make sure that every bit of you got bathed in dragon's blood?"*

"No," the sword whispered. *"Please don't do that, Robin Grima. Some day you might want to break me."*

Knut and Bookwyrm went to wash off in Hel River and came out cold but clean. Then they kept watch for Helfolk, looking politely away from the trunk of the World Tree where Robin Grima was bathing herself in dragon blood. She took off her shoes and sword belt, her tunic and breeches, and she took off my beautiful linen napkins and hung them all up on a branch of the World Tree. I checked my napkins and only found two fang marks, both in the same napkin.

Robin Grima didn't have any wounds to heal, not because she was a better fighter than Bookwyrm and Knut but because Frostbite was; he'd shared his magic powers with their swords but not his intelligence or his ego.

Afterwards Robin went down to Hel River and rinsed off the blood, looking at the little sharp knives flowing between her fingers without wounding her. Her hair flamed in the darkness like a comet, and the knives didn't cut it either. Hair and fingernails may not be alive, but they're still a part of a person, and now Robin's were proof against any weapons. Anyone who tried to trim the Valhallans' hair or fingernails was going to find it quite a challenge from now on. So would anyone who tried to trim the Valwolf's claws. I tried biting through my napkin with the fang holes in it, but my sharp teeth couldn't pierce it. I decided to keep it as a souvenir instead of trying to have it rewoven.

"Did I fight well enough to suit you?" Robin asked

Frostbite as she got dressed again, slowly pulling her pants up over her wet legs, wishing she'd thought to ask Knut to bring along a towel from the bathroom.

"I helped out a little now and then," her sword whispered, *"but you didn't make any serious mistakes. But keep practicing, Hero; your next opponent might be more of a challenge. Are you going to rinse me clean too, or do I have to stay bloody?"*

"I'm sorry." Robin Grima drew her sword and started to dip it into the river, but it screamed wordlessly in her mind and she remembered its boast that it could freeze the river with its touch. So instead she knelt on the river shore and cupped out a handful of water, warming it in her hand, spilling the water over her sword and repeating the process again and again, till its bright blade shone like starlight. The sharp knives in the water slid out between her fingers onto the river bank, forming a low pile beside her like a sand castle of steel. Icicles dripped off her sword point as it froze the water that washed it.

She waved her sword in the air but it didn't seem to get any dryer.

"You can put me back in my home," Frostbite whispered. *"I won't rust."*

"The Helfolk are coming!" yelled Knut, and Robin ran back to the World Tree to join her friends, her sword in her hand, ready for battle.

"Be polite to Lady Hel," whispered Frostbite, *"but don't offer her your obedience. She's queen of this world, but you're not her subject; you're from Asgard where Odin rules. Claim social equality with her, Hero: call her sister."*

Hel Lokisdaughter wasn't coming to the World Tree trunk by horse or on foot; she was riding Garm Hel-hound, his legs ten feet high, galloping swiftly towards them across the frozen land. Garm didn't wear saddle or bridle; Hel rode bareback, a leash in her hand attached to a choke chain collar around her mount's throat. She didn't look like the skeleton of red fire and white ice that Robin Grima had seen in Blind Hall. Her face and hands were flesh: livid blue on the left side, pale white on the right side. Her eyes were yellow, like a wolf's or like Loki her father. Her hair was pale blonde under a silver crown. Behind her came a troop of Helfolk carrying black axes. And behind them walked bright-haired Baldur Odinson, leading his twin brother, dark-haired Hodur, whose eyes were white and blind.

"I see you've killed Nidhog and bathed in her blood," Hel said, her voice cold and sharp as a winter wind, harsh as a raven's call, loud and clear as a wolf's howl. "Did you drink her blood and eat her heart?"

"We're not berserks or cowards," said Knut Valwolf Friend. "We don't want to learn the language of birds, and we aren't looking for valkyries to seduce. We bathed in the dragon's blood, but we didn't drink it." He glanced down at the Valwolf, its muzzle red with blood and wondered if his friend could say the same thing.

Robin remembered enough of the story of Siegfried and Fafnir and Brunhilde to know that was what Knut was dropping references to. She wondered what Bookwyrm would have to say to Lady Hel, but Bookwyrm wasn't looking at Loki's daughter; he was walking toward the Helfolk, toward a woman with long golden hair, toward his dead wife Drifa. Lady Hel didn't seem to notice him. Drifa was holding out her arms to him.

"And we're not as stupid as Siegfried," Ratatosk called out. "We're not even as stupid as your brothers. You talked Odin into giving you a world to rule, Lady Hel, but your serpent brother only gets to swim round and round in the ocean, and there's so little there worth eating that he spends most of his time biting his own tail. Your wolf brother has an even smaller domain and even less freedom, now that Lord Tyr has fettered and chained him so he can't leave Heather Island."

Lady Hel smiled. "Greetings, little tusked rat," she said. "Welcome to Dead Shore, where all slanderers must come at last. Insult me or my people or my kinsfolk once more tonight, and you'll never leave here." Ratatosk fell silent.

Hel's hand was on her sword hilt but she hadn't drawn her weapon. Robin Grima put Frostbite back into its sheath and looked up at Hel towering over her, remembering Blind Hall and the heavy black sword coming down to split her skull. Her neck muscles tensed, but she tried her best to smile. "Good day, Sister," Robin said.

"It's after sunset," Lady Hel said, "and tonight may not be good for either of us, Sister. What are you and your friends going to offer me as compensation for spilling Nidhog's blood?"

"Nidhog was gnawing the World Tree's roots, Sister." Robin Grima said, wondering with each word whether Frostbite was about to take her over and make her apologize to Lady Hel for her rudeness, wondering whether she could climb the World Tree fast enough to escape Hel's sword. "If the tree grows weak and dies, then what will happen to the worlds?" She looked up at Ratatosk and saw that he'd climbed a couple of branches higher while Hel was looking at her instead of him.

"I found Nidhog already here when Odin outlawed me from Asgard," Hel said. "It was hard enough to protect myself and my hall folk from her; I had no chance of protecting the World Tree. But now you've spilled her blood, little sister, and all the worlds will suffer if evil folk come here from Dead Shore and bathe in it. What did the Lord of the Gallows instruct you and your followers to do after the fight? Did he tell you how to turn Nidhog's blood into poet's mead? Or did Prince Baldur's mother send you to tell me that she'll wash my land clean with her tears if I send her fair son home again? Or did Brother Fenris tell you to bring him the dragon blood so he can bathe in it once he's broken free of his chain?"

"Nobody asked me and my friends to come here," Robin Grima said. "It was all my idea, and we came here without asking anyone's permission or advice. What I want to do next is—Sister, I know you've heard all the prophecies about Ragnarok. We came here to talk with you and work out a better future than a battle where everybody dies. What else do you want besides cleaning up Nidhog's blood? Maybe we can help you."

Frostbite was silent, so apparently she hadn't said anything unforgivably rude, but the others were all staring at her. Back in the old days, Barney's golden dragon would have handled this sort of thing because of his high Charisma. Grima's highest stat was her Strength; her Charisma was only average, and she didn't have any special abilities or spells of charm or diplomacy, and neither did her sword. *Frostbite, is there something else I should be saying to Lady Hel?* Robin thought.

The sword didn't answer.

"I could drink up Nidhog's spilled blood," said the Valwolf. "I may have already swallowed some drops of it while we were butchering her." He sniffed the bloody ground beneath his feet, his ears laid back, his tail low.

"Drinking Nidhog's blood will increase your strength and your size and your appetite," said Lady Hel. "You might even become as powerful as my hound." Garm Hel-hound threw back his head and howled, as loud as a thunderstorm. The World Tree trembled and shook under me, and I held onto it tight with my claws.

When the last echoes of Garm's howls had died away, Hel said, "Once Garm could speak to me just as well as you can, Sister, but then he killed Nidhog's sons and drank their blood. Follow in his steps, and you'll lose your speech the same way he did. Are you willing to pay that price to clean up the blood you've helped spill today?"

"We'll find another way," Robin Grima said hastily. "We won't drink it."

"Thank you," Hel said. She got down off Garm's back and held out her right hand toward Robin. "You may stay in my realm for as long as you wish," she said, "but I won't offer you my hospitality. You may not enter my hall and you may not eat or drink anything that you find here. Help my folk guard this ground till the cock crows from my hall roof to say that it's dawn. By then Nidhog's blood will be cold and powerless, and we'll have time to talk about what we can do to shape the future."

"Thank you for your kindness, Sister," Robin said. She reached out and took Hel's icy white hand and shook it firmly.

The Valwolf growled at Nidhog's carcass, then walked over to stand at Knut's side.

Knut dug an apple out of his bag and held it out toward Hel. "You're welcome to share *our* food, Lady Hel," he said.

"What do you want in exchange for an Asgard apple?" asked Hel, looking at the apple. It shone in the darkness, as gold and as bright as Baldur's hair.

"Whatever you can give me in good will that does honor to me and my friends," said Knut. He took a deep breath and said, "For instance, you might let my friend Bersi Bookwyrm Beornson's wife Drifa join us when we leave here."

"We'll discuss that in the morning, too," Hel said. She drew her black sword and walked away from them toward the river, and Baldur and Hodur followed her.

Valhalla: Absent Without Leave

It may have been after sunset, but the world was getting brighter, not darker. I looked up and saw the sky was bright with falling stars—no, with falling snowflakes. One of them landed on my nose and another on my left paw. I watched them lie on my fur, cold and glittering, till they finally melted away.

"It wasn't like this in Blind Hall," Robin Grima thought to her sword, but Frostbite was silent, and she eventually remembered that she'd only visited Blind Hall's Hel in the daytime, never at night.

Lady Hel's hall folk had formed a ring around Nidhog's blood. Beyond them, by the light of the falling snow, I watched the Dead Shore folk cross Hel River, some of them wading through the icy water, some of them suddenly falling to their knees as the knives cut them, till they reached our side of the river and came running and hopping and crawling toward us: toward the ring of black axe blades and Hel's black sword, towards Baldur and Hodur and their bright swords, towards Frostbite and the swords with which he'd shared his power.

"I should have brought a spear," Knut muttered. He picked up one of Nidhog's incisors that had been pulled out during the fight and waved it at the approaching Dead Shore folk. "I dedicate you as sacrifices to Odin," he said, and threw it like a spear toward them.

The air got colder, and a breeze began to shake the World Tree's branches. I decided to go check my email. It was only a few miles climb up the trunk to my basement, and then I could have some nice hot cider and nestle down on a soft mattress underneath my electric blanket.

I hadn't expected to find the Valwolf following me.

"I'm not running away," I told him. "I just want a few bites to eat and a few bytes to read." He growled. He used to like my jokes back when she was young, but he lost his sense of humor after Odin drove him berserk, or maybe you say rabid for canines. I understand that it's embarrassing to wake up one evening and not recognize yourself when you look in a mirror and then slowly start to remember that you went crazy yesterday and ate your best friend—but after all it was centuries ago, and you'd think he'd have gotten over it by now, and it certainly wasn't my fault: Odin's the god of intoxication and madness. The Valwolf should have been sulking at Odin, not me, but there he was, guarding the entry door for Odin's hall of warriors. Or at least there he was until he decided to go off on this expedition and make me come along with him.

And now, there he was, following me. All the way up to my basement.

CHAPTER EIGHT

I made myself a midnight snack, and then I looked through my cupboards and the refrigerator and the freezer to see what I could offer the Valwolf. He turned down the first dozen things I suggested, but eventually ate some hardboiled duck eggs I'd put aside for a rainy day, plus some sautéed mushrooms, along with a bowl of hot cider. While he was eating, I checked my email and then brought up the 9www.wiki and reread the section on Asgard Apples.

They don't grow on trees in orchards like the apples I pick for my pantry. Lady Idunn keeps her golden apples inside a little wood chest that's small enough for Idunn to hold it in one hand, and when she opens it up, you see hundreds of little apples the size of pearls. If you take an apple out, it'll grow in your hand till it's normal apple size. The Aesir have an apple feast each year at Winter's Eve, and any of them who doesn't show up and get one of Idunn's apples starts getting old and weak and tired, just like the winter sun.

Idunn's husband is Bragi the poet, Odin's son, but she used to go off and visit the frost giant Thiazi. Nobody objected, not even Bragi, till one summer Idunn took her apple box with her and Thiazi said she wouldn't be coming back to Asgard any more. Then Odin sent Loki after her, and he spoke sweet words to Idunn and brought her and her apple box back to Asgard. Thiazi turned himself into an eagle and followed him, but Loki lit a fire and Thiazi got his wings charred off. Now Odin and his Aesir are all young and strong and energetic again, while Thiazi sits on top of the entry door to Valhalla and his eyes sit in the sky and watch the Nine Worlds for Odin. And oh yes, every morning at Valhalla they put out bowls of Idunn's apples for Odin's heroes. And now Knut was offering one of them to Lady Hel.

The Valwolf wolfed down his food (obviously, but I didn't want to say that he gobbled it because he's not a turkey) and then had me fetch him loaves of bread and wheels of cheese to take to the heroes. I packed them up in a big bag and offered to tie it around his neck, but he said he'd hold the bag's neck in his mouth. Then he asked me what I had hanging around *my* neck, so I tried to explain night vision goggles—and why high tech wasn't the same as magic—and then how high tech only works if you're touching the World Tree's trunk or one of its branches or roots because the Nine Worlds are all dead areas. Eventually he realized he wasn't going to be able to understand what I was saying without taking out time to study, so he told me he expected to see me in Hel before sunrise and ran off.

I snuggled into my bed and set the alarm for an hour before sunrise in Hel.

Meanwhile, Robin and Knut and Bookwyrm were fighting Dead Shore folk. I'd say they were fighting for their lives, except that everyone involved was dead. Instead I'll just say that Robin and her friends were fighting as if every moment might be their last. Lady Hel and her folk fought desperately, too. The Dead Shore folk were less concerned. If you cut one down, it wasn't the way it had been in Blind Hall: no blood, no lopped off heads or arms. They just fell down on the cold ground, and their flesh changed into a great gray snake that wriggled away from the combat, back to Hel River. And running forward across the retreating serpents, the Dead Shore folk kept coming.

Robin Grima's sword arm was getting tired from killing them. She'd asked Frostbite for help, but the sword was silent. It hadn't said anything since Lady Hel had shown up. Speeches from Shakespeare kept running through Robin's head, but that wasn't new, though up till now it had usually happened during final exams or while waiting for a doctor to give her a biopsy result: "Once more into the breach, dear friends, once more," and "Woe to the hand that shed this costly blood," and "I have heard the cock that is the trumpet of the morn," but the cock hadn't crowed; it was still night.

Knut and Bookwyrm were also getting tired. At first they'd shouted battle cries, calling on Odin to help them and send them wisdom and fetter their enemies with battle panic, calling on Tyr to send them strength and to punish their enemies. Now they were silent, just like Lady Hel and her folk, just like the Dead Shore folk, just like Frostbite. Robin Grima's lips were parched and dry, and so was her throat, but she'd promised not to drink anything she found in Hel, and Knut's bag was yards and yards away, at the foot of the World Tree.

Lady Hel's folk didn't seem to tire, but every now and then one of them fell. After a minute or two their lopped off body parts rolled back together, making them whole again, but they didn't open their eyes and get up and continue fighting; they just lay there. The number of defenders around Nidhog's blood kept getting fewer. Robin Grima wasn't sure how many hours had gone by.

The bright snow kept falling, its flakes glowing like little stars on the Dead Shore folk's hair and skin, then trampled to darkness beneath their feet. There was a cold breeze, and every time Lady Hel's black sword swung, the air got a little colder. Robin Grima's feet were cold and wet in spite of her shoes. *"Why didn't Valhalla give us boots?"* she asked Frostbite, but the sword didn't answer. She wondered if she could catch a cold now that she was dead. The answer is you can't catch a cold or any other diseases in Asgard or Vanaheim or Light Elfland, but the folk in the middle and lower levels aren't that well off. Most new Helfolk are sick when they come, and it takes them centuries to get over it. Even the ones that just died of old age catch cold quickly enough in the cold, damp climate; they spend their first century or two with stuffy noses and post-nasal drip and a fever. It doesn't mean they can't fight.

The snow smothered the sound of the fighting, the sound of the bodies falling. And then the silence was broken by wolf howls, soft and far away at first but coming nearer, getting louder. There were a lot more than two of them, so Robin Grima knew it wasn't Odin's wolves. She shivered at the memory of the Hel wolf tearing out her throat but didn't miss her aim at the short, dark-haired woman with long fingernails who was trying to claw her eyes out.

There was a wolf howling behind her. She spun around and started to charge towards it, but her feet froze in place.

"Don't tempt me," whispered Frostbite. *"And don't try to kill it. It's Knut's friend, the Valwolf."*

The Valwolf leapt toward her, high in the air, over her head.

(What happened to that big bag of Ratatosk's good food you ask? How nice of you to care. The Valwolf dropped it by the foot of the World Tree.)

Robin Grima spun back to face the charging Helfolk and saw the Valwolf land in front of her and Knut. The Dead Shore folk turned away from him, some towards Lady Hel and the twin Odinsons on the Valwolf's right, some towards Bookwyrm and Drifa on his left. Robin Grima had a minute or two to catch her breath.

Then the Dead Shore folk drew away, and the wolves came forward.

She hadn't gotten a good look at them in Blind Hall. She could see them better now by snowlight. Their eyes weren't yellow like the Valwolf's but dead white. That's because Hel wolves are blind. It doesn't interfere with their fighting ability; they find their prey by scent and sound.

The Valwolf growled loudly, his ears pricked forward, his hair standing on end, his tail high in the air, lashing stiffly from side to side. Then the Hel wolves charged forward.

The alarm was screaming. I reached over and turned it off, but the noise didn't stop, and the clock said it was still a couple of hours before sunrise in Hel, and I realized that it was my perimeter alarm. Someone was crossing between the worlds and coming near my haven.

I checked my monitors. There weren't any valkyries flying down to Hel to pick up Robin Grima and her friends and take them back to Valhalla. Nobody was riding Odin's eight-legged horse down the World Tree (he'll gallop for Odin: Asgard to Hel in nine seconds or maybe a little less, but when anyone else tries to ride him those eight legs move as slow as the four men carrying a coffin to the grave, and it's a nine day journey). It wasn't a fire giant trying to climb up the World Tree to Asgard—or falling back down again, flaming through the sky.

It was someone riding down Hel River, his horse almost the same gray as the Niflheim fog, but with little silver stars shining in the horse's mane and tail. The rider's armor was mist gray too, but a silver star shone on his helmet and he held a silver-bright sword in his left hand, with blood runes written on it. The runes were too small to read in the screens, but I knew they said JUSTICE on one side and VICTORY on the other side. The horse didn't have reins; the rider steered it with his knees and still didn't have a hand to spare. What was Tyr doing, riding Silver Mane to Hel? I ran down the tree trunk after him to find out.

There are a lot of rivers in the Nine Worlds, and only a few bridges. Most of the gods wade their horses across when they come to a river. Thor's too heavy to ride a horse so he wades across shallow rivers or looks for a ferryman if the water's too deep. Odin's horse jumps across the rivers; it'd jump across the ocean if he told it to. Tyr doesn't have to do any of that. His biofather Hymir is a sea giant, and he rides a sea horse. Silver Mane doesn't wade or swim across water; he just walks across it.

The *Lokasenna* (the edda that Robin Grima read in Saga's Hall) says that Loki bragged that he took Tyr's wife to bed and had a son by her. That's because Snorri Sturluson was writing in the Christian Era, in the 13th century, relying on faded memories and faded manuscripts. Snorri read that Loki bragged that Tyr's woman went to bed and gave Loki's family a boy, and he jumped to conclusions. But it was really Loki's son and Tyr's mother who had a son together, if that's the right term to use for having the puppy who grew up to be Garm Hel-hound.

Lady Hel had told me not to insult her or her people or her kinsmen tonight, or I'd never leave her world. Tyr's foster father, Odin the Deceiver, was foster brother to Loki who gave birth to Hel. Was that a close enough tie to make him Hel's kinsman? I decided to play it safe and just chat with Tyr's horse.

"Did you have a good time on your way down here, Silver Mane?" I asked. "Did you stop by Hymirstead and get to drink your fill of beer? Oh no, that's right, Hymir doesn't have that big cauldron any more, does he? It's at Aegirstead now so the Aesir and Vanir don't have to walk so far to drink from it. Well, I hope you had some fun at the seashore anyway. Did Hymir—?"

"Shut up, little rat," Tyr said coldly, and somehow I didn't feel like saying anything for the next few minutes.

And then Silver Mane was galloping toward the World Tree, towards the pack of howling Hel wolves. Tyr's sword shone like the full moon, lighting up the wolves' white teeth and the Valhallans' bright swords. Even Lady Hel's black sword glistened with light along its point and edge, and so did her hall folk's black axe blades.

The other thing you saw was the red of blood. Nidhog's blood was fading away by now, but the defenders' blood blazed like fire in the light of Tyr's sword. Garm's left foreleg was red, and he ran on three legs, but it didn't slow him down. Lady Hel's right cheek wasn't pure white any more but rouged with her own blood. Bookwyrm wasn't wounded because he'd rolled in Nidhog's blood, but his wife Drifa had dropped to one knee, her sword arm scored, her right calf red with her own blood.

The Hel wolves weren't bleeding red, but that didn't mean they weren't hurt. Their blood was as gray as their fur, but their fur wasn't spotless gray any more; their muzzles and claws were red with blood from Lady Hel and her people. So far none of them had managed to break through the ring of defenders, but now Tyr was coming, and I wasn't sure whose side he was going to fight on.

Once upon a time Tyr was great friends with Fenris, (that's the giant wolf who's Lady Hel's brother), but that was back before Asgard folk heard the prophecies that Fenris was going to kill Odin, Tyr's foster father. And it was back before Tyr's pretty mother came up to Asgard to visit him—and Fenris turned out not to be as housebroken as everyone had thought. Ten years later (giants take their time getting things done) Tyr had a new baby brother with fur and fangs and a tail. Tyr's mother said that she had to go home to her husband but she wasn't taking the puppy along with her. Odin had the valkyries drop the puppy in Thunder River, and that was how Lady Hel got Garm for a house pet. Fenris didn't make a fuss about it, maybe because he was afraid of Odin, maybe because he was afraid of losing Tyr's friendship. He didn't even make a fuss when the dark elves started showing up every Yule with a new chain for him to try on. He said he trusted his friend Tyr to protect him. He doesn't say that any more, of course. It's hard to talk with a sword stuck between your upper and lower jaws, not to mention the aggravation of having to wear a fetter and chain you can't break. And of course Tyr doesn't drop by and play with him every day any more. Tyr hasn't visited Fenris since the giant wolf bit off his right hand.

"Good evening, Lady Hel," Tyr said courteously.

"Good evening, Lord Tyr," she said. "Have you come to bring me a gift of jewelry as fine as the one you gave my brother?"

"You're fighting my enemies tonight," he said. "I've come to offer you my help if you'll condescend to take it."

She didn't ask him how he'd heard about the battle even though she must have been nearly as eager to find out as I was. She just said, "I'll take any help you can give me tonight against the Hel wolves and the Dead Shore folk," stating her alliance terms in enough detail to show that she didn't trust him.

He didn't take offense, or at least if he did, he didn't say so. He waved his sword and its blade got longer and brighter. It's a magic weapon, of course. No, I don't know its name. No, I don't know who forged it. No, I don't know how Tyr got it. I'm not a know-it-all; I'm just a know-a-lot.

Garm was looking at the sword, probably trying to figure out how to handle it when they had their duel to the death at Ragnarok. Ten Hel wolves took advantage of Garm's distraction and jumped him, one chewing away at his throat, trying to get past the dense fur and into the jugular, two trying to pull off his ears, and the rest biting at his sides. He shook them off like bath water, though each of them was almost half his size.

Then Tyr's sword swept out, a hundred feet long and shining, like a scythe woven of moonlight, and cut through the Hel wolves. Hel stepped back and called to her hall folk to do the same. She had to call three times to get Garm's attention, and Bookwyrm had to help his wife Drifa limp away from the fight.

In another minute, most of the Hel wolves had run off and the rest were lying motionless on the ground, and Tyr's sword was only a few feet long and back in its sheath.

Bookwyrm was stripping Drifa's clothing off, and I wondered if he'd missed her so much over the centuries that he was going to have sex with her then and there, but instead he put her down in the mud by the World Tree's roots and rolled her over and over in it, till her pale skin and her long golden hair were both brownish red.

"Nidhog's blood is not as strong as it was when you bathed in it at sunset," Lady Hel said. She cleaned and sheathed her black sword and walked toward the two of them. She reached out a pale hand and fingernails as long as my claws and pulled Drifa up to her feet. The woman's right leg was still bleeding a little, but she seemed able to stand on it. She made no attempt to cover her nakedness, just stared into Hel's cold face.

"Do you want to go with these heroes, hall guest," Hel asked, "or do you want to stay here where it's safe?"

"I want to go with my husband," Drifa said, her voice

quiet but firm. "If I'd wanted a safe life, I wouldn't have chosen to be a leech and treat people sick with contagions. I thought my fever was just a bad cold and my fatigue was just because I was getting old. If I'd realized I was dying, I'd have found some better use for my last hours than sitting in bed, sneezing and coughing. Give me a second chance to die, Lady Hel, and I'll use it so I never come here again."

"Very well," Hel said. "From now on you're free, and the oaths you've sworn to me no longer bind you. Your feet may take you to wherever you like, and your hands may wound and heal, bind and unbind, as you wish." She turned away from Drifa to Knut and said, "I'll take your gift now, Valwolf Friend." Knut sheathed his sword and pulled out the Asgard apple and gave it to her. Hel ate it, all except for the core, then held that out to Drifa, who carefully picked out the seeds and put them in a bag she'd had tied to her belt, then swallowed the rest of the pulp.

"Hold out your hands," Hel told her. "I want to see what you're made of."

Drifa held out her right hand. Hel drew her black sword and slashed down with all her strength at the woman's right wrist. Bookwyrm ran forward, his own weapon drawn—and tripped over the Valwolf. When he stood up again, his wife was crying, but she still had two hands, even though one of them was bleeding profusely. Robin Grima gave her a napkin —*my* napkin!—and Drifa bound her wrist with it.

"She can still bleed," Hel said, "but now she'll be harder for enemies to kill. Do you want to roll in my mud too, Lord Tyr?"

"No, thank you," he said, his voice as cold as hers. "But for the sake of this woman's courage, I'll accompany her and her friends when they leave your kingdom, and I'll stay with them till they weary of my company or till Odin summons me to return to Asgard or till Cousin Heimdall blows his horn to warn us that Ragnarok is at hand."

"I'm the party leader," Robin Grima told him (catching herself barely in time before saying, "My player character's the party leader"). "Our oath is, 'All for one, and one for all.' We swear it every morning, and if you'll swear it with us, then we'll welcome your company. Just remember that our party is Knut and Bookwyrm and Drifa and me and the Valwolf and Ratatosk."

"And your magic sword Frostbite," said the Valwolf. "It would weigh heavy on my heart if I forgot Frostbite. Lord Tyr, what's your magic sword's name?"

"Its name is Two-faced," said Tyr, drawing his sword and showing them its rune inscriptions. "JUSTICE is its face for law courts and law assemblies. VICTORY is its face for duels and battles."

"Lady Hel," Bookwyrm said, "I bathed in Hel River yesterday afternoon when the only hazard I found there was knives, but now it's also full of treacherous snakes. I won't ask you for food or drink, but do you have a bath house near here where I can take my wife to cleanse herself before we set off?"

"Kykkeliky," crowed the rooster on top of Hel's Hall roof, and the bright snow stopped falling, and there was a dim glow on the eastern horizon.

"It's sunrise," said Lady Hel. "Sister, swear your party to their oath and then take them away from here. I won't give you anything to take with you except my promise that when Ragnarok comes I won't lead my folk against you and your friends or against any of the folk who live at Valhalla."

"Thank you, Sister," Robin Grima said. She wasn't sure exactly what Hel's oath meant but it seemed like some kind of an improvement on the prophecies. She drew Frostbite, its silver glow lost in Two-Face's light. Bookwyrm and Knut drew their swords and crossed them against Frostbite as they'd done every morning since they'd known Robin Grima. Drifa picked up her axe and touched it to Frostbite. "All for one, and one for all," they all said, and the Valwolf and I said it too. And then Tyr said it too, though he didn't touch his sword to Frostbite. After all, his weapon had its own magic powers.

Hel got back on Garm's back and rode away, without answering Bookwyrm's question, and her hall folk followed her, all of them except Drifa.

"I know a place not far from here that's got a hot spring you can bathe in comfortably," said Tyr. "It's got good food and drink too, and soft beds with warm blankets, and the sky is brighter by day than by night."

"What's its name?" asked the Valwolf.

"Mist Hall," said Tyr, "in the heart of the hills of Niflheim."

"Mist Hall is halfway between here and the forge fires of Svartalfheim," I said. "That's a long day's walk."

"Or a short ride on a long horse," said Tyr, and waved toward Silver Mane. "Mount up, everyone. He's got room enough for all of us."

Robin got his word that the horse would stop whenever she asked and let everybody get down safely. I scrambled back up the World Tree and untied Odin's rope and Knut put it in a bag that he hung at his back. Then we let Tyr lift us one by one onto his horse's back. Silver Mane got longer and longer with each new rider, till at last Tyr mounted up in front of us and dug in his heels, and Silver Mane galloped off, taking a mile with each stride toward Niflheim.

(What happened to the Valwolf's bag full of Ratatosk's good food, you ask? How nice of you to care. We left it at the foot of the World Tree, red with Nidhog's blood. We didn't want to risk losing our ability to talk.)

CHAPTER NINE

Mist Hall only has one bath, but it's a lot prettier than any bathroom in Valhalla. You sit in a pool of steaming hot water and you can look out at the mountaintops green with fir trees, with white snow in the shadowed areas under the branches and bright spring flowers in the open areas and dense fog flowing through the heart of each valley like a river. The sky is bright blue with patches of white here and there as the winds push the clouds around: hot, dry winds from the forges of Svartalfheim and cold, wet winds from Hel. At night the clouds rise up from the valleys and cover the mountaintops and the only light is the moon—except at new moon when everything's black if you're not carrying a lantern. The gray Nifl wolves stay down in the valleys during the daytime, and don't come up the mountain slopes till after sunset.

Tyr said that we were all welcome at Mist Hall for his sake, and nobody there contradicted him, but that didn't mean much because there was nobody there to be seen or heard or smelled. The hall doors were opened when Silver Mane stopped in front of the steps, and the riders got off his back, watching him shrink a little when each of them dismounted until he was back to his normal length. "Go to the stables," Tyr said, and Silver Mane walked away from us. Tyr started up the steps to the hall and we followed him.

Inside, the hall was bright with candles whose silver flames twinkled like stars, and still not a person in sight. There was a table on one side of the room that held a bed of boiling water with no flames visible under it and plates of hot food on top of it. There was a table on the other side of the room that held a bed of ice and plates of cold food on top of it. There was a warm hearth behind the hot table that held bright white flames with no wood or coals or peat to feed them.

Knut lifted up a plate of bacon from the hot table and put it on the floor, and the Valwolf started eating breakfast, daintily picking up the bacon one slice at a time.

"You promised us a hot bath," Bookwyrm said.

"Follow me," Tyr said, and he led us out the hall's back door and down a gravel path, and there it was: a bubbling hot spring as big as a longboat or an Olympic swimming pool. The floor was smooth granite rock, and there were oak benches to sit on, one of them with a pile of soft white towels. The air was warm and still. A few minutes later, the Valwolf joined us, still licking bacon grease off his lips. Tyr went back to the dining hall to have breakfast. The humans stripped off their things and plunged into the clean water, and the Valwolf followed them.

I glanced at the things they'd dropped on the bath room floor: belts and bags, clothes and shoes, three scabbarded swords and a Hel axe—everything spotted with blood drops and dirt and acrid with sweat. Everything except for Frostbite, with his snow white scabbard and his silver hilt. I suppose you could say that Robin Grima's sword approached fighting as good clean fun.

Bookwyrm was helping Drifa wash her hair, and Robin

was showing Knut how to do the front crawl (which Robin's parents had called the Australian crawl), and the Valwolf was dog paddling around the bath, trying to stay out of everyone's way, when I suddenly noticed that most of the humans' things had disappeared and the floor where they'd lain was as clean as Frostbite's scabbard and hilt and blade. (I could see his blade now because Frostbite had come an inch or so out of his scabbard, as if someone had started to draw him and then thought better of the idea.) The only dirty thing left was Knut's back bag, and its strings were untied so you could see the coil of rope inside it stained with Odin's blood.

The humans were too busy bathing to notice what had happened, and I didn't see any point in getting them upset when there was nothing they could do about it. The Valwolf didn't say anything either, just got out of the pool and shook himself dry and went over to sit in the doorway.

I sniffed the air, but all I could smell was wet Valwolf and underneath that wet humans and my own clean dry fur and underneath that Odin's blood dried on his rope. Considering that a squirrel can smell a cache of old seeds buried under twelve feet of snow, that meant the sneaky Nifl folk were using strong magic.

A few seconds later, the Valwolf growled quietly and I followed his gaze to see that one of the benches now held two sets of sky-blue women's clothing and two piles of blood-red men's clothing. And there were four mugs of ale sitting on the rocks around the rim of the bath. And oh yes, the floor was dry where the Valwolf had gotten it wet shaking off the bath water.

I found my mouth rather dry too, so I had a few sips of ale from the top of a mug but didn't drink any deeper for fear of falling in. Then I looked around the room a third time and saw that the Valhallans' weapons were all back on the floor again, except that now they were clean. The Valwolf was lying down with his head on Knut's bag, maybe trying to protect it from mist elf trickery, maybe hoping Odin's rope would protect him. I looked up at the misty sky and saw a black raven hovering far over us and wondered if it was Thought or Memory. Nifl ravens are gray so they blend into the clouds.

Knut picked up a mug of ale. "Skoal," he called out and took a couple of gulps. "Do you want some?" he asked the Valwolf, who politely declined. Knut took another gulp—and found the mug was full of ale again. He mentioned it to the others, who found that their mugs behaved the same way.

"It's good that Lord Tyr told us that we're welcome here," Bookwyrm said, "because we'd have small chance of defending ourselves from our courteous hosts if they chose to attack us." His irony was thick enough you could slice it up and spread it on crackers, though it would burn as you chewed it.

"They're good housekeepers as well as courteous," said Drifa with just as much sincerity. "If they attacked us, I'm sure they'd mop up all the blood afterwards."

Robin shivered, remembering Grima's fight with an Invisible Stalker in Malik's dungeon when her character nearly died. She got out of the water and dried herself, then put on the sky-blue clothes that the Mist Hall folk had given her.

Robin's hair was dark. I don't mean that it was dark brown, because it was always dark brown. I meant that starting with that bath and for the rest of the time we were in Niflheim, Robin Grima's hair didn't shine with light the way it had ever since she'd walked through the fires in Blind Hall. The bath water had damped its light.

We went back to the hall and found Tyr working on a

plate of cold roast beef, but there was still a lot of breakfast waiting for the rest of us. Robin horrified her Norse friends by filling her mug with ice from the cold table and resting it on the hot table till the stuff melted into water and then dropping even more ice into it. "It's the Vinland national drink," she told them. Nobody else was willing to sample it.

When everyone was done with breakfast, Tyr showed them how to get to the bedroom. (Walk up to the right wall and knock three times, and an archway appears. Go through it and there's a hallway. Go down it and there's a room with stone walls that holds a dozen wooden rowboats with goose feather mattresses, warm blankets and swansdown pillows.)

The bedroom had a hearth full of burning firewood, bright with silver flames, but there wasn't a chimney and there wasn't any smoke billowing out into the room. One of the bed rowboats was twice as long as the others and hung with a canopy of silver stars on a midnight blue sky. Nobody was very surprised when Tyr said that one was his.

Tyr said that he had a few things to do but that he'd be back for dinner, and rode away on Silver Mane.

Drifa said she wanted to go gather herbs. "I'll help you," Bookwyrm said, and they strolled off toward the forest.

"I want to take a look around Mist Hall," Robin said.

"Bare is back without brother behind it," Knut said, and then, when Robin looked puzzled, "It'll be safer if I go with you." The Valwolf didn't say anything, but he followed them.

First they checked the bedroom and feast hall for more hidden doors. Then they checked out the other walls. Then they went outside and walked around the building.

Ratatosk jumped up to the nearest branch of the World Tree and tried to watch everyone at once, especially Tyr, who was riding Silver Mane up through the air, from cloud to cloud, looking like a falling star in reverse, till he finally disappeared from sight and entered the middle worlds.

"My question," said Robin, "is why we can't see anyone who lives here."

"They wear mist caps," said Knut. "Or at least that's what the stories say. If you knock off the mist cap, then you can see the elf. Some say there's an ointment that'll let you see them when they're wearing the hats, but if they find you out, they'll strike you blind. Siegfried found a mist cap in Fafnir's hoard but he didn't use it much, and it didn't bring him much luck." It brought him a night in a valkyrie's arms, but seeing that afterwards they both married other people, and the valkyrie's jealousy ended up killing Siegfried, I suppose Knut had a point there. "My question is where we're going to go next," Knut said.

"I want to talk Fenris into giving me Tyr's hand," Robin Grima said, "but there are lots of other places I want to visit too. Do you think our friends here would give us some of those mist caps? If we had them, we could go to Mimir's Fountain and try fishing for Odin's lost eye and the giants wouldn't see us."

Someone giggled. Knut drew his sword and spun around, but he didn't see anything, and whoever it was didn't speak up, not even when Robin Grima politely said good morning. "Can you smell anyone here besides us?" she asked the Valwolf.

"Just horses," he said, "and...." He trotted over to a pair of stone pillars and pushed his head between them, then slowly backed away. "I just found the stables," he said. "There's a couple of horses in it and a dozen Nifl wolves, all of them sleeping."

"We're only halfway around the hall," said Robin Grima. "Let's keep going."

The Valwolf went off to investigate some more stone pillars.

"First tell me why my sword doesn't feel cold any more,"

Knut said.

Robin Grima drew Frostbite and touched Knut's blade with it. *"It's a good sword blade,"* the sword whispered. *"No curses or weaknesses. But it's not from Valhalla. And it's not one of the blades I lent my power to this morning. They took those two away and they didn't bring them back. They laid their hands on me too, but I discouraged them from going any further."*

"I've found the door to the bath," said the Valwolf, coming back. "And there's another room full of firewood: broken spears and broken benches and broken chairs." The light elves would sing songs of healing over that wood until it grew back together. The dark elves use fires of burning bones for their forges. Only the mist elves use wood for baking and heating.

"Anything there we can use for oars?" asked Robin.

"Maybe the spears."

"What do you want oars for?" asked Knut.

"To take to bed with me," said Robin. "In Vinland it's bad luck to be in a boat without a paddle."

"When I was alive," Knut said, "you didn't go to sleep in a boat that size except when you were dead and they buried you in it, or at least set stones around your grave in the shape of a boat."

"We put a stone at the head of the grave," Robin said, remembering the cemetery where her parents were buried.

"We used to put a Hel stone on *top* of the grave," Knut said, "but only if we wanted to make sure the body wouldn't climb out as a draug and kill us. And now one of our companions is a Hel woman from Hel. Odin, protect us till we're home in Valhalla again."

"Amen," said Robin, and the Valwolf said something similar in Old Norse. Then they picked out eight spears long enough to use as oars and lashed small chair backs to them with lengths that Knut cut from Odin's rope. No, the rope didn't bleed, and it didn't scream.

All this time Knut had been wondering whether Robin was going to suggest finding somewhere quiet where they could be alone and take off their clothes and do what they'd sometimes done in Valhalla after they'd had a bath together. And whether he'd say yes, given that there might be mist elves watching them, giggling at them, spreading gossip about them and ruining Robin Grima's reputation. But what Robin said was, "Let's finish walking around Mist Hall and see what else we find."

Knut picked up all eight of the oars, hoping she'd admire his strength, and they finished walking around Mist Hall and then went back to the bedroom, but the door wouldn't open.

"Open up in there!" Knut called out.

"First tell me your door number," answered Bookwyrm.

"Thirteen," said Knut, and they heard the sound of something scraping along the stone floor. Then the door opened, and they saw that Bookwyrm and Drifa had pushed a bed up to the front of the room so it blocked the door from opening. Knut set down their oars (two to each bed a human was going to sleep in), and Robin drew Frostbite and crossed it with Bookwyrm's new sword.

"I like this chopper better than the one Lady Hel gave me," Drifa said, and crossed its blade with Frostbite. "Do we swear our oath again?"

"Our oath still binds us," Bookwyrm said, and Robin Grima agreed.

They moved the bed back up against the door and set up a watch schedule, with the watcher sitting on the floor to get a good view of the door and notice if invisible people lifted the bed up and moved it aside. The silver candles didn't burn down, and the walls didn't have any windows so they couldn't look outside and see the sun, but they agreed that each team should watch till they'd yawned three times or till it seemed like half of the eighth part of a day had gone by. (Robin thought of that as ninety minutes and wished she had a wristwatch.) They agreed that Robin would take first watch, along with Frostbite and Ratatosk, followed by Bookwyrm and Drifa, and then Knut and the Valwolf.

Knut took an Asgard apple out of his bag and cut it into six pieces: one for each of the humans and one for the Valwolf and one for me. Then the people who weren't on watch got onto their beds and closed their eyes, weapons ready to grab if something happened, but nothing did.

After their naps, they opened up the door to the corridor —and found a bench out there, waiting for them, piled high with what looked like the rest of their belongings. The clothes were clean and neatly folded, the shoes were clean of blood and mud. Leaning up against the bench were two sheathed swords and a black-bladed axe. Robin shook out her tunic from Valhalla and found that all the rips and tears that the Dead Shore folk had left were now neatly mended with tiny stitches.

The Valhallans picked up the things and dumped them at the foot of their beds. Drifa picked up the axe and closed her eyes. "Yes," she said, "this is the weapon I was given in Hel." She put it in her belt, next to the new one she'd gotten in the bath.

After that they went back to the feast hall and found the tables spread for dinner and Tyr sitting at a table, devoting himself to a plate of venison roasted with sweet red lingonberries and a side dish of russet potatoes spread with butter. His red gold hair looked like sunset clouds.

"They didn't have potatoes in Europe back in your day," Robin said to Knut.

"Not even imported from Vinland," Knut said, taking one of the biggest potatoes, cutting it in half with his eating knife and then putting a spoonful of hot lingonberry sauce onto each half. "We've only been getting them in Valhalla for the last century or so."

"What meat would you like?" Bookwyrm asked, but Drifa didn't answer. She was standing in front of the hearthfire.

"I brought you a leech's box," Tyr told her ("first aid kit" Robin heard) and held out a small wooden box with a clasp of ivory. Robin thought it looked like a wooden version of her old pill box that had seven columns for the days of the week and four rows for breakfast, lunch, dinner, and bedtime, though this box had more than twenty-eight compartments. Knut and Bookwyrm thought it looked like a fish hook box.

"That was very kind of you," Drifa said, taking the chest and setting it down on a table. Then she turned around and threw the Hel axe into the hearth.

Darkness billowed out through the hall, choking out the silver candlelight and the white hearthfire. There were light footsteps running across the floor—and the sound of high-pitched screams and sobbing, like terrified women and children.

Robin Grima's hand fell to her sword hilt, but Frostbite had nothing to say, and before she could draw it Tyr had drawn his sword, filling the room with light. For a second, Robin and her friends actually saw the mist elves, dozens of them: little men and women no higher than Robin's knees, their long gray hair floating in the air as they ran out of the room. Their hands clutched their heads like the little wide-eyed man in Edward Munch's painting "The Scream."

Then there was a thunderclap and a burst of light that dazzled Robin's eyes like a lightning bolt.

When Robin Grima could see the dining hall again, Tyr had sheathed his sword and there was only the soft glow of the silver candles and the hearthfire, and Drifa's axe was all burned up.

"Tonight is a time for celebrating," Drifa said. "I want horsemeat for dinner," and she took a ladle of a rich stew that Robin had been thinking of sampling.

Robin took a slice of what Knut said was venison instead. Eating Bambi seemed better than eating Black Beauty.

"Drifa's always loved horsemeat," Bookwyrm said. "She used to tell Christian missionaries that she didn't object to worshipping their White Christ but she wouldn't give up eating horsemeat."

"Yes, I remember you telling me that," Knut said. "What did they feed you in Hel's Hall, Drifa?"

"Beggars food," she said shortly, and then, after she'd swallowed the chunk of horsemeat she'd been chewing on, "We each ate the food that we'd fed visiting beggars, and we couldn't choose which meal came next any more than a beggar can. I'd rather not talk about Hel's Hall. What sort of food did you eat in Vinland, Robin Grima? Besides these potato roots, I mean."

Robin told her, trying to like the woman for Bookwyrm's sake, but not sure if she did or if she should.

After dinner, Drifa opened up the box Tyr had brought her and put the herbs she'd gathered inside it: the white petals of Baldur's brow (which people from Robin's time more prosaically called false chamomile), the smaller white petals of Freyja's hair (yarrow), some light brown cubes of Njord's glove (sponges), and dozens more.

"I won't need Baldur's brow to sleep tonight," Drifa said.

"None of us will," said Bookwyrm.

"I have more things to do before I rest," Tyr said, "but we'll eat breakfast together."

They bade him good night and returned to the bedroom. Once inside the room, they shoved Tyr's large bed up against the door—it took all four of them to do it. After all, he'd said he wouldn't see them till morning. Then they set up watches again, this time with each team to try to watch for the eighth of a day, and got onto their rowboat beds. They didn't lie under the warm blankets, because that would have made it harder to get out of bed if a fight started.

Knut and the Valwolf lay down with their heads side by side on the pillow. Odin's rope was there too, neatly coiled up at the foot of the bed. But Knut didn't dream about wolves or rope climbing. He dreamed about a woman who stood in the shadows and asked him to sing the story of the binding of Loki and sang along with him on the choruses.

"What do you think of Loki's children?" she asked him when he'd finished. "Did the one who got eaten die a valiant enough death to deserve going to Valhalla? Is eating your own brother because you're a starving animal enough of a sin to deserve going to Dead Shore?"

"The gods turned Vali Lokison into a starving wolf who devoured Narvi," Knut said, "so they could take Narvi's guts and use them to bind Loki. I don't think Narvi was a hero, and I don't think Vali was a murderer, but I think it would take more centuries than I've been dead before I could forgive a brother who killed me and feasted on my body, even if it wasn't by his own choice."

"You're probably—" the woman said, and then the world started shaking because Bookwyrm had taken hold of Knut's shoulders and was shaking them, and Knut woke up to take his turn watching the room, while Bookwyrm and Drifa slept together.

Robin Grima dreamed that she was climbing down the

World Tree. She lowered herself from one branch down to another one and found something under her right foot that didn't feel like bark; she looked down to find herself stepping on a man's hand. "I'm sorry," she said, and the stranger swung himself up on the branch, and then he was standing next to her, his gray eyes staring into hers, smiling.

"Thank you," he said. "I know we haven't known each other long, not even a century, but I think I'm falling in love with you. At least we've been in enough worlds together by now that you can't claim it's love at first site."

"That's a pun," Robin said.

"Yes. Is it mightier than the sword? Please don't scream, Robin. I promise not to make any more puns if you don't like them. I'm only doing it because I'm nervous."

"You don't have to be—" she started, and then her bed started shaking, and she woke up.

I sat on top of Tyr's bed for a while, but I didn't feel comfortable there. It was too big, and Tyr might come back in the middle of the night, and it didn't have any oars, and I wasn't big enough to row. I finally settled down on the foot of Robin's bed, since she was the shortest one there and so the least likely to kick me.

I dreamed of reading email until one message I clicked on turned out to have a virus that my software didn't catch in time, and it infected my computer until I couldn't see any of my icons because my desktop was just a picture of a sick cow dying in the stable, mooing wildly because it knew it was a slanderer and it was going to go to Hel, and when I finally got rid of the cow and clicked on my antivirus software, things got worse because the runes turned into Chinese ideographs—every single thing that I clicked on turned into Chinese ideographs—and I can't read Chinese.

It was quite a relief when the bed started shaking and I

woke up, even though it was to the sound of Drifa's screaming.

"The walls are gone!" Drifa screamed. "The ceiling's gone!"

The bedroom was pitch black, but I could feel a cold wind blowing, which was odd in a room with no windows and the door jammed shut, and the bed was rocking under me, which was more than just odd.

"Earthquake!" yelled Robin, but it wasn't. Quakes don't last that long, especially when they're that soft and rolling.

"Waves!" yelled Drifa. "The tide's carrying us away."

Robin drew Frostbite, and its silver light let the rest of us see that Drifa was right: the rowboats were floating on a stream of water, the rolling swells rocking the boats gently to and fro, the water driving the boats uphill in a climb so Robin feel as if she was riding a roller coaster on the long slow climb uphill just before things get exciting.

"Taste the water," whispered Frostbite, and Robin dipped her fingers over the side of the boat into the cold water and licked them and tasted saltwater.

"We're in the ocean," she said.

"Then wash the Nifl water out of your hair," Ratatosk told her. "Otherwise you'll have to choose between rowing in the dark or rowing while you hold your sword between your teeth."

Robin ran her cold wet fingers through her hair, and they left streaks of light behind. She shivered as the water dripped down her back. The blankets weren't warm any more.

When her hair was all wet and shining, she picked up her oars and started rowing. Knut followed her, with the Valwolf sitting behind him, and Bookwyrm and Drifa followed them. They looked for Tyr's giant bed, for all the other beds, but didn't see them.

"How did you see the room wasn't around us any more?" Bookwyrm asked his wife.

"I can see in the dark," Drifa said. "Can't you?" And then, after he said no, she said, "I thought it came from being dead, but if you can't, then I guess that living in Hel's Hall had something to do with it."

After that they were all too busy rowing to speak for a while, but Robin Grima still had time to wonder if Drifa had picked up any other special abilities in Hel besides being able to see in the dark.

CHAPTER TEN

World Geography can be a simple or a complex subject, depending on how many worlds you're considering and in how much detail. It's easy to say that Jotunheim is a cold place where it's always winter and the sun seldom shines and the ground is covered with snow and ice and the rivers and lakes are all frozen and the only naturally occurring liquid water is Mimir's Fountain. It's easy to say that Jotunheim borders Midgard, that the borders are the towering mountains oo its south and the ocean on its coasts. Then you start wondering why the ocean doesn't freeze. It's not all that salty, a lot less salty than pickle brine, and certainly no more salty than blood, and blood freezes fast enough when you spill it in Jotunheim. (Yes, I know that most ocean water is a lot more salty than blood. That isn't true of the Arctic Ocean where the glaciers keep gliding down into the waters and dropping off chunks of freshwater ice, and it's even less true of the ocean that lies between Midgard and Jotunheim.)

One reason is that the ocean is so deep, and another is that the other side of the ocean borders Midgard where it's not always winter, and a third reason is that the ocean is fed by a stream of warm water. No, not the Gulf Stream (which goes to warm the east coast of Canada) or even the North Atlantic Drift (which breaks off from the Gulf Stream and goes west across the Atlantic to warm Europe all the way north to Norway); those stay strictly in Midgard and its workaday reflection. The ocean between Midgard and Jotunheim is fed by a stream of warm water from Niflheim, and Robin Grima and her companions were riding it.

Or maybe the right word is geyser. Did you know that the English word "geyser" comes from the Great Geysir, an erupting spring at Hawk Dales in Iceland? It sits on the side of a glacier, and it hurls boiling water two hundred feet high, and its name comes from *gjósa*, "to gush." Of course the Niflheim water carrying us uphill wasn't boiling, but it was going a lot higher than two hundred feet, all the way from the low worlds to the middle ones. Robin Grima steered her rowboat up the stream, sometimes using her oars to fend off rocks (from Niflheim) or burning lava (from Muspelheim) or ice (from Hel) that were tumbling uphill along with us.

And then the water was over our heads, cold and wet and impossible to breathe. Robin Grima and her friends could get by without breathing because they were dead, but I couldn't, and I wanted to pray to someone for help, but I know too much about the gods to ask them for favors and they know too much about me to grant them, so I just held on to the rowboat and my breath as tight as I could.

And then there was air around us again—and under us, until the rowboat beds splashed down onto the ocean.

I shook as much water off as I could and then started licking my fur dry. The Valwolf was doing the same sensible thing. The humans didn't even take their wet clothes off and wring them out.

"Whale's land is the kenning for ocean," Knut said, "and sun land is the kenning for sky."

"Air is the lungs' food," said Drifa. Her hands held the

box Tyr had brought her. I wondered what sea water would do to the herbs inside, but it turned out that the box was watertight when the ivory clasp kept it closed.

"The night sky is the star hall," said Bookwyrm, looking up at the bright stars and finding his way from the pointer stars at the back of Thor's Wagon to the North Star. "We're heading west toward Jotunheim, Robin Grima. Is that where you want to go, or should we head for Midgard?"

"Is there anyone or anything in Midgard that's involved in Ragnarok?" Robin asked.

"Loki is bound in Midgard," said Knut. "When Ragnarok comes, he'll break his bonds and go to Muspelheim. The Midgard Serpent will rise up out of the ocean—this ocean— and go to Asgard to kill Thor. The red rooster Fjalar will crow and wake the giants, and the giant Eggther will sit on a hill in Jotunheim and strum his harp joyously. The ship *Naglfar* will sail up from Niflheim to Jotunheim, and Hymir and his giants will climb aboard and sail it to Asgard. Heimdall will come to Mimir's Fountain in Jotunheim and take up his horn and blow it. Odin will come to the fountain too and ask Mimir's Head for its last counsel. And then Ragnarok will begin."

"The Midgard Serpent might be near us," said Robin Grima. "Do we have anything we can use to bargain with it? Do we have anything we can use to threaten it?"

"There are poisons in this box," said Drifa, "but not enough of them to kill anything as big as the Midgard Serpent, and none of them are as deadly as his own venom."

"Then we'll head for Jotunheim," Robin said, and rowed her boat east, with the other two boats following her. The ocean air was cold and damp, and the only reason the humans didn't catch their death of cold was that they were already dead.

As the hours went by we began to see chunks of ice floating in the water, glowing a cold blue-white under the starlight. The small ones were the size of a man's head, the big ones the size of an island. The humans used their oars to fend off the small chunks and to row their way around the big ones. The only light was the stars and Robin Grima's hair. Then, hours later, there was a dull red glow on the eastern horizon.

Drifa shaded her eyes against the sunlight that slowly grew brighter and brighter. Eventually, maybe an hour later, a golden fraction of the sun disk edged up over the horizon. "The giants call the sun Ever-Bright," Knut said, "or that's what the dark elf Alvis the All-Wise claimed in the eddas."

"Alvis ended up turning to stone in the sunlight," Bookwyrm said. "A lot of the dark elves and frost giants have the same weakness."

"Do you have a spell equivalent to sunlight?" Robin asked, thinking of the game when Grima had fought a vampire.

"No," said Bookwyrm. "The hottest I can do is dragon fire."

"And besides," said Knut, "sunlight only hurts frost giants and dark elves, not hill giants and sea giants and fire giants."

The golden sun lingered for a few minutes, and then retreated below the horizon again, the sky slowly darkening. An hour later, we were back to nothing but starlight again.

Robin Grima's arms were growing tired, but she kept rowing.

An hour or two later we found ourselves surrounded by a circle of orcas. (Those are killer whales, not orcs. They are shaped like dolphins, but they're a lot bigger and nastier.) Drifa threw pinches of something from her box into the water, and the orcas quickly swam away.

"Did you poison them?" Robin asked. "Will they die?"

"No," Drifa said. "It just made the water taste unpleasant to them so they went away."

"I hope that's all it did," said Robin, remembering going to SeaWorld and watching Shamu leap in time to the music, sometimes jumping through hoops, sometimes letting a woman ride on his back. Of course the Sea World entertainment didn't show Shamu jumping up onto a sheet of ice to eat seals and penguins, which is one way that orcas (also known as killer whales) get their meals in the wild.

A little after that, the eastern sky started turning black, the stars disappearing: one by one at first, and then twenty by twenty, and we realized that our view of the sky was being cut off by a range of mountains.

An island of ice drifted toward us with two huge walruses on it too busy fighting each other to notice us. The humans rowed around it carefully. Then a polar bear clambered up onto the island from out of the sea, and both of the walruses dove into the water and swam away, but one of them didn't do it fast enough (the one with the most wounds), and the polar bear swam after him and tore off his tail and took it back onto the ice to eat. Another piece of ocean life that doesn't get shown at Sea World.

And then we saw a bright blue-white circle of light on the shore, a little to the north, twice the size of the full moon and getting bigger and brighter and closer.

"That's Hymirstead," I told them.

"Good," said Robin Grima. "We can ask Hymir to stop building *Naglfar*." She rowed toward the light, and Knut and Bookwyrm followed her.

Imagine a sand castle built out of blocks of ice that glow blue-white as if they had starlight trapped inside them. Hymirstead is something like that. The great waves roll up along the beach and break against it when it's low tide, but its ice blocks don't crumble, though sometimes the sea water splashes in through a window. When it's high tide, the waves are higher, but the castle grows taller then, so the tops of its towers always stay high and dry even when the ground floor is half full of saltwater.

The rooms are lit by silver lamps in the shape of fish, or by silver fish swimming in crystal bowls. The benches are soft with white ermine fur. Aegirstead, where Heimdall grew up, is bigger, but Hymirstead is lovelier and the things there are better. Except that Hymir doesn't have his greatest treasure any more, a cauldron big enough to brew enough ale for everyone in Asgard. Hymir got into a dice game with Aegir and lost it, but he wouldn't hand it over until Odin sent Thor and Tyr Hymirson to fetch it. That's how Aegir got to be king of the ocean.

But even without his cauldron, Hymir still had treasures finer than anything you'll find at Aegirstead, and the best of them was his wife, the loveliest woman and best hostess in the Nine Worlds. He wouldn't tell anyone her name, and he wouldn't say where he found her. Maybe the light elves made her out of moonlight or the mist elves made her out of silver. I didn't understand how a lady who gave birth to someone as handsome as Tyr and to a woman as beautiful as Gerd Freys-wife could turn around for her third child and give birth to someone as ugly as Garm Wolfson. Then again I also didn't know what she saw in Hymir. Some gossips said she was afraid that if she left Jotunheim, Fenris would break his chains and come get her.

Our three boats rowed into Hymirstead's harbor and we found Lord Tyr standing there on the docks, waiting for us.

"You're late arriving, Drifa Hel woman," he said, "but I told my mother that you and your friends would be coming, so breakfast is still being served."

"Thank you, Lord Tyr," Drifa said politely. Tyr held out his hand to her, and escorted her up to his father's stead with the other folk following her.

The stead lady welcomed her guests at the door. Her red-gold hair shone with its own light, which her son Tyr's hair didn't do even if it was almost the same color. Maybe it's a female thing; Tyr's big sister's golden hair burned through the shadows of Jotunheim. which is how Lord Frey came to notice her.

The stead hall was well lit enough that we could see that Tyr's mother wore a blue-green dress and that her slender wrists were enclosed by ice-white circles of ivory. She washed our hands (and paws) with warm water and offered us breakfast, but she begged us to eat our meal where we'd be safe if her husband returned unexpectedly, and showed us the way to the hearth where we could hide under the cauldron if her husband returned.

"We'd rather not hide if it means being burnt," Drifa said, but Tyr assured her that we'd be comfortable there. The hearths in Jotunheim burn iron, not wood. Hymir's hearth was piled high with broken eating knives and swords, cracked cauldrons and helmets, all of them glowing rust red in a fire that was about as hot and as bright as a midsummer sunset. That's because Hymir's a sea giant. In a hill giant's home, the hearths are as hot and as bright as a midwinter noon, and a frost giant's hearths are like a midwinter midnight.

So there the heroes sat in the great hall's hearth, thankful to have a steady floor under them again. Don't imagine them huddled together and crouching by the fire. Their table was twenty feet long and they had to climb up the rungs to take their seats on the benches. Their plates were as big as Valhalla serving platters, and the serving platters were ten times that size. Of course, by giant standards, the whole affair was still dollhouse small. The stead lady had shown her hospitality by shrinking herself to human size, but once she'd made sure they had everything they needed, she walked away growing taller with each step until she was the size of a full-grown fir tree. And Tyr walked alongside her, his shoulders level with her head.

The heroes ate and drank their fill of roast seal and fish chowder, and shared out one of Knut's Asgard apples for dessert. Then the stead lady came back, her arms full of pillows and sheets.

"Go to sleep," said the Valwolf. "I'll keep watch." He hadn't spent the night rowing.

"*I won't sleep either,*" Frostbite whispered.

Robin Grima had already lain down on the white-furred benches, her head on the soft pillow, but she forced herself to sit up and draw her sword.

"All for one, and one for all," Drifa said, and touched her bright weapon blade to Frostbite, and Bookwyrm and Knut did the same.

"All for one, and one for all," said the Valwolf, and walked forward to touch his teeth to Frostbite's blade.

"*Those teeth were sharp enough already,*" Robin Grima overheard Frostbite whisper. "*I'll never forget how sharp they were.*"

Robin didn't hear the Valwolf make any reply. He just walked away, ears back, tail stiff. She lay down on the bench again and soon fell asleep, Frostbite's hilt cool and firm beneath her right hand.

They woke up to the sound of the stead door slamming shut and then, nearly as loud, the thunder of Hymir's footsteps. "Welcome home," said the stead lady. "Did the hunt go well?"

Robin listened, wondering when Hymir was going to say "Fee fi fo fum" and ask his wife to grind their bones into bread, but the tale of Jack the Giant Killer isn't trustworthy: giants don't eat bread. Except for drinking ale, they're strictly carnivorous.

"The wolves were slow," Hymir bellowed, "but they finally caught up with the white tiger we were after." There was a thump as he flung down his kill, and the floor shook, and one of the knives in the fireplace fell, though luckily nowhere near the heroes. Scientists say the Siberian tiger is the largest feline, but that's because they've never seen the Jotunheim tiger. It's white and about as tall as an elephant, and it's in no danger of extinction. "Make me a coat from his pelt," Hymir said, "and a stew from his meat and give his bones to Mother to chew. Hello, Mother. How did your day go?"

There was a babble of women's voices, too many for me to pick out all of them. I've only got two ears, and Hymir's mother has nine heads. (The *Hymiskvitha* claims she has nine hundred heads, but I've never seen more than nine.) Hymir didn't bother to listen to any of her heads. He just grabbed Tyr in a bear hug that would've killed anyone who wasn't at least half-giant.

Why hadn't Hymir's mother ever figured out that people would understand her better if only one of her heads spoke at a time? Ocean giants are nearly as stupid as frost giants and hill giants. Even Tyr, who obviously takes after his mother's people, whoever they are, isn't as bright as the Aesir or he wouldn't have stuck his hand in Fenris's mouth.

When Hymir finally stopped hugging Tyr and thumping him on his back, he growled, "And what did the Aesir send you here to steal from me this time?"

"I didn't come here from Asgard," Tyr said. "The guests I brought you are a woman from Hel and her followers."

"Tyr's almost as clever as Loki and Odin," Frostbite

whispered. *"The prophecies say that Hel and Hymir are going to be allies at Ragnarok. Robin Grima, if you want to stay safe in this hall, then remember that your host thinks Drifa is your leader and you're one of her followers."*

"Come out, brave Drifa Hel woman," Tyr called, "before Father starts looking for you and breaks the cauldron and the beam that it hangs from and we don't have pot luck to eat for dinner."

Drifa walked out of the fireplace and craned her neck back to look up at Tyr and his parents. "Good evening, Lord Hymir," she said politely, "and thank you for your hospitality." She clapped her hands and called, "Come out, everyone, and greet our host," and the rest of us came out too, trying to avoid the mounds of snow and ice that had fallen off Hymir's shoes when he came inside. The heaps of snow were as tall as I was, but of course that's only a few inches high. A wave splashed in through a window, and I jumped onto the Valwolf's back so I wouldn't get wet and hoped he wouldn't shake me off into the cold saltwater.

I'd seen Hymir time and again from a safe perch on the World Tree, but this was the first time I'd ever gotten this close to him. His eyes were sea color, always changing: sometimes blue, sometimes green, sometimes gray, sometimes black. His face wasn't craggy (that's for hill giants) or cold (that's for frost giants) but smooth and smiling, and his teeth were clean and white, but of course that didn't mean you could trust him not to sink your hopes and swallow you down.

"Are any of you kin to the Vanir or taken oaths to serve them?" Hymir asked, his voice a soft growl, and we all said no. "Then Lady Drifa and her followers are welcome here in my home," he said. "I'll protect you as long as you're under my roof. When is dinner going to be ready, beautiful treasure?"

"Right away," said the stead lady, and clapped her hands. A dozen servants came running in, each of them carrying an iron platter that held a huge roast male walrus, weighing two or three thousand pounds. Hymir cut off the heads and the servants took them away. Then he sat down at the table and started eating. The *Hymniskvitha* says that when Thor came visiting, he ate two of Hymir's "oxen," but all of our party together only managed to eat a dozen pounds or so of walrus. Hymir and his mother each ate three walruses, but most of his hall folk only had one apiece. Tyr and his mother shared one between them.

"I'll take the boy and his friends out fishing tomorrow," Hymir said. "Maybe we can catch something more to his taste than your cooking, my treasure."

"I'd love to go fishing with you, Father," Tyr said.

After dinner, Hymir yelled, "Now let's have a ball game." A servant ran off and came back tossing a small walrus head from hand to hand. It was steaming hot with fat dripping off of it, and it must have weighed at least fifty pounds. Its ivory tusks were a couple of feet long. The hall folk stood up from the table, all except for the old nine-headed lady who was still drinking—one bowl of ale for each head—and the stead lady who was making sure that the ale bowls stayed full. They lined up along the sides of the hall. We stood in front of the fireplace.

"Catch!" shouted Hymir, picking the head up off the platter and throwing it at Tyr, who caught it one-handed and threw it at one of the hall folk, who....

After a while one of the giants threw the walrus head at Drifa. Drifa caught it by its long white tusks, but they broke free at her touch, and the head started to fall, but Bookwyrm stepped forward and caught it before it touched the floor and threw it to the nearest giant. At first I thought that Hymir's mother yelled something at us, but she was only snoring. The stead lady kissed her good night and took the ale bowls back to the kitchen and must have gone to bed after that because she didn't come back to the party.

After that, the giants left us out of the game, and we didn't object. Drifa picked up the tusks and threw them into the fireplace behind her and sat on the floor, dipping her hands in the cold sea water and made Bookwyrm do the same. Finally one of the hall folk dropped the walrus head, and they made him stand in the center of the room and threw bones at him till he was standing up to his knees in them. It's an old Norse after-dinner game. King Hrolf Kraki's hall-folk played it with poor Hott till Bodvar made them stop. And about a thousand years ago, a bunch of Vikings played it with a Saxon Archbishop of Canterbury who refused to let his folk ransom him, just stood there in the hall night after night getting hit by bones till he finally got put out of his misery by a blow from an axe. But this sea giant was tougher stuff (or the hall folk throwing the bones at him were friendlier) and when the sport was done, he laughed and called for a drink.

The maidservants swept up the bones and brought out the drinking horns, each of them at least ten feet long. I drank close to my body weight in ale. The humans and wolf didn't do that well, but they each took care of two or three pints. Then we left the rest of the ale in our horn for whoever wanted it and returned to our haven in the hearth.

Knut recited the edda about how the Aesir threw things at beautiful Baldur Odinson. They threw spears and knives and burning torches and poisoned arrows at him, and they laughed because it was such fun, and Baldur laughed too, to show he was a good sport. He didn't take any hurt from any of it till his blind brother, dark Hodur, threw a spear of mistletoe, and its touch killed Baldur, and everyone in Asgard claimed to be shocked and horrified. Everyone in

Asgard claimed to be heartbroken. Everyone in Asgard wept for Baldur the Beautiful.

Drifa got out her box and it fell open, spilling bags of herbs on the floor of the hearth. Its ivory clasp was broken. She picked up the bags carefully, one by one, sometimes opening the bag and smelling the herbs inside. Finally she took out a few pinches of pink petals from one bag and added some more pink petals from another bag and some dry roots from a third. She crushed the petals on a plate with the back of her spoon, then chewed up the roots and spat the pieces onto the petals and crushed that in too, along with some of the fat from our breakfast seal meat. Then she dipped her fingers into it and put it on her reddened palms and counted to nine times nine.

"I just wish I had honey and cod liver oil to add," she said, her voice thick because chewing the root had numbed her lips and tongue. "It'll do, though. Hold out your hands, Husband."

Bookwyrm obeyed and we saw how his palms were blistered from holding the hot walrus head. Drifa smoothed the herb paste lightly on them and said, "You should be able to go to sleep in an hour or two, and you'll feel better in the morning."

"I'll take first watch then," Bookwyrm said, and the rest of us soon fell asleep, in spite of the noise from the hall where the giants were singing drinking songs and bragging about how much they'd catch in tomorrow's hunting.

An hour later, I woke up when a hand pushed a jar the size of my body into our haven. "I hope this will help," the stead lady whispered, and then we heard her footsteps going away.

Drifa picked up the jar and smelled it and said, "I can see how she'd have cod liver oil handy, but where did she ever find honey in this frozen land?" Then she rubbed some of it on her hands and then did the same for her husband. What she didn't say and what Bookwyrm didn't say and what I didn't say was that having that jar show up meant that the stead lady had been listening to us talk in here, and maybe Hymir and his hall folk could hear us too.

Breakfast in Hymirstead was cold, and even colder because the stead lady only stayed at the table long enough to explain that she couldn't eat with us because she had a heavy task that would take all her time for the next few days. She wore a new dress, the same sea color as she'd worn last night, but its long sleeves fell past her wrists. She kissed her son and husband, and then bade us farewell, apologizing because she had so little to offer us for breakfast. The table had a platter of sliced cold walrus meat that was as long as a man, flanked by dishes of cold seaweed and cold pickled herring and bowls of cold boiled eggs. There was cold deep-fried whale skin and cold raw blubber to spread on it. There were two kinds of cold milk, but neither was what the humans were used to. Walrus milk is 30% fat, and seal milk is over 50% fat (and sea giants use it for cream). Cow milk is less than 4% fat. Squirrel milk? How nice of you to ask. It's a lot richer than cow milk and a lot lighter than walrus milk, and only baby squirrels drink it, so I haven't had any in dozens of centuries.

The sky was still black when we went outside. Once Hymir dragged his rowboat out of the boathouse, though, we had plenty of light to see by: it was made of shining gold. (That meant it was probably dark elf work. The light elves prefer to work in wood, and the mist elves prefer to work in silver.)

"It's beautiful," Robin Grima said, but she was using a word that's not in most giants' vocabulary.

"It's watertight," said Hymir. "The dark elves forged it so

it won't ever sink or take on water. Beyond that, it's just an ordinary rowboat. I'm having a bigger ship built in Niflheim. Stick around long enough and I'll show it to you, Hel woman. Or go away if you want to: you're still sure to see it when Ragnarok comes, and I sail it up to Asgard to fight alongside Hel's army."

He pushed the rowboat off the dock into the water and got into it, sitting down on the front bench and picking up the oars. Tyr took the back oars, and we took the middle bench, with Knut and Bookwyrm sitting on the outside so they could each take an oar. That still left plenty of legroom. Robin thought the rowboat was about the size of a tennis court. Knut and Bookwyrm thought it was big enough to hold four longboats, two in front and two in back. Drifa thought it was about the size of Lady Hel's high table.

There were leather bags under the benches. Knut and Bookwyrm dragged them forward so they could brace their feet on them when they rowed. The Valwolf sniffed the bags and lay on the floor of the boat, as far away from them as he could get, and Ratatosk perched atop the middle bench between the Valhallans, eyes darting here and there from danger to danger: the Valwolf's teeth, the swords and axe, Tyr and his sword, Hymir.

"The prophecies say that when Ragnarok comes, Tyr and Garm Hel-hound will kill each other," Robin Grima said. "That'll be a fight worth watching, but nobody will have time to see it; they'll all be too busy fighting their own battles."

"Listen to the Hel woman, son," said Hymir. "Don't kill Garm; he's not to blame for his father's bad manners. Lady Hel's going to be so grateful to me for helping her conquer Asgard that she'll promise me anything I ask for, and I'll ask her to give me Garm. Then you and your mother can strike a bargain over whether I take in her second son as a house pet or whether I feed him poisonous herbs to put him to sleep and skin him into a lap rug. Either way you'll do better fighting beside your own father in the last battle than fighting besides the Lady and her heroes."

Robin had thought about mercy killing now and then when the pain from her cancer was bad, but she'd never made plans for it. Now at the mention of poisoned herbs, she glanced over at Drifa who held her box of herbs by her right hand. Drifa was smiling. A cold shiver ran down Robin's back.

"I won't fight beside the Lady or the other Vanir," Tyr said, "but I won't fight beside you either, Father. I've sworn to kill Garm. And when that's done, I'll kill Fenris and wipe out the shame he did to my mother."

"Stubborn as sunlight and as hotheaded as a wildfire," grumbled his father, but he didn't seem very angry. After a while, he started singing "A Hundred Barrels of Ale in the Hall," and Tyr joined in, the two of them keeping stroke to the song and Knut and Bookwyrm following along.

"I'm not going to waste my time asking Hymir and Tyr to help us outwit the prophecies," Robin Grima told Frostbite, *"but maybe when we get back to Hymirstead, I'll ask Tyr's mother to help us."*

"Be careful," Frostbite whispered. *"Make sure that the stead lady's mother-in-law isn't listening."*

After an hour or so, Hymir pulled up one of the bags under his bench and dumped out what was in it: a seal head, a walrus head, a human woman's head. "Oops," he said, "I hope nobody's offended. She was a trespasser, not a guest." He baited a hook with the woman's head and threw it overboard, her long blonde hair trailing through the ocean swells.

Three narwhales jumped at it, their horns clashing as they bit at the head, until finally one of them swallowed it.

Hymir leaned back and pulled the whale up and threw it over his shoulder into the boat. The Valwolf growled, and Robin jumped up, Frostbite gleaming silver in her hand, but the whale landed neatly between the benches, its tail inches from Robin's toes.

"One of you humans cut it in quarters and bait the hooks for something worth catching," growled Hymir, without bothering to look back.

Frostbite slashed out and cut off the narwhale's horn and pushed it toward Hymir. *"Now leave the rest of the job to the woman from Hel's Hall,"* the sword whispered, and Robin Grima sat down.

Drifa stood up and used her axe to chop down the whale's spine, turning it into a blood eagle as the ribs broke free and stood up like wings. Then she chopped through it crosswise, behind the flippers. Her axe still bore Frostbite's power, and the carcass froze at her blows instead of bleeding. Robin shivered at the sight of the mutilated whale.

Hymir picked up two of the quarters and baited a hook with each of them and lowered his lines gently over the side.

"Bait my lines too, Drifa Hel woman," Tyr said, and Drifa fetched them and slipped his hooks into the narwhale's hindquarters. A Midgard narwhale with a tusk is a male, and it weighs two or three tons, but everything in and near Jotunheim is bigger. The narwhales Hymir caught probably weighed four or five tons. His steel hooks were as long as Frostbite. I don't know what his fishing line was made of, but it didn't break when he took Thor out fishing in his old boat and they caught the Midgard Serpent, and Hymir cut the line because he didn't want to risk sinking the ship.

Tyr flipped his fishing lines into the water. The saltwater splashed up high into the cold air when the pieces of bait hit it, and the rowboat rocked from side to side, but the dark elves' work was well done, and the rowboat stayed dry.

The wind began to blow a little faster, a little colder, and I wished that I'd asked Robin Grima to let me stay behind in Hymirstead. I could have had a nice long chat with the stead lady. Or I could have hidden in the fireplace and had a nice long warm nap. I got down on the nice dry floor of the boat and snuggled up in between Robin Grima's ankles and wondered what Hymir's plans were.

You fish for a narwhale with a walrus head that weighs about fifty pounds. What are you fishing for when you bait your line with a ton of narwhale meat? The largest creature in Midgard's ocean is the blue whale, which runs up to a hundred feet long (as long as a tennis court) and nearly two hundred tons, but they won't eat anything bigger than tiny shrimps and they get those by straining seawater for them, not by chasing them down and biting them. We were too far out to sea to meet water trolls or polar bears. Maybe sharks, though that didn't seem exactly Hymir's style. Maybe....

Then the rowboat shuddered, and a man's voice whispered, "I'm not going to bite at your bait today, Hymir." I looked up and saw two bright yellow eyes, each as big as a giant's serving platter. They were set in a wedge-shaped head as wide as Hymir's rowboat, its black scales outlined in red. The head towered over us, and then sank gracefully to lie on top of the boat, both eyes looking towards the bow at Hymir. His breath was warm and sweet, but the prophecies said he could breathe poison. I wished I was sitting on a branch a thousand feet in the air, and I wondered how long I could hold my breath, and I stared up at the Midgard Serpent, Orm Lokison.

"Awhile ago I heard somebody say my nephew Garm's name and poison in the same breath," Orm said. "I know a little about poison, too."

"Of course you do, old friend," said Hymir. "Don't be modest. You know a lot more about poisons than a dumb giant like me. If you promise not to bite me with your poisonous fangs, we could have a friendly wrestle. If something goes wrong, and I accidentally kill you, then I could use your bones to build *Naglfar* and your skin for its sails. Or you could drag me underwater and keep me down there till I drowned, except that I can breathe water and we've already proved that my ribs are too thick for your hug to break them. Oops."

Orm laughed, opening up his mouth wide enough that you could see not just his long forked tongue (which he used for smelling) but his long fangs and sharp incisors.

Tyr quietly put down his oars and drew his sword. It lit up the night like a full moon, and the blood runes that faced us said Victory.

"The prophecies say I'll still be alive when Ragnarok comes," Orm said. "Thor and I will fight one another, and he'll kill me with his hammer, walk nine steps away, and then die of breathing my poison. And I trust the prophecies more than I trust you, Hymir old friend." He hissed out a cloud of sweet warm air. "And more than I trust your son from Asgard. I can smell you clearly, little Tyr. Put down your two-faced sword, or we'll see how long Justice lasts when you use it to backstab someone who isn't attacking anyone, and we'll see just who ends up with Victory after you've inhaled my poison. Maybe my little brother would like your other hand too, so he could have a matched set."

"Thor told the rest of us not to kill you," Tyr said. "He's looking forward to doing that at Ragnarok. I just drew my sword so my human friends here could see you better."

"You're so kind to your friends, Tyr," said Orm. "Do your father's human friends have any of his hooks in them?"

"They're not bait, old friend," Hymir said. "They're my guests. I took them out fishing so they could see the wonders of the ocean, especially you."

"I told you when you brought Thor out to see me that that was the last time I'd respect your guests."

"I'll fight you to protect my guests!" Hymir yelled.

"Will you? Suppose I offer you weregeld for them in advance? Suppose I offer... " Orm's yellow eyes swiveled to look down at the four humans "to let your hall folk go down to the sea bottom and harvest the shipwrecked bones that lie there? That would let you finish building your ship in weeks or months, not in centuries and millennia."

"Don't do it, Father," Tyr yelled. "You promised them your protection as long as they were under your roof."

"Oops," Hymir said. "They're not under my roof any more, are they? All right, Lokison, go ahead and take them."

Orm laughed too. "So much for trusting your host, humans. What will you offer the Midgard Monster not to eat you? Gold and silver? Magic swords and magic poisons? What do you have that I want?"

"Our respect," Robin Grima said, standing up so her eyes were on a level with the huge serpent's head. "For showing us your intelligence and your honor. And we'll respect you more if you're smart enough to stay away from Ragnarok and not fight Thor. What do you have to gain from a fight like that besides dying?"

"Be silent, insolent thrall!" Tyr yelled. "Speak up, Drifa Hel woman. Maybe your courage can persuade the monster to spare you and your followers. But I swear by both my sword's faces that I'll fight Fenris's brother here and now rather than let him hurt you."

"I can offer you my clothes and an axe from Mist Hall," Drifa said, "and a box of herbs. That's everything I've got right now so that's all I can give you—unless you want my thanks for sparing my husband and his friends, and I'll give you those if you earn them. If that's not enough, then go ahead and kill us, but you'll have to take my axe and poisons in exchange. Then decide what you're going to tell your sister when she asks why you killed her hall woman."

Nobody else said anything for a while after that.

Robin Grima wished she had a wristwatch. *"Do you know when the sun will rise?"* she thought to her sword. *"And what will it do to Hymir?"*

"He's a sea giant," Frostbite whispered. *"It may dazzle his eyes, but it won't turn him to stone."*

"Should I try to cut the Midgard Serpent's throat, or cut out his tongue?" she asked. *"Or should I call him brother and ask him to protect me and my friends from Hymir?"*

"Your choice," Frostbite whispered, *"but Orm's heart is colder than Hel's. It's almost as cold as the Valwolf's teeth."*

Knut's hand was on his sword, ready to draw it and do his best to protect Robin Grima and his friend Bookwyrm and his friend the Valwolf. Bookwyrm's hand was on his sword too, ready to tell Hymir to fight to protect them or find out if his rowboat would stay afloat with a hole cut in its bottom. The Valwolf crouched at Knut's feet, teeth bared but silent. And brave little Ratatosk huddled down among the leather bags, ready to leap up and fight to protect his oath-brothers if that's what it came to.

"She's outbid you, little Hymir," Orm said at last, swiveling his eyes back toward the front of the rowboat.

Hymir stood up abruptly and strode toward the serpent. It only took him half a dozen steps to cross the distance, but the boat rocked heavily with each one of them. "Eat the humans, or go away!" he yelled. "You're scaring the fish!"

Orm laughed, then slid silently off the rowboat and down into the depths of the ocean.

Hymir and Tyr pulled the narwhale quarters back into the rowboat and baited their hooks with smaller things from another leather bag: seal and walrus heads. They fished till sunrise, catching another narwhale and a dozen sharks. Then they turned away from the sun disc and rowed back to Hymirstead.

When they got there, Hymir offered Drifa his hospitality again for her and her friends, and renewed his promise of his protection as long as they were under his roof. Tyr offered them a ride to Mimir's Fountain, and they decided on that instead. But first they stood in the doorway of Hymirstead and told a maidservant to tell the stead lady that they bade her farewell and thanked her for her hospitality.

"She sends her apologies for not bidding you goodbye," the giantess said, "but her good wishes go with you, and she sends Lady Drifa a present to remember her by," and she held out a black leather sealskin bag tied with knotted red cords. Drifa tied it to her belt, and then let Tyr lift her up onto his horse's back.

"Farewell and fare far and fend for yourselves," Hymir said, and walked back under his stead roof.

CHAPTER ELEVEN

Silver-Mane galloped across the icy plains and snowy mountains of Jotunheim, sometimes leaping over a mound of rocks that marked a frost giant's grave, sometimes slowing down to thread his way across a rock moraine at the foot of a towering glacier. The stars were bright overhead, and Robin Grima's hair was bright where she sat nearest the horse's tail, but the land was as dark as the ocean depths, which was where Tyr's horse was bred and raised. Seafolk can see in the dark just like Helfolk and Jotunheim folk.

For a few hours Robin Grima and her friends could look back across the land and see the blue-white glow of Hymirstead growing smaller and smaller behind them. Then they crossed a range of snowy mountains, and lost sight of where they'd slept last night.

The humans were crowded close enough to one another that the wind didn't claw at their furless skin, but even so the night was cold enough that the Valhallans' warm breath turned to frost. Tyr's breath did too, another argument for his mother being something other than a frost giant. But Drifa's breath was clear and cold, even though her skin felt as warm as Robin Grima's, even though Bookwyrm hadn't found her cold when they shared a bed in Mist Hall.

The starlight didn't show them much detail of the landscape, but there wasn't much worth seeing. Jotunheim was still and barren, except for the occasional sight of a frost giant or troll out hunting. There are stories of cities and castles in Jotunheim, but few people find them in the same place twice except for the sea giant steads on the coast. Cold fields of ice can cast mirages just as well as hot fields of desert sand, and prankster magicians can weave illusions.

Finally, after long, cold, boring hours, Silver Mane crossed another mountain range and his riders looked down to see a bright geyser spurting up thousands of feet into the clouds. There was a pit of dull red flames at the geyser's feet.

"There it is," Tyr said, "Mimir's Pillow and the Nine Worlds' Pillar and Wise Odin's horse that he rode for nine days and nine nights when he went to get the runes." When he said the third kenning the illusion disappeared, and we saw the great World Tree looming before them, its middle roots nestled in the red waters of Mimir's Fountain.

"Where are you heading for next, Drifa Hel woman?" Tyr asked, and his head swiveled around on his neck to face Drifa, who sat just behind him. Robin shivered and thought of *The Exorcist*, but being able to look down on his own buttocks didn't mean that Tyr was possessed by a devil. Sea giants can do tricks like that, because their bodies aren't rigid like dirt lying on top of stones or like leaves growing on branches; they're flexible like sea waves rising and falling. "Do you want to go visit the dark elves and ask them to forge scalpels so you can cut up your patients?" Tyr asked, "Or do you want to climb up the World Tree to the gardens of the light elves and gather herbs there?"

"I'll leave the choice of where we go to my companion," Drifa said. "Grima, where does your heart call you?"

"Heather Island," Robin Grima said, remembering how she'd seen it in Blind Hall, with Fenris Lokison chained to the rocks, remembering how the Norns had asked her to bring them Tyr's right hand. "After all, we've seen Hel and Orm now, so it's only fair to see their little brother too." She thought that seeing the monster who bit off his hand would scare Tyr off, or at least make him think of pleasanter places to be, but he surprised her.

"I'll come along to protect you, Drifa Hel woman," he said, "unless you would rather win more praise for your bravery by making the journey with no one but humans, an effeminate wolf, and a cowardly squirrel to fight at your back."

"Ratatosk has sharp fangs to bite with," said Drifa, "and so does the Valwolf, but we all know that your sword is sharper, Lord Tyr, and that it bites deeper. We'd be honored if you took the time and trouble to protect us."

Tyr called out a loud greeting to the giants surrounding Mimir's Fountain. Tyr has never been accused of cowardice. On the other hand (though Tyr doesn't have one of those), it's not easy to sneak up on something when you're riding a horse long enough to carry five people plus a wolf, not to mention when your helmet has a star shining on it, and so does your horse's mane and tail, and one of your riders has hair that shines in the dark like firelight.

"Free fine food yum!" a frost giant yelled. "Don't come any closer, Hymirson, or I'll eat you and your children for breakfast."

"Stay away from the fountain!" yelled a second giant. "It's fresh water, not saltwater, so you won't be able to breathe it."

"It's Mimir's blood," yelled a third, "and you're not allowed to drink from it unless you pay us. Heimdall gave us his horn for a drink, and Odin gave us his eye. You don't have a hand to spare, do you, Hymirson? Will you give us your sword or your horse?"

Tyr got off Silver Mane and grew tall enough to look the giants in the eye. As the humans jumped to the ground, they only came up to his ankle. "Hello there, friends," Tyr said, his voice booming like thunder. "You keep a good watch, but we're not thirsty enough to sink to drinking blood. I've got a flask of my father's ale in my saddle bags, and I'll let you each have some of it if you're interested. You won't have to pay for it, either. I'm a generous visitor even if you're not generous hosts."

Knut stepped forward, next to the Valwolf, ready to fight to protect him if the war of words changed to something fiercer. Bookwyrm stepped in front of Drifa, who was sitting on the ground, going through her box of herbs. Robin Grima stood between Knut and Bookwyrm. Ratatosk? How nice of you to ask. I sat on the open lid of Drifa's herb box.

Robin looked up at the angry giants and remembered the time in the dungeon when Grima fought a Cloud Giant, twenty-four feet high and twelve thousand pounds, and would have died if it hadn't been for the Potion of Extra Healing she'd gotten from the old wizardess.

"There aren't any cloud giants in the Nine Worlds," Frostbite whispered. *"Just frost giants and hill giants and sea giants and fire giants. I can burn frost giants up with one blow, and freeze a fire giant or a sea giant just as quickly, but hill giants like these will take longer to kill, especially when they're on land."*

"Dirty little treacherous thieves!" shouted a voice behind us, and I looked back to see Hymir standing behind us, next to Silver Mane. "Don't let them get away, old friends."

"We left Hymir hours ago, hundreds of miles ago, when we left the seacoast!" Robin Grima thought at Frostbite. *"How did he get here?"*

"There's a well here," Frostbite whispered. *"Did you think Hymir was only an ocean giant? He can show up at a lake, a river, a well—wherever there's water."*

"We'll hold them for you, Hymir!" yelled a giant. "Don't move a foot, little humans, or we'll smash it off and you'll have to crawl on your hands and knees."

"Don't try to steal away!" yelled a second

"Don't try to steal an anything!" yelled a third.

The rest of the giants weren't smart enough to talk and do anything else at the same time, but they all jumped up and started waving their weapons at us. Not very impressive weapons if you judged them in terms of technology. Nothing with elf-forged magic like Tyr's sword. A few swords and axes, but mostly stone clubs or chunks of ice with jagged rocks inside them. Of course the weapons *were* impressive if you judged them in terms of size.

"I promised Lady Drifa and her followers my protection," Tyr said.

"That was back when you thought Drifa was brave and honorable," his father yelled. "You didn't know they were thieves."

"We didn't steal anything from you," Robin Grima yelled, and Knut and Bookwyrm said the same thing.

"We took nothing from you or your lady except what she gave us freely and generously," Drifa said.

I looked at Drifa's hands and rubbed my eyes and looked again, but I still couldn't see her fingers. "Put your cap on," she whispered to me, "and hand out the others." I put out my forepaw and touched something soft, and my paw vanished.

"Thieves and oathbreakers!" Hymir shouted. "They've deceived my poor innocent son, the same way crafty Fenris did when he swore he'd be my boy's foster brother and then raped my poor boy's mother."

Drifa brought up her hands to her belt, her fingers visible again, and untied the bag that Hymir's wife had given her and pushed it to me. I touched it with my forepaw and pulled back. It was cold as ice! Drifa tied its cords into a loop and slipped it over my neck so the bag would dangle in the air and I wouldn't have to touch it. I put one of the mist caps on my head and felt it shrink till it fit snugly. Then I took the other caps in my mouth and scampered toward the fountain.

"My poor innocent boy met Drifa in Hel's Hall," Hymir shouted, "but the thieving beggarwoman carries an axe that she took from Mist Hall. Go ahead, crafty lady, go ahead and deny that you stole things in Mist Hall."

I jumped onto Bookwyrm's head and unfolded a mist cap. He disappeared from sight, but I could still smell him.

Drifa closed her box and stood up, facing Hymir. "The Mist folk stole from me first," she said. "Turn about is fair play. But you and your lady never took anything from me, Lord Hymir, so I never took anything from you or her except what was freely given."

"One of the little folk vanished!" thundered a giant. "Guard Mimir's Fountain!"

"Guard Mimir's head and Odin's eye and Heimdall's horn!" cried another giant.

"Kill the rest of them before they get away!" roared Hymir and pulled his axe out from under his belt.

I jumped onto Robin Grima's head, clinging with my hind feet to her shining hair, and unfolding her mist cap with my forefeet. Then I jumped down onto her shoulder and whispered in her ear, *"Don't look now, but you're invisible."*

"Run for the tree!" Robin Grima yelled. She ran past Tyr and in between Hymir's feet and circled the fountain toward the World Tree.

The Valwolf picked up Knut by the neck—like a mother dog carrying her puppy—and leapt up onto the lowest branch of the World Tree. Tyr grabbed Bookwyrm and threw him up high into the air, and he caught hold of a World Tree branch on his way down, but he was nowhere near Odin's rope and had no way to get back down. Then Tyr reached out for Drifa, but he was too late; Hymir was holding her up to his face.

"What did you find in the bag my lady gave you?" Hymir bellowed.

"Pieces of ivory," Drifa said. "You and your hall folk had too much fun at your ball game to notice that my touch on the walrus head caused the ivory tusks to fall free. Every other ivory binding in your hall fell free, too, even the clasp on my box of herbs, even the bracelets you'd locked on your slave girl. I didn't steal her from your stead, sea lord. I shared Hel's last gift to me; I freed her."

"If you're not a thief, then give me back my woman's bracelets!" Hymir yelled.

Robin was rounding the fountain. The stead lady's bag kept bumping against my chest, threatening to knock me off my perch on her shoulder, but I held on for dear life. The giants couldn't see her because of the mist cap, and they didn't hear her because they were too busy listening to Hymir.

"Here's what the stead lady gave me," Drifa said, waving the herb box. The lid came open, and the box was upside down, and everything inside fell out onto the ice-covered ground. "Oops," she said as Hymir looked down, and then she slammed the box into his face, breaking his nose.

He screamed in rage and pushed her head into his mouth and bit it off (a quick death) and then pushed the rest of her body into his mouth and chewed her up, spitting out the crushed bones.

Robin Grima reached the trunk of the World Tree and found Odin's rope waiting for her. It was a little shorter than it used to be because of the pieces they'd cut off to make the oars, but it was still long enough to reach the ground.

I scrambled up the trunk, as Robin grabbed the rope and started climbing.

"That was ill done," Tyr said quietly, coldly, to Hymir, not specifying if he meant eating Drifa or binding ice bracelets on his mother. "When Ragnarok comes, I'll kill Garm first and Fenris second and then I'll kill you third. When were you planning to tell me that my mother was your slave concubine and I was your bastard? Were you going to wait till you took a wife and had legitimate children by her?"

"I offered to marry your mother!" Hymir yelled, talking with his mouth still full of some of Drifa's bones; nobody has ever claimed sea giants have good table manners. "But she wouldn't tell me her name or her kinsmen's names, so we couldn't draw up a marriage contract, so my only choice was to take her as a slave and make her my concubine. Yes, I had the mist elves forge her bracelets to freeze her memories so she wouldn't remember anything before she met me, but that was all I ever did to bind her. I even let her go visit you and your sister in the high worlds when she swore she'd come back to me. She was my best treasure, and your little thieves robbed me of her. If you're not going to help me get her back, then I'm going home." He turned away and dove into Mimir's Fountain and disappeared under the water.

The giants sat back down around Mimir's Fountain, picked up their laptops and went back to watching porn.

I got to the lowest limb of Yggdrasil and gave Knut his mist cap. Then I kept on climbing till I reached my home and checked my email and found that some people were wondering whether I was dead. My oath bound me not to even hint at what I'd been up to—or should that be what I'd been down to?—so I wrote that I'd been doing an inventory on the nuts I'd put aside for winter and would add their names to my list.

Meanwhile Knut was pulling Robin up to the lowest branch over Mimir's Fountain. Bookwyrm did his best to help, but he was too busy crying for Drifa to be of much use. Even so, it wasn't long before Robin was standing on the branch next to them. She off her mist cap and put it safely away in a bag at her belt.

Tyr mounted Silver Mane, and she trotted up through the air toward the Valhallans. "I'll bring Mother back to Hymirstead before Ragnarok comes," Tyr told them. "For my own honor, not Father's. But I promised brave Drifa that I'd protect you folk on your way to Heather Island. Do you want to climb the rest of the way, or to get back on my horse?"

"We'll climb till we meet Ratatosk once again," Robin Grima said loyally.

"Well thought," said Tyr. "He might tell tales on you if you left him behind."

"Ratatosk has enough room in his lair for us to sleep there," the Valwolf said.

"A good night's sleep before a good day's fight is a good idea," Knut said, and smothered a yawn.

By the time they reached my home, it was a little after high day, and the Valhallans hadn't had any sleep in nearly two days. I gave them their breakfast, and then they lay down on my benches and fell asleep. Tyr stood in my doorway and admired my computer setup, but said he'd be staying outside where he could keep an eye on Silver Mane. I looked out once or twice and saw Silver Mane nibbling the World Tree's leaves and flowers, while Tyr helped himself to lumps of ash honey. I offered to bring him a plate of bread and cheese and a mug of ale, but he politely declined.

The Valwolf lay in my doorway catnapping (or should that be wolfnapping?), going out now and then to water the tree. My home has an indoor water closet, but it's not really set up for wolves. Every time Tyr or Silver Mane moved to another branch, I'd notice the wolf's ears prick up, even when his eyes were closed.

I reset my security system so my guests wouldn't trigger it unless they went away and so Tyr and his horse would only trigger it if they came inside. Then I went back to my email, with a little catnap (squirrelnap?) now and then myself.

The Valhallans woke up around nightmark (about nine in the evening). I gave them dinner, and Knut cut up an Asgard apple and passed out the pieces.

"Last time we did this, Drifa was with us," said Bookwyrm. "When we've got time, I'm going to give her a proper funeral."

Knut went over to the doorway to give the apple core to the Valwolf and glanced outside. "The sky's full of fires," he said. "The valkyries must be dancing over Midgard."

"Or the frost giants are playing ball with a comet's head," Bookwyrm said.

"Or there was a great battle," the Valwolf said, "and Hel Falls is overflowing with ghosts."

"Or maybe it's electrons colliding with particles of gas," Robin said, but everyone ignored that, even Frostbite.

We looked at the aurora for few more minutes, then the Valhallans drank to my health and the next day's journey, and went back to sleep. Half an hour later, my perimeter alarms woke us all up: Tyr had ridden Silver Mane off to go get a closer look at the auroras.

CHAPTER TWELVE

The next morning we had breakfast at daymark. We went outside well before noon. Knut was getting ready to toss the rope up over an overhanging branch when Tyr galloped up across the clouds and offered us a ride the rest of the way.

Robin Grima accepted, and we got up onto Silver Mane's accommodating back and held on as the horse vaulted from cloud to cloud, then jumped onto the Rainbow Bridge.

But he wasn't walking up the bridge to Asgard, but downward. I tried to jump off, but I couldn't move, and I remembered that this morning nobody had remembered to touch their swords to Frostbite. Tyr started reciting the last lines of the *Lokasenna*: "'Skadi took a poison-snake and fastened it up over Loki's face, and the poison dropped thereon. Sigyn, Loki's wife, sat there and held a bowl under the poison, but when the bowl was full she bore away the poison, and meanwhile the poison dropped on Loki. Then he struggled so hard that the whole earth shook therewith; and now that is called an earthquake.'" Silver Mane stepped off the rainbow bridge and we were under a blue sky dotted with puffy white clouds but no sight of the sun; it was blocked out by a dark mountainside.

"Before you call on Fenris Wolf," Lord Tyr said, "I think you ought to visit his parents."

He kneed Silver Mane, and the horse walked toward the mountainside, its ears pricked back in discomfort. Before us lay the mouth of a dark cave that I hadn't noticed at first. It was barely wide enough to let us enter. Once we were inside, our only light was the horse's shining mane and tail and Robin Grima's hair. I looked back at the blue sky and saw a black bird circling the cave mouth. Ravens do that when they think someone might die soon.

The cave bent to the left and then to the right, and after a while we couldn't see the sky any more.

Then we were in a large chamber pierced by spears of white stone from the ceiling and the floor. Silver Mane stepped cautiously between the stone spears, threading his way to the chamber's back wall and into the darkness until we emerged into a chamber as bright as sunlight, where a naked woman with long dark red hair lay on the black floor, her mouth open like a silent scream, her arms and legs outstretched, tied to stalagmites. Over her head, a golden snake wriggled down a stalactite toward her, shining gold drops of venom dripping from its fangs and onto her face and splashing down onto her white breasts, leaving glowing red trails like embers. Her eyelids were shut tight, but she wasn't asleep; she was writhing against her bindings.

"She's not swallowing all of the snake's venom," snarled the Valwolf. "Some of it is dripping on the floor."

"Clever wolf," Tyr said, "but that's a very special snake, and walking on its venom won't hurt you. Wyrmtongue's been drinking it for centuries, and see how pretty she is."

The snake suddenly struck, its head diving downwards deep into the woman's mouth—and the room blazed bright with gold light, like being inside an aurora.

The Valwolf howled. Robin Grima squeezed Frostbite's

hilt, feeling him warm and firm against her flesh. Knut was sitting behind her, his breath warm on her neck. Bookwyrm fixed his thoughts on a song he'd written for Drifa and sung to her on their wedding night.

"You like that, don't you, Wyrmtongue?" Tyr asked. He got down off of Silver Mane's back and walked over to stand next to the bound woman.

Her body was shaking, her red nipples erect, as the snake pushed deeper and deeper into her mouth. Then her body was flowing like an avalanche of flame. The snake slowly withdrew from her mouth, its blood mixing with its venom as her teeth clenched to hold it. Except that her breasts were shrinking to taut male muscles, and her hair was only long enough to reach his shoulders, and a phallus was growing at his crotch, weeping red drops of fire from its tip. His eyelids flew open, and his bright gold eyes stared coldly at Tyr.

"Skadi's pretty snake didn't hurt you at all, did it?" Tyr asked. "You like having a snake entwine with your tongue, don't you, Loki? You've been doing it for a long time now, and you'll keep on doing it till Ragnarok comes. And if these brave humans have their way, there won't be a Ragnarok, and you'll keep on doing this for ever." His hand reached down and grasped the man's phallus, squeezing it smaller and smaller.

"Loki was the cleverest person in Asgard," he said. His hand let go of the phallus and glided down under the pale white buttocks. "Clever enough to trick Thiazi into attacking Asgard and clever enough to burn Thiazi to death." His thumb was pushing up in between the buttocks. "You like that too, don't you, Wyrmtongue? Does the pretty snake penetrate you there too sometimes so things don't get boring? You don't like being bored, do you, Loki? Was that why you tricked blind Hodur into killing bright Baldur? Were things in Asgard going so well that you were getting bored?"

The man—no, there were breasts again, and the phallus was gone—the woman moaned softly, wordlessly.

There were footsteps behind us. A wrinkled hag hobbled into the room, her long-sleeved white robe in tatters, her cane a long white bone, her sky-blue eyes the only color in her face. Her fingers were withered and blackened, and her fingernails were bitten down to the quick.

"And here's our hostess at long last," Tyr said. "Beautiful Baldur's oldest sister, Slain-Father's oldest daughter, the first valkyrie to fly over a battlefield and bring the best heroes. Who have you seen die lately, Sigyn?"

"Greetings, Lord Tyr," she said, her voice harsh and strained. "Welcome, here—" Her voice choked off into coughing. She finally spat whatever she'd been choking on out onto the floor and said. "You are all welcome here. I don't have much hospitality to offer you, but you may take the best of all that we have. Would you like raven stew or roast squirrel?"

"No fruit for your guests?" Tyr asked. "No, of course not. Idunn doesn't come here to bring you apples, does she? And your husband doesn't want to share his snake venom with you, does he?"

"Loki has to stay young," Sigyn said. "Ragnarok might come any day, and he has to be ready for it. If you don't want raven or squirrel, would you like me to fry you some rats?"

"No, thank you," Tyr told her. "We can't stay long enough to enjoy your cooking."

"I'd like a little raven stew," Knut said.

"So would I," said the Valwolf.

I suppose that was more polite than asking for roast squirrel in front of me.

"I'll wait for you outside," Tyr said and walked away.

"I'll be right back with your meal," Sigyn said and

hobbled away, leaving us alone there with Loki.

Robin Grima and Knut got down off of Silver Mane's back. Knut went to Loki's left hand and Robin Grima to Loki's right hand and they tried to undo the bindings, but the cords were knotted too tight.

"We could cut them," suggested Knut, his hand on his sword hilt.

"No!" screamed Frostbite, though of course only Robin Grima heard him.

"No, please don't," whispered the Valwolf. "If you do that you'll kill Narvi, and then Vali will become a true killer and kinslayer."

"And you'll be setting Loki free!" Bookwyrm yelled. "Freeing the mischief-maker who plotted beautiful Baldur's death and who wouldn't shed a tear to bring him back. Ragnarok starts when Loki gets free! Have you two been listening to giant songs?" ("Have you gone crazy?" his voice echoed in Robin's mind.)

"That's what the eddas say," Knut agreed. "And they say that Baldur went to Hel when he died, but they don't say why he went there; Dead Shore is for oathbreakers and murderers and slanderers, and Hel's Hall is for folk who died in their beds of sickness or old age. There's no place in Hel for folk like Baldur who died honorably in combat. The eddas say that Baldur is imprisoned in Hel's Hall, but we saw for ourselves only a few days ago that he and his brother stand at Lady Hel's side to fight her enemies, like her lovers or her husbands or her champions. And the eddas don't say what Odin whispered in Baldur's ear before he set fire to the burial ship. Don't be so sure you know what's going on here, old friend."

"There are things I've learned that I promised not to talk about yet," Robin Grima said, "but I think I know what I'm doing, and I think Odin approves of it."

"All for one, and one for all," Bookwyrm said. He got down and tried to write runes on the bindings but his blood wouldn't stay on them, just dripped off like rain running off oiled parchment in a window frame.

Sigyn brought her stew to us, one by one, holding it in her cupped hands. "I'm sorry," she said. "I used to have a bowl, but it cracked a long time ago."

I took a sip of the hot broth but didn't find it tasty enough to take a second one, and neither did Bookwyrm, but Knut and Robin Grima drank all that Sigyn's hands held, and the Valwolf licked her fingers clean.

"Thank you," Knut said. "Here's something you can add to your pantry," and he gave her a golden apple.

"Thank you, heroes," she said, her voice quavering. "Bless you, children," and she hobbled away from us.

"Does anyone want to do anything else before we go on?" Robin asked, remembering the D&D games in the hospital when Barney always used to ask that before going on to the next scene.

"Yes, but there isn't time," whispered Frostbite.

"Yes, but not here and not now," said the Valwolf.

"Yes, but not till I have something better to bring here," said Knut.

"You've already brought us hope," Wyrmtongue Loki said, the first time I'd heard his voice—no, her voice—in centuries. "Good luck, heroes." Then the snake dove down into her mouth again, and she was silent.

Robin Grima waited, but nobody else spoke up, so she climbed back on Silver Mane again, and so did the rest of us, and he took us outside to where Tyr was waiting for us.

"Does anyone have anywhere else they want to go in Midgard?" Tyr asked, but nobody spoke up, and a moment later, Silver Mane was running back to the Rainbow Bridge.

It was mid-afternoon when we got to Asgard, and the sky was red with curtains of light. You don't often see the aurora that bright by daytime. Silver Mane ran swiftly across Asgard, past Fensalir, Marsh Hall, where Odin's wife Frigga lives and where Fenris (that means "marsh giant") grew up. Then he headed down the banks of a slow-flowing river to the dark lake of Amsvartner (that means "black grief" or maybe "black trouble") that lies on the far edge of Asgard. In the center of the lake was a rocky island, red with heather.

Silver Mane trotted along the lakeshore till he came to a thicket of oak trees where a rough hut sheltered a small rowboat. "You can make your own way to Heather Island," Tyr told them, "and you'll do better there without me. Fenris still hasn't forgiven me for tricking him into letting himself be fettered and chained."

"Thank you for all your kindness to us," Robin Grima told him after we'd gotten down off of Silver Mane.

"I did it in the name of Lady Drifa's courage," Tyr said, "and in the hope that you can save Asgard from the attacks of Loki's children just as bravely as you saved the World Tree from Nidhog. You've gotten Hel and Orm to rethink attacking Asgard, but the only way you'll stop Fenris Wolf from killing Odin is to kill the wolf before Ragnarok comes. I swore by the Sun and the Moon that I wouldn't ever raise my sword against Fenris, but it wouldn't be breaking any oath if you killed him today, and he can't hurt you because you've bathed in dragon's blood. Killing Fenris is the only way to stop Ragnarok, Robin Grima."

"We won't forget your good advice," Robin said, and Tyr smiled and rode away.

Knut and Bookwyrm dragged the rowboat down to the lakeshore and made sure it was watertight and its oars were sound, then pushed it into the water and helped the others get on board. The dark water was steaming hot and salty.

The poets say it's like that because it's fed by Fenris's tears or his saliva, but the hot spring that bubbles up into it helps too.

"We could put on the mist caps that Drifa gave us," Bookwyrm said.

"We didn't come here to sneak up on Fenris and kill him," Robin Grima said. "We came to ask him why he's so set on fighting at Ragnarok when the prophecies say he'll kill Odin but then he'll get killed by Odin's son. We can do a better job of persuading him to trust us if we're not invisible."

The sun was setting by the time the rowboat reached Heather Island, but the auroras were still bright. The only wolf they noticed was the Valwolf.

"Fenris can't have escaped," Bookwyrm said. "The chains will hold him till Ragnarok, and we haven't heard Garm howling or Heimdall's horn blowing."

"And the valkyries haven't heard it blowing either," said Knut, looking up at the Asgard sky, where the valkyries were flying around lazily in ones and twos. "Can you smell him, Valwolf?"

"I can smell him everywhere we go," said the Valwolf. "After all, he's been living here for centuries."

"Fenris Lokison!" yelled Robin Grima. "We've talked to Hel and to Orm, and now we're here to talk to you. But first we've got to find you. Where are you, Fenris?"

"The eddas say that his fetter is as thin and delicate as a silk ribbon," Bookwyrm said, "and it's tied to a thin chain, but the chain goes through a massive slab, and the slab's got a big rock on top of it."

"There are a lot of big rocks around here," Knut said, surveying the landscape, which consisted of boulders of lava littered with smaller rocks the size of a man's head, with an occasional clump of red heather.

"We talked to the lady who used to live at Hymirstead," yelled Robin Grima. "Her bracelets are broken now, and she's free. We might be able to set you free too, Fenris. Where are you?"

"Where?" snarled a voice from somewhere in the growing darkness. "Where?" The word was fuzzy like someone too busy eating to speak clearly. "Where is she?"

"My wife Drifa's dead," Bookwyrm said. "She set the stead lady free, and Hymir killed her for it."

"We don't know where Garm's mother went when she left Hymirstead," Robin Grima said. "Maybe she went home to her parents. Maybe she went to Hel to see her son. Her bindings are broken. She's free to go wherever she wants."

"Tyr swore to take her back to Hymirstead," the Valwolf said, "but we're not going to help him."

"Where would *you* go, Fenris, if we set you free?" Robin Grima asked.

"Who?" the voice growled, its mouth still full. "Who are you? Where are you from?"

"We're from Valhalla and, before that, from Midgard," said Robin Grima. "We went down the World Tree and killed Nidhog, and Hel promised us she wouldn't lead her folk against Valhalla when Ragnarok came."

"Odin's our leader," said Knut, "and one of his names is Loosener of Bindings."

"Another one of his names is Binder," said Bookwyrm, as if it was a scholarly discussion instead of an attempt to persuade Fenris to come out of hiding but not eat any of the Valhallans. Ratatosk decided that the best help he could offer was to go back and guard the bags they'd left in the rowboat.

"My name is Robin Grima, and my friends are Bersi Bookwyrm and Knut Valwolf Friend, and we sit at Table Thirteen at Valhalla," Robin said. "I swear by all I hold sacred that I won't attack you, Brother Fenris, except to defend myself and my friends. Where are you?"

"Here," growled the voice, and Robin climbed up on a boulder and looked down to see Fenris Wolf lying there, his feet fettered together by a chain that was also wrapped around his neck so pulling on it would strangle him. The chain was dark elf work, its six braided strands as thin and fine as silk thread. It glittered in the sunset light like fine jewelry, and it looked as if a child could tear it apart.

Fenris was only five pounds or so when he was born. A week later he was ten pounds, and a week after that twenty pounds, and he kept on doubling each week till he met Tyr's mother. After that he slowed down, but he still kept on growing. He was twice as tall as a man and over a thousand pounds when the Aesir finally got a chain that would fetter him. He was still that tall, but he probably didn't weigh more than four or five hundred pounds; fur and skin and bones don't weigh very much, and he didn't look as if there was much more to him than that. His yellow eyes shone like firelight as he looked up at Robin Grima.

She waved an arm, and the others came up to join her.

"I know the Valwolf," Fenris growled. Dark drops fell from his mouth as he spoke.

"And I know you, Brother," said the Valwolf. "And we both know Ratatosk." He looked around for the brave squirrel.

"I'm guarding the rowboat," Ratatosk cried out bravely, "to make sure that nobody runs off with it and maroons us here."

"Thank you," said Robin Grima. *"Does Fenris get stronger after sunset?"* she thought to her sword.

"Fenris gets stronger the more he swallows," Frostbite whispered.

"What are you chewing, Brother?" Robin Grima asked, walking toward the huge wolf.

"Tyr meat," Fenris snarled, and then broke into a fit of coughing that went on and on till the monster was gasping for breath.

"Serve you right for biting off Tyr's hand and swallowing it," yelled Ratatosk from the rowboat.

"No," Fenris moaned, in between sickening noises that sounded like he was vomiting. "Mischief maker and truth twister and loathsome little liar. I didn't...."

"It's what the eddas say," said Bookwyrm. "In the *Lokasenna* Loki taunts Tyr that Fenris Lokison bit off Tyr's right hand. And in *The Deluding of Gylfi*, the High One says that the wolf bit off Tyr's hand at the wrist and that's why it's called the wolf-joint."

"If you trust something called *Deluding*," Knut said.

"I didn't swallow it," snarled Fenris. "I can't! It won't—" He started coughing again.

"*The Deluding of Gylfi* says the gods jammed a sword between Fenris's jaws so he couldn't shut his mouth," said Knut. He walked towards where Fenris lay and knelt down by the gaping mouth. Robin Grima's glowing hair illuminated the twilight scene.

"The hand's still in his mouth," Knut said. "The thumb's dug into his lower jaw and the little finger's dug deep into his upper jaw and the rest of the fingers are gripping the base of his tongue, and the fingernails are knives."

"Good old Tyr," said Bookwyrm after a while, when nobody else had said anything.

"Will you let me try taking it out?" asked Robin Grima, remembering her promise to the Norns.

"Why should I trust you?" snarled Fenris.

"I don't know," Robin Grima said. "Hel trusted us, and so did Orm, and so did the lady who was bound at Hymirstead. Sigyn blessed us, and Loki wished us good luck, but you don't have to trust us if you don't want to, Brother." She knelt down next to Knut and put both of her hands deep into the wolf's mouth, seized Tyr's index finger and pulled it slowly back from the wolf's tongue.

"The eddas say that at Ragnarok Fenris will break free and devour Odin," Bookwyrm said, "and most folk in Asgard would say that breaking his chains is breaking our oath of allegiance to Odin."

"Most folk in Asgard approve of Ragnarok where everyone loses and dies," yelled Robin. "And they approve of torturing Loki and Sigyn and Fenris. But Odin has his own views, and he goes his own way, and he's smarter than most folk in Asgard, and he doesn't trust them enough to share his plans with them." The finger kept wriggling around, trying to cut her palms and fingers with its knife-sharp nail, but she gripped it tight and pulled it back till she finally heard something crack. "One down," she said, "and four to go!"

"Pass it to me," said Knut, and she let him grab hold of the index finger. He wiggled it back and forth to keep its bones from healing, while Robin went on to the middle finger. It came free quickly, and the ring finger with it, and they seized Robin's right wrist and squeezed it as she screamed in pain and surprise.

Fenris was coughing, shaking Robin and Knut; and someone warm was sitting on her other side, steadying her; but she wasn't sure who because all she noticed was the blinding pain in her wrist; it felt as if the bones were being crushed.

And then it stopped.

"The harder the bone, the sweeter the marrow," said the Valwolf, standing beside her, spitting out little white bits of crushed bones and little shining bits of crushed silver fingernails from the bone that had gripped her.

"I've got the thumb loose," said Knut, and Bookwyrm

seized him by the waist and pulled him back, and Tyr's hand came out of Fenris's mouth, its fingers red with clotted blood.

Knut and Bookwyrm wanted to bury Tyr's hand down by the lakeshore and pile rocks on it, the way they'd have buried the body of a dead witch or a monster, to make sure it didn't come out at night and haunt people. But Robin insisted on taking the hand to the Norns, so they tied all the pieces up in a napkin that didn't have any holes yet and put it in the boat for brave little Ratatosk to guard because, of course, it was *his* napkin that they'd brought along without asking his permission because they knew how generous he was..

Robin Grima drew Frostbite, and her sword felt as heavy as a five pound dumbbell four weeks after starting chemotherapy. Drifa wasn't with them any more, with her box of poisons and healing drugs, so Robin went back to the rowboat and cut off a piece of Odin's rope and tied it around her wrist and hoped she wasn't going to get tendonitis and wished the fight had been before sunset so she could go back to Valhalla and let the sunset horn heal her.

"You trusted me not to kill you," Fenris said, his voice softer and clearer now, "and you risked your life for me." He looked up at her, his yellow eyes bright in the growing darkness. "I could drink your shining hair like firelight and your sword like moonlight, Robin Grima. Or I could bite off your head and suck out your sweet brains like honey. Or I could swear blood brotherhood with you if you'd trust the word of a Lokison."

"Our oath is, 'All for one and one for all,'" said Knut. "If you take Robin Grima as your blood sister, then as long as we're all on this quest, you have to take the rest of us, too."

"Including me!" called Ratatosk.

"What are the terms of the quest?" Fenris asked. He didn't use to be so interested in legal details before he took

Tyr's oath about the chain Gleipnir. Tyr had promised that he'd set him free if Fenris couldn't break it, but he didn't mention the detail that he wasn't going to do it until Ragnarok came.

"The quest is to change things so the World Tree doesn't die," Robin said, "and so there isn't a Ragnarok."

"So the Lokisons don't go to war with Asgard," Knut said, "and so the Valhallans don't get defeated and die."

"And so you don't kill Odin, and so Vidar Odinson doesn't kill you," Bookwyrm said.

"Odin didn't lie to me and fetter me," Fenris said. "If you set me free, I'll join your quest and I'll swear your oath."

"No!" screamed poor little Ratatosk. "Don't trust him. He'll break an oath just as easily as he broke all the fetters he wore before Gleipnir."

"We trusted *you*," said Robin Grima, "and you haven't betrayed us. Bookwyrm, do the stories say that Fenris is a liar and an oathbreaker?"

"Tyr was the one who twisted the words of his oath," said Bookwyrm slowly, "not Fenris."

"I trust Fenris more than Tyr or Ratatosk," whispered Frostbite, *"but then I'm prejudiced."*

"What will you swear your oath by?" asked Knut. "What good is an oath by the Sun and Moon when the prophecies say that you and Garm are going to swallow them?"

"I don't want to swallow the sun," Fenris said, "just a share of its light. There'll be enough left for everybody else even if I drink my fill." He turned his head up to the sky, where the starlight from the Milky Way arched across the sky like a great length of rope. "I swear by my fears of my nightmares and by my hopes of my dreams, and may the World Tree cast me out from all Nine Worlds if I break my oath or twist my words or betray my oath-mates. I swear to protect the World Tree and to protect Asgard and to protect

Odin and his family and his followers. And I pledge my blood and my heart and my brains to brotherhood with Robin Grima, to protect her honor and to aid her in her quest. All for one, and one for all."

"And I swear to protect your honor," Robin Grima said. "Now lie still, so we can see what needs to be done to set you free."

They untied Fenris from Heather Island, but they couldn't remove his fetter.

"Nobody can break Gleipnir," Bookwyrm said. "The dark elves forged it from materials that will never exist and so cannot be broken: the sound of a cat's footfall and the beard of a woman, the roots of a mountain and the sinews of a bear, the breath of a fish and the spittle of a bird."

"There are a few women who have beards," Robin said, "and a sharp enough microphone can hear a cat's footfall. All bears have sinews, and fish may breathe through their gills, but they still breathe, and birds have saliva; they use it to glue their nests together. What was the final one?"

"The roots of a mountain," said Knut. "I can't tell you what it means. I can tell you that bear *sinum bjarnarins* might mean bear's sinews or it might mean bear's withered grass, and the last one is rarer."

"I've seen Skraelings make rope out of a bear's sinews," Bookwyrm said. ("*Indians*," whispered Frostbite in Robin's mind, then, hastily correcting himself, "*Native Americans*.") "It was as strong as rope made of linen or hemp or walrus hide."

"What do bears eat when they wake up from hibernating?" Robin asked.

The two men stared at her in shocked silence at her ignorance before Knut said, "Anything they can find: from reindeer to rats and from beached whales to fish."

"They eat plants too," said Bookwyrm, "but not withered

grass buried under the snow. Cows and horses will scrape through the winter snow and eat last summer's withered grass, but bears won't do that. Bears will chase away wolves and eat their kill, and they'll eat nuts that squirrels hide, but they won't eat last year's grass; they wait for the plants to bring forth new growth. If they kill too much to eat all at once, they'll hide their leftovers by covering them with dirt and leaves."

"And they might even cover their leftovers with withered grass?" asked Knut.

"Oh," whispered Bookwyrm. "I hadn't thought of that. Yes, they'll do that too."

None of them were the least bit upset at the thought of thievish bears stealing the nuts that squirrels carefully gathered and hid for the winter famine. Fenris had the excuse of being half-starved, but the rest of them should have shown a little compassion.

Fenris shook himself, and the chain that had fettered him came free of his legs and loins, but it still clung stubbornly to his neck. "Five out of six isn't bad," he said, "but you still haven't broken through the roots of the mountain." He stood up, looming over them. His paws were wider and longer than a man's foot, his claws as long as a woman's fingers.

"Well, at least now you can walk," Robin Grima said. "Knut and Bookwyrm, with Fenris on our side, are we strong enough to go back to Niflheim and destroy the *Naglfar*?"

"Ask the Norns when you give them Tyr's hand," Knut said, and Bookwyrm agreed.

"Ask the Norns to promise not to give Tyr's hand back to him unless he swears not to attack you and your companions," whispered Frostbite.

"I already promised to give it to them," Robin Grima thought back. *"It's too late to set conditions on my promise. And besides, it would be insulting to show I don't trust them*

to do the right thing."

"Did you talk to Orm about destroying the *Naglfar*?" Fenris asked.

"We only saw Orm while we were out fishing with Hymir and Tyr," Robin said, "so I thought we'd wait until later to discuss destroying Hymir's ship."

"We could stop by the Midgard Ocean on our way to Niflheim and ask him," the Valwolf said, "but I don't think he'd be able to swim up a frozen Niflheim river."

Fenris laughed, but the laughter turned into a scream of agony, as he fell to the ground writhing in pain under the light of the rising moon. His shape was twisting, deforming, into something awkward and angular, his fur disappearing to reveal scarred skin. His mouth gaped open, drinking in the pale moonlight, and no, that's not a metaphor. He was gulping it down like water, and his hair and skin got brighter with each swallow, till at last the transformation was finished and he lay there silently, his long hair starshine silver and his skin snow white and his eyes silver.

"You're a human," Robin Grima whispered.

"Only when the full moon shines on me," Fenris said softly. He didn't smell like a human now any more than he'd smelled like a wolf before. He smelled like his father, like Loki Wyrmtongue and like his mother's father, like Odin Battle-Frenzy.

"What's the right word for it?" wondered Bookwyrm. "Not *ham-hleypa*, skin-walker, because he doesn't need a wolfskin or a human skin to change form. Daywolf?"

"The opposite of a lycanthrope," said Robin Grima. "Anthrolykos?"

"*Tungl-ljos kappi*," said Knut, "moonlight champion."

"Are we going on with the quest," Ratatosk called, "or do we have to stay here till we've written the dictionary definition?"

CHAPTER THIRTEEN

The full moon was nearing its zenith by the time they got to the Norns' well, by the upper root of the World Tree. Robin Grima gave them the pieces of Tyr's hand, and they thanked her and her companions for the gift. Silver-haired Skuld bathed their hands in well water and dried them with napkins as white and as soft as summer clouds. She untied the rope from Robin's wrist, and Robin Grima drew her sword and found it light again.

"Thank you," Robin said.

"Thokk *fyrir*," Skuld said. "Thank *you*, Robin Grima." She reached up over her head to wash Fenris's hands (even in human form he was twice as tall as a normal man) and said, "Your companions are welcome for your sake, and for the sake of their own deeds of glory."

"Drink deep," red-haired Verdandi said, and handed each of the humans a silver-bound drinking horn. Robin raised it to her lips, wondering if it was going to be mead or wine or ale, but it was cold fresh water, and she drank it gratefully.

"This is wonderful cider," Bookwyrm said, and Knut praised the mead, and Robin realized that each drinking horn held what the drinker wanted most.

Verdandi set down a small silver bowl in front of Ratatosk, who found the cider in it even better than his own, and a larger silver bowl in front of the Valwolf, who dipped his muzzle deep into the white liquid and thanked her for the milk.

And then finally she gave a drinking horn to Fenris, who lifted it up into the air over his face and poured down a flood of golden light into his mouth. "I told you," he said, after he'd drunk his fill, "I don't want to swallow the sun, just drink my share of its light."

Meanwhile, Urd was busy weaving. The loom leaned up against the trunk of the World Tree, and its frame was made of fallen branches. The weights at the bottom of the gray warp threads were skulls, and the heddle rods that pulled the warp threads up so the weft threads could pass through were spears, and the shuttles that drew the weft threads were arrows.

Urd's sisters sat down beside her, and the three of them hummed as they wove, like a hive of bees, like a nest of snakes. They were weaving the battle of Ragnarok. There was Odin falling to Fenris, and Tyr and Garm killing each other, and Thor and Orm killing each other. There was Hymir leading an army of giants off of the *Naglfar*, and there was Hel sailing her own ship up to the battle, and there was dark Surt's ship, steered by Loki and crewed by fire giants, and the Valhallans running forward bravely to meet their attacks. The closer you looked at it, the more details there were to see; the more deaths there were to see.

"'An axe age, a sword age,'" Bookwyrm chanted. "'A wind age, a wolf age.'"

"'Brothers shall fight and slay each other,'" sang Knut. "'Garm howls in Hel, and the wolf runs free.'"

"'The sun darkens,'" sang the Valwolf. "'The earth sinks

beneath ocean waves. Stars fall from the sky, and the World Tree is falling.'"

"No," whispered Frostbite.

"No!" yelled Robin Grima.

"No," agreed Skuld. "Not yet, and maybe not ever. Go and make a new future for us if you can, heroes." She turned back toward us and she was taller than Fenris, taller than the World Tree. Her hands reached out for us and we couldn't move. She picked us up in her monstrous hands and raised us into the air—and threw us down into the depths of the Thunder River.

The cold waters around us were full of falling stars and falling souls, as they tumbled down the Hel Falls, to the lower worlds. We fell past Midgard and saw Orm encircling the human lands.

"Good journey, Brothers," he called to us.

"Go to Hel," yelled Fenris.

And then the burning stars streamed off to the red fires of Muspelheim, and the frozen souls streamed off to the icefields of Hel on our right, and we were engulfed in the cool mist of Niflheim.

The farther we fell, the thicker the mist grew until we could barely see each other's faces, until we could barely see Robin Grima's glowing hair. The moonlight died out, and Fenris's scream told us that he was changing back to wolf form again.

And when we finally stopped falling, it wasn't like hitting ground or even like diving into water; it was like falling down on a feather bed of cool gray swirling mist.

In the middle and upper worlds, the sun was rising. It had been a full day since Robin Grima and her companions had had any sleep. Fenris? He hadn't had any real sleep for centuries, not since he bit off Tyr's right hand and found its fingers clutching his tongue and its fingernails digging into his jaws.

Knut took an apple out of his bag and passed it around, each person taking a bite, including Fenris. Robin held out Frostbite, and Knut and Bookwyrm crossed their swords with it and everyone swore the oath. Then the Valhallans sheathed their swords, and Robin Grima tied a napkin over her hair, and everything was gray mist. And everyone lay down in the Niflheim mist and fell asleep.

Knut dreamed of his beautiful dark-haired maiden with sky-blue eyes. She stood by a bonfire, holding out her hands to him, and he could see her face well enough this time to tell that she wasn't Robin Grima.

"You've given my parents magnificent gifts," she said, "and your name and honor are still yours. I wouldn't have stayed with you if you'd given up your name and honor."

The bonfire blazed up to show her parents standing beside her, "I want to marry your daughter," Knut told them, "but I don't trust you."

"We don't take offense at that," the red-haired man said. "Appearances are against us, and so is all the gossip you've studied for so many years. And besides that, I'm so charming and clever that you wouldn't believe me if I spoke up for myself. But just to show that I approve of my daughter's choice, I'll give you and your friends a piece of good advice: kill something native to Niflheim and drink its blood so you can see through the mists."

"I won't eat raw meat or drink blood!" Knut yelled.

Robin Grima dreamed of fighting Tyr. She cut off his left hand and saw chunks of blue-green ice spurt from the wound. His sword fell out of his fingers and shattered into pieces.

"Not JUSTICE any more, but JUST ICE," Frostbite

laughed.

Then she held Frostbite up to her face and kissed his cold blade and said, "I like you, Sword, even if you do make horrible puns. Does that one work in Norse, or just in English?"

"Only in English," he whispered. *"I like you too, Robin. Please break me into pieces when the right time comes."*

Eventually people began waking up. Robin Grima uncovered her hair, and the travelers ate breakfast by its light: sharing out an apple plus some cheese and flatbread. Except for Fenris, who only took a bite of apple.

"Is there anything to drink?" the Valwolf asked.

"Not unless you count the mouthful of mist you got every time you opened your mouth," Knut said.

"I smell water below us," said Fenris and started digging his way through the mist till he finally got down to the surface of Niflheim, the smooth ice of a frozen river. Robin Grima drew a circle of fire on it with Frostbite, and it melted into a small pool of cold, mist-gray water, and the travelers drank their fill of it.

After that, the mist grew thinner, or at least they could see through it better, and eventually Knut remembered his dream and told the others about it.

"Well, nobody would deny that this ice is native to Niflheim," Bookwyrm said, "and we've destroyed it and drunk all the blood it had to offer. That fellow's advice sounds worth trusting, Knut."

"I think so too," said Knut, "once you've unknotted his kennings and figured out what they meant." That was the first time they'd ever heard him criticize kennings, and that included Bookwyrm who'd been his tablemate for centuries.

They stood on the shore of Niflheim's frozen river and looked downstream (well, downhill) to see a shining light.

"That's the *Naglfar*'s mast," said Robin Grima, "with her star-crowned captain standing on top of it. Let's get closer and see how many giants are working on her today."

"Even if we'd brought Thor Giant-Killer with us, we wouldn't be able to kill all the giants," said Fenris.

"And whatever damage we do to the *Naglfar* today, the giants can mend it," said the Valwolf.

"What about sneaking in, sabotaging the ship, and sneaking out again?" Robin said.

"Sabotaging?" asked Knut, his face puzzled.

"Turning the bone ship into wooden shoes?" asked Bookwyrm. Valhalla's translation system can easily handle foreign words, but it's not very good at handling foreign concepts.

"Damaging the ship so they won't notice it until they set sail and it sinks and they drown," Robin Grima said.

"That's dishonorable," said Fenris and Bookwyrm together.

"It's dishonorable to use tricks in a duel or battle," explained Knut. "But it's all right to out-trick someone's who's trying to trick you, like letting a berserk take a look at your sword and then, after he's blunted it with his eyes, pulling out a club from under your cloak once the duel actually starts."

"But it's honorable to go take a look at the *Naglfar* and look for her weak spots," said Bookwyrm. "'He must early go forth, who's eager for blood or to seize the goods of his enemy.'"

"Back when I was alive," said Robin, "we were taught that sabotaging an enemy's weapons is an honorable act of war, but robbing someone isn't honorable, even if you're enemies."

"Welcome to the Nine Worlds," said Fenris, and the other men laughed, including the Valwolf and Ratatosk. Robin decided not to ask them about pre-emptive attacks on civilian population centers because she didn't want to shock them any more. She'd have been surprised to learn that that they thought it was honorable to break into an enemy town and loot its treasures and enslave its people. It was even honorable to use tricks to get inside the town gates, like Hastings, the Viking warrior who had his men carry his coffin up to the gates of an Italian town and say his last wish had been for a Christian funeral. The Italians were surprised when the coffin fell open, and Hastings jumped out of it and led his men to loot their city. Hastings was surprised too, of course; he thought he was looting Rome, but it was only little Luna in northern Italy, and Rome was hundreds of miles south.

They set off along the river shore toward the light of the *Naglfar*.

"If the mists drift away so the full moon shines on us and Fenris shape-changes, and if we find a frost giant with a sword, is it honorable to steal it so Fenris can use it?" Robin asked, worried because she'd set the man free but hadn't found a weapon for him.

"It's dishonorable to steal from a host or a guest," Bookwyrm said.

"Or from a friend or a kinsman or a battle companion," Fenris agreed. "But we're not likely to find any of those in Niflheim. And I was never trained in swordplay when I grew up in Lady Frigga's home of Fensalir. An eating knife is the most deadly weapon I know how to use in human form."

"I can teach you how to use a sword," said Knut, "but it'll take months. Better to steal a giant's shirt for him, Robin Grima. He'll know how to use that, and it's not proper for us to be clothed and him to be naked."

"I'm not cold here," Fenris said, "but I'll want a warm shirt if I go to Hel to look for my son."

"We saw your son Garm when we visited Hel," Robin said slowly, "and there's something we learned there that we should have told you before this. He didn't speak to us, and Lady Hel says he can't speak any more because he killed the dragon Nidhog's sons and drank their blood."

"I'll take him to Lady Frigga," Fenris said. "She'll have a cure for—"

"Shush, everyone," Ratatosk whispered. "I can hear them, and if they stop singing, they'll hear us."

They listened and heard the giants singing. "With a knick-knack, hammer-whack, nail another bone," they sang, "soon we will be sailing home." Robin waited for the verse, wondering how high the giants could count, but all they did was sing the chorus again. And again. And again. Fire giants are sometimes brilliant (a pun) and the stupidest of them is fairly bright (another pun), and hill and sea giants are almost as smart as the Aesir, but frost giants are dull-witted, which probably explains why they were willing to go down to Niflheim and spend their time building a ship for someone who wasn't their lord or their kinsman. It also explains why they ate the traveler whose singing they liked so much before bothering to learn more of his song than the chorus.

"Does hearing them sing mean we're going to go crazy?" Robin Grima whispered.

"After a week or two of hearing that song, it probably will," Bookwyrm whispered back.

"*Hearing giants sing won't hurt you,*" Frostbite whispered. "*That's just a superstition. But don't let frost giant music lure you into the heart of a mountain, or you may not be able to get out again.*"

"*I'll be careful,*" Robin told him, then asked, "*What's the difference between a mountain's heart and its root?"* Frostbite didn't answer, unless silence was the answer. Robin tried to remember the Geology survey course she'd taken back when she was a freshman. "A volcano pops up where tectonic plates are pulling apart or coming together," she said out loud, "and the place where the tectonics plates meet is where the lava wells up to make the volcano grow, so you could call it the mountain's root."

The slender chain fell off Fenris's neck. Robin Grima picked it up and put it onto her belt.

"I'll want to get that back from you someday," Fenris said. "I want to put it on Tyr and see how he likes wearing it."

"All for one, and one for all," Robin said.

The giants' singing was becoming more than just slightly annoying.

"I wish I'd braved the World Tree's bees and taken a honeycomb," Robin said. "If I had one, I'd squeeze out the honey and make earplugs out of the wax. If this gets worse, we'll all go deaf."

"It can't be much farther," said Knut, but he'd been saying that every half hour or so.

"We could go faster if we had skates," Knut said.

"I'll keep an eye out for bones," Ratatosk said. "If you hadn't left your oars in Hymir's harbor, you could have used them for poles." The medieval Norse made their ice skates by tying cattle or horse toe bones to the bottom of their shoes, and then pushed themselves along the ice with a wooden pole. They didn't do axels or lutzes or sit spins or flying camels, but they did skate fairly fast—except when they fell down.

Robin Grima melted another pool of water so they could wet their throats.

They'd just finished drinking when the giants stopped singing.

"Maybe they heard us," whispered Ratatosk.

"I'll go see," whispered Fenris, and tiptoed away (nothing new; wolves are digitigrade, which means they walk on their toes, not flat-footed the way humans do), his silver-gray fur and his Asgard smell drowned by the swirling mist as soon as he'd gone a few steps away,

"There's a pile of bones to our left," the Valwolf said, "but I don't think you can make good skates out of them."

Ratatosk ran over to the heap of white bones. "They're all skulls," he said.

The Valhallans went over to look at the bones. "Mostly aurochs and elk," Knut said, "but not all of them." He pulled out a skull. "This was a human once. It has a hole punched in it. Someone was hungry for brains."

Bookwyrm and Knut sorted out the human skulls, and Robin Grima helped them lay a layer of rocks and gravel over the skulls for a grave. "Rest in peace," she said quietly.

"And if you do walk," said Knut, "may your draugs pursue those who killed you and ate you." Robin knew a little about draugs; Grima had fought them once. The dungeon monsters were Norse undead, sort of like a cross between zombies and berserks but more intelligent. Real draugs are even nastier, because they're not intimidated by priests or holy symbols. Norse tradition says that the best way to prevent a corpse from turning into a draug is to bury it between the high tideline and the low tideline, so it's not in the land or under the sea. Cutting out its bones and making a ship out of them isn't one of the approved burial methods.

"Shush," whispered the Valwolf, "someone's coming."

"The ship's only a couple of miles away," said Fenris, emerging out of the mist a few minutes later. "The frost giants aren't singing because they're too busy eating their dinner, and they're too busy with their food to notice anything else." He sniffed the bone mound the Valhallans had built, "And it won't come as a total surprise to you that some of their food has the same shape that you do, but it's all thoroughly dead so it doesn't need rescuing. Even so, we should all get ready for a good fight."

"How many giants are there?" asked Robin Grima.

"Too many to count on my fingers and toes, or even on my forty-two teeth. Luckily I was educated well enough to count higher than that. There are an even thousand frost giants eating frozen flesh on the *Naglfar*'s deck, plus their star-crowned captain who sits on the forecastle and eats fresh-roasted walrus and drinks warm mead."

Suddenly Fenris stiffened and growled. That was all the warning they had.

Robin Grima drew Frostbite just in time to defend herself as the mist elves attacked, but the sword didn't do her much good because she couldn't see them; they were wearing their mist caps. They jumped on her, and she couldn't count how many of them she was fighting, just that they were pulling her hair and pinching her ears and nose, and pulling off her clothing so they could pinch her arms and legs and nipples and belly. Then the pinches turned sharper—like hypodermic needles. And after that her flesh began to go numb as if she was getting Xylocaine injections.

"Sleep-thorns!" Bookwyrm yelled.

Robin swung Frostbite about wildly for as long as she could, and heard them mocking her. "Clumsy blind human!" they yelled. "Couldn't see a white cat on new-fallen snow at midsummer noon. Couldn't hit a hummingbird if it wasn't nailed down." Then her fingers went numb, and they pulled the sword out of her hand.

She heard someone screaming and wasn't sure if it was Knut or Bookwyrm. She heard growls, and wasn't sure if it was the Valwolf or Fenris.

"Filthy dead trespassers!" yelled the mist elves, their high voices piercing Robin's ears like icepicks. "Walked into our nice clean home," cried one, "and sat in our nice clean bath," cried another, "and lay down in our nice clean beds and had filthy necrophiliac sex there!" cried a third one. "And never said thank you for our hospitality," screamed a fourth. You couldn't see which of them was speaking, and from now on I'm not going to bother mentioning when one of them stopped screaming and another one started.

"You stole my sword," yelled Knut.

"Blind filthy dead people with filthy weapons from filthy Death Hall," they yelled. "We robbed you blind, and none of you stupid people said a word to stop us except for filthy Frost—son of Evil and brother of Evil. We wouldn't dirty our nice clean hands to touch Frost! And except for plaguey Drifa who threw her filthy Hel axe into our nice clean fire and put out its flames with her black magic and stole our nice clean mist caps!"

"That's my hero wife!" yelled Bookwyrm.

"She's your filthy corpse!" yelled the mist elves. "We'll never let any of Hel's filthy dead folk into Mist Hall again. We'll never let any of Odin's filthy dead folk into Mist Hall again. We're going to punish you for what you did to us!"

"How much do we owe you for your gracious hospitality?" asked brave little Ratatosk. "I don't think the five of us ate as much together in your hall as Lord Tyr did by himself, and we didn't get to spend a full day in your beds, only from sunrise till midnight, and then we found ourselves all at sea. I don't know how many mist caps Drifa borrowed from you, but we've got five of them that we've kept safe, and we'll gladly give them back to you."

"And what about the treasures you stole from our woodshed?" screamed the mist elves. "No, the bill for the injuries you've done us can't be paid in silver. We've declared you all outlaws, and we're going to punish you."

"What are you going to do to us?" Robin asked, trying to think of the right brier patch to beg not to be thrown into. She and Knut and Bookwyrm and the Valwolf had bathed in Nidhog's blood, but she couldn't remember if Ratatosk had, and she knew that Fenris hadn't.

"Guess!" screamed a mist elf. "Guess and guess and guess, and whatever you guess, it'll be worse!"

"Whatever you do to me, give me my sword back," Robin yelled, "or else you'll be worse thieves than we are, because you know you're stealing someone else's treasures, and we didn't. We didn't steal your beds from Mist Hall; they kidnapped us. Yes, we took some of the pieces of wood we found in your shed, but we thought that was just firewood. If you treasured that stuff, then we'll apologize and we'll bring you ten times its weight in a wooden bench from Valhalla."

"Thieves and outlaws and plague-carriers!" screamed the mist elves. "Draugs!" ("*Walking dead*," Frostbite whispered in Robin's mind.) "We don't bargain with outlaws!"

"Good for you," said Hymir's familiar voice. "If I'd known they were thieves, I'd never have welcomed them to my stead. I'd have sent them to the kitchen and had them chopped up for a midnight snack. Come to think of it, I'm hungry now. Can I have one of them to eat?"

"Sea giant, we're not surprised that you'd eat filthy dead bodies," the mist elves screamed. "We know what the fish do in your filthy ocean water. Tell your son that he owes us compensation. He summoned the sea tide to carry his gang of filthy dead folk out of our world, and we had to spend days mopping up our nice clean floors after that filthy water flowed over it. And you owe us compensation too if you want to go on building your bone ship in Niflheim and having your filthy high tides wet our land. Where's your rent, sea giant?"

"Here it is, my fine little fellows," Hymir said, "all the skulls from today's hunt. And besides that I've brought you back the fine things that these outlaws stole from you. Here's your three little beds and the oars they fashioned out of your kindling wood."

"Nice sea giant," the mist elves cooed. "We'll give you the outlaws' arm and leg bones just as soon as their filthy bodies stop moving. You can build their bones into your ship so they'll help it find its way to Asgard."

"Thank you," said Hymir politely. "With helpful allies like you, I know we'll triumph at Ragnarok."

"Look at this filthy stuff the outlaws were carrying!" the mist elves yelled. "Blood-stained rope and blood-stained napkins!"

"I'll take all that filthy stuff away if you don't want it," Hymir offered. "And they made their oars by strapping pieces of your nice clean wood together with their filthy rope. Just let me untie it, and I'll take the rope away too."

"No, no, no!" screamed the mist elves. "It was the filthy thieves' rope, so now it's our rope, and we'll use it to punish them! We'll hang them with their own filthy rope!"

"Good idea," said Hymir. "I'll hang all the folk who resist me when I conquer the upper worlds. But what are you lords of Niflheim going to do with this big bad wolf that you've caught? Fenris Lokison isn't an outlaw in Niflheim; he never trespassed in your hall or stole any of your things."

"He wore a cap that Hel Drifa stole from us!" they yelled. "We can smell his filthy scent on it! Son of Evil and brother of Evil and father of Evil!"

"Yes, but he probably didn't know the cap was stolen. He was led away from Asgard by bad companions. I'll bring you his weight in skulls if you let me take him away with me. Remember, the prophecies say we're both going to be fighting on your side when Ragnarok comes."

"Take Fenris Lokison away and keep him safe till Ragnarok so he can swallow filthy Odin!" the mist elves yelled. "And here's the filthy fetter the dark elves wove to bind him. Take that away too."

"No problem," said Hymir. "Take a last look at your bad companions, Lokison, and be glad you're not one of them."

"We'll hang the filthy outlaws with their own filthy rope!" screamed the mist elves.

"It'd be safer to run them through with a spear," advised Hymir, "or just cut their throats with a knife."

"Don't shed their filthy blood," yelled the mist elves. "Don't let their filthy blood stain our nice clean world. Hang them, hang them, hang them!"

"Great idea," said Hymir.

The mist elves pulled Robin's jaws open and stuffed rope in her mouth and then tied her jaw up again so her tongue was rasped by the rough rope. They tied her wrists together, and they tied her ankles together, and they tied a blindfold over her eyes. "Gag them and blind them and hang them up high!" the mist elves chanted. "Now they can't curse us with words or with lies."

"You could stick her filthy magic sword up inside her so she can feel how sharp and cold it is," Hymir suggested.

"Don't shed her filthy blood or it'll contaminate our nice clean world!" the mist elves yelled. "Tie Frost Son of Evil on her back so she can feel him but never use him again, never do anything again, just hang in the air."

"Are you going to hang them from the ceiling at Mist Hall?" Hymir asked.

"They don't belong in our nice clean hall!" the mist elves screamed. "They don't belong in our nice clean world! We're going to hang these filthy dead outlaws outside our world!

Where's the nearest branch of the World Tree?"

"I'll show you," said Hymir. "I'll even throw the filthy rope up over it for you."

Now of course, Robin Grima's travels weren't the only thing that was happening in the Nine Worlds that week. People got born and grew up, made friends, made money, made trouble, made mistakes, and died. The valkyries kept dropping dead souls into the Thunder River, and one of them swam out, and Valhalla got a new warrior. Odin's ravens flew far and wide, and their one-eyed master smiled at the news they brought him. Orm Midgard Serpent explored a new stretch of water he'd never traveled before, and Lady Hel made her own travel plans and started packing. The Aegirstead folk started preparing for a party, and they were so busy that they didn't notice Orm's disappearance. The Hymirstead folk did, though. They swarmed out through the ocean depths, gathering bones, now that Orm wasn't there to stop them.

I take out time now to mention these things because Robin Grima and her companions weren't going anywhere interesting, weren't doing anything interesting, weren't saying anything interesting, weren't even hearing anything interesting. For an hour or two they heard the frost giants singing as they hammered away at *Naglfar*, but that stopped when the giants went home for the day, and after that all they could hear was the winds blowing between the worlds.

CHAPTER FOURTEEN

Even dead folk find it unpleasant to be hanged, and poor little Ratatosk didn't even have that to reduce his discomfort, though the fact that the mist elves didn't know how to tie a slip knot did help to keep things from being much more than an agonizing pain in the neck. Odin's rope squeezed the poor squirrel tighter than it did the Valwolf who'd kept watch at his hall door, let alone the Valhallans who'd pledged their word to follow Odin in battle.

"I'm sorry for failing you, Robin Grima," Frostbite whispered.

"It's not your fault," Robin told him. *"It's my fault. I was the leader. I should have been prepared for an ambush. I shouldn't have taken us back to Niflheim without getting more people. Nobody knows we're here, and—"*

"Odin knows. He won't forget us, not after spending all that time waiting for someone to be my companion."

"If you want to keep up my morale," she thought, *"then show me a way I can talk to Knut and Bookwyrm and the Valwolf and tell them we're going to be all right."* She shivered in the cold wind.

"Nine nights he hung on the wind-swept tree," a voice sang. "He was a sacrifice, dedicated to Odin, himself offered up to himself, the god of the gallows hanging all alone on the World Tree, no food to fill his mouth and no drink to wet his lips. He reached out to the runes. Screaming, he seized them."

"That's not the way it goes in the Havamal," whispered Frostbite. *"Odin's rope is singing its own song about the time it hanged him."*

"Great," Robin Grima thought grimly. *"At least we'll have something to entertain us, and my door-mates will appreciate the poetry."*

Then there was something warm and wet licking her face until the blindfold fell off, and she could see a white cow with golden horns staring at her. The cow's tongue licked raspingly across her face and into her mouth till the gag fell out. She took a deep breath and tried to decide how to apologize for being a bad leader. Bookwyrm was whispering something about a fee. And then the cow lowered her head and drove her horns into Robin's palms. The sleep thorn on her left hand fell out, so she felt the horn pierce her instead of just seeing it, and the rope around her neck was loose enough that she could scream in pain. Then the cow walked away, leaving Robin's hands full of blood and a gold coin in each of them.

The same thing happened to each of her oath-mates, except that the Valwolf got gold rings in his pierced ears.

What happened to Ratatosk? How nice of you ask. Squirrels have thumbs, and squirrels in the Nine Worlds have opposable thumbs, so he held onto his wound compensation.

"It's the rune ordeal!" Knut yelled.

"It's the first step of the rune ordeal," Bookwyrm corrected him. "Feoh means Cow and Wealth."

"It's disgusting!" the Valwolf yelled. "This is no time to get French kissed, especially by a cow!"

"I can stand the French kissing!" yelled Ratatosk. "It's the bling-bling stigmata I object to."

"The true wealth we've been given isn't gold," said Knut. "It's air: the lungs' food, the fuel that burns in speech's fire."

"Get ready," said Bookwyrm. "The second rune is Uruz, and it stands for Wild Ox and Health. Say 'Uruz,' and maybe you won't have to learn it the hard way."

"Uruz," Robin whispered, and saw the wounds in her hands heal as the wild ox licked them.

There are three sets of eight runes in the oldest rune alphabet, twenty-four of them in all.

The eighth rune is Wunjoh which stands for Comfort, and it caused ash honey to drip into their mouths so they weren't hungry and thirsty any more. The sixteenth rune is Sowilo which stands for Sun, and it opened the clouds so the sunshine poured through and warmed them against the world winds. The last rune is Othalan which stands for Inheritance, and it covered the three humans in warm clothing and hung sharp swords at their sides (except for Robin Grima, who still had her sword even if it was tied at her back). Their new clothes were dark blue, the color that Vikings used to wear when they rode out to kill an enemy.

But none of the runes untied the ropes around their wrists and ankles and necks, and none of the runes made the rest of the sleep thorns fall out.

"I'm sorry," Robin Grima told her friends. "I asked you to follow me, and then I failed you."

"You didn't fail us against the dragon or against Loki's children," Bookwyrm said. "It's true that you underestimated the mist elves, but the rest of us made the same mistake, so we're all equally to blame."

"It's been a great adventure," Knut said cheerfully, "and it's not over yet."

"And after this you won't need footnotes when you read runes," Frostbite whispered.

"There are times I'm willing to break you even when you haven't asked for it," she thought back to him.

"So you do remember sharing dreams with me," he said. *"This is the first time you've mentioned it, and I wasn't sure. If you could break me now, Robin, then I'd tell you to do it, because it would let me untie you and set you free."*

"I wish we had one of Lord Heimdall's windows," Knut said. "We could have a great view from up here."

"I wish we were back in Mist Hall," Ratatosk said. "I'd piss in their nice clean fireplace and shit in their nice clean bath, and—"

"That's not filthy enough to repay them properly," Knut said. "I'd kill Lord Hymir on their nice clean dining table and then I'd keep the wolves and ravens away until all the mist elves could smell was rotting flesh. Then I'd set fire to their kitchen till their food was nothing but ashes, and the only fresh thing they had to eat was each other. And then—"

"What sort of host leaves his doors unlocked but despises his guests?" the Valwolf asked. "What sort of host sets out food for his guests that he doesn't want to eat himself?"

"I can answer that riddle," said Knut. "A hunter setting out traps, but they didn't want our fur, not even yours, old friend. They wanted our brains and our bone marrow. Now tell me why they gave us weapons?"

"Who did you fight with their weapons?" asked the Valwolf. "Drifa used her axe to butcher a whale, and that was all you did with them. Do you really think that your nice clean Mist Hall weapons would have wounded the elves who made them?"

"We never found where they forged their weapons,"

Robin Grima said. "I agree about the fireplace and bath house and dining room and bedroom and kitchen, but we've got to trash their smithy too."

"That's why you've got to be the leader," Knut said, "because you remember the details."

"I'll follow you anywhere as soon as I'm able to set one foot in front of another one," the Valwolf said.

"And as soon as you can hold your sword in front of you instead of behind you," Bookwyrm said.

There wasn't much else to say after that, so they were silent, and the hours went by, and nothing happened. Robin tried to think of six impossible things that were really impossible, and wondered if Lewis Carroll's White Queen had been trying to weave her own version of Gleipnir and what she'd wanted to fetter.

If you've ever tried gnawing at a rope that's binding your ankles, you'll know it's difficult. Having no feeling in your torso and legs doesn't help. And doing it while hanging from a rope around your neck so you have to double up to get your ankles up to your head makes it impossible. Even for a lithe little squirrel, let alone for big clumsy humans or a big awkward wolf.

Once we'd gone through the rune ordeal, there wasn't much to do except to watch the ravens wheeling in the air. One of the raven flew down and sat on Robin Grima's shoulder.

"Are you Thought or Memory?" she asked.

It cawed loudly. Then its beak stabbed down at her right eye, but she twisted away, and it just got her cheek.

"Shoo!" she yelled at it and tried to bite its wing, and it flew away, but not as far away as she'd have liked.

"Did it wound you?" Knut asked.

"I don't think so," Robin said, trying not to let her voice shake, trying not to scream. "I can still see out of both eyes, and I don't think I'm bleeding, but I can't really tell because I can't touch my face."

"If you're bleeding, then more ravens will come," Bookwyrm said. "After a battle, the ground is thick with wolves, and the air is thick with ravens."

Down below them, someone started howling. Fenris?

"'Now Garm howls loud before Hell's mouth,'" Bookwyrm recited. "'The fetters will burst, and the wolf run free. Loud blows Heimdall; his horn is on high. The World Tree shakes, and its branches shiver. The giants are groaning, and the elves are roaring. Hymir is coming; the *Naglfar* is loose.'"

"No!" screamed Robin Grima. "Heimdall hasn't blown his horn, and Ragnarok isn't starting! We haven't lost, and we're not going to lose!"

"No, we're not," agreed a woman's voice.

"Drifa?" said Bookwyrm, torn between delight and disbelief. "But you're dead, Wife. I saw you die."

"We're all dead," Drifa said matter-of-factly.

"Welcome back," said Knut. "I'd shake your hand, but I'm stuck full of sleep thorns and my hands are tied."

"Welcome back," said Robin, still unsure if she could trust the Hel woman who knew so much about poisons, even if she was Bookwyrm's wife.

"We're all dead except for Ratatosk," said the Valwolf, paying tribute to the cleverest person there.

"Who killed *you*?" Knut asked his friend.

"I killed myself," the Valwolf said. "I was so hungry that the dearest meat in the Nine Worlds couldn't satisfy me. It was all I could do to keep myself from cracking open the white spine and sucking out the marrow, but I controlled myself enough to feed on my own flesh instead. I bit and swallowed it till I bled to death. Afterwards Odin said I'd died a hero's death and sent me to keep watch on his Slain Hall."

"Nobody ever told me that," Frostbite whispered, *"But I'm glad he knows what it's like to be wolf-bitten. Turn about is fair play."*

"Well, I'll free Ratatosk of his sleep thorns first," said Drifa, "because he's the lightest of us and he'll find it easiest to do the same for the rest of you." She didn't bother to ask if gallant Ratatosk was willing to help, but of course she'd heard him say, "All for one and one for all."

Once freed, Ratatosk pulled out sleep-thorns with his teeth and then brought them up to Drifa, who stored them away in a bag that hung from her belt. She pulled up the Valwolf (who only weighed about a hundred pounds). Then the two of them pulled up the humans, one by one.

Bookwyrm looked at Drifa. She was wearing a blue tunic and trousers—men's clothing, and a sword sheath hung from her belt. "Back when we were alive, Wife, those clothes would be grounds for me to divorce you," he said. (And of course the same thing applied to a man who wore women's clothes, like a shirt cut so low it showed his nipples. The old Norse laws may have been sexist, but they were even-handed.)

"Go ahead and name witnesses then, if that's what you want to do," Drifa said.

"I stood by and let the giant eat you. Do you want me to pay compensation for that? Do you want to be free of me?"

"I told Lady Hel that I wanted a second chance to die," Drifa said, "and she gave me permission to go seek it. My death by Mimir's Fountain pleased Odin well enough that he said I could enter Valhalla, but I didn't want to waste my time in feasting and mock fighting. I signed the Hero List, but I chose to turn away from Valgrind and come after you instead, and I chose clothes fit for your quest, not for keeping house or nursing patients."

"You look good in them," he said, "and I find no fault in your reasoning. Wear them for as long as it pleases you."

"How did you get here from Valhalla?" Robin Grima asked.

"Climbed down the World Tree," Drifa said. "I didn't stop to sleep, but it still took me a while, because I didn't have any rope. Odin said you took it all with you."

"Can I trust her?" Robin asked her sword.

"She's telling the truth," Frostbite whispered. *"You can trust her as much as you trust Odin."*

"We don't have much rope left," Knut said, but he tied the five pieces together. Altogether it was about twenty ells, 33 feet, not long enough to reach from the branch they were sitting on to the next one below it. "The mist elves have the rest of it."

"Did Odin tell you what to do after you found us?" Robin asked. "Did he give you any message for us?"

"Odin said that you were our leader," Drifa said. "What do we do, Robin Grima?"

"We have one companion left in captivity," said Robin Grima. "Fenris Lokison is tied up somewhere below us, maybe in Mist Hall or maybe by the *Naglfar*, but wherever he is, we're honor-bound to find him and free him. But first we've got to make sure the mist elves can't catch us again."

"I can't stop them hearing us," said Knut, "but we all saw a remedy against their invisibility."

"I don't have another Hel axe," said Drifa. "My sword's from Valhalla."

"The Mist Hall hearthfire burned white and their candlelight was silver," Bookwyrm said, "so maybe a normal fire with yellow flames and black smoke would be enough."

"I hate relying on maybes," said Robin Grima, "but we may have to. How do we get down without jumping?"

"We didn't take any harm from our landing when we fell all the way from Asgard to Niflheim," the Valwolf said.

"That was when we fell down the Hel Falls," Knut said. "Don't count on the same good fortune twice."

"We could go back to the World Tree's trunk," Ratatosk suggested. "The branches are closer together there."

"Whatever we do, let's stop here long enough to swear our oath," Robin Grima said, and she pulled out Frostbite. They all pledged their words and crossed their swords with hers, including Drifa.

"Tell the Valwolf he can touch me too," whispered Frostbite, *"and tell him not to kill himself a second time unless it's absolutely necessary."* Robin repeated the message, and the Valwolf agreed to both parts.

"We could unbraid Odin's rope," Drifa said.

"That means untying it again," said Knut, but he did it, and the humans and Ratatosk set to work. (Wolf teeth and claws aren't much use at that sort of thing.) They ended up with a rope three times longer and still strong enough to bear a man's weight, and now it was long enough to reach the next branch. Knut tied a loop at one end of the rope, and slipped it over the Valwolf's head and then over his forelegs so it girded his body.

The Valwolf looked down at the dizzying distance below him. He leapt down and landed on the branch and steadied the rope as the humans climbed down the rope one by one. Finally, gallant Ratatosk untied the rope from the upper branch, then grabbed the end in his mouth and leapt down to the branch on which his companions were standing.

Then they did it again—only that time the Valwolf missed the branch on his first three tries, and Knut had to keep pulling him up to jump again.

The problem, of course, was that tree branches aren't like steps or bookshelves, nice parallel flat surfaces. That hadn't mattered so much last week when Robin Grima and her companions were climbing down the tree trunk. Now they were far away from the trunk, and sometimes the next branch down was fifty or a hundred feet to the left or right.

After a while the sun began sinking toward the west, and then it drowned in the mist. A few minutes later, there weren't any branches to see when you looked down, just thick Niflheim mist with a few faraway mountain peaks sticking up from it like ocean islands.

"We could stop here for the night," Knut said.

"I remembered you like apples," Drifa said, and brought one out from a bag that hung at her belt and gave it to Robin, who took a bite and passed it on. It was the first bite of solid food they'd had since being captured.

"Now if we could just wash it down with water from melted Nifl ice," Knut said, "we could see our way down to the ground."

"I can smell the ground," said the Valwolf. "It's not far below us, just another thousand feet or so. But I can't smell how far down the next branch is, or which way it angles."

"I can see in the dark," Drifa reminded them, "and through the mist too, and I can see the next branch down. It goes off a little to the right." She picked up the rope and tied it around her waist and jumped down into the mist.

Bookwyrm held the rope, waiting for her to call out that she'd reached the branch or that he had to pull her up so she could try again, but there was only silence, and the rope hung straight down, not off to the right.

Knut cleared his throat, but the Valwolf took his hand gently between his teeth, and Knut decided not to say anything. Robin started to ask if something was wrong, and felt Frostbite's power surge over her muscles and hold her silent. Even Ratatosk was quiet, but then he could smell the people below them just as well as the Valwolf could. And then everyone heard the voices.

"The mist elves caught your runaway brother," yelled Tyr, "and now Father's got him safely tied up on the bowsprit. He's got as many sleep thorns in him as a hedgehog has spines. I found my runaway mother waiting for me in Asgard, and she's promised that she'll come back to Hymirstead and bring me my missing hand, but I don't need two hands to deal with you, Corpse Queen. I can do that left-handed, if you'll come to the island with me."

"I don't believe you, Oathbreaker," said Lady Hel, "but I'll meet you on the island anyway."

"What's all this stuff about meeting on an island?" Robin asked Frostbite.

"Duel fighters go to an island," the sword whispered. *"They draw a circle in the dirt, or they make a ring of hazel wands, and then they go inside it and fight. If Hel or Tyr dies, then the prophecies—"*

"My son's telling the truth about your brother," boomed Hymir's voice. "Here's a rope braided from the fur I got on my curry brush. Let your dog smell it, and he can tell you that it's his father's fur."

Garm howled, and the World Tree shook, and Robin Grima and her companions held on with all their might.

"My nephew's never studied dueling rules," Hel said. "If I take him to the island, he might bite your other hand off."

"Take him home then," Tyr said. "And just to be fair, I'll send my mount away too. Go back to where you had breakfast, Silver Mane, and I'll meet you there when the duel's over. My father will bear my shield for me."

"My shield holders will be Baldur and Hodur," Hel said.

"Let's get this over with quickly," Hymir said. "It'll be

sunset soon, and my workmen will be coming down from Jotunheim. They'll build your bones into a doghouse for your brother, and once my woman is home again, she can weave a rug out of your hair for your brother to lie on. I'll cut up your flesh and use it to bait my hook; maybe I'll catch your other brother with it. And I'll give your head to the mist elves. They've promised me that after they eat your brains, they'll forge your spine into a magic sword that I can use when I conquer Asgard."

Robin heard Frostbite scream in horror.

The Valwolf walked over to Robin and opened its mouth silently—and then closed its teeth gently on her hand, his tongue licking out to touch her sword hilt. *"When this quest is over, you can kill me,"* his thought whispered in her mind.

"I have other plans for what I want to do when this quest is over," Frostbite whispered, *"and they involve both of us staying alive."*

Of course, the three of them were the only people who could hear this touching conversation. All that the rest of the party could hear was Silver Mane galloping away. And then they heard the other folk walking off toward the border where Niflheim touches Hel. After that, the only person below us was Drifa.

When she didn't say anything, I ran down the rope and found her dangling in the air, silent and motionless. She wasn't breathing. Valhallans are dead and don't need to breathe except when they want to say something. They usually do it anyway out of force of habit, but Drifa was trying to be utterly silent, for fear that someone below would hear her.

I sat on her shoulder and whispered in her ear, "The only people I can smell nearby are us."

She took a deep breath. Then she climbed back up the rope to the branch and jumped off again. This time she landed on the next branch down.

"At this rate, we won't touch ground till sunrise," Robin Grima said, "and we still have to walk to the *Naglfar* and try not to let the mist elves catch us."

"I'll see what I can do to speed things up," Bookwyrm said. He wrapped his legs around the rope and began to climb down. We could hear him reciting: "'Men call it Fire, and the Aesir say Flame, and the Vanir say Wildfire. The Giants say Biter, and the dwarves say the Burner, and the folks in Hel hall call it the Swift One.'"

When Robin got down to the next branch, she found a black dragon with fiery red eyes standing there next to Drifa. "Climb on," it told her in Bookwyrm's voice.

"I thought the shape was just illusion," she said.

"I seem to get a little more power out of the runes now that I've learned them with Odin's rope around my neck," he said dryly.

"He's gone up a level," Robin thought, "or maybe he's just improved his Self Polymorph spell. I wish I knew what rules our game is using. Have I earned a new power also?"

"This isn't a roleplaying game!" Frostbite whispered. "The only rules you need to worry about are the ones Odin used to build the Nine Worlds. We're safe from some of them. Fire can't burn us, and lack of air can't suffocate us. But there are other ways to die, and they'll be real, and don't count on getting a second chance the way Drifa did."

"I know that much," Robin Grima thought. "I haven't had a good night's sleep in days, but I still know this isn't a dream or a game of imagination. Don't worry. I'll be careful."

She climbed up onto the dragon's neck, feeling the warmth beneath his black scales, and the others followed her, Knut coiling the rope around his waist.

"Everybody holding tight?" Bookwyrm asked, and then

spread out his wings and dove down into the mist.

"Knut, can you do shape-change too?" Robin asked.

"I've never been comfortable with illusion," Knut said, "let alone with skin walking. But maybe I can summon something real." He switched to the edda that Bookwyrm had been quoting, the *Alvissmal*, Alvis's Song. "'Men call it Wind, and the gods say Wafter. The high ones say Whinnier, and the giants say Wailer. The elves say Wake the Dead, and the Hel-folk say Whistler. Welcome, wild Wind, and waft away the Mist. Blow warm, Wind.'"

"The Dutch call it the Foehn," the Valwolf said, "and so did the Helvetians."

Robin was familiar with Southern California santanas, the hot dry winds that blow away the Los Angeles smog and fan forest fires in the autumn or bring summer temperatures to the people who sit on the stands overlooking the New Year's Rose Parade. This wind was stronger and hotter. It caught up the dragon and whirled him across the land, as he flailed his gold-edged black wings to keep his balance. His snakelike neck doubled back for a moment and his red eyes glared at Knut. Then the neck whipped forward again, as he dove down towards the shining light on top of the mast of the *Naglfar*.

"There's a giant wolf tied to the bowsprit," Drifa said. "Was Tyr telling the truth? Is that really Fenris? How did he get loose from Asgard?"

"We set Fenris free from his fetter," Knut said.

"He swore our oath," said Robin Grima.

"Then he's my oath-mate too," said Drifa, but her voice shook a little as she said it.

Bookwyrm circled the shining masthead, and they saw that this time the light didn't come from the captain's helmet but from a sea horse with bright stars in its mane and tail.

"First, we take care of Fenris," said Robin Grima. She

squinted her eyes against the wind and looked again. "Where are the giants? Hymir said they'd get here after sunset."

"Maybe Knut's wind blew them away," called Bookwyrm, trying to land by the ship but getting swept up by the wind and carried up into the air again.

"Slow down, wild Wind," said Knut. "Blow slow, blow silent, blow soft, blow sweet."

The wind died down to a gentle breeze, and Bookwyrm spiraled slowly down and landed on *Naglfar*'s deck near the prow. He let his riders get off, then closed his eyes and shook himself and dwindled back into a man.

It was the first time they'd seen *Naglfar* close up, and they felt dwarfed by her. She was over a mile long. In front of the first foremast and behind the last aftmast, her prow and stern rose up into the forecastle and aftcastle. When she went into battle, archers and swordsmen would stand there. She didn't have any oars. You can't get a group of giants to do anything in unison, let alone row without tangling their oars up. Even the sails did not need to be fully functional: the prophecies said *Naglfar* would get to the upper worlds by riding a flood tide of melted ice and fresh blood. She didn't have a row of shields along her sides, the way Robin had seen in pictures of Viking ships. (Even the real Vikings didn't put their shields on their ships for thieves to steal or for the waves to knock down, though they sometimes hung them on the side of the ship when they were nearing shore and ready for battle.) She didn't have a figurehead. (And the real Vikings only put a figurehead up on their ship when they were nearing an enemy coastline. If a ship came into a Norse port with a figurehead, the locals would muster an army against the enemy. If it turned out to be a Viking trading ship, the owner would be given a heavy fine for upsetting the land spirits with his figurehead.)

Knut unknotted a length of the rune rope and tied up his

jaw with it.

"Are you hurt?" Robin asked. He shook his head.

"He's afraid he'll say something and it'll turn out to be magic," Bookwyrm said.

"Don't speak in meter," said the Valwolf, "and don't alliterate, and don't use kennings, and don't quote the eddas."

"And don't mention any runes," said Bookwyrm.

Knut nodded but he didn't untie the rope.

"Don't say *anything* till I get Fenris untied," said Robin Grima, "unless you notice the giants coming back." She went over to Fenris. His eyes were wide open, staring at her, but he didn't speak and he didn't move. She put her hands on the fetter that Hymir had wrapped around his legs, and it came off at the touch of her fingers, but he still didn't move.

"That fetter was strong magic once, until you unbraided it," Frostbite whispered.

"I've got my own list of impossible things to tell you someday," Robin said out loud, and she picked up the fetter and tied it back on her belt. Then she began pulling out sleep-thorns.

"Thank you," Fenris said, once she'd pulled the sleep-thorns out of his muzzle and ears. "I've had a lot of time to think about it since we last spoke, and I've decided you were right. Hymir and his captain aren't honorable, and we should feel free to sabotage their ship."

"I agree," said the Valwolf, and so did Ratatosk and Drifa, and Knut nodded fervently.

"What do *you* think?" Robin asked Bookwyrm.

"I think it's a fine idea," he said, "but don't weaken the center mast. I want to set up a scorn pole." He turned to Drifa. "Did Odin give you a grappling hook, Wife?"

"No, Husband," she said. "Only what I've already given

you and a box of herbs that I like more than the ones I found in Niflheim.”

A normal Viking longship stretched eighty feet long with a mast forty feet high, and sides that were only a little taller than a tall man, and she only mounted one sail on her mast. *Naglfar's* sides were a hundred feet high, and her center mast was a couple of hundred feet high, topped by a small platform for her giant captain to keep an eye on things. It must have been crowded when he was standing up there; it was barely wide enough for his sea-horse.

Bookwyrm craned back his head to look up at the shining sea-horse. Then he muttered a line of poetry under his breath and was a dragon again. This time he kept his wings furled close to his body and wound his way up the mast.

“You’ve been having adventures without me,” Fenris said, still unable to move his legs or tail or anything below his neck, but looking higher and higher as Bookwyrm spiraled his way toward the masthead. “What did I miss?”

“We had a run in with the runes,” Robin Grima said, pulling out a sleep thorn hidden deep in the fur of his chest. “Now Bookwyrm can turn into a real dragon, and Knut’s afraid to speak for fear his words will have too much power if he says them in poetry.”

“Tyr and Hel have gone off to fight a duel,” the Valwolf said. “We heard them agree on the terms.”

“He’ll cheat,” Fenris said. “With any luck, big sister will cheat back.”

There was a roar from above, and we looked up to see the sea horse stepping daintily down off the masthead.

The black dragon breathed golden-red flames, hot enough that we could feel their warmth as we stood on the deck. The sea horse screamed like a raging wind and struck out with its hooves, opening a bleeding slash along the dragon’s side.

"That's impossible!" Robin Grima. *"Bookwyrm bathed in Nidhog's blood. His skin should be invulnerable."*

"In human form, yes," Frostbite whispered. *"But Bookwyrm Dragon didn't bathe in Nidhog's blood, so he's still vulnerable."*

The sea horse's mane and tail foamed with mist and with stars, and its breath was gray sea mist, drowning the dragon fire. Then, as it came level with the dragon, it opened its mouth wide and wider and impossibly wide. There was row after row of teeth—some broad like horse's teeth and some pointed like shark's teeth and some rough and jagged like rocks that tear out the bottom of a ship and send its crew under the waves. Its jaws gaped wide enough to swallow the dragon in one bite.

The dragon disappeared.

Drifa screamed in anguish.

And then we saw that Bookwyrm was back in human form again, hanging upside down, with both of his legs wrapped around the mast, a long bleeding slash down one of his sides. The shining gray horse roared again and rushed at him, jaws wide—and he swung his sword against its neck, two-handed, and cut off its head.

It fell on the deck with a loud thump, barely missing Knut, who jumped hastily out of the way. Its great teeth were still snapping, and the force sent it spinning around on the deck.

The sea horse's body turned into a cloud of blue-green hailstones that rattled down like drum beats onto the white deck, too cold to melt, glowing like scattered stars.

"Bring me the horse head," Bookwyrm called down, after he'd finally managed to get his sword back into its sheath. (It's a lot harder to do upside down, but he didn't want to try swinging himself right side up again one-handed, and he didn't want to drop his sword.)

"The head's still trying to bite us!" Robin Grima yelled.

"You can wait till it stops," Bookwyrm said. "But don't chop it up into bits. I want it whole."

Robin Grima and Knut stood watch as the sea horse died. The head spun near a pile of hailstones, and Knut dashed forward and kicked its jaws closed, just in case swallowing its frozen blood would heal it. Finally the horse's jaws stopped moving and the light in its eyes went dark, and so did the stars that shone in its mane. The Valwolf came over and sniffed and said, "He's dead."

Knut untied his jaw and said, "I'll take it to Bookwyrm," carefully choosing his words for their lack of poetry. He carried the head up to the masthead and gave it to his door-mate, while Robin and the Valwolf stood guard below, and Drifa carefully pulled out the last few sleep-thorns from Fenris's fur.

Bookwyrm held the head up to look its last at the sky, then jammed it down on top of the center mast. "I set up this scorn-pole!" he yelled. He turned the head around three times and left it facing the World Tree. "I turn this pole's scorn upon this ship and upon Hymir who brings down the bones to build her. I turn its scorn upon the captain who rode this horse and who oversaw the giants who built this ship and who looked forward to steering her on her way to Asgard. I turn its scorn upon the *landvaettir,* the guardians of this land, until they no longer give any welcome to this ship and her folk."

By now Knut had recognized how Bookwyrm's words were echoing the curse that Egil Skalagrimson had said against the tyrants of Norway who had robbed him and persecuted him and murdered his kinsfolk. He said the old words along with his door-mate, "I turn this post to send the land guardians all astray so that none of them will find a resting place in this world by chance or design until they have driven this ship and her folk from their land."

Fenris shook himself and stood up, huge besides Drifa, dwarfed beside the ship. "Well spoken," he said. Then he threw back his head and howled at the sea horse's head on top of the mast, at the stars.

"Are you all right, Fenris Lokison?" Robin Grima asked.

"I'll be better soon," he said.

"Do you need any help climbing down?" Knut asked Bookwyrm.

"Not yet," he said. "I'm not done here yet. Keep watch to see if anyone comes." He wiped the blue-green blood off of his sword onto his left sleeve, then began using its tip to carve his curse into the bone mast. After that he stained the runes once with the sea-horse's blood, and then once again with his own red blood.

Meanwhile Drifa stood with Fenris at the prow of the ship, and the Valwolf stood at the stern, and Ratatosk ran up and down the ship. And while their comrades kept watch for giants and elves, Robin Grima and Knut pulled up the bones of the deck and climbed down to the ship's keel and began weakening it here and there: sometimes pulling out a nail or splintering a bone, sometimes knocking a bone loose altogether and replacing it with ice.

Drifa had the Valwolf bring her a branch from a nearby fir tree and used it to sweep the hailstones of sea horse blood into a chamber pot she'd found at the stern of the ship.

An hour later (runes take a while to carve properly, especially when it's not into wood but into bone, and it was a long curse), Bookwyrm finally slid down the mast onto the deck of the ship.

"Welcome back, Husband," said Drifa, and washed the blood from his wounds and anointed them with salve and bandaged them.

"Something's coming!" Ratatosk yelled. "It's heading

toward us from starboard." (That meant from the right side where the steering oar was fixed to the steering board.) "It looks like a snake. A big snake. It's wriggling straight toward us!"

"I'm tired," Bookwyrm said quietly, but he drew his sword and went to stand by the starboard side of the ship, with Robin on his left and Knut on his right.

"I haven't seen big brother Orm in a long, long time," said Fenris.

"It's not anywhere near as long as the Midgard Serpent!" yelled Ratatosk. "It's only a furlong or so long."

The humans could see it now, a thin dark line wriggling across the land and down onto the frozen river, coming straight toward them. Knut shrugged and walked a few yards to his right, and the thing changed course and came toward him.

Robin Grima fingered the fetter the dark elves had forged for Fenris and remembered her list of six impossible things, starting with the sound a stone hears when a tree falls in the forest and ending with the turd that a bear dropped while it was hibernating.

The snakelike thing got to the side of the ship and began wriggling its way up, still heading for Knut.

"Don't attack it!" Knut yelled. "It's our rope, coming back to us." He sheathed his sword and stepped back from the side of the ship. The rope crawled to his feet and lay still, like a well-trained dog.

"Are you sure it's safe?" Robin Grima asked.

Knut unwound a length of rope from around his waist and touched it to the end of the newcomer. Nothing noticeable happened. He shrugged and said, "In Odin's name, bind same to same. Bind fast and strong; hold true and long." The drops of dried blood glowed red along both pieces of rope, and they grew together as if the mist elves had never cut them apart. "I think it's safe," Knut said.

"Is there anything else we have to do here?" Robin asked. "Maybe there's still time to see the last round of Tyr's duel with Lady Hel."

"Let's go," Bookwyrm said. "But don't expect me to fly you there. I'm tired. You may have to carry me some of the way."

"Lift him onto my back, and I'll carry him," said Fenris.

They tied the rope around the steer board and climbed back down. Then Ratatosk untied the rope and climbed down the side of the *Naglfar*, carefully digging his claws into the cracks where one bone overlapped another.

When he finally got down, the others were all gone. "I thought it was all for one, and one for all," he said plaintively. Then he saw that they'd left the rope behind them, and it was stretching up into the sky.

He ran up it and found them waiting for him on the World Tree branch. Bookwyrm sat on Fenris's back and the others behind him. All except for the Valwolf.

Knut pulled up the rope and wrapped it around his waist.

"Pick your mount," said the Valwolf. "We're going to race to see who gets to Hel first." Ratatosk jumped up and held on tight as the Valwolf raced into the night.

CHAPTER FIFTEEN

Ratatosk won the race, and the Valwolf and Fenris tied for second. Fenris would have won except that he slowed down so he wouldn't jolt his riders. The Valwolf came to a sudden stop when he crossed the finish line and that sent Ratatosk flying off his back, so he landed inside the ring of hazel wands on the dueling island.

The moon was sinking toward the West, but the brightest light on the dueling island was from Baldur's bright hair, as he knelt on the ground, weeping. The dark silhouette next to him was his blind killer, his brother Hodur. The red spots that sparkled here and there on the dueling island were blood drops.

"The duel's over, and my son won!" boomed Hymir. "Does anyone else want to use the dueling circle?"

"Yes," said two voices. One of them was the Valwolf's; the other was one we hadn't heard since we left Hymirstead. We could see her clearly in the sudden flood of bright moonlight. It didn't come from the sky; it streamed from her face and pooled out around her feet. ("*Light, twenty foot radius,*" Robin thought.)

240

Fenris fell to the ground, his fur disappearing, his shape changing from wolf to man, so we knew she had brought the full moon with her even though the sky moon was several days past full.

"What's going on here?" yelled Hymir. "I left Fenris at the *Naglfar!*"

"We unchained him," said Robin Grima.

"Did he seduce you with his honey tongue?" Tyr asked, "Or did Hel do that before I met you? I thought I could trust Valhallans even if you did have a Hel woman in your party. You swore not to betray Odin, but you've unchained Odin's killer."

"Don't be rude, son," Hymir said. "Say hello to your mother before you talk to strangers. Remind her that she promised to give you your right hand back."

"I remember my promise," she said. She looked the same as she had at Hymirstead, except that her gown wasn't sea green but the shimmering white of moonlight, and her red hair burned with the colors and warmth of a bonfire so that she stood in a blaze of moonlight, and red flames danced in it like ripples dancing on a wind-swept lake. Fenris stood up in human form, and she took his hand and kissed him.

"You're a fire giant!" the Valwolf said.

"I'm from Muspelheim, Firehome," Tyr's mother said. "I went swimming one night when the auroras were burning, but Hymir caught me in his net and bound ice bracelets on me."

"I broke those bracelets and set you free," Drifa said.

"If I'm alive when the sun rises, you can ask me for my help," the woman said. "Right now I want to see what my son did here." She walked up to the ring of hazel wands, and Fenris walked beside her.

In her light, we saw Baldur and Hodur kneeling on the blood-spattered ground, each of them holding half a woman's body in his arms. Baldur held Lady Hel's light side, her right half, and Hodur held her dark side, her left half.

"Was it a fair fight?" Fenris asked, as he looked at his dead sister.

"He cut through her shield," Hodur said, "and then he cut through her sword."

"And then he cut through her," said Baldur.

"Take her home," Fenris said, and Baldur and Hodur stood up, each holding his half of Hel Lokisdaughter, and they set off toward Hel's Hall.

"I've come here to challenge Hymir to a duel," Tyr's mother said.

"I won't fight you until you tell me your name," Hymir said. "And I won't fight you here, on the border of Hel, even if you are my runaway thrall."

"My name is Tide Fire," Tyr's mother said. (No, she'd said "Tidefyr," which means Time Fire, the fire they kindle in Muspelheim at midwinter to mark the end of one year and the start of another. It probably wasn't a coincidence that if you dropped out the middle letters, you got her son's name.) "My mother's brother is Surt, King of Firehome." (Surt means soot-black, and I don't go to Muspelheim often enough to know if the fire giants think their king's name means Charcoal or Dark Energy.)

"I've come here to challenge Tyr to a duel," said the Valwolf. "This place is fine. Any place I find him will be fine."

"Odin assigned you to guard the door to Valhalla," Tyr said, "but you've run away, and you've betrayed your master by helping set Fenris free. I'll kill you gladly, as soon as you tell me your true name."

"My name stays my secret for now," said the Valwolf.

"Then I won't fight you for now," Tyr said.

"Will you be my champion against your father?" Tidefyr

asked.

"No!" Tyr screamed. "I swore I'd kill Father when Ragnarok came, but not until after I'd killed Garm and Fenris. The prophecies all say I won't live long enough to do that, and I'm not going to kill him any sooner than that."

"Then I'm not your mother anymore," Tidefyr said, "and you're not my son. I disown you."

"Don't worry, Son!" bellowed Hymir, "I won't kill her. Now that I know her name, I can marry her and you won't be illegitimate anymore. I'll bring her back home, and I'll put new bracelets on her, and they'll make her forget that she was ever anything but my wife and your mother."

"You'll have to step across my dead body to marry her," Fenris said, his voice low and growling. Even when he was in human form, it was easy to remember that he was a wolf.

"No, no," Hymir said, laughing, "not your dead body. We need you alive to kill Odin at Ragnarok. But I'll stick you full of sleep thorns again, and lay you across my threshold, and we'll step across your body when we get married. And after I'm married, I'll tie you to the foot of my bed, and we'll step across your body every time we have sex."

"I'll agree to wrestle you to the first clean fall," Tidefyr said. "I stipulate that there may be no weapons and no biting, a fair fight, one on one." She got down off her horse.

"No!" Tyr screamed. "Father, you said you wouldn't fight her here."

"Yes," boomed Hymir. "We'll go back to the beach where we first met and wrestle it out there. I'll agree to all your stipulations. We can meet there in three days' time."

"Agreed," said Tidefyr. "Invite the neighbors. I'll want to name witnesses." That meant that she was going to go through the legal form of divorcing Hymir.

"Agreed," Hymir said. "They can be our wedding guests."

"What I want to know," Robin Grima said, "is why Hymir and Tyr are both still here. I can see why they didn't go across the border into Hel; the folk there are angry with them for killing their queen. But why didn't Tyr call Silver Mane and ride back to Asgard? Why didn't Hymir go back to the *Naglfar*?"

"I can answer those questions," said the Valwolf. "Tyr may have called Silver Mane, but his horse didn't come. It's too busy sitting on top of the *Naglfar* mast, looking scornfully down on Niflheim, and Hymir can't go back to his ship—or go anywhere in Niflheim—as long as Silver Mane's head stays there."

Tyr screamed in grief for his horse. Then he drew his sword. "I'll drown that insult in blood," he said. "Choose a champion who's got a name, you son of a bitch!"

"Now!" screamed Frostbite.

Robin Grima drew her sword. "My name is Robin Grima Jonson," she said, "and the Valwolf is one of my followers and so is Fenris Lokison. You swore our oath too once, Tyr Hymirson *Naglfar*'s Captain. It doesn't seem to have bound you very much, but now I release you from it, and I challenge you to a duel to last for as long as we both have swords." She walked into the dueling circle. "I don't want a shield, but you can have one if you like, Lord Tyr."

"I don't need a shield to fight a Valhallan," Tyr said. "All I want is...." He turned away from Robin to face Tidefyr. "You may not be my mother anymore," he said, "but you still promised that you'd give me my hand back."

"I know when I'm not needed," said Hymir, and stepped out of the dueling circle on the far side. "Try not to hack her up too much, though. I want her bones for the ship."

"If you promised him his hand, then keep your word," said Fenris. "Don't tell him that he'll have to wait for it till Ragnarok. Only someone without honor would say something like that."

"Here it is," said Tidefyr. She stepped out of the dueling circle and threw something at Tyr.

Tyr's right arm reached up into the air for it, and his wrist touched it and clung to it, and now he had his hand again: its silver fingernails as strong as steel, as sharp as knives. He waved his sword, still holding it in his left hand, and ran toward Robin Grima.

She swung Frostbite down in a desperate parry.

The two swords met with a flash of light and a crash of thunder.

And then the swords both shattered.

****

"Kykkeliky," crowed the rooster sitting on top of faraway Hel's Hall roof. It was sunrise.

"You treacherous Valhallan!" Tyr screamed. "You've broken your oath to Odin and allied with the Lokisons! I'll strangle you and—"

"Great idea," said Hymir, "but you can't kill her now, Son. You agreed that your duel would only last as long as you both had swords. Both of your swords are broken so the duel's over; you have to wait till tomorrow before you can challenge her again."

"Tyr Hymirson should have broken his sword after he broke his oath of blood brotherhood to Fenris," Tidefyr said. "He had no right to a sword that said Victory and Justice. It should have said Treachery and Lies."

"My sword is no concern of yours," Tyr said coldly, turning away so he wasn't looking at her, so she couldn't see his tears. "You're not my mother anymore; you said so. I'll find elves who can forge me a better sword."

"'A wind age, a wolf age,'" Fenris sang. "'Brothers will

fight and slay each other.'"

"And if the mist elves won't let us into Niflheim anymore," Hymir said, "then I'll start over again and build myself a new ship in Jotunheim. I can go anywhere there a river or a beach or a well. Anywhere there's water." He looked up at the sky. "Here, horsie!" he called. "Come take me and my son back home to Hymirstead."

"Hymirstead's not my home anymore," Tyr said. "I live in Asgard now and—"

A sea horse erupted out of the ground at Hymir's feet like a spouting geyser. Hymir jumped onto its back, and Tyr jumped up behind him, and it galloped up into the sky.

Robin Grima knelt down in dirt and found it was wet now with saltwater from the sea horse's passage.

She picked up a silver hilt with a jagged blade no longer than an eating knife. When her fingers touched it, it glowed faintly, faded to darkness and then slowly glowed again. *"Frostbite,"* Robin thought. *"Love,"* But there wasn't an answer. She picked up the pieces of her sword and wiped them clean and put them in her scabbard.

Drifa was holding out a napkin to her. "Wipe your eyes, Robin Grima," the woman said. "Where do we go now?"

"To the bottom of Rainbow Bridge," Robin Grima said. She wiped away her eyes' tears and then gave the napkin back to Drifa. "I'm hoping for a family reunion."

Fenris laughed. I didn't understand that it was a black-humored pun until later on. "I've sworn an oath to go on this lady's quest with her," he told Tidefyr.

"I've heard their oath," Tidefyr said, "and I'll swear it too if they let me. May I come with you, Robin Grima?"

"What do you—" Robin Grima thought, but there was no one there at her side who could hear her thoughts anymore,

no one there to advise her. Frostbite had made his choice, and now she had to make hers. *"I'm too busy to cry right now,"* she thought. *"Maybe later, when I've got time."* It was what she'd told herself when her parents died and she had to arrange the funeral and sell their house and make plans to move away to college. It was what she'd told herself when she got cancer and when the cancer came back and when her cancer patient friends died one by one, some because they'd gotten sick of chemo and radiation and surgery and refused further treatment, some because they'd run out of insurance, some because they'd done everything the doctors recommended but it wasn't enough. Robin had gotten used to having her friends die long before she came to Valhalla.

She thought about the broken pieces of Tyr's sword and decided she didn't want to have her companions swear on Justice or Victory and wished that she knew someone with a sword named Peace or Safety or Common Sense or even What Would Odin Do. "We're from Valhalla," she said aloud, "all of us except for Ratatosk and Fenris, and we've all pledged to fight for Odin if Ragnarok comes. We won't ask you to do that, but—"

"You set me free," Tidefyr said. "And you set Fenris free. Who else are you planning to set free? Do you really think that you're going to stop Ragnarok?"

"I'm doing the best I can," Robin said. "I don't think we betrayed Odin by setting Fenris free, but I don't know if Odin's angry with us or pleased with us. I don't know if I'm right or if I'm making a terrible mistake."

"One prophecy at least won't come true," Fenris said. "I'm not going to attack Odin. But I also won't attack my relatives or their friends. If you want me to fight on your side, Sister, then you have to persuade the rest of the Lokisons to join you or at least persuade them to stay out of the fight."

"Thank you, Brother," said Robin Grima. "I'll try to

protect your honor too." She held out her scabbard with the broken pieces of Frostbite in it and said, "All for one, and one for all," and the others touched it and repeated the oath.

Tidefyr spread out her arms, and the circle of moonlight that flowed from her grew more clearly defined, like a spotlight. "The moon won't set over Midgard for another ten minutes," she said, "and until it does I can walk there in one step and anyone who stands in my light will come there with me."

"I don't have claws or teeth anymore," Fenris said. "I need a weapon to fight with."

Robin picked up the two faces of Tyr's sword and handed them to him, wet with saltwater and dark with dirt and red with Hel's blood drops. Fenris slapped the two sword faces against one another, and "Victory" shattered like a smashed glass, into small shards that turned into flames, into dying embers, into dark coal. "Justice at my side is all I really need," Fenris said, "though I may want to pick up some clothes and a scabbard before I go to a formal occasion."

"Is introducing me to your father a formal occasion?" Tidefyr asked.

"Knowing him, it probably won't be, but we can always hope. Do you know someone who might lend me a shirt long enough to come down to my knees?"

"There's no point in visiting your father before we visit Skadi Thiazisdaughter," Tidefyr said, "and a hill giant home should have some clothing we can cut down to fit you."

Robin Grima didn't remember seeing Thiazi Eagle guarding the door at Valhalla, but she remembered Skadi's snake burrowing into Loki's mouth, and she was happy she wouldn't have to fight it, especially when all she had now was her bare hands. And she remembered something else.

"It's after sunrise, Lady Tidefyr," she said. "Come with us and protect Drifa—and the rest of us too, if you're willing to swear our oath."

"I pledge to protect—" Tidefyr started, and then hesitated, because you can't protect the life of someone who's dead. "I pledge to protect Drifa and Robin Grima and everyone they accept as companions on their quest from any threat to their bodies and to their minds and to their honor. May Odin's spear run me through, and may Surt's flames burn me to ashes, and may everyone I love hate me if I break my word."

"That's a strong oath," said Bookwyrm, "and I'm sure we all trust it. But there's one thing you said that I don't understand. Why should Skadi Thiazisdaughter welcome a gang of wandering Valhallans? What hold do you have over her?"

"She's my daughter's stepmother-in-law," said Tidefyr, "so we're relatives. Beyond that," she paused a while, choosing her words, and then said, "She's eager to help you in the hope that you'll help her strengthen her ties to her husband and her stepchildren."

Fenris laughed again (and I didn't get that joke at the time either). "By all means then," he said, "if Robin Grima agrees, let's go to Bifrost by way of Skadistead."

I was expecting Tidefyr to call a horse from Muspelheim and wondering how safe it would be for the rest of us. Riding Silver Mane hadn't gotten me wet, so maybe riding a flame horse wouldn't burn me to death, but I wasn't going to be the first one to climb on its back. Or even the first one after Fenris. Loki may not be the god of fire, but he's on closer terms with flames than I am.

But instead Tidefyr just walked forward, and the circle of moonlight slid forward with her and took us with it. We stood there and watched Hel and Niflheim fall away below us. The pink and gold-tinted sunrise clouds encircled us, but Tidefyr's moonlight was brighter than the rising sun shining through the branches of the World Tree.

We ended up in the cold world of Jotunheim, and the sunlight faded away behind us, but Tidefyr's moonlight was brighter than the bright stars and glittering icy mountains, brighter even than the glowing hair of Gerd Tidefyrsdaughter Freyswife who sat in the golden garden of Skadistead.

A garden in sunless Jotunheim? Skadistead's garden was rich with gold roses and gold sunflowers and gold daisies. None of them would ever lose their petals unless a thief stole them. None of them would ever grow. They were all cold metal, forged by dark elves, but they shone bright in the fire-gold glow of Gerd's hair.

A raven sat on the garden wall, watching Gerd comb her hair, watching us. Robin Grima looked at it and winced, remembering the raven who'd nearly pecked out her eye as she hung on the World Tree, but then she felt a wave of knowledge sweep into her mind and realized that it was Memory, one of Odin's ravens. Odin never forgets Lady Skadi and her house guests.

Gerd's lips moved, but we couldn't hear her, just the Jotun wolves howling. A ring of white wolves circled Skadistead like lookouts standing guard at a castle, and I saw why the place's other name was Thrymheim, Noise Home. One of the wolves came forward and sniffed us, one by one, and at his touch the noise grew soft and we could hear ourselves think, hear other people speak, the way you stop hearing the ocean waves after you've spent long enough at the seashore.

"Good morning, Mother," Gerd told Tidefyr. "Everything here is still under control." She had her mother's sweet smile and bright hair but her father's changeable sea color eyes. "Welcome to Skadistead, everybody."

She stood up, towering over us, even over Fenris who was twice as tall as Knut and Bookwyrm, but with each step she took, she shrank, till she was the same height as her mother

Tidefyr, who only came up to Fenris's shoulder. Fire and sea are never the same shape twice in a second, and their giants are like them.

"You're all our welcome guests," Gerd told us. "You can speak freely here, Sheep-horned Heimdall's too afraid of our wolves to listen to what's said here." Then her left arm snaked out a dozen feet and caught poor little Ratatosk by the neck. "All of you may speak freely here except for Ratatosk Honeytongue. Swear by anything you hold sacred that you won't open your mouth while you're here and insult my dear husband or his father, sweet little Ratatosk. Swear that you won't gossip to anyone about what you see here."

"I won't say a word to them or about them to anyone in the Nine Worlds," the squirrel said, gasping for breath. "I swear it by my hope of getting home alive and in one piece."

"Then you're welcome here too," Gerd said. "Please come in, everybody, and let me serve you breakfast."

We followed her into the hall whose rooms were bright with candles and warm with wood fires, and she fetched a golden basin of warm water to wash our hands and feet and brought us each a golden cup of ale to wet our throats. By then Skadi Thiazisdaughter had come to greet us too. She wore a gown of white wolfskin trimmed with white beads that might have started out as wolf's teeth or walrus tusks; Skadi's cloak was woven of eagle feathers. Her skin and her teeth were white as snow and her hair was black as the night sky, and her lips were blood red, but she didn't look anything like Disney's pretty little Snow White; she looked more like the beautiful stepmother queen, but her speech was soft and gentle and Tidefyr seemed to trust her.

Skadi led us to her dining hall where her man and his son already sat, eating their breakfast off of golden dishes.

Njord looked up from cracking the speckled brown shell of a ptarmigan egg and courteously wished us a good meal and a safe journey onward, and Frey Njordson put down his slice of bread spread with honey and added, "And may you find your homes warm and your bedmates warmer when your journey is done."

"Thank you for your welcome," Robin Grima said.

Skadi's table was spread with food: plates of roasted ptarmigan in berry sauce and salty smoked chicken and cold pickled fish, warm bread and cold cheese and butter, and pitchers of warm cider and cold milk. The travelers toasted their hostess, and ate and drank till they were too busy yawning to do either. Then their hostess showed them to a room with dark curtains and soft beds, and they slept till it was nearly dinnertime.

By then Lady Gerd had found clothes for Fenris: a shirt of blue wool and loose trousers of black wool, with a red silk belt for his waist and a leather-wrapped wooden scabbard into which he stuck the Justice blade. His belt buckle was carved wood, stained red to match the belt. She offered him socks and shoes too, but he said they'd be more of a hindrance if he changed back to wolf than a help while he stayed human, so she put them away again. There were cloaks too: long ones for Fenris and Tidefyr and shorter ones for the Valhallans. I don't know what the clothes were woven from except that it was light but warm. The cloaks fastened at the neck with ivory brooches in the shape of snowflakes.

But before the humans put on their clothing, they insisted on going to the bathhouse. It was a separate building of packed snow, at the back of the garden. The ceiling looked like air or maybe fine crystal, till Ratatosk climbed up and touched it and found it was only ice. The water was warm but not hot enough for the humans till Bookwyrm knelt down and spat on the circle of stone that ringed the bath and wrote runes of heat on it.

"I thought you had to dye it with your blood," Fenris said.

"We went through the rune ordeal when the mist elves hung us on the World Tree," Bookwyrm said, "and now I know them by heart in my blood, not just in my word treasure chest, in my mind."

Tidefyr waited till the humans had all bathed and gotten dressed. Then she took off her robe and slipped into the bath, and the water started boiling. Fenris threw off the shirt he'd pulled on and dove back into the pool of bubbling water.

Robin remembered breakfast on top of Mount Shasta in California, where it took longer than usual to boil an egg, and then learning in a Physics class that water boils at a lower temperature when you climb higher and the air pressure gets lower, one degree lower for each five hundred feet over sea level. She wasn't sure how high up they were, but she stuck a finger into the bath water. Her skin didn't burn, because she had walked three times through the fire ordeal, but she was convinced that the bath water was hot enough to boil an egg in three minutes.

"Isn't that a little hot for you, Fenris?" Bookwyrm asked.

"My mother may not have been able to stand much heat," he said cheerfully, "but I'm a Lokison."

"There's hotter fires in Jotunheim than Loki's," Bookwyrm warned, "or at least that's what the eddas say."

"I've heard the story," Fenris said, scooping water up in his hands and watching it dance and bubble on his palms.

"I haven't," said Tidefyr, so they told her how Loki and Thor and a boy from Midgard traveled into Jotunheim long ago and met a giant who ruled the city of Utgard and who set contests for them.

"The boy ran fast," Bookwyrm said, "but he lost, and later he found out that he was racing against Thought. (That was Utgard-Loki's retainer Hugi, not Lord Odin's raven Hugin, two supposedly different Thoughts.) Thor couldn't outwrestle an old lady, who turned out to be Old Age."

"He'd have done better if he'd brought along one of Idunn's apples," Drifa said.

"The Aesir have to eat those apples at least once a year or they start getting wrinkled," Ratatosk said. "Grandmother Old Age would still have won."

"And Thor couldn't lift up the cat," Knut said, "but it wasn't really a cat; it was the Midgard Serpent."

"And he couldn't empty the drinking horn," Bookwyrm said, "but that was because it held the ocean."

"And the fire hotter than Loki?" asked Tidefyr.

"Father lost his eating contest to a fellow named Logi, who was really a forest fire," said Fenris. "It was all tricks and illusions. The Utgard king called himself Utgard-Loki because he'd tricked Father, but he ended up admitting that he'd been terrified the whole time, and nobody's ever seen the city of Utgard again."

"Are there many illusionists in Jotunheim?" Robin Grima asked.

"Utgard-Loki's the only one the eddas mention," Bookwyrm said. "And the only other illusions I know of in Jotunheim are the ones that hide Mimir's Fountain."

Clean and clothed, we went back to the dining hall and found Njord and Frey already sitting there, and had dinner which was much the same as breakfast except that it started with soup and ended with cracked nuts and fruit. By now we were all better rested and less hungry, and so more willing to make conversation with our hosts. Knut told the story of how we'd met Orm Lokison, the Midgard Serpent, hoping it would interest Njord, who folk used to pray to as the god of sailing and fishing. Bookwyrm told how he and Drifa had been separated for centuries and then scandalized the mist elves by making love as soon as they found themselves a bed, hoping to interest Frey, who folk used to pray to as the god of fertility, but the Vanir didn't seem interested in either story and didn't tell any of their own.

Robin told how we'd found Lady Hel lying dead in the dueling circle, cut in half, and how Baldur and Hodur had carried her away, and that got our hosts' attention.

"Did you hear that, Skadi?" Njord said. "Baldur finally escaped from Hel, but he went back again, carrying his dead mistress, like an obedient thrall. Do you think he'd have done the same for you if you'd married him?"

"I don't know," she said. "Does it matter? I had my choice, and I chose you."

"No, it doesn't matter," Njord said. "What matters is that you chose me out of a lineup of every available male in Asgard. Of course Odin's condition was that you couldn't look any higher than our ankles. I'll never forget how you said that no one could have such handsome feet but beautiful Baldur. But it wasn't Baldur you chose; it was me. And you're still fond of my handsome feet, aren't you? Why else would you have given me such pretty jewelry to wear on them?"

He pushed back his chair and put his feet up on the table, kicking the platters aside so we could see them.

His feet were long and fine and beautiful, and his toenails were painted sea green. There were rings on his toes that linked to chains as thin and delicate as silk ribbons that wove together to circle his ankles and then linked to another chain that that went down into a slot in the stone floor.

"Isn't my jewelry beautiful?" Njord asked bitterly. "Didn't the Aesir honor me and my son as guests in Asgard?"

Ratatosk opened up his mouth to comment—and then remembered his oath and was silent. But he hadn't sworn not to *think* of insults, and there were several that came to mind. After two terrible Worlds Wars, the Vanir had sent Njord and Frey and Lady Freya to Asgard not as honored guests but as hostages, and Odin had sent his two brothers in exchange to try to ensure a lasting peace. But it turned out that the Vanir didn't understand complicated words like "hostage" or "peace"—words that even Jotunheim giants understand. The gossip—Ratatosk's *reliable* gossip!—was that the Vanir had killed Hoenir and Mimir and feasted on their blood and flesh, all except for Mimir's head. And after the Vanir sent Mimir's head back to Asgard, Odin and his foster brother Loki decided not to trust the Vanir anymore.

"My jewelry is just as beautiful as yours," Frey Njordson said, "and that makes sense because it came from the same generous benefactor." Robin Grima peeked under the table and saw that Frey's ankles were also chained to the floor.

"Our guests thought we were rude when we weren't impressed by their tales," Njord said. "It's been centuries since either of us got near enough the seacoast to smell the salt sea air, let alone took out a rowboat and went fishing."

"It's been centuries since either of us lay down on a bed," his son said. "There are things you can do with a woman while you're sitting down under her, but it would be good to try another position for a change."

"I spent centuries chained on Heather Island," Fenris growled. "I had no one to keep me company and barely enough nourishment to stay alive. The gods said it was a splendid sport to chain me up each new year's day and watch me break free. You two were both there when I broke my first two chains, and you two were both there when I couldn't break the third one. I remember how you laughed when I begged my blood brother Tyr to keep his promise and set me free."

"The gods came to watch you bound," said Gerd, "not the goddesses. None of us laughed at you."

"What really matters is that you've broken free of your third chain," Frey Njordson said. "Tell us how you did it,

Lokison, and I'll give you sanctuary in Light Elfland when Ragnarok comes."

"The Aesir gave Light Elfland to you when you cut your first tooth." Njord said. "You let your light elf servant trick you out of it. You gave him your world and your magic sword in exchange for that golden-haired woman from Jotunheim."

"She's the warmest and loveliest thing in this world," Frey said loyally.

"She doesn't have much competition," Njord said dryly. He turned to Fenris. "Tell us how you broke free, Lokison, and we'll swear blood brotherhood with you and stand by your side against Odin at Ragnarok."

Outside the wolves began howling louder than usual, and Njord shivered at the sound.

"I have enough blood brothers already," Fenris said. "I don't want any more. Did a light elf trick you into wearing that jewelry?"

"My son and I aren't as foolish as my pretty daughter," Njord said. "The dark elves showed her a necklace to match these chains, and she wanted it so much that she spent three nights keeping their hammers hot to buy it from them."

"She looked beautiful in that necklace," Frey said. "She wound it around her slender neck and draped it down over her honey-gold breasts and the sweeter honey that lies between her legs. She caught her lovers in it like a fishing line and she rode them like bridled horses. Every year, Odin sends his ravens here with new year's greetings. Memory says that my sister still loves us, and Thought says that my sister still sits in her hall, busy playing with her lovers, and still hasn't noticed that she's chained there and can't leave."

"My son and I were tricked," Njord said. "Skadi and I agreed to spend half our time on the seacoast and the other half in the mountains, and when I complained of how bored I was in the dark howling wilderness of Jotunheim, my son said he'd come with me to keep me company. We found a keg of winter wine waiting for us and spent the night toasting our benefactor. We woke up chained to the feast hall floor and saw Loki Wyrmtongue laughing at us."

"I gave Loki a proper punishment for his trickery," Skadi said. "I hung a snake over his head to torture him." Robin Grima shivered, remembering Loki bound and writhing, the snake's head buried deep in his mouth.

"They're beautiful chains," Gerd Hymirsdaughter said. "I'm not surprised that the Lady fell in love with hers. And Loki said they'd fall apart at Ragnarok."

"When that happens, I'll run away from here as fast as I can," Frey said. "I'll turn into a stag and go fight the sons of Muspel. The prophecies say that Loki's going to be piloting their ship to Asgard. With any luck, I'll be able to help Heimdall kill him before I have to fight Surt."

"I'll run away too," his father said. "I'll leave these disgusting dark mountains with their horrible howling wolves. I'll go back to my beautiful seashore and send my ships out to help the sea giants defend themselves against their enemies. And when Ragnarok's over, I'll spend the rest of my days listening to the waves crashing on the shore and the gulls screaming in the sky."

"I'm glad to know that my father loved me enough to make you wear the same chains that you and your friend Tyr Hymirson bound on me," Fenris said, his voice quiet at first but getting louder as his anger grew. "I just wish he'd made you bite off Tyr's feet so you'd have known how good your friend tasted. My father told me that he wouldn't help me break free. He told me to just lie still and be patient and wait for Ragnarok and to trust him and Uncle Odin. Then he laughed and told me never to trust him and he ran away."

Ratatosk thought of saying that Fenris had gotten to stay in Asgard a lot longer than Orm or Hel and hadn't been in nearly as much pain as Narvi Lokison when the starving wolf ate up everything but his guts and spine. He thought of asking Fenris if he'd have preferred being eaten up or being the one who did the eating. Then he looked at the Valwolf who knew all those stories even better than he did but wasn't saying anything, and he stayed silent too.

"No wise man trusts Loki," Gerd said, and passed Fenris the bowl of walnut meats.

"That's right," said Skadi. "Don't ever believe anything Loki tells you."

"If blind Hodur Odinson had been that wise, he'd still be alive," said Njord, "and so would bright Baldur his brother, but Loki tricked them, and now they're both dead and Odin has learned not to trust his foster brother."

"There are rules about bindings," Frey said. "Our chains were just as tight as yours, Lokison, and then last week they started fraying. Yesterday they were loose enough that I could have gotten my right foot free if I'd cut off my big toe, but I thought I'd be patient and wait another day. And then, last night," he shook his feet and we heard the chains rattle, "last night they got rewoven, and now they're tighter than ever." He glared at Fenris. "I warn you now, Lokison, there are rules. You can't bind us with secrets. We told you that the dark elves forged your fetter from women's beards and cats' footfalls and the rest of it. You have till sunrise tomorrow to tell us what our chains are made from, or else I'll have the right to put up a scorn pole against you and your gang."

"Does anyone here know what he's talking about?" Bookwyrm asked. "Because if anyone does, please tell him what he wants to know. I value my honor too much to have someone put up a scorn pole against me."

"I know what he's talking about," said Robin Grima, "and I know the new set of impossible things because I thought them up. The sound that a stone hears when a tree falls in a forest. A hair from the beard of a barber who shaves all and only the men in his village who don't shave themselves. A tree with the square root of minus one flowers. The biggest number that can only be divided by itself and by one. The tears of a bird. The turd that a bear dropped while it was hibernating."

"Who broke your chains, Fenris Lokison?" Frey asked. "That's the man we need to talk to."

"I broke his chains," said Robin Grima. "But you shouldn't trust me any more than you'd trust Loki. I'm a Vinlander, and all Vinlanders are liars." Her hand touched her scabbard, but Frostbite was broken. Knut and Bookwyrm and Drifa laughed at her joke, though; and so, eventually, did her other oath-mates. Even Fenris smiled wryly.

"She's a valiant Vinlander from Valhalla," Fenris said, "and I trust her, and she broke my fetter. The proof of my words is that it hangs on her belt."

"Why have you come here, Valhallans?" Njord asked. "Did Odin send you here to free us?"

"Not today," Robin Grima said. "Today we're on our way to Midgard to look for a hero."

"The valkyries used to do that for Odin," Frey said, "but now they spend half their time seeking men to keep my sister distracted."

"And the other half of their time dancing in Asgard's pretty skies," said Njord.

"And one spends her days and nights in Midgard," Knut said, "keeping an eye on Loki."

"A bleary eye, fuzzy with cataracts," Bookwyrm said.

The two Vanir laughed.

"Sigyn was Odin's first-born daughter," Frey said. "She was the brightest and most beautiful of his valkyrie, and the proudest, too. She turned down every god who asked for her hand, and then she lost her mind and asked her father to give her to Loki Wyrmtongue. Now Sigyn's son and daughter are dead, and her husband's an exiled outlaw." He reached out for a bowl of fruit and held up an apple. "Every midwinter Idunn brings us a basket of apples, so we stay young and handsome, but nobody brings them to Sigyn, do they? Have you seen her, Valhallans? What does she look like?"

"Wrinkled face and bleary eyes," said Knut. "White fingers crooked with arthritis and spotted with age. White hair thin and tangled, with the scalp showing through. Bent back and hobbling legs so she needs a cane to walk surely. Dirty ragged clothes because she's got no time to mend them or wash them."

"If she's half-blind with age, then she's not a safe guardian," Skadi said. "Loki's so tricky that he killed my father and then made me laugh. I'd better go take a look at his bindings and make sure that nothing's gone wrong. May I come with you, Tidefyr?"

"I'd welcome your company," Tidefyr said, "but I'm not the one you should be asking. Robin Grima, the Valhallan from Vinland, is our leader."

"We'd all welcome your company, Lady Skadi," Robin Grima said, "but it's not likely to be an easy trip."

Skadi laughed. "I took my first steps wearing skis," she said. "I can outrun wolves and outfight them. I'll never forget what I owe Loki for killing my father, and I couldn't forgive myself if he got free and I didn't know it." She turned to golden-haired Gerd. "Keep watch over our menfolk, Daughter, and make sure they have everything they need. Remember we don't want a third Worlds War with the Vanir."

"I promise," Gerd said. "Fare safely, mother and foster mother. Fare safely, all of you."

CHAPTER SIXTEEN

Robin Grima and her companions left Skadistead as soon as they'd finished dinner. Nine days ago, Robin Grima and her friends had set out to prevent Ragnarok. They'd left Valhalla and gone down Yggdrasil to the world of Hel and killed the Dragon Nidhog, and they'd gotten permission for Drifa to leave with them. The next morning, Tyr had taken them to Mist Hall, and they'd ended up rowing to Hymirstead, where they'd met Orm and where Drifa had freed the beautiful stead lady from Hymir's ivory bracelets, but Hymir had killed Drifa.

A week ago, they'd freed Fenris on Heather Island by the light of the full moon. Three days after that, the mist elves had hung them on the World Tree, but clever Ratatosk untied them, with a little help from Drifa, who was now a Valhallan. They'd captured the *Naglfar*, and Bookwyrm had carved her mast into a scorn-pole. Then they'd traveled to the Hel River dueling island and found Hel lying there, her two halves severed by Tyr's sword. Robin challenged Tyr to a duel, and both of their swords shattered. Fenris had taken one piece of Tyr's blade, the piece that said "Justice". Robin Grima had taken all the broken pieces of Frostbite and put them in her scabbard.

Now the moon was at his waning crescent, and he wouldn't rise until midnight. Even so, Tidefyr cast a circle of warm moonlight around her, bright enough to keep Fenris in human form and warm as a summer sunset. But it didn't melt the snow and ice of the Jotunheim mountains or silence the howling wolves.

Skadi wore snowshoes, and so did Knut and Bookwyrm and Drifa. Fenris said there had never been enough snow in Asgard for him to learn to walk on it. Robin Grima said the closest she'd gotten was using a Nordic Track at the gym. Nobody understood that except for Ratatosk, but the others had gotten used to Robin speaking Vinland gibberish now and then, and they didn't bother to question her. Tidefyr lent a hand to Fenris and to Robin, and they walked safely in her orbit. The Valwolf scampered along lightly over the snowcrust as Skadi led the way.

The Milky Way hung like a ribbon across the sky, and there was a stream of meteors falling from the two brightest stars of Gemini. Yes, I know that in human lands Gemini is a winter constellation and its meteor swarm falls in December. The seasons are different in Jotunheim, and so is the sky.

"Father is crying," Skadi said, waving a hand at the meteors.

"Odin's got a way with eyes," Ratatosk said. "Look at how he took out his own left eye and threw it into Mimir's Fountain. When his twins were born, folks said that blind Hodur took after his father's left side and Baldur—"

"I wasn't born yet when Thiazi died," Fenris said, rudely interrupting the witty squirrel, "but if you feel that I owe you compensation for my father killing your father—"

"The Aesir paid me full compensation," Skadi said. "Odin gave me my choice of a husband, and your father made me laugh, which was more than my own father ever—"

Valhalla: Absent Without Leave

A Jotun wolf suddenly leapt into sight and knocked Skadi down into the snow that was the same color as his fur, the same color as her white skin and wolf fur clothing.

Knut and Bookwyrm drew their swords and ran forward to attack the wolf.

"Idiots!" yelled the Valwolf and leapt up to attack the real danger, an ice snake the size of a glacier, its head as wide as a Valhallan feasting table, its body a hundred miles long if it was an inch. It had lain there motionless, watching us walk nearer and nearer to its mouth, but it wasn't motionless any more; it was flailing its head about, trying to shake off the Valwolf, and gnashing its white teeth.

The Valwolf dug his fangs deeper into the ice snake's nostrils, and the Jotun wolf leapt at the snake's throat and tore off a strip of scales. That was more than anyone else managed.

Skadi was back on her feet and holding her longbow. She sent arrow after arrow at the ice snake, but they all bounced off without harming it. Knut and Bookwyrm flailed away with their swords, but they couldn't pierce the ice snake's skin, and Fenris found that the Justice blade was just as useless.

Drifa turned away to watch the empty land, ready to warn her friends if any new danger appeared.

"It's like a berserk," Knut said at last. "The sagas all agree that you can't wound a berserk with steel. You need to strangle it with your hands or bite it with your teeth or maybe hit it with a club fresh-cut from a tree."

"What about fire?" Robin Grima yelled. "Maybe a meteorite..." but the Geminids had stopped falling.

"Father never was around when I needed help!" Skadi said, laughing grimly.

"Neither was mine," said Fenris.

"I'm here," Tidefyr said, "but all I can give you is light and warmth."

"Those won't help," Knut said, "and neither will fire or moonlight or boiling water. You have to attack a berserk with something that's alive or used to be alive."

The ice snake shook the Jotun wolf loose from its throat.

Robin Grima's hands were empty, but she ran to her ally's side, hoping to drag it out of danger.

The ice snake bent down over them, its white eyes blind and indifferent, but its huge mouth gaping open, and its forked tongue swinging to and fro. And then its mouth darted down and closed around them, and they were trapped inside it and the only light in the darkness was Robin Grima's hair.

Robin reached up her empty hands and tore out a handful of her hair with each of them and ran forward to hit the snake's tongue.

The ice snake screamed in agony at the touch of Robin's shining hair. The Jotun wolf howled in triumph, then leapt at the base of the forked tongue and began to chew it off.

The ice snake tossed its head about wildly. Robin Grima braced her feet against a row of its teeth, scouring her bright hair against the snake's tongue. The snake bled cold hailstones that battered her body like a landslide of rocks. She buried her face in the Jotun wolf's warm fur and fought on.

Then the ice snake fell onto the snow and lay there, motionless. Robin struggled out from under its severed tongue. The Jotun wolf walked at her side, but one of his eyes was gouged out, and a white hailstone rested there instead.

"Come here, brave wolf," Drifa called. "Let me help you." She gently eased the hailstone out of his eye socket and packed the bleeding wound with herbs from the box of medicines she'd brought with her from Valhalla.

"I've never seen anything like that in these mountains

before," Skadi said.

"It's an ice snake," Ratatosk said. "They live in the mountains of Hel, and their task is to keep oathbreakers and murderers on Dead Shore and not let them escape." He thought back over the oaths he'd sworn and decided he hadn't broken any of them, but he still kept his distance from the ice snake's dead body.

Bookwyrm was picking up icy rocks f and dropping them around the ice snake's head in the outline of the prow of a ship. Skadi picked up a huge boulder and dropped it on the snake's head. "Stay anchored here," she said, "or sail back to Hel where you belong, and tell any friends who came here to Jotunheim with you to do the same."

"You need a weapon, Robin Grima," Knut said. His hand fell to his waist, and she thought he was going to offer her his sword, but instead he unwound a length of Odin's rope and cut it off. "Strike straight and sharp," he said. "Stay true and trustworthy. Cut keen against evil enemies, but never forget friends or loyal allies." The rope stood stiff in the air, and Knut smiled. "I think I'm beginning to understand how to use the power the runes gave my poetry," he said, and held out the rope to Robin Grima.

She took it and ran her fingers cautiously down her new blade's razor-sharp edge and touched its keen point. "*Sword?*" she thought, but nobody answered.

"Let's go on," said Tidefyr, and Skadi walked forward to lead the way across Jotunheim to Midgard.

About an hour later, they reached the top of a mountain pass and looked down to see a forest of twinkling lights.

"*Christmas trees,*" Robin thought, and then realized there wouldn't be any of those in the Nine Worlds, especially not in Jotunheim.

"It's too cold here for fireflies," Bookwyrm said.

"The lights shine like night-snow," said Drifa, "but why can't the birds fly away from the branches?"

"Jotunheim snow doesn't shine," Skadi said. But as the party went downhill they found themselves surrounded by glittering snowflakes, just like the ones that fell from the skies of Hel.

A few minutes downhill walk brought them to the trees, and they saw the birds that Drifa had been talking about. The branches were covered with them. Robin recognized pigeons and ducks, eagles and ravens, but there were other bird species there she didn't recognize. Her friends told her they were ptarmigans and grouse, plovers and woodcocks, puffins and skuas: white feathers and gray, blue and red, brown and black—all of them desperately flapping their wings but stuck on the branches.

"Like the sacrifice trees below the Dnieper rapids when we went down to Micklegard," Bookwyrm said. (*"Down to Byzantium,"* whispered a voice in Robin Grima's mind.) "The traders boiled mistletoe down to bird lime, and spread the trees with it, and dedicated the sacrifices to Odin, the same way a warrior would when he looked at the enemy forces before a battle."

"Like the wood at Uppsala," Knut said, "where every ninth spring they held a blood feast to Frey. They say in the old days it was bulls and men, but when I went there it was only birds."

Normally, Norse households only had two blood feasts, and neither one featured birds. One was on Winter's Eve, the first Freya's Day after the Fall Equinox, the start of the six months of Winter. That was when they brought the grazing animals down from the mountains and saw how many cows and sheep and goats and horses and pigs they had. That's when people who were good at mathematics counted how much hay and other fodder they'd gathered in their fields over the summer and brought into the barn, and then they figured out how many grazing animals they could keep alive during the winter. That's when they killed off all the extra animals they couldn't feed to keep alive.

A few of the animals were sacrificed to the gods, and the humans ate them at the Winter's Eve blood feast. It was the last time they'd get to eat their fill until the Midwinter blood feast. The rest of the slaughtered animals were salted or wind-dried or baked or boiled or otherwise preserved to be eaten, little by little, during the winter months.

The midwinter blood feast was Jul (pronounced Yule). Scholars say Jul is one of Odin's names, but scholars are dedicated to Odin, and they think that everything is about him, including birds heading south for the Winter. Jul was when farmers sacrificed a stallion or boar to Frey because he was the god of fertility, and he ensures lots of new piglets and foals at winter's end.

The sacrifices at royal courts or big trademarts were bigger. The kings sacrificed to Odin, because he was the god of warriors, and the traders sacrificed to Njord, because he was the god of ships. Thor was the god of farmers, so most farmers sacrificed a bull to him. Frey was the god of Fertility, and every nine years a special sacrifice was made in his honor.

"The giants don't make sacrifices," said Skadi, when knowledgable Ratatosk finished. "Not to Odin, and not to Frey, and not to anybody else, and I've walked this way a thousand times before tonight, but this grove was never here."

"Illusions?" asked Robin, but Bookwyrm drew runes on the nearest tree and it didn't disappear.

"Let's go on," said Tidefyr, and Skadi led them around the strange grove and up a mountainside to a pass. At its top stood a tall tree, its branches cut off, and blood running down its trunk from a dark shape impaled on its top.

"A scorn-pole?" asked Robin.

Bookwyrm walked slowly around it and said, "I don't see any runes."

Drifa knelt down and touched her finger to the red pool of warm liquid that was melting the snow. "There's power in the blood," she said.

"Then maybe it comes from whatever's bleeding," said Fenris. He gripped the pole with his hands and knees and started climbing. A few minutes later, he was high enough to lift the body off the sharpened tip. He threw back his head and howled. The sound echoed through the pass. Far away, a pack of wolves howled back in response.

"It's someone I know," Fenris said, his voice harsh. He laid the body across his shoulders and slowly climbed back down the tree.

When he got down to a few feet over the ground, he leapt off the tree, over the pool of blood, to land in clean snow, then laid down the great gray body of Garm Hel-hound. "Is there anything you can do for him, Lady Drifa?" he asked.

Drifa gently touched the bleeding wounds. "None of the blood has stayed on him," she said. "His fur's still gray."

Garm's eyelids drew apart, showing his yellow eyes, the same color as Fenris's and the Valwolf's. "It's not my blood," he said softly. "It's the dragon blood I drank when I ate Nidhog's children. There may still be power in it, but I don't advise bathing in it. It's not fresh-shed."

"You're talking," Robin Grima said. "Does that mean the dragon blood is out of your system, and it's safe to bandage your wounds?"

"I don't know," Garm said. "Nobody told me. They just said I owed Hel a sacrifice for taking me in when Asgard threw me out, and they were going to take me to a world where people could die. They brought me here, and they tore the tree branch off, and then they pushed it up my rear end and out my throat, and I waited to die, but I didn't. Everything hurt but I didn't die, and after a time I started thinking clearer."

"Who brought you here?" Skadi asked, but Garm didn't answer. His eyes had closed again.

"You're my son," Fenris said, kneeling down and touching the hound's cheek. His clothes were all stained with dragon's blood but he didn't seem to care.

"And you're my son, too," said Tidefyr.

"I'm cold," Garm said, panting for breath between each word. "I'm cold, and it hurts." A trickle of dark blood dripped out of his muzzle, staining his fur.

"That's his own blood," Drifa said. "His wounds are clean, and I don't smell any dirt from his intestines. He's got a good chance to live if we can keep him warm." She took off her cloak and wrapped Garm's body in it.

Tidefyr picked Garm up and carried him in her arms. "I'll keep you warm, my son," she said.

"Do you know anything about all this?" Knut asked the white Jotun wolf. It gazed at him silently. "If we pushed a spear through you, would you learn how to speak?" It tucked its tail between his legs and ran a few yards away from him.

"This is the third sign of Hel we've met on this trip," Skadi said. "That's too many to be just chance. The Hel snake came to take me to Dead Shore because I'm an oathbreaker. I swore to take vengeance on Asgard for my father's death, but I settled for a man in my bed and a smile on my lips. And I broke my marriage vows to Njord when I let Loki Honeytongue chain my husband's feet so Njord wouldn't send his ships to join *Naglfar* at Ragnarok."

"You can always settle a loss with compensation instead of vengeance," Drifa said, "even for a parent. Your marriage is another matter. You owe your husband compensation for keeping him prisoner all these years."

"It depends on her marriage vows," Bookwyrm said. "Did you take them in Frigga's hall or at Njord's hall or here in your home in Jotunheim?"

"We were married in Asgard," she said, "but not in any hall. We stood on a tall hill in front of Odin's silver throne."

"Hlidskjalf," muttered Bookwyrm. ("*Awe Gate*," Robin heard.)

"Was Lady Frigga at your wedding?" Knut asked. "Did Lord Thor hallow it with his hammer?" Frigga Odinswife is the goddess of marriage, but Thor's hammer was the symbol of law, so the Norse used to put it on a new bride's lap or tuck it into bed with the new-married couple.

"None of the Aesir came to our wedding," Skadi said. "It was just the two of us and Odin."

"What about Njord's children by his first wife?" Drifa asked. "Were Frey and the Lady Freya there to witness their father's vows?"

Skadi shook her head.

"Was that your first marriage, Lady Skadi?" Knut asked and then, when she nodded, asked, "But what kinsman declared your marriage terms, since your father was dead and you were a maiden? Did Odin adopt you as a foster daughter?"

"Odin told me I was always welcome in Asgard," she said, "but he didn't offer to make me his daughter. Nobody declared my marriage terms with Njord. We settled them privately between the two of us. We spent one week by the sea, where the salt air burned my eyes and the seabirds' cries were harsh in my ears, and the next week in the mountains, where the air was crisp with cold and the wolves howled in chorus to give us privacy from Heimdall's spying. But now we live all our weeks in Jotunheim. What compensation should I offer my husband for letting Loki chain him,

Valhallan lawyers?"

"You could return him his bride price and veil price for a start," Drifa said, and Bookwyrm and Drifa nodded.

Skadi laughed. "He didn't bring me any money," she said.

"Did he give you a share in his ships or trade goods?" Bookwyrm asked.

"Did you give him a share in your land or your hunting?" Knut asked.

"Do you have any community property?" Robin asked.

"Did you agree where your children would be fostered?" Drifa asked.

Skadi shook her head to all four questions.

"Did your relatives declare the match to their friends in Jotunheim?" Tidefyr asked.

"My relatives all quarreled with Father over who inherited Grandfather's stead," Skadi said. "None of them came to our home to stand between me and Father, and none of them came to visit me after Father died, and none of them came to my wedding. Njord and I made our vows in front of Odin, but no one else from Asgard was there except for Frey Njordson. Isn't Odin's word enough to make a marriage in Asgard?"

"The Prose Edda made it all seem like a normal wedding," Bookwyrm said. "It should have said more—or less." That was the first time anyone there had ever heard him criticize the eddas.

"I grew up in Frigga's hall," Fenris said, "and one of the things she taught all her foster children was all the marriage customs throughout the Nine Worlds. What vows did Uncle Odin ask you and Njord to swear?"

"Odin said, 'I bind this man and this woman together, to share table and bed, day and night, sea and land, and to watch each other through good times and bad. Swear you'll be faithful and true,' and I said I would, and so did Njord."

"That's not a marriage," Fenris said. "Not by Asgard customs or by Jotun customs. You may be Lord Njord's bedfellow, but you're not his wife nor his concubine, and you don't owe him any compensation."

Skadi laughed. "I'll tell Njord the news when I return home, and ask him if he already knew and just forgot to tell me. If I can find my way back home from this place. Do the wolves howl in Hel's world? Is the ground covered with snow and ice there?"

"Sometimes the Hel wolves howl," Drifa said, "but usually they're silent. It snows a few inches every night, but the snow melts when the sun rises and then freezes to ice when the sun sets."

"I don't like sunlight," Skadi said. "It dazzles my eyes."

"Last time we saw my sister Hel," Fenris said, "she was cut in two pieces by Tyr's sword, but the sword's broken now, and perhaps my sister is mended. I pledge you my word that if you help us on this quest, I'll speak to Hel on your behalf and ask her to pardon any fault she finds in you and let you go home."

"Speak to her for me too," Tidefyr said. "I was Hymir's concubine, not his wife, but I still betrayed him when I went to another man's bed. And I betrayed my lover when I didn't speak up for him against the gossips who said that he'd raped me." For some reason she was glaring at poor little Ratatosk.

Fenris laughed. "I'll speak to my sister on your behalf too, love. Any more confessions?"

The white Jotun wolf howled, but that was all. Drifa adjusted the bandage on its empty eye socket, and it fell silent. Skadi took up the lead, and the group started off.

"We're nearing the border to Midgard," Skadi said, as she led them around a conical mountain. A plume of light smoke rose from its top. There wasn't any snow underfoot, but she still wore her skis to cross the drifts of volcanic ash. "If we can keep up this pace, we'll reach Mimir's Fountain by midnight, and from there it's all downhill."

"Can't we take another route?" Drifa asked. "I had bad luck the last time I saw Mimir's Fountain."

"There's no danger waiting for you there this time," a woman's voice said from behind a pile of boulders to the right of their path.

"The only danger waiting for you in Jotunheim is right here," a woman's voice said from behind a pile of boulders to the left of their path.

Two directions but the same woman's voice.

The two women stepped forward to stand in front of Skadi, blocking her path, and both of the women were Hel: one of them fair-skinned and blonde, one dark-skinned and redheaded, both grown back to normal human shape with left and right arms and legs. The light-skinned one held a black two-handed sword. The dark-skinned one's sword was sheathed at her side, and she held a gray cat. Behind them stood bright-haired Baldur and dark-haired Hodur, their hands on their sword hilts.

"Things have changed since the last time I saw you, Robin Grima," the light Hel said. "You've lost one of my brothers, and you've taken two giantesses as companions."

"They've lost one of our brothers, but they've gained another one," the dark one said. "Some people might not recognize Fenris in human form, but that's him, standing beside the fire giantess."

"Why are you carrying Tyr's sword, Fenris?" they both asked together.

"They were left lobe and right lobe," Robin thought.

"They can both speak, so it wasn't like severing the corpus callosum, or at least it means the lobes weren't specialized. They've each got their own body now, but they're still close enough to speak in chorus. Are their thoughts linked the way mine were with Frostbite?

"I'm carrying this face of Tyr's sword because I know more about Justice than he does," Fenris said. "I've taken Tidefyr and Skadi under my protection, and I won't let you hurt them unless you know greater wrongs they've committed than those they've told me about."

"Who else do you speak for, little brother?" the light-skinned Hel asked.

"My son," Fenris said, laying his hand on Garm's neck, "and for everyone else here who's joined Robin Grima's quest and sworn her oath."

"That doesn't include the Jotun wolf," Hodur said, stepping forward to stare at the wolf, and they saw that only one of Hodur's eyes was still white and sightless. The other was dark and seeing.

"Did you find an eye nobody was using?" Bookwyrm asked.

"I've sworn allegiance to Odin," Drifa said, her hand on her sword hilt. "He didn't tell me you were free to take his eye from Mimir's Fountain."

"We didn't take Father's eye," Baldur said, turning to them, and they saw that now one of his eyes was missing. "I gave my spare eye to my brother as compensation for his injured reputation."

"It was Father's plan," Hodur said, "and I never felt insulted, but it's only fair for our ladies to have equally good husbands."

"Have you set the date for the weddings yet?" Fenris asked.

"Next year," Baldur said.

"On Summer's Eve," Hodur said. (That's the first Thor's Day after the spring equinox, the day that starts the six months of Summer.)

"We gave Garm back his speech as the first payment on the bride price," they said together, and Robin wondered if they were linked too, and whether it had started with the gift of an eye or went further back.

"Our dowry took longer to put together," the two Hels said. "But then we know more about what kills people than Uncle Odin's wife. We got oaths from everything not to hurt our men."

"Not just the mistletoe," said the light-skinned Hel. "We talked to roses and nettles, peanuts and potatoes."

"Asbestos and pitchblende," said the dark-skinned Hel, "snow and tornadoes."

"Plasma and lightning," they said together, "and everything else in the Nine Worlds."

"But the little mistletoe was the hardest bargainer," said the dark-skinned Hel.

"We gave it a thousand birds," they said together.

"We saw them coming here," Skadi said. "And we saw your snowflakes falling, and we saw your ice snake. Odin exiled you from Asgard and sent you down to the lowest worlds, Lady Hel. What right do you have to come to Jotunheim?"

"My heart's blood came here," the light-skinned Hel said. "Hymir's sea horse brought it up into the ocean that washes the banks of Midgard and Jotunheim."

"And Tyr brought it on his hands and his clothing," said the light-skinned Hel.

"And our brother is carrying it with him on his sword," they said together.

Fenris drew Justice and looked at Hel's blood shining on

the sword. "What do you want from me, Sisters?" he asked.

"You can keep the sword to remember us by," the two Hels said together. "All we want from you is your promise to come dance at our weddings."

"I'll promise that gladly," Fenris said.

"Farewell then," the two Hels said together.

"Say hello to Father for us, if you see him before we do," Baldur and Hodur said together. "And say hello from us to your father, too," Hodur added.

"I promise," said Fenris. "Say hello to Brother Orm if you see him before I do."

"I promise," said the dark-skinned Hel, stroking her gray cat's chest. Then she and her sister stepped aside, one to each side of the path.

"Onward, then," said Skadi, and led the way forward. There was a moment of cold silence when the party crossed between the two Hels. It wasn't just that the wolves stopped howling; you couldn't hear the sound of skis gliding through the snow, you couldn't hear the wind blowing through the trees, you couldn't hear yourself breathe. It wasn't just the wind that was cold, and a shiver ran down your spine; your breath felt cold as it came out between your lips and the blood felt cold in your veins. For a moment, everything was as cold and silent as the grave.

And then everything was back to normal again, and Skadi was leading the way up the mountainside.

The steep path finally leveled off and widened into a small valley between the towering Jotun mountains. In the center of the valley stood an oak tree, some of its branches bright with red leaves, some of them bare. A pile of red and brown leaves lay at its feet, encircled by a low stone wall.

The white Jotun wolf stopped in his tracks and growled:

his ears back, his legs stiff.

"Do the tree leaves in Hel's world grow the color of fresh blood?" Tidefyr asked.

"Hel trees bear green leaves," Drifa said. "This tree is almost as red as some of the ones I saw in Glasir Grove, outside the western gate of Valhalla."

"Some of us have been here twice before," Bookwyrm said impatiently, "and it's still trying to fool us. Where's Mimir's Fountain?"

"It's there in front of us," Skadi said, and the illusion shattered. There was the fountain of blood jetting up into the sky, but....

"Where are the giants?" Knut asked.

Ratatosk bravely ran forward and scampered around the unguarded fountain. "They're all gone," he yelled, "but they left their laptops." He fingered a keyboard and hit the ANY key (giants use special keyboards designed for Clue-Challenged Lusers) and the screen lit up to show the last message received.

ELEVENTH MONTH, TWELFTH DAY

BUILD THE SKIP THAT'LL CONQUER ASGARD AND VANAHEIM!

RUSH PROJECT! <u>MUST BE DONE BEFORE SUMMER'S EVE!</u>
BUILD THE BIGGEST SKIP IN THE NINE WORLDS!
ALL THE WORK YOU CAN HANDLE!
ALL THE **ALE** YOU CAN DRINK!
ALL THE **FOOD** YOU CAN EAT!
HYMIR WANTS EVERYBODY'S HELP!

HILL GIANTS AND FROST GIANTS AND SEA
    GIANTS!
LAND TROLLS AND WATER TROLLS!
MALES AND FEMALES!
OLD AND YOUNG!
EVERYBODY IN JOTUNHEIM!

**BRING BONES! BONES YOU HAVEN'T
    BROKEN! BONES YOU HAVEN'T
    CRACKED OPEN!**
BRING VANIR AND AESIR AND HUMAN AND
    ELF BONES FOR THEIR WEIGHT IN GOLD!
BRING GIANT AND TROLL BONES FOR A
    POUND OF GOLD EACH!

THIS MEANS YOU!
YOU AND ALL YOUR FRIENDS!
YOU AND ALL YOUR RELATIVES!
YOU AND EVERYBODY YOU KNOW!

THIS MEANS NOW!
RIGHT NOW!
NOT NEXT YEAR AND NOT NEXT WEEK AND
    NOT TOMORROW AND NOT AFTER
    DINNER!
NOW!

**COME TO HYMIRSTEAD FOR A PARTY
    YOU'LL NEVER FORGET!**
**HELP BUILD A SKIP THAT'LL WIN YOUR
    NAME! GLORY THAT WILL LAST
    FOREVER!**

For giants, it seemed a little understated but amazingly well proofread once Robin remembered that "skip" was Norse for "ship".

"He's building a new *Naglfar*," Fenris said grimly after reading the message. "He can't undo Bookwyrm's scorn-pole."

"He spent centuries building the old one," Bookwyrm said, "and it's still not ready to sail."

Ratatosk shrugged and ran over to check out another laptop. His inbox had over six hundred messages. He didn't bother to reply, just brought up the Nine Worlds News.

"It wasn't the eleventh month when we passed Midgard," Knut said.

"The Jotun year starts with Winter's Eve," Skadi told him. (In the upper worlds, that's the first Lady's Day after the Autumn Equinox. In Jotunheim, it's the first Moon Day.) "The next new moon will start the month of Autumn, and when that's done, it'll be half a year till Summer."

"There's not enough of us to fight all the giants in Jotunheim," Bookwyrm said. "Maybe we should go back to Valhalla and—"

"First we're going to the foot of the Rainbow Bridge," Robin Grima said. "After that we'll decide where—"

Ratatosk started laughing loudly.

"What's so funny?" the Valwolf asked, but the squirrel didn't have the spare breath to answer; he just pointed at the laptop screen and kept on laughing.

Robin Grima went over to look and read out the headline: "POETIC JUSTICE." Below that was a picture of a hillside covered with pieces of splintered wood, like a suburban block that's been hit by a tornado. Ratatosk's nimble thumb spun the trackball to raise the literacy level a bit higher (it was already way up from the frost giant's setting) and the headline changed to "Rune Rope Ruins." Robin read the first sentence and started laughing too.

"What does it say?" Drifa asked.

Bookwyrm read it aloud to her.

The rope Odin hanged himself with eons ago showed up in Niflheim recently with no visible means of support and was promptly seized by the mist elves on charges of vagrancy, necrophilia, lack of hygiene, and illegal border crossing. But the last laugh turned out to be on the mist elves, when Odin's rune rope sneaked (or should that be snaked?) out of confinement and coiled around Mist Hall, blocking all the exits. It tightened its grip till nothing was left of the mist elves' treasured home but a pile of rubble. Many of the mist elves died in the collapse, and the rest have gone into hiding. Odin was unavailable for comment, but his son Bragi says that the Aesir king hasn't had anything to do with that rope since he got his neck out of its coils and took the runes back home to Asgard. The rune rope was last seen crawling across Niflheim, destination unknown. Travel agencies are warning clients to avoid Niflheim until further notice. Discussion: Will the mist elves be missed?

(712 comments)"

"Well done, Rope," Knut said, patting the coils that circled his waist.

"How many days ago did it happen?" asked Fenris.

"The story's dated today," Bookwyrm said. "It doesn't say when the rope destroyed the mist elves' nice clean hall, but we got it back...." He paused to count; it's hard to keep track of days when there's no alternation of day and night, especially if you don't have a wristwatch. "The rope came back to us nearly two days ago. Does it matter?"

"I was just wondering whether it attacked the mist elves because they annoyed it by calling it 'filthy'," Fenris said, "or because you put up the scorn-pole and wrote that the land guardians of Niflheim would be sent astray so they couldn't find a resting place till they drove the *Naglfar* away."

"Who *are* the land guardians of Niflheim?" Robin asked.

Her companions looked at her in surprise at her ignorance. "The mist elves are," Bookwyrm said, and Knut and Skadi agreed.

"Someone's coming," the Valwolf warned. He was standing on the Jotunheim end of the pass, staring across the icy wasteland. "A dozen or more of them. Riding wolves."

Skadi strode to his side, then laughed. "It's only trolls. They won't dare challenge you to a fight you once they see that I'm with you."

But the trolls kept coming.

"I won't let then kill anyone under my protection," Fenris said.

Robin Grima put her hand on the hilt of her rope sword. "All for one and one for all," she said. "We've all sworn to protect one another."

"There's a Jotun wolf here with us," Drifa said. "Will you speak for us to your cousins, valiant wolf? Tell them that we treated you well." The one-eyed wolf didn't say anything, but then he'd never said anything.

"Maybe he's too dumb to speak," said Bookwyrm. "Or maybe he's under a curse to be silent. Or maybe he's just waiting till we all take him for granted and think we can safely turn our backs on him."

"He doesn't have to say a word to make me trust him," Drifa said. "He fought the ice snake for us." She turned away from the one-eyed wolf and walked over to Tidefyr, reaching up to put her hand on one of Garm's forefeet. "His pulse is stronger," she said. "I'll watch him for you if you want to be free to fight."

"You said he needed to keep warm," Tidefyr said. "I'm from Muspelheim, Valhallan. I'm warmer than you are."

The trolls galloped their white wolves up the mountainside toward us like a tidal wave cresting. The leader's wolf howled, and the rest of the pack took up the cry.

Some of the wolves were riderless with pack saddles strapped to their backs, not riding saddles, and they bore high piles of white bones.

They reached the head of the pass, and there they stopped. All but the leader, a female troll with long tangled white hair. She'd wrapped a white wolfskin around her hips, but her breasts were uncovered, hanging down to her waist. Snakes coiled down her arms like spiral armbands and another snake wrapped itself around her neck like a necklace, and they all three raised their heads and hissed at us. Her fingernails were long and pointed, and so were her teeth. She held a long white legbone in her left hand.

She rode forward to just a few yards away from Robin Grima and Skadi and Fenris. Then she drew back on her snakeskin reins, and her wolf-mount reared up on his hind legs, bringing her head up to a level with Fenris's.

"Hail, wisdom well watchers," she called. "We've lost our bearings. Which way is Hymirstead?"

"Down the mountainside again," Skadi said, "and then east to the seacoast."

"East is where the moon will be rising soon," Fenris added helpfully.

"Hymirstead's walls are built with blue-white ice," Robin Grima said.

"Thanks, wise ones," said the troll-wife. "We'll bring you a keg of ale once we've got Hymir's skip built." She let the reins slack, and her wolf went down onto four feet again. She kicked it in the side, and it galloped away, the other wolves parting to let it through, then turning to follow it.

Robin Grima put her rope sword back on her belt.

"What sort of bait do you use to catch an eye?" Knut asked. His companions turned to look at him and found that he'd thrown a few hundred feet of the rope into Mimir's Fountain.

"You don't have a hook on that, do you?" asked the Valwolf.

"I know better than that," Knut said. "It'll hold on well enough if it wants to. But what do I use for bait?"

"Try poetry," suggested Bookwyrm. "Odin came here wishing wisdom, thirsty for knowledge. He traded his eye for a drink from the fountain of Mimir's knowledge of the world's last days."

"'A better burden no man may bear when wandering wide than wisdom,'" Knut said, quoting the *Havamal*, Odin's own advice. "'It works better than wealth when you walk a strange way, and it grants a good refuge from grief.'"

"Baldur is risen," Drifa said, "beautiful and bright-eyed, next to his bride. His dark brother Hodur walks close beside him. Their father might need two eyes to see both of them."

"The rope remembers the beat of Odin's blood," the Valwolf said, "and the burden of his breath. Has his left eye forgotten them? Has it quarreled with his right eye, so it doesn't want to go home?"

Then they were all silent, staring at Robin Grima. "You've got to say something too," Knut told her. "You're our leader."

"I'm not a poet," Robin said.

"Then recite a Vinland poem about eyes," said Bookwyrm.

Robin could write term papers about a poem's meaning and meter, its social context and philosophical implications, but she'd seldom bothered to read a poem aloud and taste it on her tongue and let it echo in her ears and in her heart. She'd liked Shakespeare's "My mistress' eyes are nothing like the sun," but she didn't think Odin's eye would appreciate the sonnet's dark humor, and besides Shakespeare was British, not American. Finally she remembered a few lines from a Robert Frost poem and said, "'My object in living is to unite my avocation and my vocation, as my two eyes make one in sight.'"

"Are you still thirsty for Mimir's wealth of wisdom, Uncle?" Fenris asked. "There's a wide world out here, waiting for you to take a three-dimensional look at it."

The eye bobbed about in the fountain, sometimes flirtatiously nearing the rope, then diving away again.

"I don't think it wants to come out," Robin Grima said finally, and nobody disagreed with her.

Knut pulled the rope out and coiled it back around his waist. "It's a long way to the foot of the Rainbow Bridge," he said. "Maybe we should have a drink before we go."

"No!" Robin Grima yelled, remembering Frostbite's voice whispering in her mind. "I was warned not to do that. If you drink from Mimir's Fountain, then you'll see the same future that he did. We're not on this quest to learn the prophecies. Our mission is to change them!"

"The moon's rising," said Tidefyr.

"Is there anything more we need to do or to learn here?" Robin Grima asked. She looked from face to face, but nobody had any suggestions, so they gathered around Tidefyr, as her moonlight circle grew brighter and more clearly defined. Tidefyr walked forward, and the circle of moonlight moved with her; Jotunheim fell away and Midgard appeared. The crescent moon shone in the eastern sky, and the Rainbow Bridge shone on the mountain peaks as it arched high up into the heavens, spanning the way from Midgard to Asgard.

CHAPTER SEVENTEEN

The last time we'd visited Loki's cave, the sun was shining and the mountainside was dark. This time it was night, and the mountainside was bright with thousands of little gold flames.

"We didn't notice anything like this the last time we were here," Robin Grima said. She bent over to look at the flames more closely and found they were small yellow flowers, each one with a center stalk of gold fire. She picked one and held it out for the others to look at.

Fenris touched it with an index finger and then jumped back. "It's not an illusion," he said. "It's a real flame."

"The outer petals look like a crowfoot," Drifa said. "If that's what they are, then their sap will blister your skin even better than the fire at their heart, and if you suck your burnt fingers and swallow the sap, it'll give you a bloody flux." Robin dropped the flower hastily, then spat on her fingers and wiped them off on her cloak.

"We bathed in Nidhog's blood," Bookwyrm said. "That ought to protect us from burns."

"It ought to protect you from normal burns," his wife said

patiently. She waved her hand at the bright flowers. "Those aren't normal."

"No, they aren't," agreed Tidefyr. "Their flames drown out the moonlight. A normal fire won't do that."

"Maybe they'll go to sleep at sunrise," Robin Grima said, "but I'd rather not wait that long."

"I'm not fond of sunlight," Skadi said.

"Maybe I can put them to sleep now," Drifa said, and unknotted a bag from her belt and spilled out the sleep-thorns she'd gathered from her companions. She cast a handful of them across the mountainside like a farmwife throwing grain to chickens, and a moment later there was a trail of darkness leading up the slope to the cave mouth.

"Fenris, have you ever been here before?" the Valwolf asked.

"No," Fenris said. "What about you, little know-it-all? How often have you been here before?"

"I came here the first time when they bound him," said the Valwolf, "and I came here again last week with my friend Knut. In between, I passed my time keeping watch at Valhalla. This door is smaller than the one I guarded. How did you get through it to hang your snake, Lady Skadi?"

"I crawled," she said, and went down on her hands and knees toward the cave mouth. Fenris did the same. Tidefyr just strode forward, growing shorter with every step she took till she was only a little taller than Knut.

Once we were inside, Tidefyr's moonlight showed the Valhallans all the details they'd missed on their first trip. There were paintings on the black stone walls and ceiling done in red and white. First there was Baldur's Ordeal, with the Aesir attacking him, and then there was Loki bringing Hodur the shoot of mistletoe, and then there was Baldur's death and the red blood flowing from his wounds.

The cave bent to the left and then to the right, and we

walked past scenes of folk weeping when they heard the news of Baldur's death and Hel's promise that their tears might bring him back again. Aesir and Vanir, elves and giants and humans, everyone wept for Baldur. And then there she was on the cave wall, smiling at us, the dry-eyed giantess who said her name was Thokk, Thanks, and cried out, "I never loved him. Let Hel keep him." And over her head the artist had written Loki's name.

We walked past the pictures and into a chamber as bright as sunlight, where Loki lay on the black floor, arms and legs each bound to a stalagmite, his eyes closed. A thin trickle of blood oozed slowly out from under his left eyelid.

Over his head, a golden snake hung from a stalactite, and shining gold drops of venom dripped down in his eyes and in his nostrils and in his mouth, leaving glowing red trails along his white skin. Fenris walked forward and held out his hand under the snake's mouth and then brought it up to his nose. "It smells like Asgard."

"Wolf nose show-off," the Valwolf muttered.

Skadi laughed. "Idunn gave me one of her apples when she found me hiding in the cellar after Father beat me. When Loki came to take her back to Asgard, Idunn asked me to come with her, but I knew I wouldn't be welcome there, so she gave me another apple and kissed me goodbye. I kept it in the cellar to smell it and think of her, but it didn't stay a golden apple long in Jotunheim; it turned into a serpent."

"Shape doesn't matter as much as most people think," Loki said. His body writhed, and he began turning into a woman. By the time the transformation was finished, her left eye had stopped bleeding.

Robin Grima sat down on the wet floor next to Loki's left foot and began taking the pieces of her broken sword out of its scabbard. They still shone silver, the light pulsing steadily between bright and dim, and the metal felt warm on her fingers. *"Sword,"* she thought, *"can you hear me?"* but there was no answer. *"We went through the fire ordeal together,"* she thought. *"We went through so much together. You came into my dreams and said, 'I think I'm falling in love with you.' Please don't really be dead. And if you are, then please don't stay dead."*

The Valwolf came over and laid down next to her and put his head on her lap. She rumpled his ears with her left hand. "Don't cut Loki's bindings," he said.

"I won't. Don't eat them."

"Not as long as I stay sane, but I can't promise more than that."

"Welcome," said a woman's voice. Robin didn't bother to look up. She was trying to untie the binding, but it was covered with frozen blood. She picked up a piece of the silver sword's tip and laid its warmth gently against the knot. "Let me wash your hands, dear," the woman said.

Robin held them up and felt the water on her fingers as warm as a kiss, and then the soft dry towel. "Thank you," she said, and looked up to see a smiling face with bright blue eyes and golden red hair like a spring sunrise. "I'm sorry," she said. "I don't recognize you."

"We met last week," the woman said, "but that was before your friend gave me an apple. I'm Sigyn Lokiswife." She knelt down and washed the Valwolf's feet. "Did Tyr bring you again? Is he waiting outside?"

"He left us after he brought us to Asgard," Robin said.

"We haven't seen him since he crossed swords with our leader, and both their swords broke," said Ratatosk.

"He refused to be my champion," Tidefyr said, "and he left the dueling circle with Hymir, even after he heard Hymir call me a runaway thrall."

"Poor broken sword," Sigyn said. She sprinkled warm water on Frostbite's silver shards, then got up and walked over to welcome her other guests.

"Odin's fetter can drive an army insane with fear or a warrior insane with battle lust," the Valwolf said softly. "Were you ever insane, Robin Grima?"

Robin remembered the way she'd felt after her breasts had been amputated and she'd had her first few weeks of chemo, when her periods stopped and the hot flashes started and a good night was when she had four whole hours of sleep before she woke up with her bald head wet with sweat and stripped off the soaked sheets and put fresh ones on the bed and had a cold shower. Everything made her angry, and the doctor said it was just a testosterone imbalance. He made jokes about how now she could appreciate the masculine viewpoint, and she knew he was plotting against her. "Yes," she said quietly. "I've been insane."

She put the rest of Frostbite's pieces back into its scabbard and then pressed the warm silver shard of her sword's tip against the ice-cold binding. *"This was all your idea,"* she thought. *"You asked me to break you against Justice. Please don't be dead, Frostbite. I think I've fallen in love with you."* She put down the metal and touched the cord. It was still terribly cold but no longer frozen. She found an end and gently worked it out of the knot and began to unwind the length of gut off the stalagmite.

"No one from Muspelheim has ever come here to visit us," Sigyn said, staring at Tidefyr. "What relation was Tyr Hymirson to you before he disowned you?"

"He used to be my first-born son," Tidefyr said, "but now Garm is my only son," she lowered her head and kissed Garm's gray-furred cheek, "and he's your husband's only grandson."

"Garm's welcome here," Sigyn said, "and so are you, and so is his father. Why did you come here, Fenris?"

"My wife-to-be wanted to meet my father and foster

mother," Fenris said. He reached out to touch Tidefyr's hand and then Garm's face. "This is Tidefyr, daughter of Burnt Moon and niece of King Surt. And this is Garm, our son. This week is the first time I've seen either of them since I was fettered." He knelt down by Loki's head and said, "Trickster, I spent centuries hating you for never visiting me in Frigga's hall, for never warning me against Tyr's tricks, for never helping me escape. But I've learned a lot in the last few days, and I think I'm beginning to understand you, and I apologize. I should have known better than to believe you when you told me not to trust you."

Loki laughed and opened her eyes, both of them bright gold, just like the snake's venom.

"I came to ask for my freedom," the Valwolf said.

Loki laughed again and shook her arms. "You want a prisoner to set you free?"

"Yes, Father," said the Valwolf.

Robin Grima unwound the binding from around Loki's left ankle and then—slowly, gently—untied the knot that held it to the stalagmite. The cord still felt ice cold in her hands. She laid it down on the stone floor, wet with the sweet-smelling venom from Idunn's apple-serpent, and then put the warm silver shard on top of it. She rested her fingers on the warm metal till they didn't feel frozen any more. *"Sword,"* she thought, but nothing answered, nothing happened.

"Don't let anyone step on this," she told the Valwolf.

"Knut," the Valwolf said, "if you love me, then guard Frost-biter for me. I'll guard Robin Grima."

Knut stood by Robin Grima's scabbard, and the Valwolf followed Robin as she crawled over to another stalagmite.

"It looks like you won't need my snake any more," Skadi said. She reached out over Loki's head, and the snake wound down her arm and then up onto her head so it was like a golden wreath in her hair.

"You look like a queen," Loki said. "Nobody's asked how I'm feeling these days, and up until a moment ago I'd have said that I can't kick, but now," the left leg moved, "I can." Her body began changing back to a man again. "That's more than your house guests could do the last time I saw them. How are their chains holding out now that Fenris walks free?"

"Stronger than ever," she said, "but I don't remember what the wordsmith from Valhalla rewove them with."

Fenris repeated Robin Grima's list of six impossible things, while Robin sat by Loki's right foot and ran her fingers over the cold cord till she found an end and began to work it free. A chill ran up her arm and down her spine, and she shivered till the Valwolf lay down beside her with his warm head on her lap.

"There might be a stone somewhere that can hear a tree fall," Sigyn said, "but the other ones sound strong."

"All the birds cried when they heard that Baldur had died," Loki said, "but only Odin's Thought could fly back in time to fetch their tears."

"That's true," Sigyn said, "and I can't think of any news that would make them cry again. How secure is Valhalla's western door now that it only has two guardians?"

"Valhalla doesn't need guarding as much as Robin Grima does," said the Valwolf. "She's our leader, and I've sworn an oath on her sword: one for all, and all for one. The sword may be broken now, but my oath still stands."

Robin got the knot untied, then stopped to get another piece of Frostbite out of her scabbard. She began to unwind the binding, wondering whether Loki would say that now he could kick twice as much, but she did Trickster an injustice; he doesn't repeat his jokes; he always has something new to offer or offend.

"There's a second wolf here with you," Sigyn said.

"Maybe he's the Valwolf's new boyfriend," said Loki.

"He is not!" said the Valwolf loudly and firmly. "We met him in Jotunheim, and he helped us fight the ice snake. You've already met my best friend, Knut Vidarson once called Knut Nine-Toes and now called Valwolf Friend, a valiant fighter and good companion."

"As are you," Knut said, not taking his eyes off of Frostbite's shattered pieces.

"Sword," Robin thought, but there wasn't an answer. She crawled over to Loki's left hand, and the Valwolf padded softly after her. Behind them, Knut experimentally brought the two pieces of silver sword together and saw them join into one as if they'd never been broken, and the two pieces of gut cord join into one longer cord.

"Welcome, Knut Vidarson," Sigyn said.

"Welcome, Knut Valwolf Friend," Loki said. "A wind told us good things about you. Would you forgive the Valwolf if he ever got hungry and ate you?"

"If we were both starving, I'd share my last bite of food with him," Knut said. "And if the gods drove him insane with hunger, then I wouldn't hold it against him if he ate me."

"Brave words," said Loki, "though you might find them hard to say after you died screaming in agony."

"I've already died once in Midgard," said Knut, remembering the duel as his enemy's sword cut him again and again till at last he found a way past sword and shield to his enemy's heart and drove his own sword into it before dying of blood loss. "It wasn't altogether painless, and neither were the deaths I suffered each day in Valhalla. Have you ever died, Loki?"

Robin Grima had picked up dozens of silver sword shards, but now there were only three pieces of Frostbite left in her scabbard, the hilt and two pieces of the upper blade.

She pulled out one piece of the blade and felt its warmth in her hands, then laid it on the floor and began to unknot the cord that bound Loki's left wrist to its stalagmite.

"No," said Loki. "I've never died. Both of Odin's brothers died when he sent them to Vanaheim as hostages, but that was after they tried seizing Asgard from him and said they'd share his wife between them. I've never threatened Odin, and I've never died."

"You killed Odin's son and then you wouldn't weep for him to bring him back to life," Ratatosk said.

"I brought dark Hodur the mistletoe that killed bright Baldur, who should have been betrothed to his father's foster-brother's daughter," Loki said, "and both Baldur and Hodur went to Hel on that account, but that's all. You shouldn't repeat false gossip, little squirrel. It doesn't hurt nearly as much as the truth, and the truth is that I wept for poor Baldur just like everyone else who heard the news except for the stone-hearted Thokk."

The Jotun wolf howled, and Drifa knelt down and took off his old dressing off and washed his eye socket and bound on fresh new herbs against pain.

Robin Grima unwound the cord off of Loki's left wrist and laid it on top of Frostbite's shard. Knut crawled forward and took it, and laid it next to the other pieces he was watching, putting the broken sword back together like a child's jigsaw puzzle.

"I'm left-handed," Loki said. "I could take care of the last one myself if you're getting tired."

"I'm not tired," Robin said and crawled over to Loki's right wrist. She pulled out the last piece of Frostbite's blade and warmed her fingers on it and on the Valwolf's warm fur. Then she began to pick the knot apart.

"There's still another new face here," Sigyn said. "Who's the new human who wears a sword from Valhalla?"

"My wife," Bookwyrm said.

"My name is Drifa Fridisdaughter," the woman said. "I died once in my bed and spent a thousand years with Hel before she let me leave her realm with my husband and die a better death at Mimir's Fountain, between Hymir's teeth. A valkyrie took me to Valhalla, and Odin gave me my sword and told me I was free to wait for my husband or go out in search of him."

"How is my daughter Hel doing?" Loki asked.

"That last time we saw her she was beside herself," Ratatosk said.

"We saw my sister two days ago," Fenris said, "in the dueling circle, between Niflheim and Hel. She lay dead and cut in two, a left half and a right half, and her blood was on Hymir's sword. Baldur held her right side and Hodur her left side, and both of them seemed grieved for her death. And then, earlier tonight, we saw her again, two women, both whole, sometimes speaking each by herself and sometimes together, and they invited me to come dance at their weddings to the Odinsons. They'll be married next year at Summer's Eve."

"I'll try to be free to attend," Loki said.

The Valwolf laughed at the wordplay. "We saw your son Orm last week," he said, "when Hymir took us fishing. Orm offered him all the bones off the sea bottom if Hymir would let him eat us, and Hymir agreed, but Orm said that Lady Drifa made him a better offer, and he let us go."

Robin Grima unwound Loki's last binding and then undid the knot that bound it to the stalagmite, and laid the cord on the last piece of Frostbite's blade.

Loki stood up and laughed, and his laughter echoed around the room. He waved his arms and legs about wildly, and then began to dance round and round the room, laughing maniacally, his long hair tossing about. "Free!" he screamed. Robin shivered, suddenly unsure if she'd done the right thing.

Fenris threw back his head and howled, and the Jotun wolf joined in, but the Valwolf stood silently next to Robin, his ears back. Sigyn clapped her hands to her ears and ran out of the room. Robin Grima's hand went to her rope sword, but she didn't draw it.

Loki's hands flew up and down his naked body, rubbing his nose, his chin, his neck, his chest. He swung his hips to and fro as he rubbed his back against a stalactite. "Free at last!" he screamed. "Three thousand years without being able to scratch an itch, and now I'm free!" He walked over to Tidefyr and asked quietly, "May I hold my grandson?"

She held Garm out to him, and he took the huge gray dog in his arms.

"He has soul and sense," Loki said, "but that's not enough, is it?"

"When Odin and his brothers made humans," Bookwyrm said, "you were the one who gave them heat."

"I still can," said Loki and bent down and kissed Garm's head, and the dog's yellow eyes opened.

"Put me down," Garm said.

Loki dropped him.

Garm landed on his feet and walked around the room, smelling people. "Mother," he said to Tidefyr, and "Father," to Fenris. He went to Robin Grima and said, "Leader. I saw you in Hel's realm after you killed Nidhog and watered the World Tree's roots with her blood." Then he went to Drifa and said, "I saw you there too, axe woman. You helped us fight off the Dead Shore folk."

"I'm a Valhallan now," Drifa said, "and I carry the sword Odin gave me."

"Don't everyone be so formal," Loki said. "It's a family

reunion." He danced over to Fenris and kissed him, kissed Tidefyr, kissed Garm again, kissed the Valwolf, kissed Skadi.

Knut took the last pieces of cord and sword blade and brought them to join the other pieces. "Stay free of the sword, or you'll get hurt," he warned Loki.

Loki stopped dancing. He stood motionless, silent, staring at the sword.

"What happens next?" asked the Valwolf. "How much longer does he have to be brave?"

"I want him back just as much as you do," Robin said. She pulled the silver sword hilt out of her scabbard and placed it at the top of the broken sword. It shone brightly, steadily. *"Sword,"* she thought, touching her fingers to the hilt, but there still wasn't an answer. The pieces all fitted together without any gaps, but the sword was still broken and lifeless.

"When I first saw you," Knut said, "you were climbing out of Thunder River, and a valkyrie flew by and gave you your scabbard and sword belt and sword. Maybe you need to put all of them together again for this healing."

"Maybe I do," said Robin. She took off her white scabbard and sword belt and laid them gently on top of Frostbite, but it didn't make any difference. "Any other suggestions?" she asked. "Should I weep for him the way people did for Baldur? Should I ask Bookwyrm to write runes on him? Should I ask Knut to write a poem about him? Should I ask Drifa to put healing herbs on him? Should I take him back to the courtyard of Valhalla and see if the sunset horn heals his wounds so he can rise from the dead? What should I do?" She wiped the tears out of her eyes and shook the saltwater onto the sword and its scabbard but nothing changed.

"Whatever you do," Skadi said, "it'll be sunrise in a couple of hours. Tidefyr, you promised to take me back to Jotunheim before sunrise."

"I promised to meet Hymir this morning," Tidefyr said,

"and wrestle him till one of us subdued the other. Shall I take you back to your home, Skadi, or will you come with me to the beach at Hymirstead?"

"I'll come with you," Skadi said. "You might need a friend to guard your back if Hymir decides to cheat."

"And what about the brave sword?" asked Loki. "He's all guts and backbone, but nothing more. Where did the rest of him go?"

"You know where it went!" yelled the Valwolf.

"Yes, but not as well as you do," Loki yelled back.

"That's true," said the Valwolf and walked away from Robin Grima's side to stand in front of Loki. "If you need to tear me apart to heal him, then go ahead," he said.

"It's not your fault," said Sigyn, coming back with an armful of clothing and four scabbards which she hung on a stalagmite.

"No, it's not," said Fenris. "The person to blame is the one who wouldn't cry for Baldur but was too much of a coward to come forward and clear Father's name."

"I agreed to the plan," Loki said. He stepped into a pair of white underbreeches and then ankle-length red trousers, and then pulled a long-sleeved, knee-length white shirt over his head, the neck and cuffs and hem bright with gold thread. He stepped into black leather slippers that were bright with gold beads. There were four white scabbards, all of them empty, still hanging on the stalagmite, but he didn't take any of them.

"Thanks for your consent," he said. Then he knelt down and began pulling out the Valwolf's fur, handful after handful of gray hair, bleeding at the roots, throwing it over Frostbite's shards until there was nothing to see but a pile of gray fur. The Valwolf stood there, silent and shivering, his white skin covered with lines of beading blood drops, looking much smaller, as if half of him had been his fur. Then he screamed in agony, as Loki reached down and pulled off his right ear, leaving a bleeding wound.

"No!" Knut screamed.

"Yes," whispered the Valwolf, and Knut took his hand from his sword hilt.

"Please, Father!" Fenris screamed. "I swore I'd protect him. We all swore we'd protect each other. He rescued me, once from the fetter and once from Hymir."

"He gave his consent," Loki said. "You heard him."

"We all heard him," Robin Grima said, surprised to find that her throat wasn't too dry to speak, that her voice didn't tremble.

Loki was smiling sweetly, like a berserk getting ready to fight a duel, like a man looking at his wife holding his newborn baby. He tore off the Valwolf's left ear, and then he tore off his penis, and after that his hands were moving too fast to see, tearing off chunks of bleeding flesh and tossing them onto the pile of gray fur. The Valwolf screamed till Loki tore out his throat, and from then on he was silent.

Fenris stared grimly at his father. Sigyn shut her eyes. Knut was sobbing.

Robin Grima stood there with her hand on the hilt of her rope sword, but she didn't draw it. She just stared at the Valwolf as his body got smaller and smaller, bloodier and bloodier, trying to make sure that she saw everything in case some day she had to testify about it in court.

And she noticed that none of the Valwolf's blood got on Loki's white shirt or on his face or even on his hands. It just clung tight to the chunks of flesh that Loki tore off and threw on top of the gray fur, on top of the white scabbard, on top of Frostbite's silver shards. Soon she couldn't see silver or white or gray any more, just bloody flesh, and there was nothing left of the Valwolf but a skeleton of burning bones.

"Don't take too long, Trickster," Skadi warned. "It will

dishonor Tidefyr if she's late to her duel with Hymir."

There was a sudden burst of intense light. (*"Like being caught inside a lightning bolt,"* Knut thought. *"Like holding a fire giant in your arms as she trembled in orgasm,"* Fenris thought. *"Like having a thousand flashbulbs go off in your face,"* Robin thought.)

When Robin opened her eyes again, at first all she could see was dancing black spots.

"Now that didn't take too long, did it?" Loki asked. "There's still lots of time till sunrise. Can Sigyn and I come with you? I love to watch duels."

"Robin Grima's our leader," Knut said. "Ask her."

"Skadi and the Jotun wolf didn't swear our oath," Tidefyr said, "but they're following us anyway."

"I haven't sworn your oath," Garm said, "but I heard it when you were in Hel's realm, and I'll swear it now if you let me."

"I never swore Robin Grima's oath," said a man's voice. "I've been with her from the start, though, and I think I heard her say once that she wanted me to stay with her."

Robin stretched out her hand toward the voice, and touched another hand, warm and strong. *"Frostbite?"* she thought, and suddenly her eyes were full of tears, which didn't make any sense because he wasn't broken any more, and there was nothing to cry about.

"My name is Kalinn," the man said. "Or you may call me Frost. And my sister's name is Kari, or you may call her Wind."

"Your sister," said Knut, and stared silently at the beautiful girl with long dark hair and sky-blue eyes in gray robes trimmed with wolf fur, with a swan feather cloak hanging from her shoulders.

I hadn't seen Kari Lokisdaughter in her true form for a

long time. I remembered her as a little girl, running around Asgard with her father, flying over Asgard with her mother. I remembered when the gods changed her from a beautiful young woman weeping for Baldur Odinson to a ravenously hungry male wolf who ate up her brother.

"She's my sister too," said Fenris, "and he's my brother, and I've been in their company for days, but I didn't recognize either of them." Garm silently went over to his new-found uncle and aunt and sniffed their ankles.

Robin was silent too, but that was because she was too busy kissing Frost Kalinn to say anything.

Knut walked over to Wind Kari, close enough to touch her, but he didn't. Norse law fined a man half a mark (that's four ounces of pure silver) for touching a free woman "unseemingly" on the wrist or ankle, and another three ounces for touching her on the knee or elbow. Kissing her in public was a lot more expensive, and made it lot less likely that her father would award her hand in marriage to someone with such bad manners and such an empty purse. So Knut just said, "I saw you in my dreams, and I hoped that someday I'd find you and introduce you to the Valwolf."

She laughed. "I can put on swan form and fly through the air," she said, "or I can put on wolf form and run across the land, but I won't guard Valhalla any more. What form do you want me in?"

"I want you," Knut said, "in any form that you like, and I want to marry you if your father will accept me, but I still don't have any gifts to bring as a bride-price."

"You brought me back my daughter," Loki said. "That's a magnificent gift. But I stipulate that the two of you have to know one another in human form for a year and a day before you announce your wedding date. And as for you two...." He looked over at Robin Grima and Frost Kallinn who were holding hands and staring into each other's eyes. Kalinn had the same starshine silver hair as Fenris, but his eyes were gray, not silver, and he had his own face, more like Sigyn's than like Loki's. He wore white clothing, the same color as Frostbite's scabbard. Robin didn't hear any violin music or see shooting stars and hearts and flowers, but her lips still felt warm where Frost Kalinn's lips had touched them, and she'd never imagined she could feel so happy.

"I'm willing to wait a year and a day as well," Frost Kalinn said. "My blood sister and I have got lots of time to get to know one another."

"No, you don't, my son," Loki said. "You won't live to see sunset if you go to Hymirstead today without a weapon."

"I made a rope sword for Robin Grima," Knut said, "and I can make another one for Frost Kalinn."

"Don't waste Odin's precious rope," Loki said. "You may need all you've got and more before the day is done." He kicked at one of the stalagmites he'd been bound to, and it broke free from the cavern floor. He swung it up against a stalactite, and the limestone coating flaked off and revealed a gleaming steel sword inside. He held it out, and Kalinn took it by the hilt. He touched its tip to the floor, and the apple snake's juice turned into gold ice around the sword tip.

"You haven't lost your touch," Loki said, and Frost Kalinn laughed. Sigyn held out one of the empty scabbards to him, and he sheathed his sword in it and tied its belt around his waist.

"Did Nidhog's blood lose its power?" Knut asked. "It was supposed to protect anyone who bathed in it from wounds, and the Valwolf rolled in it from nose to tail."

"It protected me from every wound," Wind Kari said, laughing. "Giving my brother back the flesh I stole from him was a healing for both of us, not a wounding."

"Anyone else want a sword?" Loki asked.

Robin Grima handed her rope sword back to Knut and

said, "Yes, please." Knut sang to the sword till it was soft rope again and joined back to the rest of the rune rope.

Loki kicked down a second stalagmite and gave Robin Grima the sword inside it, and Sigyn handed her a scabbard.

"Anyone else?" Loki asked. "Speak up if you want a sword. We don't want to be late to the party at Hymirstead."

"I fight best in wolf form," Fenris said. "And I plan to marry Lady Tidefyr as soon as we can."

"I told Hymir to bring the neighbors to our duel so I could name them as witnesses to the divorce," Tidefyr said, "but there are enough people here even if he goes back on his word."

"Grandson," Loki said, "do you give your consent to your parents getting married so soon? Or do you think they need to spend longer getting acquainted?"

Garm wagged his tail stiffly. "I think you're trying to make us all nervous," he said, "I think that they should get married whenever they want to, but that we ought to invite Uncle Orm and Aunt Hel. Both Aunt Hels."

"You're a wise fellow, Grandson," Loki said. "Last chance for a sword."

"I don't need a sword, Father," Wind Kari said. "I have my own skills."

"As do I," said Tidefyr.

Loki laughed and kicked down the other two stalagmites he'd been bound to and freed two more swords. He took one in each hand, and hit the left hand sword against the right one, like a stage magician playing with interlocking rings. Once, twice, three times—and then suddenly both swords were gone and his hands were empty, and Sigyn's hands that had held the last two scabbards were empty too.

"I've got everything that I want," Loki said. "Let's go."

"First we'll swear our oath," said Robin Grima. "People

who don't want to swear it may still come with us, but we aren't pledged to protect them." She held out her new sword, and Kalinn laid his sword across it, and both swords flared bright silver, and the air hummed around them. (*"Like a hot foehn wind sweeping across the forest,"* Knut thought. *"Like the valkyries singing,"* Fenris thought. *"Like a high tension wire,"* Robin thought.)

Knut and Bookwyrm drew their Valhallan swords and touched them to where the two swords crossed, and Drifa followed their example.

This time everyone swore the oath except for the one-eyed Jotun wolf.

Robin looked at her party and thought about their strengths and their weaknesses. They didn't have anyone with healing magic, though Drifa's box of herbs was better than nothing. Frost Kalinn hadn't bathed in dragon blood, and he didn't have any armor. They didn't have any thieves—well, maybe Loki, but his real strength seemed to be Fast Talk, not Open Lock or Pickpocket. (If she'd known clothing design better, she'd have realized that the modern world is the only one with locks or pockets. Back in the old days people didn't put padlocks on chests or carry house keys or sew clothing with pockets, so there weren't any lock picks or pickpockets yet, but there were already robbers and sneak thieves. You put your valuables into a chest, and you put warriors to guard your chest—and robbers tried to beat up the warriors and steal your valuables. You kept your silver and gold and jewels in a bag tied on your belt, and a sneakthief used a little knife and cut your bag. Robin should have remembered her Shakespeare. Hamlet called his uncle "a cutpurse of the empire." A beginning cutpurse would cut a purse off a belt. A skilled one could cut the purse at the side and light finger out the best items from it.) Well, at least they had Knut and Bookwyrm for magic users, and there were lots of fighters.

Outside the cave mouth, the sky was still dark except for the faint light of the crescent moon. The burning flowers were still there. As Loki came out of the cave mouth, the flowers suddenly blazed up as tall as a man. The Jotun wolf stood up on its hind legs and howled, its ears erect and its fur bristling. Fenris howled too, and so for a moment did Wind Kari who used to be the Valwolf. She stopped abruptly and shook her head. Knut reached out and touched her ear, then changed his target to stroke her long silky hair. Fenris didn't seem embarrassed at having joined in the howling, but then he was born in wolf form, not like Kalinn and Kari who were both born in human form.

Drifa cast a handful of dark sleep-thorns down the mountainside, but it wasn't enough, and she had to use up all she had in the bag before there was a dark trail. We walked warily downhill, till at last we were out of the mountain's shadow and standing in the moonlight. Then Tidefyr gathered us around her, and she walked with the moonlight, out of Midgard and into Jotunheim, back once more to Hymirstead.

CHAPTER EIGHTEEN

"The beach where we first met," Hymir had said. It wasn't at Hymirstead but a little down the coast, out of sight of Hymirstead's blue-white glow. The sea was down to low tide but starting to rise. Did that mean Hymir's powers were at their lowest but starting to grow?

"Hymir caught me at moonset and bound ice bracelets on me," Tidefyr had said. The crescent moon hung at the top of the sky. Did that mean Tidefyr's powers were at their highest but starting to lessen?

"Bring the neighbors," Tidefyr had said, and there they were. Aegir, king of the sea giants, stood in the sea up to his knees, along with his nine daughters and their son Heimdall, who doesn't always stay home in Asgard. No, that doesn't mean that one of the girls bore a head and two bore the right and left arms, and so on, and then they sat down and sewed them together. It means that one morning the nine girls came to breakfast with a baby, and said they'd all sworn to be his foster mothers and not to tell which of them gave birth to him. They also never admitted who the father was, and Heimdall got teased enough about that little detail that he left home and went to Asgard, taking his kinsman Tyr along with him, and they both became Odin's foster sons.

Some of the other sea giants were there too. Kott and Osgrui and Alfarin, Vind and Vindsval and Vipar, Vidblind and Vignir, Rangbein and Leifi.

"I told you she'd be early," Leifi said, and held out his hand for Alfarin to pay off his bet.

Then they went back to setting the terms for the rest of their wagering. Not that any of them thought Tidefyr had a chance of winning. They were betting on how long it would take, on what hold Hymir would use to throw her, on which part of her body would touch the ground first.

Hymir's nine-headed mother was there too, each of her heads placing its own bets.

Tyr stood next to his grandmother, but he wasn't betting. A blood-red scabbard hung from his belt on his right side so he could draw it with his left hand—even though the Norns had given him back his right hand, the one that Fenris had bitten off.

"I see you've got a new sword," Ratatosk yelled. "Have you got a new horse too, or did all the stallions you've asked turn you down because they wanted a rider who wouldn't let his stablemate's head get chopped off?" Tyr didn't answer.

"The new ship's nearly finished," Robin Grima said, pointing up the beach, away from Hymirstead, to the white shining length of the new bone ship. She was the same length and width as the old *Naglfar*, but her sides were already higher. Her center mast towered up into the sky, and a great sail hung from it. The giants and trolls were busy putting up the lesser masts, one every thousand feet.

"Where's Hymir's party?" Drifa asked. "I see the sea waves, but I don't see any cauldrons of ale. I see benches on the sand, but I don't see any feasting tables covered with platters of meat. I see the bones Hymir asked for, but where's the gold he promised?"

"All the water here is Hymir's ale bowl," Tidefyr said, "and his feasting tables are set up on the waves. The gold's in the chests you mistook for benches. I've dusted those chests every month for centuries, and—"

"I can see you standing over there, bedmate!" Hymir yelled. "Don't be shy. Come wrestle a fall with me, and then we'll go back home and start making plans for our wedding."

Tidefyr kissed Fenris, and then walked away from us, toward Hymir. Fenris fell to his knees and his shape changed back to wolf. Wind Kari helped him struggle out of his human clothing once the change was finished. Garm was whimpering, his tail tucked between his legs, his ears back.

Once it was quiet again, Loki said, "I'll bet a hundred ounces of gold that there aren't any wolves in this group when the day's over." Nobody took his bet.

Down the beach, Hymir and Tidefyr were drawing their wrestling circle on the wet sand.

"I don't like that sail," Drifa said, pointing at the new *Naglfar*.

"I can't see it well enough to know what I think of it," Robin Grima said.

"The warp threads still have weights hanging from them," Drifa said, "and they're human skulls. The weaving shows the battle of Ragnarok, everybody fighting and everybody dying."

"It's the cloth we saw the Norns weaving," Knut said. "They gave Tyr's hand to Tidefyr, and they gave their tapestry to Hymir. If the Norns are against us, then Ragnarok's going to happen!"

Loki laughed. "I'd better go to Muspelheim then," he said, and ran off.

"Father's a generous fellow," Fenris said. "He's giving us another chance to distrust him."

"'An axe age, a sword age,'" Knut chanted. "'A wind age, a wolf age.'" He stopped and stared at Wind Kari. "The Valwolf's gone," he said, "and so is my nickname."

"Knut Nidhogsbane," said Wind Kari. "Knut Rune Rope Bearer. Knut Windfriend. Knut Karislove."

"If I take one of those, you'll owe me two nickname presents," Knut said, "but I'll wait to collect them till we've declared our betrothal."

"Quiet down, everybody!" yelled Skadi. "The fight's about to start."

In Midgard, they'd have started out the wrestling match by asking Thor to bless it and see that justice was done, and then they'd have shaken hands. But Hymir and Tidefyr were both giants. She held out her hand to him, but he didn't take it; he just rushed at her and gripped her tight. Sport wrestlers grip each other at the thigh and hip, but Hymir caught hold of Tidefyr by her left breast and her right elbow, and she caught hold of him by the left side of his neck and his right thigh. The good news was that he hadn't set up a fang-hella, a waist-high wedge of stone to throw her down on and break her back or her neck.

They circled round and round, deosil, sun-wise, looking over each other's shoulders. It's bad luck to look down at the ground because it means you might fall. It's bad luck to see your opponent's eyes because your soul might get fettered and you'd panic.

A wave crawled in, wetting their feet up to the ankles, and then crept out again. Hymir tried an elbow lift, but Tidefyr wriggled out of it. She tried a backheel trip (pulling his foot forward with her leg and pushing his body back with her arms), but he raised up his leg and kneed her in the crotch and pushed her back and got out of it.

Fenris growled.

"Foul!" Knut yelled. You're not supposed to kick or punch

or knee an opponent any more than you're supposed to bite or head butt or jump on them once they've fallen.

"Oops," Hymir said. "I didn't do that on purpose. I was just trying to get out of your hold."

"Let it go," Tidefyr called. "He didn't hurt me. I'm the only one here with the right to complain if he fouls me."

After that, none of the watchers spoke up when Hymir kicked her right knee or, later on, when he let go of her elbow for a moment and punched it instead. The moon slowly crept down the sky toward the west, and the waves slowly crept higher and higher on the sands, and the wrestling went on and so did the betting.

Hymir managed to trip Tidefyr once, but she kicked out her legs as she fell so he tripped too, and they both fell on the sand together.

"Brother fall," yelled Knut, and so did Aegir. That meant nobody had won.

Tidefyr let go her hold, and they both stood up.

"See what a good sport I am," Hymir said. "It's against the rules to pull your opponent down on top of you, but I know you didn't do it on purpose so I won't object."

"Thank you for your courtesy," said Tidefyr, and they took hold of each other, and the match started again. By now the waves were coming in a foot high, which probably favored Hymir. If it came in much higher, he could try pushing Tidefyr's head under water. That's all according to the rules.

Hymir tried a backheel trip of his own, but Tidefyr stepped around it, and the fight went on.

"If she loses," Fenris said, "I'll wait till it's full moon and then I'll challenge Hymir to a duel, and kill him."

"The full moon won't come back to us for another three weeks," Frost Kalinn said. "I could him challenge him today, elder brother."

"You've got the sword Father gave you," Fenris said. "Do you trust it?"

"Yes," Frost said. "I trust my sword, and I trust Father, and I trust my sister Kari, and I trust you too, Brother, in spite of all the prophecies. The only prophecy I've ever trusted was when Memory flew back across the centuries to tell me that a hero woman was going to climb out of Thunder River and enter Valhalla, and that she'd have spent her last few years playing let's pretend games where she carried a magic sword named Frostbite that froze whatever it touched."

"Was that before or afterwards?" his sister Kari asked.

"Afterwards," he said. "After you'd fed on me. Uncle Odin asked my permission to send my spine to the dark elves and have them forge it into a sword, but I wouldn't agree till Memory told me I'd be meeting Robin."

"All the valkyrie told me," said Robin Grima, "was 'Here's your death day present.'" She looked up, but there weren't any valkyries or ravens to be seen in the sky. The crescent moon hung halfway between midheaven and the mountains on the western horizon. The Geminids had stopped falling. A warm wind blew in off the ocean; in Midgard, it was a hot summer day, and the sun was nearing the midheaven.

Then Tidefyr bent at the knees and got Hymir up into the air, her left hand sliding from his thigh to the small of his back, as his arms and legs thrashed wildly about, trying to hit her. She stood up, growing taller and taller, spinning round and round, and then flung him up the beach, onto the dry sand.

He raised his knees up to his stomach and tucked his head into his chest, trying to somersault so he could land on his feet. Cats can do that easily, but Hymir wasn't as agile as a cat. He landed on his feet all right, but he overbalanced and fell on one knee. He reached out, but Tidefyr stepped back, and his flailing arms missed her.

"You cheated!" he yelled. "It's not fair! The fair thing was for me to win!"

"You lost the fight," Aegir said calmly. He held out his hand and Vind put a bag of gemstones in it, to settle their bet.

"I call on Hymir's neighbors to hear me," Tidefyr said. "Hymir took me to his home and to his bed by outfighting me, and he locked magic bracelets made by mist elves on my wrists to freeze my memories, so I wouldn't remember anything that happened before he took me as his thrall concubine. When the bracelets were broken, I left his bed and his home, and I named my nine maidservants and Hymir's mother's nine heads as my witnesses. Now I have outfought him, and I name you all as my witnesses that I am divorcing him. I did not bring any property to him, not even my name and my family's names, and I do not seek any property of Hymir's. I do not ask for any share in Tyr Hymirson, and I will not contribute any support to him, and I do not grant Hymir any share in my son Garm Fenrisson, and I will not seek any support for him. Hymir has no claim on me, and I have no claim on him, and we are divorced, and I'm going to marry Fenris Lokison."

"I disown you too!" Tyr yelled. "When Ragnarok comes, I'll kill your son Garm and bear out the prophecies that say brother will kill brother!"

The crescent moon was setting, and there was a small pinkish glow on the eastern horizon. In Midgard, the sun stood at the midheaven.

"No!" Hymir yelled. "Don't let sunny Sol come any closer when she's naked like that. It's not decent. Bring the clouds up to cover her. And don't let her brother moony Mani get away either. It's time for both of them to fall into the ocean and drown, and the stars along with them. Kill her! Kill him! Kill all of them!"

The Valhallans drew their swords, but the giants weren't attacking them. Hymir's orders weren't for the giants.

There was a loud howl. Not from the land but from the ocean.

A sea wolf leapt out of the ocean and up, high up, into the sky, No, I don't mean a little wolf eel, that grows up to seven feet long and weighs up to fifty pounds. This was more like the orcas Robin Grima had seen at SeaWorld, except it wasn't a mere thirty feet long with a weight of a mere six tons. It was over a hundred feet long and weighed over thirty tons, and the higher it got, the wider its jaws gaped. Another sea wolf leapt up after it, and then a third one. Their huge black bodies blotted out the sky.

And then they splashed back down into the ocean, but the sky was still black.

The sun was gone, and the air was suddenly midwinter cold.

The moon was gone, and Tidefyr's light was gone too.

The stars were gone. The North Star, and all the stars that circle it, and all the stars that rise and set with the seasons, and the planets that wander among them. There were just a few hundred glints of light here and there, the crumbs left over from the sea wolves' dinner.

The sea wolves had stopped howling, and everything was quiet, dead quiet.

"The eddas didn't say anything about the stars dying," Bookwyrm whispered. "They said a wolf will swallow the moon and a wolf will swallow the sun, but they didn't say the stars would die, too."

Fenris growled and ran off into the darkness, off toward the wrestling circle and Tidefyr.

Valhalla: Absent Without Leave

Then the meteorites began to fall, one by one, burning across the sky. And by their light, as they fell into the ocean, we saw the saltwater pulling away from us, the waves crawling farther and farther back till they didn't reach up to the low tide line any more, till they didn't come within a hundred feet of the low tide line.

"Tsunami!" Robin Grima yelled. ("Huge wave!" the others heard.) "We've got to get to high ground before the sea comes back!"

"The nearest high ground is those mountains," Skadi said, pointing at the inland horizon, "and they're a hundred miles away."

Then the earth started shaking under our feet. Robin Grima had lived long enough in California that she reflexively looked for a table to crawl under, a doorway to stand in, but there was nothing to fall on her but the sky. Hymir and the rest of the sea giants sat down on the wet sand. Up the beach, Hymir's workmen fell off the *Naglfar*. Some of them sat up; some of them lay motionless, which with any luck meant they were dead or at least seriously hurt.

When the earthquake finally stopped, the sea draugs began walking up out of the ocean. Some of them were naked, with seaweed as their only covering. Some of them still wore clothing, but the fabric was torn and rotten. Their arms were full of bones, as they shambled up onto the beach, lurching uncertainly from leg to leg. They hadn't walked on the land in a long time. There were thousands of them: fishermen and traders and pirates, raiding gangs and royal soldiers—centuries' worth of men and women who'd sailed out to sea and drowned and were never found, never buried. ("*Zombies*," Robin Grima thought, but that was wrong. Yes, draugs are walking corpses, but they're a lot nastier than zombies. They're strong enough to tear a man apart the way bad boys tear the wings off butterflies, and they're immune to weapons, just like berserks.)

By now most of the meteors had fallen, though every minute or two a falling fireball lit the world up for an instant like a flash of lightning.

A spear flew out of the darkness, barely missing Robin Grima's head. It was thirty feet long, with a spearhead that weighed half a pound, a giant's weapon. Another spear hit her right shoulder. The spearhead didn't break through her skin, but its force left her bruised.

Drifa ran forward to stand in front of Robin Grima, sword drawn, her face barely visible in the light of Robin's hair. Frost Kalinn stood at Robin's left. A spear flew out of the darkness towards them, and Frost Kalinn reached out and grabbed it and threw it back, and a giant screamed. Skadi took up her longbow and started shooting a cloud of arrows into the darkness. Someone stepped on Ratatosk's tail, and the poor squirrel whimpered in pain. Someone else barely missed stepping on his head, which would have been a lot worse.

The poor little squirrel smelled his way over to Wind Kari and jumped up onto her left shoulder. "Get off quick, or hang on tight," she told him. And then she jumped up into the air and didn't come down, The brave squirrel clung to her long hair and felt it change into feathers, as she spread her swan wings and flew up into the sky.

Then, far above them, the aurora spread through the darkness, shimmering gold pillars of light like a great palace, and Sigyn was gliding across the sky in swan form, her white feathers gilded by the light of the auroras she was dancing into existence. Wind Kari followed her, a little more clumsy, a little slower; below us a sheet of red gold light hung in the darkness like a curtain of fire. Ratatosk held on tight and looked down.

Valhalla: Absent Without Leave

The sea giants had thrown all their spears. None of them had wounded the Valhallans, but a spear had hit Skadi's left arm, and Drifa was bandaging her wound.

The draugs didn't seem interested in joining the fight. They were walking over to the *Naglfar* and dumping the bones they'd been carrying near the workmen, who were picking the bones up to nail on the ship.

Then the draugs smashed Hymir's treasure chests, and the shining gold spilled out on the dark wet sand. There were gold coins, minted in Christian lands, but there was more hackgold from Viking raids: broken links from gold chains and broken bits of gold armbands, and torcs, each piece carefully cut so it weighed exactly one ounce. And there were whole pieces of gold work too, gold chains and armbands, gold brooches and hairpins, gold torcs and crowns, gold cups and belt buckles. There were gilded squares of parchment cut out of illuminated manuscripts and gilded spines cut off of leather-bound books. The draugs sat down on the sand and helped themselves to the treasure, throwing the coins and ounce pieces back and forth to one another, draping the chains over their heads and clasping the torcs around their necks and slipping the armbands up their arms and putting the crowns on top of their heads.

On the seabed, there were fish flopping about on the wet sand. Seals rushed about, swallowing as many fish as they could. Robin had always thought of seals as fast swimmers and slow walkers, but that was based on seeing them lazing about in their enclosures in SeaWorld. Fur seals can move across the land at five miles an hour. Earless seals aren't quite that fast, but they can still put on a burst of speed if they're in a hurry and outrace a human being.

But the fastest runner on the beach was Wolf Fenris. The sea giants tried to catch him, but they couldn't keep up with him. Tidefyr sat on his shoulders and held onto his neck fur, as he raced back toward his friends.

"The sea's going to be coming back soon," Robin Grima said. "The longer it stays away, the higher the waves will be. Even if we can't get to the mountains, we've got to get off this beach."

"Will the waves be higher than the *Naglfar*?" asked Fenris. He sat down on his haunches, and Tidefyr slid off his neck and onto the sand. Her red-gold hair had lost its light, but she managed to stand up.

Robin Grima looked up the shore at the towering ship of bones. The tapestry hadn't made it look that big on the Norns' loom, but sometimes you have to get far away from the Norns' weaving to realize just how big their scope is.

"I don't know much about ships," Robin said. "If a wave a hundred feet high comes out of the sea and hits it, what will the *Naglfar* do?"

"I sailed out thirty summers as a trader," Bookwyrm said, "but the ships I sailed were all made of wood. If that were a wooden ship, she could ride out a wave that came up a few feet over her sides, but it would be safer to turn her head to the ocean and row her out as deep as she could get."

"Living bones are stronger than wood," Robin Grima said, remembering a karate class where the instructor told them that before assigning them to break a piece of wood with their bare hands. "But I don't know about dead bones."

"Dead bones are heavier than wood," Skadi said, "but they're stronger too." She sounded as if she was speaking from experience, and nobody felt like asking her for all the gory details. "Hymir's bone ship won't break apart at the seams if a great wave hits it, and it won't capsize. As long as the hold stays watertight, it'll float."

"We'll have to fight our way past every giant here to get to *Naglfar*," Robin Grima said. "Or else we'll have to sneak past them or run around them or fly over them. We don't have the mist caps any more. How many people can you carry, when you're in dragon form, Bookwyrm?"

"Let's find out," said Bookwyrm. He closed his eyes and began reciting the *Alvissmol*. "'Men call it Heaven, and the Aesir say Height, and the Vanir say Wind Weaver. Giants say the Up World, and the light elves say the Fair Roof, and the dark elves say the Hall of Raindrops.'" He skipped the verses for the sun and the moon and the clouds and went on to "Men call it the Wind," and then skipped the verses for the calm and the sea and went on to "Men call it Fire." And as he spoke, his shape changed. His clothing faded away and so did his sword and scabbard, and he was covered with black scales. His legs shrank away, and then split into two pair of small, clawed feet. He fell on his belly, and his body grew longer and longer. His arms stretched out into long, black wings. His head turned into a wedge that was mostly jaws, and he opened his mouth and there were rows of sharp white teeth inside, and his eyes glowed like small bonfires, and spurts of red fire blew out from his nostrils. The only thing that stayed the same was his voice.

"Climb on," he said.

The ground shook again, not as hard or as long as before. ("*Aftershock*," Robin thought.) Once things seemed steady again, Skadi stood up and walked over to Dragon Bookwyrm. Tidefyr walked after her, her arms stretched out in front of her like a child who's learning to walk and is afraid of falling, like a fire giant half-drowned in darkness.

"Stupid draugs," yelled Hymir, "stop playing with my gold!" His voice was loud enough that even Wind Kari and Sigyn heard him as they danced in the sky. "Go after the Valhallans. They can't be wounded or killed, but you can take them down into the sea and bind them there."

The draugs stood up and walked across the wet sand toward Robin Grima, their hands still full of Hymir's gold, their limbs still bright with it. If they kept on at that pace, they'd get close enough to attack in another minute or two. Sooner than that if their idea of attacking an enemy was to throw gold at him.

Looking down from Wind Kari's shoulder gave Ratatosk a great view of the upcoming battleground. Of course, one of the things that made it especially wonderful was that there was no way any of the fighters could attack him that high up. And none of them could accidentally step on him.

Ratatosk also got a great view of the ocean. The tsunami swell was starting to crawl toward Jotunheim. It was still hundreds of miles away from the coast, and it wasn't breaking yet, just a low swell, only a foot high. It would get higher and faster as it got closer to shore.

Another set of draugs was walking out of the ocean, carrying a battered rowboat with a pile of bodies lying inside it. They laid it down gently on the sand and stood in a ring around it, facing outwards, like warriors forming a shield fortress to protect their king. A cat who'd been lying in the rowboat got up and stretched, and went to stand at the prow, like a figurehead.

Skadi and Tidefyr clumsily climbed on top of Bookwyrm. Fenris leapt up after them and, after a few shaky moments, found his balance on top of Bookwyrm's scaly back, and Garm followed him. The Valhallans got up easily. The only one who couldn't seem able to manage it was the Jotun wolf. He ran round and round the great black dragon, sometimes growling and sometimes whimpering, but he wouldn't jump up, not even when Fenris called him.

"Leave him down there," said Knut. "He didn't swear our oath, and we're under no obligation to him."

"He saved my life," Skadi said, and reached out her good arm and picked up the Jotun wolf by the scruff of his neck and pulled him up to sit in her lap.

Then Bookwyrm ran forward, flapping his wings faster and faster, and suddenly he was airborne, flying easily over the onrushing draugs. Getting past the *Naglfar* workmen wasn't as easy. The trolls just threw things: sticks and stones and bones and hammers. The missiles bounced off of Bookwyrm's scales the same way the spear had bounced off of Robin Grima's skin. But the giants reached up to grab hold of the dragon and tear its wings off, tear its passengers off. Their arms stretched longer and longer the same way Skadi's had when she picked up the Jotun wolf. The first wave of draugs, the ones that Hymir had ordered to bind the Valhallans, looked up and saw the dragon getting away, and they turned around and walked back toward the *Naglfar*.

Bookwyrm soared up higher than the masts, higher than the giants could reach, and then he lowered his head and breathed fire. In its light, you could see the Norns' weaving clearly, and the wind from the dragon's wings blew the tapestry so it looked as if the woven figures were alive and moving. Fenris's huge jaws gaped and swallowed Odin. Tyr's sword pierced Garm's chest as Garm's teeth bit Tyr's head off. Thor's hammer thudded down on Orm's head as Orm blew out a cloud of venom. The *Naglfar* sailed up to the Upper Worlds with an army of hill giants, and Hel's ship sailed with an army of the dead, and Loki steered Surt's ship up from Muspelheim with an army of fire giants.

Dragonfire licked across *Naglfar* three times as Bookwyrm circled the ship.

"I won't be able to do that again soon," he said afterwards, his voice harsh and grating. "Was it enough?"

They looked down and saw *Naglfar*'s bones were still white and her sail hadn't burned up (the Norns weave their tapestry from human lives, not from wool or cotton or linen, and it's not easy to destroy what they weave), but the trolls on her deck were dying. Their hair had caught fire like wicks, and they were blazing up like oil lamps. The rest of the trolls had jumped on their wolves and were racing away from the ship.

The frost giants flinched from the dragon flame, but they didn't die from it, any more than a campfire could melt a glacier. They cowered down on the sand, but they didn't run. This proves that frost giants are braver than trolls. And more stupid. Though at least they weren't stupid enough to climb up onto a ship with a fire-breathing dragon on board.

But there were still the hill giants. Some of them clambered up the sides of the *Naglfar*, howling in anger, while the others threw a barrage of stones and bones up at the dragon. A few of the missiles fell short and hit hill giants, but nobody minded, not even the victims. You can't injure a hill giant with dirt or any of the things that lie in the dirt.

Bookwyrm had bathed in dragon blood, and he wasn't wounded either, though he started panting in short breaths after a boulder that must have weighed five hundred pounds hit him in the ribs.

"Time for me to do something," Wind Kari said, and she swooped down from the sky, screaming. The *Naglfar*'s sail billowed out before her—and the ship's head slowly turned to face the retreating sea.

"And then the foehn hit the ship," said Frost Kalinn.

Robin Grima laughed—and then remembered that he'd told her he made puns when he was nervous.

Naglfar trembled in the wind, and some of the hill giants fell off her side and onto the wet sand, but most of them managed to get onto the deck. A few started climbing up the center mast, which would bring them up to within a few dozen feet of Bookwyrm.

Down on the beach, Hymir's draugs had lost all interest in the *Naglfar*. They were throwing their gold onto the sand around the rowboat. The cat arched its back and hissed at them. The four bodies inside the rowboat stood up and clapped their hands, like kings accepting their vassals' tribute. The two women searched through the shower of treasure till they found gold crowns and put them on their heads. The two men drew their swords.

The frost giants got to their feet and ran away, back to the mountains.

"Treacherous frost giants!" Hymir yelled. "I'll send the fire giants to melt you if you don't come back and help me. Stupid draugs! I've got a lot more gold than that, if gold is what you want. Go climb onto my ship and bind the Valhallans, stupid draugs, and I'll give you each nine thousand pounds of gold. But if you don't help me, I'll send you back under the sea again for another nine centuries!"

CHAPTER NINETEEN

"Someone take the steering oar!" Bookwyrm yelled, gliding down to land on the *Naglfar*'s deck, near her stern. His passengers jumped off and drew their weapons, but it was Dragon Bookwyrm who led the way toward the steerboard (on the right if you're facing the prow), shoving hill giants out of his way.

Kari's gale filled the *Naglfar*'s sail, and the great ship glided down the beach toward the shrinking ocean, its speed picking up as the sand beneath its keel got wetter.

"Don't let the pirates get her!" bellowed Hymir. "She's ours! Our bone hoards and our work! Take her back from them!" He started walking down the beach toward the *Naglfar*. He was limping on his right leg, the one Tidefyr had thrown him by.

"Who's going to steer?" yelled Dragon Bookwyrm.

"I know how to row," Knut said, "but I've never been a steersman on a rowboat, let alone on a longship."

"I've never been on a ship before," Skadi said, and Tidefyr said the same.

Frost Kalinn shook his head, and so did Robin Grima.

Fenris Wolf and Garm Hel-hound and the Jotun wolf plainly wouldn't be able to handle the steering oar.

"You'll have to do it, Husband," said Drifa, and Bookwyrm shrank down to human size again and took the steering oar, as the ship keel lifted on a ripple of seawater. Drifa put her healer's box under her husband's feet and kissed him, then drew her sword.

The *Naglfar* was pitching wildly as she skipped across the wet sand and onto the little curling waves whose reach was still receding, minute by minute, back into the heart of the ocean. Bookwyrm clung to the steerboard, trying to keep the ship on course with the steering oar (think of it as a right-side rudder). The hill giants tromped aft toward the steerboard, some of them barehanded, some holding sticks and stones, bones and hammers.

Knut picked up a legbone and waved it back at them. "I dedicate you as sacrifices to Odin," he said and threw it like a spear toward the mob of giants.

"I wish we had my old battle standard," Bookwyrm said. "It showed a trader's balance scale with a bowl of gold on one pan and a bowl of blood on the other pan, and its name was Blood Scale."

"I wish we had the Jotunheim Table from Valhalla with us," Robin Grima said, "and a battalion of Marines with machine guns and flamethrowers." None of her companions asked her to explain the untranslatable terms that turned the second half of her wish into gibberish; they didn't think they had time before the fight started.

Robin stood a few yards in front of the steerboard, with Drifa and Knut on her right side, and Frost Kalinn and the Jotun wolf and Fenris on her left side—a six-man shield wall to defend Bookwyrm.

Skadi still wasn't up to using her longbow, but she picked up a bone lying on the deck and stepped in between the onrushing giants and the Valhallans, and Garm and Tidefyr went with her. A huge stone hammer hit Skadi's head but it's just as hard to hurt a hill giant with stone as it is to hurt a frost giant with icicle spears or a dark elf with gold. Skadi threw her bone spear back at her attacker, and it went through his forehead and out the back of his head, and he fell dead.

A stone hammer hit Tidefyr's knee, and she fell down on one knee. Skadi knelt down beside her and whispered something to her.

Garm leapt at the giant who'd thrown the hammer and tore his throat out, but a dozen other hill giants gathered around the gray hound, punching him, kicking him, hammering him.

Fenris ran towards them and opened up his massive jaws and breathed out a cloud of fire, scorching the giants who were attacking his son. The giants backed away from Garm and began muttering to each other. Garm stood up and shook off flames, like a dog wet from the bath shaking off drops of water.

"Fenris never said that he could breathe flame," Robin Grima said.

"'Fenriswolf will go with mouth agape,'" Bookwyrm said, quoting *The Deluding of Gylfi*, "'and flames will burn from his eyes and nostrils.'"

"You left out 'His upper jaw against the sky, his lower jaw against the ground/ He would gape wider if only there was room,'" Skadi said. "Njord and Frey recite the prophecies to each other often enough that by now I know them by heart." She stepped back and took Fenris's place in the shield fortress.

Tidefyr ran toward Fenris. She still didn't have her aura of moonlight, but her red-gold hair was as bright as Fenris's fire breath. She was wearing a gold armband that spiraled up her left arm. Were the draugs throwing Hymir's gold onto the *Naglfar* deck? No, it wasn't dead gold but living treasure; Skadi had taken off her apple snake and given it to Tidefyr, and the snake's fangs were deep in the fire giant's arm, pumping youth and vitality into her blood to make up for the sun and moon being eaten.

When Tidefyr reached the hill giants, she began pulling them away from her son and lover. Her fingers left black burns on their skin, and they screamed in agony.

Wolf Fenris stood at her left side and Hel-hound Garm at her right side, and they ran toward the prow of the *Naglfar* like a wildfire racing through a drought-dry forest. The hill giants scattered out of their way, and so did the draugs.

"Don't anyone kill the big gray wolf!" bellowed Hymir, leaping up onto the prow of the *Naglfar* with a great splash of saltwater. "He's going to kill Odin for me when Ragnarok comes. Don't anyone hurt the pretty flame-haired lady. She's going to keep my bed warm for me." He wasn't limping any more now that he was on a ship and not on a dry beach, now that *Naglfar* was fully afloat with at least half a foot of water under her keel. He ran sure-footed down the deck. The *Naglfar* was over a mile long, but at Hymir's speed, he'd reach the steerboard in only a couple of minutes.

"Don't anyone hurt the dog!" yelled Tyr, jumping up onto the prow after his father. "I'm going to kill the bastard at Ragnarok." He ran to the center mast and began to climb it; that way he'd be the safest person on the ship with the best view.

"You're going to find it harder to stick sleep-thorns in me this time," Fenris said grimly. "The mist elves could do it because they were invisible, but I can find you hulking giants by the smell even if I couldn't see you."

"This time we've got something better than sleep-thorns for you and your friends," Hymir said, stopping a few hundred feet in front of the center mast.

Tyr laughed, and so did the three sea giants climbing onto the prow of the ship: Osgrui and Alfarin and Vipar: Roarer and Far Strider and Viper. The rest of Hymir's neighbors were still back on the beach with Aegir and Heimdall, walking toward Aegirstead, where the Asgard folk go when they want a drinking party. That cut down the number of Robin Grima's enemies from a dozen sea giants and thousands of hill giants to merely five sea giants and hundreds of hill giants: a step in the right direction, but not a very big step.

There was deep-throated laughter on each side of Wind Kari, and Ratatosk looked up to see Vind on the right and his brother Vindsval on the left. The last time he'd noticed, they'd been standing on the shore, talking to Hymir. Now they'd put forth their sea eagle wings and taken to the air.

"Time for us to do something for Cousin Hymir's ship too," said Vindsval, and the two of them blew a freezing gale that sent the *Naglfar* speeding away from the shore, across the breaking waves, into the calm of the swells and toward the onrushing tsunami. The ship yawed and pitched and rolled as the waves tossed her about, but Bookwyrm clung tight to the steering oar and kept her course as steady as he could.

"Thank you for your help," said Kari politely, and the two sea giants laughed and reached out to stroke her and pinch her and run their long wet fingers through her black hair.

"Pretty little swan," Vind said (yes, his name also meant "wind"). "Maybe I'll put you on my ship as a figurehead."

"Strong little swan," Vindsval said (and his name meant "frozen wind"). "But you'll be stronger once I take off your clothes and teach you to make love on an iceberg to the rhythm of the ocean swells." His fingers tore at her cloak, and a feather came loose and blew away.

"Come down here and cross swords with me," Frost Kalinn yelled, "and we'll see how strong you bullies are. You can fight me two against one if it'll make you feel better."

"Or two against two if you feel like being honorable," Robin Grima yelled.

"Don't be impatient, dead folk," Vind called. "We'll come down and attend to you before the night's over."

"Unless Cousin Hymir's already killed you by then," said Vindsval. He tore a strip of wolf fur off the hem of Kari's swan cloak and caught one of her ankles and tied the fur around it.

Kari screamed at the touch of his long blue fingers. She broke free from his grasp and dove down toward the *Naglfar*, though there wasn't anyone there likely to be able to help her, and the two sea giants flew down after her, taunting her with cowardice. Suddenly she shook herself, and poor little Ratatosk fell off her shoulder and a long dizzying way down, at least a dozen feet, past the swaying platform at the top of the ship's mast, and then sliding down the sail till his claws caught hold of a patch of green threads and he clung to it for dear life. Later on, he realized he was sitting in the middle of the Midgard Serpent's cloud of venom, his red fur blazing against it for any eyes shaped to see by sunlight. Of course, dark-skied Jotunheim giants have eyes shaped to see in the dark, and even sea giants are a little dazzled by daylight, and yes, they're all colorblind. (And bright Muspelheim's fire giants can see all the colors a human can plus three shades of infrared, but the only fire giant on the *Naglfar* was on our side.)

There was a sudden flash of golden light in the sky, and Ratatosk looked up to see if the sun had come back, but it was Sigyn the valkyrie flying to her daughter's side, her white swan wings trailing a curtain of aurora that glowed like a bonfire. Wagner claimed that Odin put a ring of magic fire around his daughter Brunhilde while the girl slept, but that's wrong; it was the valkyrie's own magic that gave her the shield of fire. Now Sigyn's flames burned the air like a dying hero's courage burns in his blood, and her talons stretched strong and sharp toward the sea giants.

The Jotun wolf raised his head and howled at the sky, his one eye glowing small but bright in the darkness. Kari howled back down at him as she stretched out her talons. The two sea giants turned and fled, back to the frozen wastes of the far north.

"Look what I've got ready for you, pretty lady," Hymir said. "You remember it, don't you? You slept in it till the mist elves made those pretty bracelets for you. Now you and your boyfriend and your bastard can all sleep in it together." He threw out his arms, and he was holding a great net wet with saltwater.

It wasn't as big as Aegir's wife's net. Queen Ran's net is over a thousand miles on a side, big enough to stretch from Copenhagen to Venice. Hymir's net was only a thousand feet on a side; just wide enough to stretch from one side of the *Naglfar* to the other, but it was certainly long enough to reach from where he stood to where Tidefyr stood with Fenris and Garm.

"All for one!" Robin Grima yelled and started running, Kalinn at her side and the other Valhallans only a step behind them, but they weren't fast enough.

Hymir cast the net out, and it covered Tidefyr and Fenris and Garm and clung to them, then a wave of saltwater rolled out of it and raced down the deck, sweeping up everything before it: stones and bones, spears and hammers. The only one strong enough to stand against that wave was Skadi, but then it only came up to her knees, not up to her neck the way it did to Robin Grima.

Tidefyr's fire dimmed and disappeared, and so did Fenris's and Garm's as Hymir's net tightened around them the way the ocean water tightens around a drowning man, pulling him down into its frozen depths where there's no light or warmth, only darkness and cold, weakness and despair and death. Tidefyr's snake armband turned dark brown, like a rotting apple.

Robin Grima almost fell off the ship as *Naglfar* suddenly pitched head downwards and then rolled halfway onto her left side as the breaking waves tossed her about. Only a few minutes ago, the ship had had fifty feet of calm water under her keel, but the oncoming tsunami was still sucking up the ocean, and now *Naglfar* was riding the waves.

Frost Kalinn grabbed hold of Robin's scabbard and held her, but what held them both on the deck was that Knut flung out Odin's rope and tied it around the rail that ran up the steps to the aftcastle, at the stern of the ship.

Bookwyrm kept both of his hands on the steerboard and his eyes fixed ahead at the waves. "Are you all right, Wife?" he called after the wave of saltwater broke over his head and then sank enough that he could speak again.

"Yes, Husband," Drifa said, as she clung to Odin's rope with one hand and her sword with the other.

Robin's head ached where a stone hammer had hit it, but she struggled onto her feet and looked around for her companions. The Jotun wolf was standing on top of the aftcastle, his teeth set in Odin's rope. But at first she didn't see Fenris and his woman and their son. They weren't anywhere on the deck.

Knut threw a loop of rope toward Bookwyrm, who stepped into it and pulled it up to his waist, never taking more than one hand off the steering oar.

"I've caught Fenris and his bastard, both on the same

hook!" Tyr called out. "And I killed Hel in the dueling circle. Now all I have to do is catch Orm Lokison, and I'll have dealt with Loki's whole brood of monsters."

He stood on the swaying platform on top of the center mast, holding a fishing pole in his right hand. Its hook was caught in Hymir's net, and he'd pulled it up into the air, so it dangled a hundred feet over the deck.

"Come down to the deck, Hymirson," Robin Grima called, "and let's fight another duel. This time we won't just fight till one of our swords breaks; we'll fight till one of us dies."

"Don't be impatient, Robin Grima Jonson," Tyr said. "I'll kill you and your followers before we're done here, and I'll send your treacherous souls to Dead Shore where oathbreakers belong!" He tied off his fishing line to the platform's railing, so he didn't need to stay there and hold it up.

Skadi walked toward the center mast, reaching up toward the net, her arms and legs growing longer with every step. "I'm no oathbreaker!" she yelled. "Come down and fight me now, Hymirson, or else I'll know you're a coward!"

Tyr jumped down from the masthead and landed on the deck in front of her and drew his new sword. It glowed blood-red, the color that Mars used to shine in the night sky, but Mars was gone now, swallowed by sea wolves, along with Mercury and Venus, Jupiter and Saturn, the sun and the moon and the North Star and Thiazi's Eyes and all the other stars.

"Does anyone want her alive?" Tyr asked.

"Thiazi's daughter belongs to us," called a hill giant.

"Thiazi's brothers were Gangur and Idi," called another hill giant. "They divided their father's gold among them, but Thiazi got the family home because he was the oldest. We're the Gangursons and the Idisons. When Thiazi died, his daughter should have offered herself and her home for us to share out fairly. Instead she went up to Asgard and pledged herself to fight with the Aesir, and what did she get in exchange? Not one of Odin's powerful sons, only a Vanir hostage."

"Thiazisdaughter, what's it like going to bed with a Vanir,?" a third hill giant called. "Did shiplord Njord bring you a mattress stuffed with your father's charred feathers, or did he insist on a waterbed, and did it make you seasick?"

"Skadi's a slut," called a fourth hill giant, "but she's our slut. Give her to us, and we'll keep her too busy to get into trouble."

"It's a bargain," said Tyr, and sheathed his sword.

Skadi spat on the deck. "If you want me so much, cousins," she called, "then come and take me!"

"Come and take all of us!" Robin Grima yelled. "All for one, and one for all!"

But Skadi shook her head. "It's a family quarrel," she said. "If you joined the fight, oath-mates, then I'd have to take their side against you. Stay out of it, and keep your eyes on Cheater Hymir."

Skadi's uncles had had a lot of sons, too many to count easily. Skadi grabbed them one by one and tore their heads off and threw the heads at Tyr, and he swung his scabbarded sword and batted them away. One of the heads hit a hill giant, and he fell down dead. Another one flew towards the Jotun wolf, but he jumped out of the way.

Skadi had just cut off head number nine when the rest of her cousins jumped on her. Some of them held her down, and the rest of them nailed her feet to the bottom of the center mast and stretched her arms up over her head and nailed her hands to the center mast too, about a quarter of the way up.

"That was a great ballgame," Hymir said. "But the next game is going to be even better."

Then there was a rumble like thunder, and a hissing like a million snakes, and "Wave ho!" Bookwyrm yelled, and the tsunami hit, higher than the *Naglfar*'s forecastle and halfway up her center mast. It smashed against the ship like a giant hammer and drove her back towards the beach.

The tsunami's crest hit the bottom of the *Naglfar*'s sail and broke off some of the skull weights that held the warp threads taut. The foam flew up higher than the center mast. It drenched the Norns' weaving and the ropes that held it to the mast and poor little Ratatosk, who dug in his claws and scrambled up to the platform on top of the mast as *Naglfar* fought her way back up from the cold dark sea bottom.

The ship finally settled back down on top of the ocean. At first there was a pool of seawater a few feet deep amidships, by the center mast, but Hymir sat down on the deck, his jaws gaping open, and gulped the water down, and a minute later a man could have walked from one end of the ship to the other and only gotten his shoes damp.

Up above, the sky was a sea of blackness lit by a dancing aurora. Down below, the seashore was barely visible as a dark line on the horizon. There wasn't a sign of the blue glowing ice blocks of Hymirstead. Hymir would have to build himself a new home when this was over.

Being underwater hadn't bothered Hymir or the other sea giants, of course. And it hadn't bothered Tyr who was half sea giant. Tyr's fishing line was still hanging from the top of the center mast, and it still held Hymir's net, and the net still held Fenris and his family. Odin's rope had held the Valhallans safely aboard. The Jotun wolf was clinging to the top of one of the lesser masts, shaking himself furiously. And Skadi was gasping for breath, which meant that she hadn't drowned either. One of the advantages of being a giant is that you have a huge lung capacity.

Most of the hill giants had been swept off the deck, but

there were still nearly a couple of dozen left, and some of the ones washed overboard were swimming back to the *Naglfar*.

Ratatosk finished licking himself dry and then looked at the tangled green threads he'd cleaned off his hindclaws. After a little thought, he climbed carefully back down the mast and onto the sail, and began to pull the loose warp threads up to the top of the sail. When he came to a splice that joined one thread with another, he set it between his teeth and gnawed it apart.

"This is what it used to be like in the good old days," Hymir said. "Dark water running free wherever it wanted, with Jotunheim and Midgard trembling before the waves."

"Wave!" yelled Bookwyrm, and the ebb wave hit, racing back from the shore of Jotunheim and dragging along all the clutter it had found there. It wasn't tall enough to crest over the *Naglfar*'s aftcastle, but it dragged the ship out deep into the ocean, and it washed over the sides of the ship at midship. This time the wave that swept the deck was only a couple of feet high, and the ship took less than a minute to recover, but after it did, the deck was littered with the ebbwave's leavings: sea-washed white bones and dragon fire-charred black trolls, heavy stone hammers and light bone nails. And at the lowest part of the ship, by the center mast, between where Skadi was nailed and where Hymir was sitting, there were four draugs and their rowboat, with the gray cat still standing proudly at her prow as if nothing in particular had happened. The four figures inside the rowboat had fallen down, but they got up now, the women still wearing their golden crowns, the men still holding their bright swords.

"Throw that evil rowboat back into the ocean!" yelled Bookwyrm, with his first breath of air. "Otherwise the draugs will swamp our ship!"

The draugs screamed. That meant someone on board

would be dying soon, but that didn't come as much of a surprise to anyone there.

"There'll be another tsunami wave soon," said Robin Grima, "probably bigger than that one. Don't waste time on the rowboat. We've got to free Skadi!"

"The rope won't reach that far," Knut said and began to unwind it from around his waist, tying a knot on the steerboard to keep Bookwyrm anchored there.

"Don't underestimate Uncle Odin's rope," Frost Kalinn said. "It was long enough to go around Mist Hall."

Knut unwound the rest of the rope from his waist and held up its other end. "Rune rope," he sang, "tall tree rope, beautiful blood rope. You bound flame-eyed Odin, the Slain Father, who wields the War Fetter of fear and of fury. Keep us safe on this ship as we dare its dangers. Stretch out your sinews and bind us aboard."

The Jotun wolf howled and jumped down onto the deck and ran to Knut's side.

Knut tied the rope's loose end around his waist and ran forward, and the Jotun wolf ran beside him, and Robin Grima and Frost Kalinn and Drifa ran after them, their left hands on the rune rope, and when they reached three hundred feet or thereabouts, halfway to the first mast, the rope began to stretch with each of Knut's strides so he never had to slow down.

It was about half a mile from the *Naglfar's* steerboard to her center mast where Skadi was nailed. Even an Olympic runner (I've seen them all: Midgard is where all deeds of heroism take place, and that includes the Olympics) would take a couple of minutes to get there, and Knut had spent his last ten centuries training as a fighter, not as a runner. He also didn't have track shoes, but his feet didn't slip on the wet slippery bone deck; the Othalan Inheritance rune did good work.

"Hurry up, draugs!" Hymir yelled. "I'll watch over your stupid rowboat for you. Get on my ship and grab the Valhallans and tie them up with seaweed and take them down to the sea bottom and tie anchors to them! Hurry up, or I won't ever let you leave the ocean again!"

"Your draugs need encouragement, not insults," Tyr said. He went to the prow and whistled till a sea horse jumped up onto the deck. Tyr got on its back and rode off across the sea, slapping the draugs with his scabbard and driving them toward the ship.

Wind Kari was blowing against the ship's sail with all her might, but it wasn't doing as much good as before because of clever Ratatosk's work at unraveling the threads in the Norns' weaving. "It's coming!" she screamed, and "Wave ho!" Bookwyrm yelled, and Ratatosk looked out to sea and saw the tsunami's crest, silhouetted against the auroras. It was already higher than the forecastle of the *Naglfar*, and the saltwater under the ship's keel was dropping as the tsunami sucked it up to grow taller and taller.

Osgrui the Roarer was screaming, louder than a thunderstorm, louder than the tsunami. The sea giant's face was set in an exultant smile so you could see all of his foam-white teeth, sharp and jagged like rocks that can tear the bottom out of a ship. Alfarin Far Strider was smiling too, and he was getting taller and taller, just like the onrushing wave. Vipar was licking his lips with his forked tongue.

Poor little Ratatosk didn't have time to scream for help or run back up to the top of the mast before the wave hit. He held his breath and clung to the sail with all his might as the great wave smashed against the cloth, tearing away more warp weights, pulling out more warp threads at one blow than the clever squirrel had done with all his work.

Knut grabbed the rune rope with one hand and the Jotun wolf with the other as the huge wave washed across the deck.

The water grabbed the Valhallans and threw them back towards the stern, but they only got as far back as the second mast, about a thousand feet forward of the aftcastle, about fifteen hundred feet back of the center mast, and there the rune rope tangled around the mast and wouldn't let go.

Dark and cold saltwater engulfed them, but they could feel the ship battling the weight of water to rise again.

When *Naglfar* finally found her way back to the air, there were light ocean swells running underneath her. Hymir was standing up on the forecastle, surveying his ship and his forces. There were only a dozen hill giants on deck, but there were hundreds of draugs, and they'd each brought an armload of sea bones, tearing up the deck here and there and throwing the bones into her hold like raiders stowing away their loot.

The rowboat still sat at the foot of the center mast. Some of the draugs were standing guard around it. The rest of them stood around the center mast, their heads about as high as Skadi's knees.

Overhead, Hymir's net swung from the end of Tyr's fishing line. Inside it, Fenris and Garm were clawing and biting at the mesh. Tidefyr's hands were over her head, her fingers busy with the fish hook. Up above them, on the sail, you could still see Odin's one-eyed face, but there was nothing left of Fenris Wolf in the Norns' weaving of the great battle of Ragnarok. And the other Lokisons were starting to unravel too. All you could see clearly now was *Naglfar* sailing across one side of the tapestry with Hymir's army of hill giants and, on the other side, Loki steering the ship from Muspelheim with its army of fire giants.

Down below, the ocean was full of more draugs, all of them swimming for the *Naglfar*. Their legs were trailing long dark chains of seaweed, and their arms were full of bones. Behind them rode Tyr, his sea horse walking daintily a few inches over the saltwater. And seated behind Tyr, facing the tail of his sea horse, was his grandmother, Hymir's nine-headed mother, all of her heads bending down on their long necks to gulp down the saltwater, four heads to the right and four to the left and one over the horse's shining tail.

"Hurry up, draugs!" Hymir shouted. "Grab the Valhallans." He picked up a leg bone from the deck (too tall to be a human's leg, probably a hill giant's) and drummed it against the deck in time to his chant, "Grab the Valhallans! Bind them and drown them!"

His sea giant friends standing at the prow of the ship beat their spears against the deck in approval.

Tyr's sea horse jumped up onto the forecastle behind them, and Tyr politely helped his grandmother get down off the horse's back and onto the deck. She joined in Hymir's chant, clapping her hands, beating her heads together. The sea horse leapt overboard, back to the sea.

Tyr stood on the forecastle, looking out over the ocean. "Hurry up, Orm," he called. "I'm going to drown your brother and his son, the way Odin should have drowned all of you when you were born. I'm going to—"

Then Osgrui started roaring, and you couldn't hear anyone else. His voice was long rolling thunderclaps with only a few words understandable here and there. "Osgrui deafens you!" he roared and started running toward the stern, towards the Valhallans, and then "Osgrui defeats you!" as he passed the center mast, and then "Osgrui drowns you!" as he got to only a few hundred feet away from the Valhallans. He threw a spear, and it hit Robin Grima's right breast. She screamed in pain and surprise as the impact flung her into the lesser mast behind her. She reached up to the spear, wondering how much of her breast would be left after she pulled it out, but her skin was unbroken and the spear had melted into warm saltwater and was running down her legs like sweat.

"I accept your challenge, Osgrui," she said, trying not to let her voice waver. She drew her sword and saw the glow of its silver blade and felt its power pulse in her fingers. "I'm Robin Grima Jonson of Vinland and Valhalla. Let's fight."

"May I join in?" Frost Kalinn asked, drawing his own sword. "There's enough of him for both of us."

"No," Robin said, remembering that he hadn't bathed in dragon blood. "Go help our captive oathmates." Kalinn ran off, dodging around sea giants and hill giants like a cat eluding lumbering humans who want to catch it and give it a bath. His silver hair glowed bright as starlight.

"I'm Alfarin," said the second sea giant. He took one stride forward and he was at the center mast, another stride and he was only a few yards away from Knut and the Jotun wolf, his spear pointing at Knut's heart. "Run away if you want to live, little Valhallan," he said, "and we'll see if you can outrun me. Stay here and fight me, if you want to die quickly, and I'll tear your flesh off to feed the orcas, and Hymir will have your bones to build his ship."

"I'm Knut Windfriend," the Valhallan said, "and I won't run away from any enemy." He drew his sword and ran past the sea giant's spearpoint to parry Alfarin's weapon by chopping through the sea giant's arm. That tactic works very well on humans, and it's also effective on trolls and hill giants and frost giants, but Alfarin just laughed as the sword swept through his arm and his flesh rejoined behind it, with no more effect than parrying a sea wave. Then he frowned in puzzlement as the blood in his spear arm froze to red ice because Knut's sword still had the ice power it had gained from touching Frost Kalinn's weapon.

"I'm Vipar," said the third sea giant, and flung himself on his belly and glided along the wet deck like a snake, like a wave. "Stay or speed off, as you wish," he hissed as he passed the center mast, "but you shan't escape me."

"I'm Drifa Bersiswife," Drifa said, "and I don't want to escape. Hurry up, slow-worm, and don't keep me waiting."

"Hurry up, everyone!" called out one of Hymir's mother's nine heads. Her other heads were busy licking the water off *Naglfar*'s prow.

"That's right, Mother," said Hymir, walking back to the prow to join her. "Hurry up, everyone. On with the show!"

Alfarin broke off his frozen spear arm and threw it at Knut's face. The Jotun wolf leapt up and caught the arm between his teeth and lay down on the deck to gnaw it. By then Alfarin had grown himself another spear arm. It's not easy to permanently injure a sea giant—or to permanently disarm one, though the Jotun wolf had done a valiant job.

"Here I am, Bersisdeadwife," Vipar said. His fingers reached out to seize Drifa's ankles and then grew longer and longer, coiling up her legs. She thrust her sword into his long blue fingers, but there were dozens of them, hundreds of them, and she couldn't freeze them all. He pulled her legs apart, shaking them violently, till she fell down on the deck, and then his jaws gaped open wide enough to swallow a horse, and his fingers pulled her left foot into his mouth and he began to swallow it. Drifa sat up and aimed a sword thrust at his head, but he jerked back and upwards, and she fell again, dangling in the air by her left leg, as Vipar grew another head and began to swallow her right leg too.

Robin Grima walked cautiously along the wet, slippery deck toward Osgrui, her left hand still holding the rune rope. The sea giant threw another spear at her, and she slapped it aside with her sword. He laughed and walked toward her, a hundred feet at a stride. Then they were face-to- well, not face-to-face; more like Robin's face to Osgrui's shins. She cut through his knees, and what was left of his legs froze to ice.

"I want fire!" Robin Grima yelled, and the runes for it

burned in her mind, and the tip of her sword seared Osgrui with hot flames. (No, Knut and Bookwyrm couldn't do that with their swords, not even after learning the runes on the World Tree. None of them had gone through the fire ordeal even once in Blind Hall, let alone three times.)

The Jotun wolf swallowed the last chunk of Alfarin's old spear arm and ran off to grab a mouthful of rune rope and then leapt up high enough to pull a loop of rope up over Drifa's head. Then he sat down on the deck to watch, as the loop of Odin's rope crawled up over Drifa's dangling neck and up past her waist and her knees and Vipar's heads and settled down snugly around Vipar's neck. Vipar pulled at the rope, but he couldn't get his fingers inside it. The sea giant wasn't laughing any more; he was shaking in a frenzy. Then his hands let go of the rope and went down to each grab one of his heads and pull with all his might till he tore his heads off and threw them on the deck. No, losing his heads didn't affect his intelligence. He was still clever enough to wriggle backwards towards the prow even faster than he'd wriggled forward. By the time he reached the center mast, he'd grown himself a new head.

Drifa cut herself free from Vipar's severed heads. "Thank you, Odin," she said and kissed the rune rope.

Meanwhile, up above, Wind Kari was still blowing the ship toward the heart of the ocean, and Sigyn was still dancing golden auroras in the sky. Ratatosk was unraveling more threads from the sail. Garm had torn a hole in Hymir's net big enough to slip his muzzle through. Tidefyr and Fenris were trying to widen the gap with their fingers. Skadi was still nailed to the center mast. And there were hundreds of cold wet draugs on the deck, some of them throwing bones into the hold and some of them kneeling around the rowboat, playing with the hackgold, and some of them shambling down the deck towards the Valhallans.

"They seem to like gold," Knut said, "and I've got some to spare." He fingered the bags that hung at his belt and untied the one that held the Feoh rune's gift. He threw the gold coins at the draugs, and Robin followed his example. The draugs knelt down and picked up the gold and took it all back to the rowboat.

Frost Kalinn came running up the deck toward the center mast, his drawn sword in his right hand.

"Catch that silver-haired fellow, stupid draugs!" yelled Hymir. "He's with the Valhallans! Don't let him get away!"

Wind Kari swooped down and caught up her brother and flung him up, over the draugs, over Vipar, and onto the Norns' tapestry. The draugs leapt up after him, but he kicked them off, and they fell back onto the deck. He grabbed hold of the sail with his left hand, but the weft threads pulled out of the tapestry, and he fell, landing with his feet on Skadi's shoulders, a bunch of threads in his left hand that had once been his sister Hel's face.

Then the ebb wave hit, hammering *Naglfar*'s stern and dragging her far out to sea. The wave splashed over the stern, sending cold saltwater up to Bookwyrm's neck as he sat by the steerboard, grimly holding onto the steering oar, up to Robin Grima's waist and up to Osgrui's ankles. The ship pitched forward and the water washed up the deck, lifting the draugs' rowboat up to Skadi's knees and then wetting Hymir's toes at he stood on the prow.

Hymir's mother waddled down to the center mast and sat in the pool of saltwater, gulping it down with all nine of her heads, like a farmer who'd spent a hot dry day reaping grain, like a warrior who'd spent a hot dry day reaping enemies, and the water level began to drop.

Up above her, Frost Kalinn was standing on Skadi's right shoulder, his fingertips reaching up toward Hymir's net, but he wasn't quite tall enough to touch it until he stepped up to stand on top of Skadi's head. "And all for one," he reminded her. A draug caught hold of his right ankle, and he kicked him off. Another draug climbed up onto Skadi's left shoulder and sank its sharp green teeth into her left fingers.

"No!" Frost Kalinn screamed, and Skadi began to scream too.

"Forget about the giantess, stupid draugs!" yelled Hymir. "Catch the silver-haired fellow and take him into the ocean, or you'll never be dry again; you'll never feel the air on your faces again! You'll spend the rest of eternity slaving away under the waves till your fingers and toes rot off!"

"Forget about the draugs, stupid sea lord," said the gold-crowned women who stood in the rowboat, their voices loud enough that everyone on the ship could hear them. "The draugs aren't stupid, and they're not your thralls, and they aren't going to obey you. They were born and named on land, and you don't know their names. They may have spent years sailing on your sea and centuries imprisoned in saltwater, but their final home isn't for you to decide. It's up to the Norns to examine their lives and decide which folk may go up to some hall in Asgard and which folk must wander forever on Dead Shore and which folk will go to Hel's Hall."

"Hel's dead!" Hymir yelled. "My son Tyr killed her in the dueling circle."

"Your son freed us from each other in the dueling circle," the two Hels said, "and then your sea horse brought our blood up to the Middle Worlds. Thank you for opening the way for us, enemy."

The Valhallans disentangled themselves and the rune rope from the second mast while Hymir's three cousins laughed at them. "You're like turtles lying on their backs and trying to turn over," Alfarin said; and, "Like beached whales stuck on the shore," Vipar hissed; and "Deep-drowning dolphins," yelled Osgrui.

"We're too honorable to attack you till you're ready," Alfarin yelled, "but we haven't finished our fight yet!"

"We'll finish it soon, and we'll finish all of you," Vipar hissed. Osgrui was roaring wordlessly, like a thunderstorm. And then Vipar spat out a cloud of green venom, not at the Valhallans but up into the sky, and Wind Kari's aurora went dark, her white swan wings crumpled down to her sides, and she spiraled down into the dark ocean.

Sigyn dove after her but too late; by the time she got there, Kari's black hair had disappeared into the black saltwater.

After that, Sigyn's aurora wasn't swaying gold curtains any more; it was dark-red spears flying downward, and *Naglfar*'s deck was cloaked in shadows. At the stern, Robin Grima's hair still glowed red and her sword still shone silver, but Knut and Drifa found it hard to see the tips of their own swords, let alone to see an enemy to attack. At the prow, the only light was the white star on Tyr's helmet. At the center mast, the only light was Frost Kalinn's silver hair.

"I'll kill you for that cowardly attack, Vipar!" Knut screamed.

"You won't kill anyone, dead man," Alfarin said, laughing, stepping forward to kick Knut in the face. Knut held onto the rune rope, so he only slid back a few feet.

"Don't rush the slaughter too fast," Vipar hissed. "Let the dead man despair. The only person you can kill here, dead man, is yourself." His head darted at Drifa, but she stepped out of its way and her sword made a long gash along his neck.

"Stop that, stupid draugs!" a hill giant yelled. "If you want nails, we'll give them to you. Don't pull them out of the mast like that!”

“I’m free!” Skadi screamed. “Don’t fight the draugs, oath-mates. The draugs set me free!”

“Grab her!” screamed the hill giants. ”Hit her legs till she can’t run away. Hit her arms till she can’t fight back!”

“I’ll help you hit her,” said Hymir.

“No!” the hill giants yelled. “This is a family fight, sea giant. If you mix into it, we’ll have to take her side against yours, and she’ll have time to run away.”

“I’m not going to run away from you, cousins,” Skadi said. She put her arms around the center mast and began shaking it back and forth. Poor little Ratatosk lost his grip on the sail, and Wind Kari wasn’t there any more to rescue him, and Sigyn didn’t show any loyalty to her children’s valiant companion, and the poor little squirrel fell down toward the deck, toward the rowboat. Dark-haired, one-eyed Hodur reached out and caught him, not in the palm of his hand which would have been graceful and gracious, but by the tail, which was painful and awkward, but yes, it was a lot better than landing on your head, and there was some excuse for a man who’d just gotten the use of one eye not being too good at eye-hand coordination yet.

“Try to stay out of the way, Wyrmtongue,” Hodur said, and put the squirrel down gently on the prow of the rowboat, uncomfortably close to the big gray cat.

“Greetings, Ratatosk,” the cat said. “What’s the latest gossip?” His eyes were bright yellow, and his breath was warm and sweet. He opened his mouth and showed his teeth.

“Skadi, have you changed your mind about accepting assistance?” Fair Hel asked.

“I don’t need your help against my relatives!” Skadi shouted and shook the mast harder.

"Are they all your relatives?" asked Red Hel.

"The ones who'll come up and fight me are my relatives," Skadi shouted. "You can kill any cowards who hang back from battle." She shook the mast harder still, and it splintered free from the deck.

About that time Hymir's net fell apart into brittle icicles, spilling out its captives.

Frost Kalinn jumped down onto the deck after them, his bright sword slashing out to cut off the head of a hill giant who was stepping forward to hit him with a stone hammer. "That's not gneiss!" Kallin yelled. The giant fell apart into a tall heap of dirt (like the special effects in a horror movie when a hero pounds a stake into a vampire's heart, except that the mound of dirt didn't blow away on the wind; it just stayed there on the deck).

"Thank you for freeing us, little brother," Fenris Wolf said, and bared his teeth at a hill giant who seemed to be heading for Tidefyr. The hill giant circled carefully around them and went on toward Skadi.

Garm laughed and ran over to Baldur and Hodur. "Thank you, Odinsons," he said. "Being impaled was the worst pain I've ever felt, but if I hadn't gone through the ordeal, I wouldn't be able to speak to thank you."

"You're welcome," Hodur said politely.

"It wasn't a pleasure," said Baldur.

"And this won't be either," said Red Hel, the one with the dark skin and red hair.

"For any of us, little nephew," said Fair Hel, the one with the light skin and blonde hair, and she reached out a hand and lifted Garm up by the scruff of his neck till he was standing on his hind legs.

"You can tell us afterwards if being impaled is still the worst pain you've ever felt," said Red Hel, and then she opened her mouth wide and breathed a cloud of red flames around him, and Fair Hel breathed a cloud of white flames that sank into it, and the fireball was bright enough to light up the *Naglfar* from one end to the other.

Some people might have used this opportunity to look around the ship, waiting patiently for Garm to start screaming in agony, waiting patiently for the fireball to explode and char everyone within range. Clever little Ratatosk ran away as fast as he could, dodging icicles and bones and hill giants and sea giants, till he was sitting near the aftcastle, a few yards behind Bersi Bookwyrm. He panted a bit, and *then* he looked back to see what was happening.

He hadn't heard the fireball by the rowboat explode, but its flames had burned out.

Garm was still standing on his hind legs, but now he looked more comfortable doing it, because now he was in human form, no longer a hound. He stood there, naked, staring at his fingers with wonder. His hair shone red gold, like his mother's. He didn't have a hound's massive jaw any more with teeth that could bite through a giant's bones, but he seemed pleased with the change anyway.

Skadi had ripped out the center mast and was sweeping it across the desk at shoulder-height, about forty feet in the air, tatters of the Norns' weaving still dangling from the crosspiece that used to be its yardarm. Some of the hill giants that it hit fell down and didn't do much for a while, and a few of them flew into the air and over the side of the ship. The rest of them ran toward Skadi, waving stone hammers and bone spears.

"That's not fair!" Hymir screamed. "Put down my mast, you stupid giant! Don't freeze my saltwater net, you stupid Lokison!"

"Oops!" yelled Frost Kalinn.

Valhalla: Absent Without Leave

Meanwhile, near the second mast, Robin Grima stood with Knut on her right and Drifa on her left. The Jotun wolf lay at the steerboard side of the ship, his good eye closed. That put him about five hundred feet away from the fighting. but it still seemed like a bad time to take a nap.

Vipar kept his distance from the Valhallans—and the rune rope—and Osgrui was still on his knees because his legs hadn't healed after Robin Grima cut them off. Now he was only thirty feet high and he couldn't move much faster than a human. Alfarin had six arms, all of them throwing ice spears, and every few minutes one of the ice spears landed uncomfortably close to where Bookwyrm sat by the steerboard. Vipar's two severed heads slid around on the deck every time the ship rolled or yawed or pitched. Their eyes were closed, but sometimes their mouths would open and emit a puff of green venom, and the Valhallans would hold their breaths. The Valhallans didn't need to breathe except to talk, and there wasn't any point in doing that because Alfarin was roaring so loudly that nothing else could be heard.

Ratatosk would have felt more comfortable watching the fight from a branch of the World Tree. Watching it on a computer screen from his safe, warm, dry home would have been even better. But he'd sworn an oath by the Sun and the World Tree, and he'd asked for Thor's hammer to kill him and for the giants to eat him if he broke faith. No one had seen Thor in ages, and the sea wolves had swallowed the Sun, but the World Tree was still around, and so were the giants, and the giants on the *Naglfar* were likely to be hungry once the fight was over.

Vipar began to grow some more arms: three on the left and three on the right, each of them with a head at the end of its wrist instead of a hand. Knut thought it made the sea giant look like a huge octopus with heads at the ends of its tentacles. Robin remembered a drawing she'd seen of Hercules fighting the hydra of Lerna, which grew two heads for every one you cut off unless you seared the necks with fire. Her Comparative Mythology textbook claimed that Hercules was just trying to dam up the Lernaean swamp and that the stagnant water flowed around his earth dams until he used baked earth. The textbook writer would probably claim that this long nightmarish battle was just an encounter with a sea storm whose clouds blotted out the sun and moon and stars.

"Are each of your heads hungry, cousin?" Osgrui roared.

"One mouth for Bersisdeadwife," whispered Vipar—at least it seemed like a whisper after hearing Osgrui roar, "and one for the bitch with the fire sword. One for the bastard who cut off your arm, and one for the one-eyed wolf. One for the pilot, and one for the squirrel. And one to speak with them as I slowly swallow them."

"The squirrel's too small to satisfy your hunger," said Alfarin, which was true, and a very good reason for not bothering to eat the squirrel.

"I'll swallow Ratatosk slowly," Vipar hissed viciously. "I'll swallow him tail-first and make him last long enough to see all the others die before him, The only enemy here who won't satisfy my hunger for heroes is the coward sitting at the steerboard. He's got a sword, but he's too afraid of us to get up from his seat and join his friends."

Bookwyrm didn't say anything, just held onto the steering oar, his face grim.

"Our brave friend back there is the one keeping this ship steered with her head toward the waves so the tsunamis won't capsize it," Robin Grima answered. "He knows we don't need his help to deal with you. There are only three of you sea giants back here, and having more than three of us fighting you would be overkill. That's why I sent Frost Kalinn forward to help the captives." (She'd have said, "One sea giant, one Valhallan," but she knew that nobody else around had heard the Texas Ranger story.)

There was a thump behind me, on the aftcastle. I whirled around and saw a pair of yellow eyes. A gray wolf shook itself furiously, then slowly stepped down the aftcastle steps onto the deck. None of the Valhallans turned around to look, not even when they heard the wolf start howling. The Jotun wolf opened his good eye to look, but he didn't join in the clamor.

The wolf ran forward, fast as the wind, past Ratatosk and past Bookwyrm, jumped over Knut's head and stood between him and Vipar.

"You're the biggest coward on this ship," the wolf said, taunting Vipar in a woman's voice. "You didn't even have the guts to challenge me before you attacked me. You didn't even ask to know my name. But now I'm back to fight you face to face, and this time we'll do it better, Vipar."

Vipar's heads all struck toward her, and she leapt into the air, twisting to avoid the writhing arms, and came down neatly on his back. "I'm Kari Lokisdaughter," she yelled, and leaned over to bite through one of the right arms, then breathed a cloud of flame that seared the wound and made Vipar scream in agony. "I'm Kari Odinsgranddaughter," she yelled and bit through a left arm. "Your poison couldn't kill me, Vipar, but now I'm going to kill you!"

Knut ran forward and hacked off the rest of Vipar's left heads. His sword's touch didn't sear their wounds with fire, but it left them frozen, which was almost as good.

"I'm Kari Knutsfriend," his girlfriend screamed, biting through another right arm, "and I'm Kari Nidhoggsbane," as she bit through the last right arm, "and I'm Kari Viparsbane," as she bit through Vipar's neck and severed his true head, the one in the middle, and then breathed fire to sear all the necks that Knut had severed.

Vipar turned into saltwater and washed overboard, and so did his loose arms and heads.

"Welcome back, Valwolf," said Robin Grima.

"Welcome back, darling," said Knut.

"Thank you," said Wind Kari, and swirled into a cloud of dancing gold light with white sparkles, then stood in human form again, her swan cloak still wet from the seawater. "Now there's only two of you left," she told Alfarin and Osgrui, "and you're facing four Valhallans. Run or die."

They started running back towards Hymir, towards the prow.

"Wave ho!" Bookwyrm yelled, and the third tsunami came, weaker than the first one, lower than the *Naglfar*'s sides, even at midship. Bookwyrm stood up and ran forward to join his friends.

The four Valhallans plus Wind Kari charged forward toward the center mast.

Ratatosk would have liked to stay safe and overlooked near the stern, but he'd sworn an oath, so he followed his oath-mates, scampering nimbly along the top of the steerboard side wall.

The midship deck was covered with dozens of mounds of dirt that had once been hill giants, and Skadi was whirling about like a berserk, holding the center mast two-handed and dashing at her enemies as they fled away from her, some of them jumping over the sides of the ship. Red Hel and Fair Hel were laughing and applauding. So were the draugs. The gray cat was silent.

Then Baldur drew his sword, and it was like the first glimpse of the sun disc when the spring comes back to the northlands. In its brilliant white light, Frost Kalinn's silver sword gleamed like white-hot metal, and even Hodur's dark blade glittered like a starry sky.

"Everybody here wept for me once out of pity," Baldur

said. "I've come here to challenge Tyr *Naglfar*'s Captain to a fight. Don't get in my way, or I'll make you weep in pity for yourselves." He walked toward the forecastle where Hymir and Tyr stood, and his brother Hodur followed him.

Frost Kalinn didn't follow them, even though they were the sons of his father's foster brother. He stood next to Fenris his brother and near Garm his nephew. Frost Kalinn was the only Lokison there with a sword, though Fenris still had his teeth and claws.

"Get out of my way, too!" Tidefyr screamed. She'd wrenched out one of the lesser masts, only a hundred feet high, Her hands were gold with fire, and the flames licked down her mast. "I've defeated you at wrestling, Hymir," she yelled, "and I've defeated you at law, and now I'm going to kill you."

"She was never a good daughter-in-law," Hymir's mother yelled, with all nine of her heads speaking together for a brief moment. "She overcooked the cattle," screamed one head, "and she didn't serve enough drink to our guests," yelled another. "She let the floors get dry," said a third, "and she shook the salt crystals out of the bedlinen," said a fourth. "She welcomed trespassers and thieves," said a fifth, "and broke her wedding vows," said a sixth, "and only gave my son two measly children," said a seventh, "and had a child out of wedlock to a werewolf," said an eighth, and then they all started screaming different insults at the same time so you couldn't pick out any of them.

"Well, I'm still going to marry her now that I know her name," Hymir said. "You can fight her, Mother, but don't kill her. And don't kill Fenris Wolf either; he's going to help me at Ragnarok."

"And don't kill Fenris's bastard puppy," said Tyr, drawing his sword. "I'm going to cut Garm and his father up for bait to catch Orm Midgard Serpent. And don't kill the twin

Odinsons, because I'm going to take care of that, too." He stepped forward to meet Baldur and Hodur. "Don't feel you have to fight me one at a time, dead men. Two of you against one of me is a fair fight." His dull red sword struck out against their swords like sunset dimming the sun disk so you can look at it without your eyes watering.

"That's my wonderful son," Hymir yelled. "Odin took him as a foster son, but Odin didn't appreciate him. Odin never made the Asgard folk pay my son proper respect. Frigga Odinswife should have given my son her fairest daughter as a wife, and Frey Njordson should have ordered the light elves to build my son a house, and Idunn should have planted her apple seeds in his garden. Forget the ungrateful Aesir and Vanir, Son, and come back home where you belong."

"What home?" Hymir's mother wailed. "The great waves smashed down the walls of the stead that I raised up when I was pregnant with you. Where are we going to live now, Hymir, my son? Are we going to have to beg Aegir and Ran to let us come to their stead as refugees?"

"The Nine Worlds and the World Tree all shook when my wolves and my waves swallowed the Sun and the Moon," Hymir said. "If Hymirstead fell apart, then Aegirstead did too. Cousin Aegir and his family will be showing up soon, begging us for shelter, but I won't let them live on my ship till Aegir gives me back my cauldron and admits that I'm his king. Then we'll build our new home, and it'll be a royal palace. That'll be worth coming back home for, won't it, Son?"

"I'll tell you again," Tyr said, "my home is in Asgard. I'm not here to fight on your side. I'm here to kill the Valhallans because they broke their oath to Odin and allied with the Lokisons. When I've done that, I'll go back to Valhalla and take Baldur along with me. When Odin sees Baldur, he'll forgive me for everything I did to help you."

"Odin won't get much conversation out of Baldur," Hymir said. "The fellow's too sleepy."

He was telling the truth. Baldur was down on his knees, holding his sword with both hands as if it was too heavy for just his right wrist to lift it. Hodur lay on the deck next to him, his eyes closed.

"He'll wake up once he's back in Asgard," Tyr said. His sword reached out and touched Baldur's right cheek. The bright-haired god's eyes closed, and he stretched out on the deck beside his twin brother. "You'll wake up back home, beautiful brother," Tyr said, "and it won't take you long to forgive me."

"Just tell us what to do, Cousin Hymir!" Osgrui roared, as he and Alfarin ran up to join Hymir.

"Go help the hill giants deal with Skadi Thiazisdaughter," Hymir said. "Mother, you can tie up my faithless concubine. My son can take care of the Lokison brood one-handed. And I'll send the sea herd up against the rest of the Asgard folk so they don't interfere with us." He screamed words that sent the *Naglfar* to pitching violently, first pointing her prow up into the dark sky and then down toward the dark sea bottom.

There was a chorus of howls from the sea: not a pack of Jotun wolves, but a pack of sea wolves, racing toward the *Naglfar*. And running before them came the sea horses, galloping across the saltwater and leaping up over the sides of the ship and onto the deck. They were screaming in fury and terror, and their mouths gaped wide open, full of rows of bright teeth. There were dozens of them, then hundreds of them, stampeding up and down the deck, their ears back, their eyes wild. The gray cat arched his back and hissed at them, and they fled away from him, away from the rowboat.

The sea wolves didn't follow the sea horses up onto the deck; they just circled the ship, round and round, like dutiful sheepdogs guarding a flock, like hungry wolves stalking a flock. The three biggest sea wolves had little bits of light gleaming in between their teeth as if they needed to floss after chewing up the lights in the sky.

By then Alfarin had reached Skadi's side. He grabbed the mast out of her hands and was beating her over the head with it, as Osgrui roared in triumph and tore at her hair, pulling a hank of it loose and twining it into rope.

"Get away from our cousin!" some of the hill giants yelled. "This is a family fight." They punched and kicked Alfarin and Osgrui, but it didn't seem to do any damage.

The rest of the hill giants leapt at Skadi and tore her bow off her back and broke it. She hit and kicked and bit as much as she could, but in a few minutes Osgrui had pulled her arms behind her back and tied her wrists tight with her hair, and Alfarin had tied up her ankles with her bowstring. Then the sea giants rolled away, up the deck to the forecastle, leaving Skadi lying on the deck, cursing.

"Silence her!" yelled a hill giant, and he climbed up the mast and threw down the tatters of the Norns' tapestry. The other hill giants used the cloth to gag Skadi's mouth.

Meanwhile, the sea horses stampeded up and down the deck, biting savagely at anything and anybody that moved: the giants, the Valhallans, the draugs, and each other. The hill giants who weren't busy with Skadi began jumping overboard and swimming back toward the safety of Jotunheim. Some of them got past the sea wolves.

And Granny Nine-heads was wrestling with Tidefyr, but not by any of the standard rules for a wrestling match. Granny's heads danced about like Vipar's, and her breath was wet, cold saltwater that clung to the skin and hair and filled up the nostrils and mouth and lungs, so being in her embrace was like being drowned, which may explain why you never hear anything about Hymir's father. Tidefyr's red-gold hair was turning gray, and her fair skin was turning livid blue.

Fenris and Garm and Frost Kalinn would have gone to Tidefyr's rescue, but Tyr was there facing them, his red sword flickering through the air like lightning. It didn't dig through skin to open a fountain of blood drops, but its victims grew more tired each time it hit them.

Granny Nine-Heads stuck out her nine tongues at Tidefyr —they were all the colors of seawater: blue and green and gray and black and foam white—and her tongues grew longer and longer, a foot long, a fathom long—and then she bit them off and spat them out and tied them around Tidefyr's wrists and around her ankles, across Tidefyr's eyes and across her mouth, and then she picked up the fire giantess and tied her to the bowsprit, to be the ship's figurehead.

By then, Garm and Frost both lay sleeping on the deck. Fenris was still wide awake, but every time he leapt at Tyr's throat, the red sword beat him back.

"Did the mist elves forge that weapon for you out of sleep thorns?" Fenris yelled. "Did you tell them you were afraid to fight anyone who was awake?"

"They gave it to me in exchange for my promise to rebuild their hall after I killed the treacherous Valhallans," Tyr said. "The mist elves forged thousands of swords like this to defend themselves against Hel and her evil dead folk. Just a touch of this sword sends the dead back to sleep again. Of course it's no good against shameless seducers, is it, wolf? But I'm not worried. Here's the right weapon for you, Lokison!" He ran forward and shoved his right arm into Fenris's mouth, then stepped back, his right arm ending at the wrist, his right hand back in Fenris's mouth once again, its fingers clutching the base of the wolf's tongue. "The mist elves charged me a higher price for my silver-boned hand than they did for my sword," Tyr said, grinning. "They took out my old finger bones and chewed them up and swallowed the marrow. But it's worth it, all the same, Lokison, to be able to stand here and watch you suffer."

Fenris screamed, wordlessly at first, and then gasped out, "This time, at least, my legs are free." He leapt at his enemy, his claws slashing toward Tyr's face.

The Valhallans had been trying to fight their way forward to help their oath-mates, but they couldn't get past the sea horses. Drifa's left arm was bleeding where a sea horse had chewed it. Another sea horse had tried biting off her head, but Bookwyrm cut through its throat and left it choking on its own frozen blood.

Robin Grima sheathed her sword and picked up a loose bone and waved it at the sea horses, at Hymir, at all their enemies. "I dedicate you to Odin," she yelled. The sea horses neighed loudly and ran toward her, their jaws gaping open. "Lasso them!" she yelled and then, when Knut didn't do anything because he didn't understand her, she yelled, "Throw the rune rope around them!"

"All right," Knut said, "but they don't look as if they want to learn to read." He pulled the rope free and flung it out, chanting, "Encircle our enemies, and end their exultation. Mash them into fragments just like you did Mist Hall."

Robin waved her bone at the rune rope and tried to think of F words. "Frighten them and hold them fast!" she yelled. "Fetter their feelings!"

"You'll never be a skald," Knut told her.

"Not skald but scholar!" yelled Bookwyrm. "She's right! That rope's not just for runes and poetry. It's Odin's war fetter! Catch our enemies in your coils, Rope, and bind them with blind panic."

"Send them fleeing in fear from us," chanted Knut, and Bookwyrm and Robin Grima joined in the chant, and the

Jotun wolf howled in time with their tempo. Knut flung the rope at the sea horses, and it glided across the deck air towards them like a greased snake.

Fenris's claws had left eight bleeding scratches to scar Tyr's face.

Tyr stuck out his tongue, and it stretched out for yards—well, after all, Old Lady Nine-Heads was his grandmother—till it was long enough to wrap itself around Fenris's legs and bind them fast together. Tyr tore it out of his mouth and tied it off, and laughed loudly as Fenris tried to squirm free. He picked the giant wolf up by the tail and swung him round and round, then bashed his head down against the deck so hard that the white bones splintered under the impact.

After that Fenris's eyes were closed, just like Garm's and Frost Kalinn's.

Hymir walked down from the prow and kicked Baldur's face. "I wept when they told me that you died," he said, "but that was because I was sad that I'd never have the chance to kill you."

"We all wept at Baldur's death," Granny Nine Heads said, following her son. "Because we wanted him as a kitchen drudge," one head said. "No, as a bed closet drudge," a second head yelled. "No, no, no," yelled the other heads, each with their own insult.

"Odin's my foster father," Tyr said when his grandmother finally fell silent, "and that makes Baldur my brother. I'll never forgive Loki for tricking Hodur into killing Baldur, and I'll never forgive Loki for not weeping for Baldur."

"So you've got your tongue again, do you?" asked Hymir. "Good boy."

Granny Nine-Heads spoke up in nine voices, one head saying that growing back a tongue was an easy thing to do once you had the hang of it and the rest screaming, "The horses! The horses!"

The sea horses were all running away from the Valhallans, stampeding to the sides of the ship and jumping overboard, some of them diving into the sea where the sea wolves tore them to pieces, some of them running across the saltwater to the dry land, and some of them running up into the sky, where Sigyn dove towards them, talons outstretched. Wind Kari spread out her arms and took to the air again, to help her mother.

Brave little Ratatosk jumped from the railing atop the sides of the *Naglfar* and ran forward along the bowsprit to where Granny Nine-Heads had tied Tidefyr and began gnawing at her bonds. They were very salty, which wasn't too surprising, given that they were the tongues of a sea giantess, but the valiant squirrel didn't quit, even though after a while his mouth felt horribly dry and he'd have traded his newest computer for a swallow of fresh water.

The third tsunami's ebb wave hit around then, only a couple of dozen feet high, but it sent the sea wolves to howling again, and it set the *Naglfar* to pitching, and the Valhallans didn't have the rune rope to hold onto any more.

When the bowsprit pointed up at the sky, Ratatosk could see the sea horses kicking and biting Wind Kari and Sigyn. White swan feathers were falling like flakes of snow, and the auroras were getting smaller.

When the bowsprit dipped down toward the dark saltwater, Ratatosk could see the sea wolves more clearly than he wanted to. Their teeth were red with sea horse blood and they were leaping hungrily up into the air. One of them tried to tear off Tidefyr's right foot, but it fell back screaming when she kicked it. Another one had better luck: it leapt at her left leg and tore off a chunk of her calf. A third was luckier yet—for Tidefyr; it bit off the binding that held her wrists together behind her back. A fourth one nearly swallowed Ratatosk, but the heroic squirrel bit him in the nose, and the sea wolf fell back into the ocean, howling in pain.

After that, the sea grew calmer, and Ratatosk and Tidefyr managed to crawl along the bowsprit, back onto the forecastle.

Down on the deck, the rune rope glided over to Alfarin and Osgrui and twisted around their feet. They ran away from it, screaming in terror, and jumped over the side of the ship. The hill giants followed them.

"It's the rope that hanged Odin!" Tyr yelled. "It's the rope that destroyed Mist Hall! My sword's no good against it!"

"You're a coward, Hymirson!" yelled Robin Grima.

"You're a traitor, Jonson!" Tyr yelled back at her.

"And faint-hearted Hymir's a coward too!" yelled Bookwyrm. "He sends his old mother into combat rather than risk his own skin!"

"I'll show you who's old, you foul-mouthed draugs from Slain Hall!" all of Granny's heads shouted in unison. She ran toward the Valhallans, screaming insults—till the rune rope bound her legs together and then climbed up and bound her necks together.

"Stupid rope," one head yelled, and "I'm stronger than your sword, Grandson," another head cackled. She bent her nine heads down to the rope and started chewing on it, spitting out little bits of rope, but her heads were turning blue as the rune rope grew tighter around their necks.

"Help me, Grandson!" she screamed, all nine heads together, and she ran toward Tyr. "I don't want to die alone!"

The rope flung a loop around a mast, but she pulled it free. It flung out another loop that caught Tyr's left arm.

"No!" he yelled.

"Yes," Granny gasped. "We can keep each other company." She ran to the side of the ship and jumped overboard, and the rope went with her and so did Tyr, all of them sinking into the black ocean.

Minutes went by, and none of them came up again.

"Now it's my turn at last," said Hymir, "and you'll all find out how cowardly I am. I'm going to wrestle Hel—one man against two women is a fair match."

"Wrestle me first," said the cat. "I hear that one woman beat you this morning, when you were fighting for your honor and family, but I'm sure you can do better than that when you're fighting for your cowardly life."

"She cheated," Hymir said, "but it wasn't a disgrace to lose to Black Surt's sister's daughter. My name is Hymir the Wave Lord. What's your name, kittycat?"

"Don't tell me you've forgotten me, old friend," said the cat, arching his back and growing a little taller and a lot longer. "A few days ago, we agreed that I knew more about poisons than you did, and that I could drag you underwater and keep you there if I chose." By then his tail had reached the aftcastle half a mile away and he was still growing, and his fanged face wasn't a cat's any more but a serpent's, the Midgard Serpent's. "My name is Orm Lokison," he hissed and breathed out a cloud of glowing green venom.

"Save your poison to kill Thor at Ragnarok," Hymir said. "I grew up playing with Vipar, and I'm immune to venom. All right, Orm, let's see how well you can wrestle." He leapt forward like a breaking wave.

A moment later a flurry of swan feathers fell from the sky and the auroras vanished, and it was pitch-black on the *Naglfar* except for the glimmer that was Robin Grima's hair. The sky rang with sea horse neighing, like battle horns, like high-pitched thunder, and I wondered how many of them it had taken to defeat Sigyn and Wind Kari.

"I can't see anything," Tidefyr whispered, and "I can't either," Ratatosk whispered back. They could both hear the sounds of conflict: thumps and bangs (was that Hymir jumping up and down, or someone pounding someone else against the deck?) and now and then Hymir yelled, but they couldn't tell if it was a cry of pain or triumph.

Then there was a sudden gust of bright fire, Orm's flame breath, and they saw Hymir standing by the rowboat. He'd grown four long arms: one was wrapped around Fair Hel's neck and a second one around Red Hel's neck and the other two held Orm's neck and tail. He was tying the Hels' hair together so they faced away from each other, and he was tying the giant snake into the same complex knot.

"Around twice," he muttered, "and then thread it back under all three loops and pull it tight." That made an overhand knot underneath two riding turns; sailors call it a double constrictor knot. It helped that Orm still hadn't reached his full size; now the thicker he got the tighter the knot got, and changing back into a cat in that position would leave him with a broken spine.

Orm's fire breath was getting dimmer.

The Jotun wolf was sitting off by the side of the ship, safely out of the way, observing the action with mild interest, like someone watching a prizefight that he hadn't bet on.

Hymir laughed. "Don't struggle, Orm," he roared. "Save your strength and your fire and your venom for Ragnarok when we'll be allies. Until then, I'm going to make sure you stay out of trouble." He grew two more arms and picked up the center mast and thrust it through Orm's body, as easily as pinning a cloak on with a brooch. Orm screamed, and his fire breath went out, and there was darkness again.

"There's not going to be a Ragnarok!" Robin Grima yelled. "The Norns wove all those prophecies up into a tapestry, and you took it to hang on your mast, but it's all unraveled now, and so are the prophecies." She walked forward by the light of her hair, with Knut and Bookwyrm and Drifa following her.

"Clever little Valhallan," Hymir said. "Odin will be angry with you for telling me that, but I'm very pleased with you. I'm so pleased with your warning that I'm not going to kill you after all. I'll just take you and your friends back home with me and chain you to a loom and set you to reweaving the Norns' threads till my sail is whole again."

"No!" Robin screamed.

Hymir reached down and scooped up two giant handfuls of unraveled Norn threads and poured himself down the deck toward the Valhallans like a great wave full of seaweed, tangling them in the Norn threads till they couldn't move hand or foot to attack him and they couldn't open their mouths to speak.

"That'll keep you out of trouble," he told them. "I'll set you free once I've built my stead again and set up the weaving room. There's no rush; I won't need my sail till Ragnarok comes."

"There's not going to be a Ragnarok!" Tidefyr yelled. I could hear her limping down the forecastle steps toward Hymir.

"I hope you're right, honeytongue," Hymir said, "because that'll be even better. I'll cut out Orm's bones, and use them to stake him down on the beach, between the low tideline and the high tideline. I'll cut his skin off in strips and tan it and use it to tie up his sisters and brothers. I'll cut out their bones too, and make a bed frame out of them. I'll take you to my bed and lock ice bracelets on you so you forget you ever did anything but lie in bed and wait for me to come join you there. I'll chain Fenris to the foot of our bed, so he can look his fill at us when we're there together. We'll have lots of time in bed together before I go conquer Asgard. I'll need nine frozen winters to get a new generation of frost giants to replace the ones that the dragon's fire breath melted, and nine centuries to get a new generation of hill giants."

Ratatosk clung to the forecastle, wishing he had a mist cap so he could sneak away and go back home, wishing that somebody would step forward and kill Hymir.

"Your mother's dead, Hymir," Tidefyr said.

"It happens to most men, sooner or later," Hymir said. "It'll mean more housework for our thralls, but I don't mind."

"Your son's dead too," she said.

"I can get more sons now that I've got you back. You were only pregnant nine years with Tyr. In another nine centuries, you can give me ninety new sons. The important thing that happened today is that the ocean swallowed proud Odin's war fetter. That'll hurt him more than—"

He stopped in surprise. There was a bright red light shining through the ocean. Not inching up over the horizon and not high in the sky, but lighting up the saltwater like sunlight lighting up clouds. Had one of the sea wolves gotten indigestion and burped up the sun?

It was a burning ship, longer and wider and higher than the *Naglfar*, red pillars of flames rising hundreds of feet up into the sky like masts, black clouds of smoke clinging to the flame pillars like sails, white-hot tentacles of flames lashing out at the water like oars.

CHAPTER TWENTY

"Better late than never," a voice on the *Naglfar* said, a man's voice but not one I'd heard recently. I couldn't see his face, and it could have been some trickster doing voice impressions. I cursed the darkness, and I wished I was on a branch of the World Tree and had my night vision goggles, but I wasn't, and the stranger didn't say anything else, and even if it was who I thought it was, I wasn't sure if he'd come here to save us or to kill us.

I reckoned up Robin Grima's companions. The Valhallans were tied up in Norn threads, and the only one of them who could see in the dark was Drifa, the one who bore a weapon she'd never been trained with. Tidefyr was injured. The last I had seen of Sigyn and Kari were falling feathers. Fenris was fettered with Tyr's tongue; Kalinn and Garm lay sleeping along with Baldur and Hodur. Orm was tied up, and so were the Hel sisters, and so was Skadi, and the rune rope was in the ocean, and the Jotun wolf didn't seem interested in fighting.

It looked as if it was all up to me. I didn't have the strength to pull Tyr's right hand out of Fenris's mouth, and I didn't want to get too close to Orm and risk breathing his venom, but there was still something I could do.

I crept down the forecastle steps, quiet as a squirrel (and that's a lot more quiet than a mouse), smelling my way toward Skadi.

"Ahoy, *Naglfar*!" shouted a far-off voice from the fire ship. "The *Muspel* will get there as fast as it can, Evildoer."

"What's going on here?" bellowed Hymir. "I'm not an evildoer, you slanderer. I'm fighting against the evil Aesir and for the good folk of Jotunheim!"

"Tell the good folk in Jotunheim that King Surt of Muspelheim is coming to visit them," the voice called from the fireship.

"Welcome to the ocean, King Surt," bellowed Hymir. "The prophecies said you'd come sailing here someday to conquer Asgard and that you'd have Wyrmtongue Loki as your pilot. I'm Hymir the sea lord, your loyal ally. Together, we can conquer the Nine Worlds and divide them between us."

There was a loud thump somewhere amidship, and the *Naglfar* rocked as if something heavy had landed on her. Three more thumps followed.

"Who's there?" Hymir screamed.

Nobody answered.

I took a deep breath and smelled Skadi nearby—and sea wolves!

"No!" Hymir screamed. "Go away! Go back to the ocean, or I'll call the tsunamis to wash you away!"

The rune rope had gotten back on deck and was slithering toward Hymir, dragging along three sea wolves (those must have been the thumps I'd heard) wrapped in its coils. Its tail still hung over the side, in the ocean.

"Don't come any closer, stupid snake!" Hymir yelled, but the rune rope didn't stop.

"Are you all right, Mother?" Hymir screamed. "Are you all

right, Son?"

Nobody answered that, either.

The fireship sped across the dark sea toward the *Naglfar*, its bright oars beating in unison against the dark water. The closer it got, the warmer the air got.

Sniffing, I found my way Skadi's feet and began gnawing at the bowstring that held her ankles together. It was tough but still better tasting than sea giant tongue.

"An army of fire giants is coming from Muspelheim to help me," Hymir bellowed. "They'll burn   up all of my enemies!"

Nobody answered.

As soon as I'd gnawed Skadi's feet free, she started kicking wildly. One of her kicks sent me flying through the air. *"Well,"* I thought, *"if that's how she's going to behave, then I won't go back and set her wrists free."* I looked around by the light of the fireship to find somewhere safe to sit, but all I could see was danger.

The Jotun wolf sat quietly on one side of the ship, observing everything but not getting involved, obviously the most intelligent person on board except for me. I ran over to sit next to him.

"Hello, Ratatosk," he said. "What do you think of our host's hospitality?" He'd picked a crazy time to start talking, but I've never turned down a chance to have an interesting conversation.

"I haven't seen any real hospitality since we left Skadistead," I told him. "But even Loki was a better host than Hymir."

"Loki's studied the *Havamal*, and Hymir hasn't. 'Fire and food and clothes must await the wayfarer.... Water and towels and welcoming speech.'"

"I didn't invite you snotty bastards here!" Hymir bellowed at us. "You're not my guests, and you're not under my roof, and I don't owe you any hospitality or protection."

"You invited everybody in Jotunheim to come here!" I yelled indignantly. "We read your invitation when we visited Mimir's Fountain."

"You promised us all the work we could handle and all the ale we could drink and all the food we could eat," the Jotun wolf said, getting up and walking toward Hymir.

"I know Wyrmtongue Ratatosk," Hymir said, "but I don't know you, Wolf One-Eye. What's your name?"

"I'm Evildoer," the wolf said, standing up on its hind legs and changing into a man—no, a woman, as tall as Hymir and a lot uglier. "I'm the giantess Thokk, the only one in the Nine Worlds who didn't weep at Baldur's death." Her form changed to a man's, and her voice deepened. "I'm the king of Utgard who out-tricked clever Loki." He changed back to wolf form again and fell back down onto four feet. "My enemies call me Shapeshifter and Deceiver." His voice changed with every form he took. The only thing that stayed the same through all his changes was that his left eye was missing. Shape-changing can work all sorts of wonders, but it can't heal your wounds.

"Welcome to the *Naglfar*, whatever your name is," Hymir said. "I can tell from your names and your deeds that you're going to be my ally. What do your friends call you?"

"I sometimes call him Flame Eye!" yelled the voice from the *Muspel*. The wolf laughed.

"That's a good name, too," Hymir said. "What can I do for you, Flame Eye? You can't have my ship or my woman or my son or my thralls, but ask for anything else you see, and there's a good chance I'll give it to you."

"There are three thieves on this ship," Flame Eye said.

"Do you want to beg me to show mercy to them? Do you want to fight me as their champion?"

"I don't like thieves any more than you do," Hymir said. "I offer you self-judgment against any thieves you find on my ship." That meant that Flame Eye wouldn't have to summon the nine nearest neighbors to sit on a jury and hear the case; he got to pass whatever sentence he thought was fair—outlawry or fines—against the thieves.

"You show all the wisdom I expected from you," Flame Eye said. He trotted over to the first sea wolf. "Put what you stole back where it belongs," he said, "and I'll let you go back where you belong."

The sea wolf blew a cloud of bright foam up into the sky from the blowhole on the top of its head. It flew apart into thousands of small bright lights that hurtled up into the sky like a meteor shower in reverse—and a minute later the sky was full of stars. The Milky Way arched across the heavens like a silver belt, and Frigg's Distaff and Thiazi's Eyes and Odin's Wagon and all the rest of the constellations were back in their places, and the North Star shone at their center, and there were blue-white spears of auroras hanging over the *Naglfar*. The rune rope eased its grip, and the sea wolf wriggled away, rocking the ship with its weight, and leapt over the side, back into the ocean.

"That was cute," Hymir said, "and you can make the second guy cough up the Moon if you want to, but I don't want any more sunlight over my ship than I'd see at sunset, and less than that would be even better."

"It's a bargain," said Flame Eye. He walked over to the second sea wolf and told him, "Put what you stole back where it belongs, and you can go join your brother." Then he turned to the third sea wolf and said, "And hide what you stole behind what your brother took, and you can go along with him."

Valhalla: Absent Without Leave

For a minute—and a minute is a long, long time when nobody's saying anything and nothing is happening—all we could see was the cloud of bright foam surrounding us. It was even denser than the Niflheim mist.

Finally the foam blew away, and there were three great glowing lights—the red fireship only a few hundred yards away from us, and the silver circle of the Moon shining on the eastern horizon, and behind it, flaring out like a golden aurora, the Sun's corona. (Yes, I know that the Moon was a waning crescent when the sea wolf swallowed it, and a solar eclipse only occurs at the new moon. That got straightened out a few minutes later.)

Anyway, there was a Sun and a Moon up in the sky again, and it was like— There aren't enough words and similes and metaphors in my wordbox to say what it was like.

The air was warm again, and it felt like going from midwinter to midsummer. Well, maybe more like going from mid-spring to midsummer if you counted the last few minutes with the fireship nearby.

And the sky was bright again. Yes, I know that a total solar eclipse is a lot darker than normal daylight, but we'd been in near-total darkness for hours, and our eyes were dazzled by even a glimpse of the sun. Suddenly, the flare of Robin Grima's hair and the gleam of her sword were just faint glows, barely noticeable in a world of light.

And the world was big again—not just a few hundred feet of twilight but hundreds of miles wide, from horizon to horizon, hundreds of miles high from the sea beneath us to the sky above us. We could see the *Naglfar*'s white bone deck gleaming from forecastle to aftcastle. The sea wolves were gone, and the only people standing on the deck were Hymir and Flame Eye Wolf and a small inconspicuous red squirrel.

And there were colors again. Not just the colors of the auroras dancing in the sky and the colors of the Norns' threads, but all the colors of the rainbow. Things weren't twilight gray any more; they were vivid. The world wasn't dreamlike any more; it looked real. The bright light hurt my eyes, but I couldn't stop looking around.

"I have wonderful gifts for you, Hymir," the man called from the fireship. "Treasures from Muspelheim that King Surt wants to give you. May I come aboard your ship and offer them to you?"

"I think I know what your name is," Hymir said, "but tell me anyway."

"My enemies call me Wyrmtongue," the man said, "and my friends call me Loki."

"Greetings, Loki," Hymir said. "The gossips say that Flame Eye here out-tricked you at Utgard. I thought you said you and he were friends."

"We were, once," said the wolf.

"We still are," Loki said. "Even when we torture each other it's out of friendship."

"Then you can come aboard the *Naglfar*," said Hymir. "And, Flame Eye, you can have your pick of the fire world's treasures, to seal our alliance."

"Thanks for your courtesy, Hymir," the wolf said. Then he turned his back on Hymir and said, "Rope, you're twisted and tricky, and I don't blame Hymir for distrusting you after the grasping way you treated his mother and his son. What did you do with them, Rope?"

The rope pulled its tail up over the side of the ship, and there were Granny Nine Heads and Tyr caught in its coils, both of them trembling in terror.

"They're not dead!" Hymir yelled happily.

"Let go of them at once, wicked rope," the wolf ordered, "and then go tie yourself up and stay out of our way."

The rope obediently let go of Tyr and Granny and glided

awkwardly off to the bowsprit, somehow managing to bump into everyone it passed. Robin and the other Valhallans, caught up in the Norn threads. Fair Hel and Red Hel, their long hair tied together. Garm and Frost Kalinn and Baldur and Hodur, all four of them peacefully sleeping. Skadi, her arms tied behind her. Fenris, with his legs fettered. Orm, tied in a constrictor knot.

It didn't seem to matter. The sleeping ones went on sleeping, and the tied up ones stayed tied up.

"There are too many enemies on this ship," one of Granny's heads whispered. "I'm going back home to where it's safe," another head whispered. The rest of them were crying hysterically.

"Mother!" Hymir yelled, but she didn't pay any attention to him. She staggered to the side of the ship and jumped overboard.

Tyr wasn't crying. He just sat there on the deck, mouth open and panting—like a man who's just run away from an enemy and isn't really sure he's safe. His hands were trembling. Well, his left hand was trembling.

"Where's your new sword, Son?" Hymir called, but Tyr didn't answer, didn't reach down to his empty scabbard, didn't even look up at his father.

Meanwhile the eclipsed Sun was drifting slowly along the horizon, sinking lower every minute. The eclipse was lasting a long time, but that was fairly normal for Jotunheim. What wasn't normal was that when the corona finally faded from sight below the horizon, the new moon didn't go with it. First it was a black circle silhouetted against gold sunset clouds. Then it was a shining crescent as thin as an eyelash, just a little above the horizon. And then it began climbing back toward midheaven, which wasn't at all normal, growing wider and brighter with every step it retraced, till it hung a little below the North Star, a three-week-old waning crescent, only a little older than the one we'd seen this morning. It was back where it belonged, and so was the Sun.

Fenris was back in human form, and Tidefyr had moved to his side, her red-gold hair bright in the moonlight, her eyes bright with happiness. Tyr's right hand lay on the deck near her, and her circle of moonlight kept growing till it covered the whole ship. Fenris opened his mouth wide to drink the last traces of the sunset; then he sat up and reached out to Tidefyr.

Both of them were too busy kissing to notice Tyr's hand crawling off, across the bone deck, to where Tyr was sitting. It rubbed against his ankle like a cat who wants to be stroked, and then, when he didn't pay any attention, it stood up on its fingertips and jumped up onto his right wrist.

Loki climbed up a twisting pillar of smoke from the fireship and then somersaulted through the air to land standing on the bone ship's deck, his arms full of shining gold chests that he laid at Hymir's feet.

"Hail, Hymir," he said. "Hail, Evildoer."

The last time we'd seen him, he'd been wearing a white shirt and red trousers. Now his clothes were all shining gold, almost as bright as his red hair. Only a sharp-eyed squirrel looked away from the spectacle and noticed Frost Kalinn turning over onto his belly, his starlight hair softly shining. He crept silently across the deck, toward the tangle of Norn threads, towards the Valhallans.

And nearer the prow, Baldur and Hodur were helping each other sit up. Red Hel and Fair Hel had gotten their hair separated and were combing it out with their fingers. Orm had managed to slither out of the knot and was coiled up, ready to strike.

"Hail, Loki," said the one-eyed wolf. "You're more polite

than you were the last time we talked. Has some woman been teaching you manners?"

"I see you're just as rude as you've always been," Loki said. "What women have you met lately?"

"I met several beautiful women just this month," said the wolf. "I held them tight, and they loved my embrace. What about you?"

"I've met just as many as you have," said Loki, "and the only thing that kept me from coming closer to them was that I didn't have a hand free."

"And now you've got both hands free," the wolf said. "Stolen anything lately?"

"Only getting my own property back again," Loki said. "And you shouldn't talk about stealing. We both know that you'll steal anything you want. I was missing an eye for a while recently, and I suspect you're the one who took it."

"Only to play with," the wolf said. "I gave it back again as soon as I was done with it."

"I can see you two are old friends," Hymir said. "What's in the boxes, Loki?"

"King Surt doesn't send you silver or gold," Loki said. "In Muspelheim, that's the gravel in their streets. Instead he sends you jewelry made with a substance that doesn't need light to glitter. It's black now, but if you scrape off its surface under water, you'll find that it's bright white in the daytime and spring green in the night and a little warm to the touch. It's name is radium. The artists of Muspelheim have fashioned it into jewelry—rings and brooches and necklaces and armbands and torcs." He opened up a chest, and the things in it glowed in the moonlight like yellow-green flames.

Hymir reached down to run his fingers through the chest. "Pretty," he said.

"And here's King Surt's next present," said Loki, opening another chest. "A cloak of spun rock that will never catch fire, even in the flames of Muspelheim. Its name is asbestos, and it's padded with spun glass to keep the wearer cool."

Hymir shook out the long hooded cloak and watched the moonlight glisten on the white cloth. "Pretty," he said again. "I'll keep this if the Aesir put a wall of fire around Asgard the way they did when Thiazi came to visit." He put it on.

"And here's a drinking horn," Loki said. "It will never go dry, and just one sip will make you forget all your troubles." Hymir picked up the curling, foam-white horn and shook it and heard the liquid inside it gurgle.

"Nice," he said, and put it back in the chest. "I'll take it with me when I sail to Asgard, to keep up my warriors' hearts."

"And here's a sword," Loki said. "It's forged from a metal that you won't easily find anywhere but Muspelheim. It's as strong as meteoritic iron but half the weight, and it won't rust in salt air or saltwater. Its name is titanium."

Hymir picked the sword up and swung it through the air. "Very pretty," he said. "I'll wear this when I go to Asgard." He dropped it back in its chest and turned to the wolf. "Which do you want, Flame Eye? Nothing or jewelry?"

"I want jewelry," said the wolf, and changed back into a hulking giant. He picked up a ring and pried out its glowing green gem with his fingernails and shoved it into his empty eye socket. "You can keep the rest of it."

"I can grow a new eye whenever I want to," Hymir said, "and I don't change into a woman." He ran his hands through the chest, picking up handfuls of glowing yellow-green things and dropping them again. "Is there anything else in here besides jewelry, Loki?"

"That's all King Surt told me about," Loki said.

"Look again," Hymir urged him. "Maybe there's something you'd like to wear. If there is, I'll give it to you as a reward for bringing me all these wonderful things."

"Well," Loki said, "I'll look into it, but don't blame me if things don't work out the way you want them to." He knelt down and peered into the jewelry chest. It was deeper than it looked. His hands went in up to his shoulders, and he leaned over—and then he was falling into the chest like a man diving into a pool, head and waist and hips and feet disappearing into the yellow-green light—and Hymir slammed the lid down on top of him and turned the chest upside down and jumped up on top of it.

"I can out-trick Loki, too," he told the wolf.

"You can't sit on that chest forever," the wolf said. "You'll need something to tie it up with."

"I don't want to keep Loki imprisoned forever!" Hymir said. "I just want him to respect me for being more clever than he is."

"I do," Loki called out from inside the chest. "I respect —"and he broke down into giggles, which didn't make him sound very convincing even after he managed to gasp out "You're much more clever."

"And I still don't trust that rope," Hymir said, standing up. "Any more than I trust you, Flame Eye Evildoer Odin. Just how stupid do you think I am not to recognize your names?"

"Don't answer that question!" Loki screamed in between fits of wild laughter.

The wolf changed shape again, to a tall, bronze-haired man, Odin's true form. He was still one-eyed. "Do you want a duel?" he asked in his own voice, the one we'd heard in the darkness when we first saw the fireship. "I didn't come here to kill you, but I will if you insist."

Something screamed up above. Not a woman's scream but a raven's. Thought and Memory were both up there, keeping watch on their master.

Robin Grima tried to sit up, and the Norn threads fell

away from her.

"No," whispered Frost Kalinn. "Let Father and Uncle Odin handle this for now. We'll wait till we're needed."

"A duel's too formal," Hymir said. "I just want to watch Fenris Wolf destroy you."

"Odin's my foster father!" yelled Tyr, jumping to his feet. "I won't let Fenris Wolf kill him until Ragnarok comes."

"Don't worry," Fenris growled. "I'm not going to kill him, now or at Ragnarok. I promised I wouldn't."

"Then I'll just have to do it myself," Hymir said. "Now is as good a time as any. Would you like to help, Loki?"

"I'd love to help you out-trick Odin," Loki called out from inside the chest. "Let me out of here, and we'll stuff him inside the chest and tie it up with Baldur's intestines. Turnabout is fair play."

"No," Hymir said. "I don't want Odin imprisoned. Not even if you promised me we'll put him into a box of of clear ice so I'll get to watch him grow old and weak and ugly. He's got to be destroyed. He's the one who sent my son and Thor to take my cauldron and bring it to Aegir. He's the reason that I'm not king of the ocean any more."

"No!" Tyr yelled. "I don't want my fathers to fight each other. Fight Loki! Fight Fenris and Orm and the Hels! They're your real enemies!"

"They're my real allies," Hymir said. "The prophecies say so."

The chest tumbled over and spilled out its contents at Hymir's feet—jewelry and silvery titanium and green glowing radium, and Loki lying in the midst of it holding two gleaming swords. "I'm your loyal ally," Loki said, in between fits of giggles, "and I'm Odin's worst enemy. The prophecies —" He broke down into hysterical laughter.

"You killed my twins, Wyrmtongue," Odin said. "You

tricked them, and they both died of it."

"Only after you banished my children! Loki yelled. "And afterwards you did the same to me, only worse. Your son Baldur died so quick it barely hurt. My son Frost died slowly, bite by bite."

"Turnabout is fair play," Odin laughed. "But there's one question I'd like to ask before Hymir tries to kill me."

"Go ahead and ask," said Hymir. "Usually you claim to know everything, so it'll be a refreshing change, and I might even tell you the answer. What do you want to know, Blind Eye?"

"It's a question for Tyr," Odin said. "Because he remembers that I'm his foster father and because he doesn't want you to kill me. Where were you planning to be when Hymir's ship sailed up to Asgard, Tyr foster son, Tyr *Naglfar* Captain, and what were you planning to do when Hymir's ship got there?"

"I was going to steer the old *Naglfar* from Niflheim up to Asgard," Tyr said, "and not stop in Jotunheim to pick up the giants and trolls. The mist elves said they'd go to Asgard with me to fight the Hel folk and the Muspel folk. But that was back before I knew that the fire giants were my mother's family. That was back when you treated me honorably, foster father. It was before you tricked me and trapped me in your war fetter and let people see me trembling in fear. Now I see why Thor left Asgard and swore he wouldn't come back till Ragnarok. I won't break my oath to you the way Robin Grima Jonson and her gang of runaways from Valhalla did, but I'll never forgive you for what you did to me today."

"Everyone has to put up with some embarrassment and frustration now and then," Odin said. "And what I've done to you today, foster son, is nothing compared to what I'm going to do your father." He turned his back on Tyr, to face Hymir. "This is your day of disaster, Hymir. The sea giants who stood at your side have all left you. Even your own mother abandoned you. You called the trolls and the frost giants and the hill giants to build this ship and follow you, but now most of them are dead and the rest have wisely run away. This ship of bones where they fought and died isn't the *Naglfar*—the wraith ferry—any more but the *Valskip*—the slain ship, my ship as Lord of the Slain."

"*Naglfar*'s my ship," Hymir bellowed, "and you don't have the right to rename it, and I'm going to destroy you!" He screamed out words of power, but this time no sea horses came running; no sea wolves came howling. But the stars and the moon tilted and spun over our heads as the ship tossed about on the angry ocean and the waves howled around us.

No, it was worse than that! The sea was motionless and silent under the ship, and the ship was motionless on top of the sea. And the stars and the moon were tilting and spinning over our heads because the world was out of balance. The howling we heard was the World Tree groaning in pain, and its branches were trembling, and the Nine Worlds were tossing about like dead leaves in a strong wind.

And something was hissing. ("*Like an angry cat,*" Knut thought. "*Like a rattlesnake,*" Robin thought.) The sound grew louder and nearer.

"Shore wave, ho!" yelled Bookwyrm as the cresting tsunami crept toward us from Jotunheim, its waters sparkling under the moonlight. From Jotunheim? That didn't make any sense. The last tsunami we'd seen was an ebb wave from Jotunheim heading back home to the ocean, and all the water in Jotunheim is frozen except for Mimir's Fountain!

"I've still got one follower left," Hymir bellowed, "and you shouldn't underestimate it."

"We'd never underestimate Hel River," Fair Hel

whispered.

"We've fed it for centuries on murderers and slanderers and oathbreakers," Red Hel whispered.

"You've starved it," Hymir bellowed. "It's nibbled lots of fingers and toes and noses over the years but not nearly enough to satisfy its hunger. You may have learned to understand dead folk, Hel queens, but I was born understanding water. I was born king of the water, and Hel River stayed mine even after I gambled with Aegir for my birthright and he cheated me out of the ocean cauldron. When I called Hel River to come, it ran to obey me—up the trunk of the World Tree to Mimir's Fountain and down across Jotunheim to my side. Wake up, Garm! The prophecies say you'll howl when the World Tree falls. Howl, Hel-dog, and I'll spare your life! Maybe I'll even spare your brother's life."

Loki laughed. "Everybody has to put up with some embarrassment and frustration now and then," he yelled, "and this is the day Odin reaps the reward of all his lies and his tricks. Howl, Garm! This is the day that my monster children triumph!"

Garm was still in human form, and he didn't howl. Instead, he sprang silently at Hymir and his small short blunt teeth—not as good as a dog's fangs, let alone a squirrel's fangs—met in Hymir's throat and tore it out, and Garm fell to the deck coughing, choking, his mouth and his lungs full of sea water.

"No!" Fair Hel screamed and drew her sword, and so did her sister.

"Go ahead," Loki yelled. "Tickle Hymir with your silly swords! We all need a laugh. Don't worry, girls. Your swords can't wound Hymir any more than my swords can wound me." He stabbed his two swords into his chest and then, giggling hysterically, pulled them out and threw them into the ocean and fell to the bone deck, choking with laughter. "No weapon can wound Hymir," he yelled in between fits of giggling. "You might as well attack the sea."

"Yes," whispered Orm and began beating his head against the deck. That didn't mean he was frustrated or insane; it meant he was getting ready to shed his skin.

"Hurry up, Hel wave!" Hymir yelled, and the tsunami rushed toward us across the motionless ocean, under the reeling stars, its crest higher than the *Valskip*'s aftcastle, its water sparkling with little sharp knives.

"No!" cried Odin.

"Now!" whispered Frost Kalinn, and ran toward the stern, toward the tsunami, and the Valhallans ran after him.

Tyr turned to follow them, holding a bright spear of sea water tipped with a star, but then Fenris was standing in from of him, growling, little gusts of flame flaring out of his nostrils.

After that, of course, there wasn't anything to worry about. We got all the loose ends tied up and checked out the available Asgard real estate, then—Yes, Urd, I remember my promise. Please don't be angry. Please don't touch my life-thread.

The Hel River tsunami flooded down from the aftcastle, its sharp knives carving lines in the *Valskip*'s bones. And then it met the ice swords—Frost Kalinn's and Knut's and Bookwyrm's and Drifa's and Robin's—and the wave froze.

Frostbite the D&D sword froze any liquid its point touched, but if the volume was over a gallon, the liquid got a saving throw. Frostbite the Nine Worlds sword didn't have to worry about saving throws; he froze anything he attacked, even boiling dragon's blood. Frost Kalinn Lokison was the child of wind and fire, but his power was cold, and going through the fire ordeal in Blind Hall hadn't altered that; it just gave him another string to his bow. Being cut down to just his backbone had weakened his power, but his sister and father had restored it, and now he was at full strength. His sword had cut through Hymir's net which was the power of the ocean. And now his touch froze Hel River.

The river froze into a glacier full of sharp little knives. The ice floated on top of the ocean like an iceberg, if you can imagine an iceberg that's a hundred feet wide and a hundred miles long. The ice lay on top of the stern of the *Valskip*.

And then Robin Grima's sword stabbed it, hot as the flames that had melted her flesh in the fire ordeal.

The Hel ice melted into steam and its knives melted too, and Sigyn and Wind Kari caught it all up in a net of auroras and carried it away.

After that, things were calm. The moon and the stars shone quietly and peacefully in the sky, and the ocean swells rolled quietly and peacefully under the ship, and the Nine Worlds hung quietly and peacefully on the World Tree.

"You've lost that follower too," Odin told Hymir. "Now you're all alone."

"He's still got me left!" yelled Loki, and he jumped up to embrace Hymir with arms and legs that turned into tongues of flame.

Hymir screamed as his white asbestos cloak from Muspelheim twisted around him, protecting him from Loki's fire, enveloping him, imprisoning him, and then Loki stepped away, but the fire didn't stop burning. By now it looked like a bonfire, like a funeral pyre.

"Beg me for mercy," Fenris growled at Tyr, "and grant me self-judgment, or else fight me. This time it'll be a fair fight because I'm not going to swallow your lies or your hand."

Tyr didn't answer, just stabbed at Fenris's heart.

Fenris laughed and tore the spear out of Tyr's hands. "You swore you'd be my foster brother and you betrayed me," Fenris snarled. "You sent Robin Grima and her oath-mates to find me in chains and kill me. And then when they set me free, you told people that they were traitors to Odin. Oathbreaker, murderer, slanderer!"

I waited for him to stab the spear into Tyr's heart, but he didn't. He dropped the spear and grabbed Tyr by the waist and threw him onto the rowboat that the Hels had come in. The rowboat narrowed and shortened and the sides closed up over him and Tyr was lying inside a coffin, as still as a corpse.

"Where's Hel River gone to, Daughter?" Odin called up to the sky, where curtains of golden auroras danced across the stars.

"Back where it belongs," Sigyn Odinsdauaghter called down to him.

"Flowing along the Dead Shore," said Wind Kari, and flew down to stand on the bone deck, next to her brother Kalinn and, by what probably wasn't a coincidence, next to Knut.

"It's time for Tyr Hymirson to go there too," Red Hel said.

"There's a splendid hall waiting for you on the Dead Shore, Tyr Oathbreaker," Fair Hel said.

"Its walls and roofs are woven of serpents as twisted as your honor," Red Hel said.

"Its drinking horns will never get empty," Fair Hel said.

"Its drinking horns are full of bitter poison," Red Hel said.

"And you'll stay there forever," the two Hels said together, "like all the folk at Dead Shore. When our ship sailed to Ragnarok, our warriors were going to be the folk who came to us because they died in bed, of sickness and old age. We were going to give them a last chance to die valiantly, fighting for Uncle Odin against his enemies."

"Hail, Tyr Hymirson, Lord of Dead Shore!" said Odin Lord of the Dead. "Go to your eternal home."

The rowboat flew off toward the World Tree.

"What do you do with a burning sea giant early in the evening?" Loki asked, walking over to stand by Hymir's pyre.

"You could tie him up with my old skin," Orm said, as he wriggled out of his molted snakeskin and emerged in cat form. "It's strong enough to hold Midgard and Jotunheim and the ocean in their proper places."

"No," Odin said. "I'm going to have my valkyries put your shed skin back into the water so it'll keep the ocean from getting out of bounds when we're off getting drunk at the victory party."

"Does that mean I don't have to stay in the ocean any more?" Orm asked.

"You can go wherever you wish, in any form that you like," Odin said, "world-girdling serpent or lap cat or even human form if you ever find that interesting. Just come to me once a year at midsummer and tell me what you've seen and what you've done." And Orm promised that he'd do that.

"You could give Hymir's asbestos cloak back to King Surt," Red Hel suggested. "Then Hymir would burn to death."

"No," Odin said. "I promised Aegir that his cousin Hymir wouldn't die till Ragnarok came, and that means Hymir won't ever die."

"You could tie Hymir up in your war fetter,' Baldur suggested, as the rune rope glided down from the bowsprit and coiled up by Odin's feet like a pet dog.

"No," Odin said. "Just because there isn't going to be a

Ragnarok doesn't mean there won't be more fighting in the years to come. My rune rope holds my power to bind and to loose, to fear and to dare. Its touch freed you and your brother from the sleep binding of Tyr's sword, and it freed Orm Lokison from Hymir's knot. It's got too much power to waste on just Hymir."

"I'm glad to hear you say that," Garm said. "I'd hate to think there wouldn't be any more fights and adventures."

"Clearly my sister Hel took good care of you, Nephew," Orm said. "I've had enough fights and adventures this year to satisfy me for the rest of my life."

"I've got a fetter you can use on Hymir," Robin Grima said.

"Give it to me," Tidefyr said, and she bound it tight around Hymir, her hands sure and deft and untroubled by the raging flames that encircled him. "Hold fast," she told the fetter. "Hold till the end of forever or hold till Ragnarok, whichever comes later."

"Ship ahoy," came a call from the fireship. "Do you need assistance?"

"This is the *Valskip*," Loki called, "under the command of Odin God of Victory, and we need a tow to harbor."

The fireship threw a line of fire across the waves, and Loki caught it and made it fast to the aftcastle, and the *Muspel* towed the *Valskip* back to the shore of Jotunheim.

The beach we landed on wasn't smooth sand any more. It was covered with chunks of ice and boulders and fir trees. Tidefyr and Skadi pulled the *Valskip* up over the debris till it was well above the high tideline. The Valhallans and their companions took everything off the ship that they wanted, which wasn't much. Then King Surt came ashore and laid his hands on the *Valskip* and started the bone fire—for the bones that had been nailed together to make the ship and the bones the draugs had brought to fill her hold.

"Ship ahoy," Loki called out, but nobody answered from the boneship flying toward us through the sky, borne up by two valkyries.

"Greetings, brother-in-law," the valkyrie at the prow called back. "We found this lying about in Niflheim. We asked the land guardians if they wanted to keep it, and they begged us to take all the filthy bones out of their nice clean world."

"Lay it on the pyre," Odin told them, and they lowered it gently down onto the bonfire.

The flames rose up bright and eager, and the souls of the drowned folk who once wore the bones flew up from the sea, and the wind blew them away up into the sky, where they'd wait for the Norns to judge them.

King Surt's shipmates came ashore: Tidefyr's mother was there and her younger brother and his two daughters—and hundreds of her cousins who'd come with Loki to rescue her from the sea. They all hugged Tidefyr, and she introduced them to Fenris and Garm, and then to her other oath-mates and friends.

After that, Tidefyr and Fenris declared their betrothal before both their families and all their oath-mates.

Tidefyr clasped hands with Fenris and Surt bound their wrists together—three times with sunlight and three times with moonlight and three times with firelight—and had them pledge to share their warmth and light and not to burn one another. After that, Fenris found he could take wolf or human form at will, whatever phase the moon was, wherever Tidefyr was.

A valkyrie flew down and brought Odin a sword that he gave Fenris and a pearl necklace he gave Tidefyr.

"You'll have to wait a few days for my presents," Loki said.

"Just having you here with me is the best present you could give me," Fenris said.

"I'll give you better presents than that before we're done," Odin said. "Meanwhile, my next presents go to my Valhallans. They've served me well and faithfully, and I'm going to answer one question from each of them."

Knut and Bookwyrm and Drifa looked at Robin Grima, but she shook her head. "You ask first," she said.

"I spent years studying the eddas," Bookwyrm said. "What happened to the prophecies?"

Odin whistled to the sky, where Thought and Memory were circling over our heads, and his ravens flew down and perched on his shoulders. "Answer his question, foster brother," Odin said. "We can trust everybody who's here to hear us."

"The prophecies were all lies," Loki Wyrmtongue said.

"Beautifully written lies," Deceiver Odin said.

"The most beautifully written lies in all the Nine Worlds," Loki agreed. "Odin and I drank mead for nine long nights, dreaming them up, writing them down. Then I went up and down the Nine Worlds whispering them into people's dreams, and my brother gave up his left eye to put them in Mimir's Fountain so everyone who drank there would see them and believe them, and so none of our enemies would be prepared for what was really going to happen. We didn't tell anyone else our secret except Baldur, and he didn't learn it till Odin whispered it to him at his funeral."

Bookwyrm and Knut looked shocked. It's hard to hear that everything you studied and memorized was wrong.

"What about the Norns?" clever little Ratatosk asked. "Did you lie to them too?"

"There's only one safe way to lie with the Norns," Loki said, grinning. "It cost me three times nine nights of long hard work to persuade them to go along with the story, and even longer to persuade my wife to forgive me for neglecting her all that time, but it worked out well, now didn't it?"

"It worked out well," Odin said. "There were too many giants in Jotunheim for even Thor to kill enough of them for Asgard to triumph. We had to lure them out onto the ocean where their powers were weakest. We had to trick the sea giants into accepting allies who turned out to be their enemies."

"Hymir said there'd be a new generation of frost giants in nine winters," Tidefyr said, "and a new generation of hill giants in nine centuries."

"And they'll all come visit Utgard," said Odin All-Father Deceiver, "and no one will challenge the authority of the lord of Utgard over the land of Jotunheim any more than they challenge the authority of Aegir over the ocean."

"We'll conquer Jotunheim slowly and softly and sweetly," Loki said. "Utgard's lord will be known for his power and his generosity. Every midwinter he'll give his folk gifts: jewelry and furs, laptops and porn, and all of it with the message that the Asgard folk are their friends and relatives."

"What will you tell them about the Vanir?" Frost Kalinn asked.

"The truth," said Odin. "We'll tell them that the Vanir lost the war to the Aesir and crawled into their burrows and fell asleep, except for a few who changed their names and moved to Ireland."

"And except for Asgard's three hostages, who live in chains," said Loki.

"Next question," said Odin.

"Do I have to spend all my days in Valhalla?" asked Knut, "or can I come out sometimes and see Wind Kari? And what about Robin Grima?”

"That's at least two questions," Loki said.

"Take my question for one of them," Drifa said. "I've got all the answers I need," and she reached out to hold Bersi Bookwyrm's hand.

"Knut Nidhogsbane is free to go anywhere in Asgard," Odin said, "as long as he comes to my side when I call him, and so are the rest of the Nidhogsbanes. And that includes Kari Valwolf, even if it does mean that I'll have to look for a new guardian for the entrance door to Valhalla."

"I stood guard on Valhalla's entry for ten thousand years," Wind Kari said. "If that makes me a Valhallan, then I want to know why the stories called me Lokison and why you changed me to a male when you made me a wolf."

"Because I knew you were going to stand guard on Valhalla for ten thousand years," Odin said, "and I didn't want you to go into heat every year of that time, when the only wolves in Asgard you could turn to for consolation were my two pets and, if they were too busy on my affairs, your brother Fenris."

And then they were all looking at Robin Grima again.

"I'll save my question till later," she said, "if that's permitted."

"Save it up for as long as you want to," Odin said. "Is there anything else anyone wants to do or ask that needs a sober head?" Nobody could think of anything, so we turned away from the eternal bonfire—the boneships' would burn down in another week or two, but Hymir would burn forever —and went off to Aegirstead to get drunk.

CHAPTER TWENTY-ONE

Aegirstead is just a short walk up the shore of Jotunheim from where Hymirstead used to be—if you're a giant. You go south past Glacier Point and the maelstrom and then across the causeway. Or you can let a valkyrie carry you, which is a lot faster and safer and maybe even more comfortable if you're not acrophobic.

Aegirstead is also just a short walk down the coast of Asgard from Noatun, where Njord used to live.

And on Midgard Aegirstead is just a short sail from the northeast shore of the Jutland peninsula to the island of Hlesey, where the folk used to reap the land for salt, not grass, and where gourmets go to buy brown bee honey (it's the bees that are brown; the honey is the usual color).

We flew there in the arms of valkyries, and we got a good look at the World Tree on our way. Its leaves were dark green and its flowers were purple and it looked healthy in spite of the thousands of sharp little knives glittering in its trunk and branches as souvenirs of its encounter with Hel River.

Aegir stood at the doorway of his gold-bright hall. "Greetings, Odin Wanderer," he said. "You're always welcome here, and your followers are welcome for your sake, and many of them are welcome for their own sake as well."

"I owe you an apology, King Aegir," Loki Wyrmtongue said. "The last time I was here, I was rude to you."

"You were rude to everyone here," Aegir said, "and I was glad you didn't leave me out."

"I offer you self-judgment against me for my insults and threats," Loki said.

"When you pronounce your judgment," Odin said, "remember that I'll help my foster brother pay it if it's too much for him to afford on his own."

"I decided a long time ago what your foster brother owed me," Aegir said, "and he won't need anyone's help in paying it. Loki Honeytongue, I ask you to say a word of praise in my honor for every rude word you spoke in my hall, and to bring me an ounce of bright gold for every drop of blood you spilled here, and to promise me that you'll come to my aid, and bring all you friends with you, if fire threatens me or my family or my home."

"I swear by the Sun and Moon and by my eyes," Loki said, "and may I lose my sight if I don't keep my oath."

"Welcome to my home," Aegir said and stepped aside, and his wife and daughters came forward, and they washed our hands and feet with warm water and dried them with soft clean towels, and then they led us to the drinking hall.

Aegir's cauldron is as big as the ocean. Depending on which path you take to it and what you're thirsting for, it might be full of waves of foaming saltwater and drifting icebergs, or it might be full of cool ale with a head of bubbling foam, or it might be full of sweet mead, or it might be full of hot ale and baked apples and floating slices of toasted bread. Whatever it has to offer you, you're welcome to drink your fill of it.

VALHALLA: ABSENT WITHOUT LEAVE

We drank to the Nine Worlds and looked around to see people there from almost all of them: hill giants and sea giants and frost giants and trolls, dark elves and light elves (but no mist elves), four-horned Heimdall, and silver-haired Skuld, the youngest Norn.

"Greetings, foster son," Odin said and embraced Heimdall.

"Greetings, foster father," gold-toothed Heimdall said. "Yesterday night, the wolves at Skadistead stopped howling, and I went down to visit her guests, and we spent the long night talking about their misfortunes. I owe you an apology for doubting you."

"I'll forgive you this time," Odin said, "but don't make a habit of it. I'm going to welcome Loki and his children back to Asgard because they trusted me, and I've sent your cousin Tyr to reign over Hel because he doubted me."

"You know best, Father," Heimdall said.

"Where's Tyr's right hand?" Skuld asked Tidefyr.

"The mist elves ate it," Tidefyr said.

"What did you do with the right hand we gave you?" Skuld asked.

"I gave it to Tyr, and when he threw it away, I helped him get it back again. He's wearing it in Hel now, unless he's picked a fight with someone on Dead Shore."

Frigga Odinswife was sitting at the head of a table, next to her mother Fjorgyn, but when she saw her son Baldur, she ran to him, her bright eyes full of tears. "It's been so many centuries," she said, hugging him, kissing him. "Is it finally over, or will you have to go back to Hel's Hall?" Then she took another look at him and screamed, "What happened to your eye?"

"We're back from Hel's Hall for good," Baldur said. "Or at least unless Father sends us there again. And your son Hodur spent almost as long away from you as I did and had a less pleasant leave taking. I gave him an eye in compensation for the centuries of slander I never spoke up to correct. Welcome him back too, Mother."

"Welcome back," Frigga said, kissing Hodur. "I'm glad to know that now you can see the beauties of Asgard." Then she looked again and saw the Hels. "What's Loki's daughter doing here?" she asked. "And how did she split into two?"

"Tyr's Justice cut her two halves apart," Baldur said, "and they gave Tyr their kingdom in payment for his skill as a surgeon, and we're going to have a double wedding, next year on Summer's Eve, and we'd like you to help us plan it, Mother."

Frigga took a deep breath, smiled at the Hels, and said she'd plan the most splendid wedding Asgard had ever seen. "But first I need to know the brides' names. Your real names, I mean, not the one you wore as Hel Queen."

"I never officially named my children by Angurboda," Loki said. "They came upon me too unexpectedly, only a few minutes after I drove off the hungry dogs and sampled the lady's half-cooked heart. I barely had time to get back to Asgard before giving birth to the three children, and then for some odd reason I felt even more tired than I did after giving birth to an eight-legged horse. I've never been good at baby names, or I'd have named the horse something better than Slippery Sleipnir. I suppose I could call my beautiful twin daughters Helga Red and Helga White, but I think I won't be seeing them nearly as often as your twins will, so I'm going to let their bridegrooms name them."

The Odinsons and the Lokisdaughters whispered back and forth for long enough for everyone else to drink a mug of wassail and get a refill. Then Baldur said, "My wife-to-be is to be named Berg-ljot" ("*Light will save,*" Robin heard). "And my wife-to-be is to be named Bo-il," said Hodur. ("*Battle will cure,*" Robin heard.) "And we ask our father and their father to come to our wedding next year on Summer's Eve," the two said together.

"I'll be there," Odin said, which was either a proud father's promise or a prophecy.

"We'll all be there," Frigga said. She turned to Fenris. "Welcome back to you too, foster son," she said. "I hear you're thinking of getting married even sooner than my boys."

"Yes, foster mother," Fenris said, and introduced Tidefyr. "We'll set the wedding date as soon as we've found somewhere to live. My old rooms at your hall are too small for me now, let alone for a family."

"What sort of home are you looking for?" asked Fjorgyn (which means "soil" or "land" and who's the lady in charge of Asgard real estate as well as being Odin's mother-in-law). "I've got all sizes and all locations." She flipped through her book and noted that Baldur and Hodur were back and that she'd have to send a flock of valkyries to clear out the squatters who'd been hanging out in Baldur's hall of Breidablik.

"Anywhere except Heather Island," Fenris said.

"But near a river or lake or seashore," Tidefyr said, "where the sun shines by day and the stars shine by night."

"Some building that nobody else has ever stayed in before," Fenris said

"Or some land where we can build our own home," Tidefyr said.

Fjorgyn flipped past Njord's shipyard hall in Asgard and dead Hoenir's hall where the sea tides swept up the river twice a day, and showed them a rocky promontory jutting into the ocean on the eastern shore of Asgard.

"We'll build you a starter home there as our share of the bride price," Tidefyr's uncle said, "and you can redesign it to suit yourself when you've got time."

"I'll host your wedding at my hall," said Frigga, "if the bride's family doesn't mind coming to the fenlands."

"We're comfortable anywhere sunlight goes," said Surt.

"And anywhere fire can burn," said his sister, Tidefyr's mother.

Once they'd agreed on the next full moon for the wedding date, Skadi spoke up to say that she was looking for a small home in Asgard with a mountain view.

Fjorgyn began looking through her book, while Frigga turned her attention at last to her husband and congratulated him on how well his schemes had worked out.

"Our schemes," said Odin. "I couldn't have done it without Loki's help."

"Yes, you could have," said Loki, "but it would have been more work if you'd had to make up all those lies by yourself. The help you really needed came from my children."

"And from my Valhallans," said Odin.

Skadi settled on a home on the northern frontier, not far from the Yewdales, where Ullur Sifson went for skiing and hunting when he wasn't practicing with his hall of archers.

"You'll still need a hostess to keep an eye on your houseguests," Odin said.

"Send the draugs," suggested Skuld. "They owe you some service for getting them out from under the saltwater," and Odin nodded in agreement.

"I'm looking for some land where I can build a home," Frost Kalinn said. "Or better yet two homes—one for me and one for my sister. It needs to be within walking distance of Valhalla."

"Close enough to the World Tree to use a computer," Robin Grima said.

"And far enough away from Valhalla and Gladsheim and Vingolf that the nights are quiet," said Wind Kari.

"And close enough to Saga's hall to drop in and read the newest hero stories," said Knut.

"There's a vacancy at the entry door to Valhalla," Odin said. "I could have a shelter built in Glasir Grove for Valgrind's new guardian, but they'd have to be small buildings. No more than ten doors and a hundred windows and ten thousand square feet between them."

"My wife and I are going to stay in Valhalla," said Bookwyrm. "At least until she's learned more of sword fighting. And besides, we can't let Door Thirteen stand empty each day when the heroes march out to the courtyard."

Skuld raised her mug. "A toast to Robin Grima Jonson and her oath-mates and companions," she said. "They unraveled our weaving and preserved our future."

"I'm the one who started the unraveling," Ratatosk said modestly, purely in the interests of accuracy.

When they'd refilled their mugs, Odin gave the next toast. "Here's to the brave heroes of Door Thirteen of Valhalla," he said. "They've gone on a great quest, and they've defeated Asgard's enemies, and they've saved the Nine Worlds and the World Tree."

"I don't remember saving the World Tree," Knut said.

"You did that first," said Odin. "You did that when you killed Nidhog and watered the World Tree's lowest root with dragon blood. If it hadn't been for that, Hel River's knives would have killed the tree, and the Nine Worlds would have fallen off their branches, and even if Ragnarok never happened, everyone would still be lost in the darkness."

I felt a cold shiver running down my back at the thought of the World Tree dying the death of a million cuts. I had another mug of wassail, and then I excused myself and went home and took a look at my inbox. There were over ten thousand messages waiting for me to read. I looked at the headers, decided that none of them were more important than sleep, and went to bed, glad to be home at last. My two weeks of fights and adventure were over, and like Orm I'd had enough of them to satisfy me for the rest of my life.

Robin Grima and Frost Kalinn Lokison didn't feel like that, which, given the new tapestry the Norns had started weaving, was a good thing.

THE END

Author's Notes

Wikipedia articles on Norse myth figures are fairly trustworthy. Marvel comics and movies in the Marvel Cinematic Universe, however, should not be taken as representational of Norse mythology.

The Norse myths as we currently have them (in the eddas) were written by poets, and they got their information about Ragnarok from Odin. the Norse god of poetry. Wikipedia has a delightful article on "Names of Odin." At first glance it looks boring, but it repays investigation.

Odin's names include "Ancient One" and "Wise One" and "Terrible One," and "Deceiver" and "Swift Tricker." Given those names, it's quite interesting to see how the poets all absolutely trusted him.

This is a heretical novel. It clashes with a lot of what the Norse myths say about the Good Guys (the Aesir, who live in Asgard and are ruled by Odin) and about the Bad Guys (the hill and frost and fire and ocean giants who are going to invade Asgard and kill the Aesir at Ragnarok). And it clashes with everything that the Norse myths say about the Evil Guys: Loki and his Three Evil Children: Hel & Fenris & Orm.

Nine Worlds Geography

The Poetic Eddas and Prose Eddas both say that there are Nine Worlds, but they don't list them, let alone describe where they are. We do know that the Nine Worlds are all connected to the great World Tree, the Yggdrasil, an Ash Tree. There's an eagle at the top of the Tree, a dragon at the bottom of the Tree, and a mischievous squirrel named Ratatosk who runs up and down the Tree carrying malicious gossip.

The highest level of the Worlds contains:

Asgard, the home of the **Aesir,** who are ruled by Odin. Prominent Asgard folk include Odin's wife Frigg, Odin's clever but unreliable foster brother Loki, Odin's strongest son Thor, and Odin's foster sons Tyr and Heimdall, both born in the Ocean.

Odin sends the valkyries (the choosers of the slain) to get the souls of heroes. He takes half of them for Valhalla (Slain Hall) and gives the other half to Freya (a Vana hostage). The other Vana hostage in Asgar is Freya's father, Lord Njord, patron of Shipping. His home Noatun is on the ocean-side. The Ocean that borders Asgard is linked to the Ocean that borders the shores of Midgard.

The Rainbow Bridge of Bifrost links Asgard to Midgard. This bridge ends at the home of Heimdall, who keeps watch for Ragnarok.

Nearby is the **Well of Urd** which nourishes the highest World Tree Root; this well is where the three Norns meet and weave the fates of men and Aesir and Vanir and giants and elves.

Vanaheim, the home of the beautiful **Vanir**. The Vanir and Aesir fought two wars, until they finally made peace and exchanged hostages. Then the Vanir killed Mimir, one of the Aesir hostages and sent back his head. No one is sure what happened to the other hostage.

Asgard still has three Vanir hostages. Njord left his sister-wife in Vanaheim. The Aesir arranged to marry him to Skadi, a frost giantess. They spend half their time in Noatun and the other half of their time in Jotunheim at Skadi's home. Freya Njordsdaughter lives in Asgard. Frey Njordson lives in Alfheim.

Alfheim, the home of the beautiful **Light Elves**. It's ruled by Frey and his wife Gerd. Frey used to have a magic sword, which could fight on its own, but he gave it to his servant Skírnir, so Skirnir would use his magic wand to get Gerd to marry Frey. And now Frey's scabbard doesn't hold a sword anymore, just a stag's cast-off antler. The prophecies say the antler won't be as good as Frey's magic sword when Ragnarok comes, and that's why the fire giant Surt will be able to kill Frey.

The middle level of the Worlds contains:

Midgard ("Middle Earth"), the home of **Humans**. It includes Europe stretching south to Byzantium—and east to the Middle East. It includes the Atlantic Ocean stretching west to Greenland and then to Vinland. The Ocean somehow reaches up into the higher level to border Asgard and perhaps down to the lower level.

Under the Ocean live the **Ocean Giants**. And the Midgard Serpent entwines the Ocean and that lets him hold the Midgard World together.

Jotunheim ("Giant Home"), the home of **Trolls** and **Hill Giants** and **Frost Giants**. It lies in the great mountains to the north and east of Midgard, where only heroes are crazy enough to go. Some of its lands are bordered by the Ocean.

Mimir's Well is in Jotunheim. It holds Mimir's Head and one of Odin's eyes and the horn that Heimdall will blow to warn the Aesir that Ragnarok is about to start. The middle World Tree Root is in Mimir's Well.

Muspelheim, the home of the **Fire Giants**, who are ruled by Surt. It lies in the Tropics where it's always warm. Its days are never very short, and its nights are never very long. Its lands are bordered by the Ocean.

The lowest level of the Worlds contains:

Svartalfaheim, the home of the Dark Elves, the magic smiths who can create wonderful magic items. These elves die and turn into stone at the touch of Sunlight.

Niflheim, the home of the Mist Elves. No one is sure what these elves can do or how they are affected by sunlight or fire.

Helheim, the home of Lady Hel Lokisdaughter, who receives two sorts of dead guests:

people who ignominiously die from illness (like a cow who dies on straw) go to Lady Hel's elaborately furnished Hall.

slanderers, oathbreakers, treacherous killers, adulterers, and other sinners go to Nastrond (Corpse Shore), on the shore of a river of snake venom, where they are gnawed by wolves and the dragon Nidhog (Malice Striker).

Frigg's beautiful son Baldur ended up in Hel after his death. The eddas don't explain why this happened. Baldur didn't do anything evil, and he died from a weapon attack, not from illness. Then again, Saxo Grammaticus tells another version of the story. https://en.wikipedia.org/wiki/Baldr#Gesta_Danorum.

There's a spring called **Hvergelmir** ("bubbling boiling spring"). The lowest World Tree Root is in this spring, and the dragon Nidhogg gnaws the lowest World Tree Root when she's not busy in Nastrond gnawing the ghosts of evil people.

Interesting Reading:

Sagas

Heimskringla, or the Lives of the Norse Kings by Snorri Sturluson

The Sagas of Iceland: a selection—preface: Jane Smiley

The Sagas of Ragnar Lodbrok: translated by Ben Waggoner

https://www.sacred-texts.com/neu/ice/index.htm#sagas

Folktales and Myth

Folktales of Norway, edited by Reidar Chrisiansen, translated by Pat Ivarsen

The Norse Myths by Kevin Crossley-Holland

Scandinavian Folk Belief and Legend by Reimund Kvidland and Henning K. Sehmsdorf

The World Guide to Gnomes, Fairies, Elves and Other Little People by Thomas Keightley

And then perhaps read the collection of Irish folktales and myths: *Gods and Fighting Men, The Story of the Tuatha De Danaan and of the Fianna of Ireland*, by Lady Augusta Gregory. (https://www.gutenberg.org/files/14465/14465-h/14465-h.htm)

Compare the Fomorians (whose chief king was "Balor of the Evil Eye") with the Aesir—and remember that the Norse conquered Ireland.

History

The Viking Achievement by P. G. Foote and D. M. Wilson

The Vikings by Michael Wilson

The Vikings by Johannes Brondsted

Ibn Fadlan and the Land of Darkness: Arab Travellers in the Far North by Paul Lunde and Caroline Stone

About the Author

Lee Gold

Lee Gold grew up in a home with lots of bookshelves. There was Hans Christian Andersen and the Brothers Grimm and Oz. There was the Iliad for children and the Odyssey for children. There were the Shakespeare plays, and there were stories about the Shakespeare plays. There was the Greek myths, and there were the Norse myths. There was a Jewish Bible. There was Kipling's *Just So Stories* and *Jungle Books* for children and his *Plain Tales from the Hills* not for children. And every week or two there was a trip to the library and library books to take home.

The summer after Lee graduated sixth grade there was a trip to Canada, and on the ferry to Vancouver Island, she bought an SF magazine. And after that she kept on buying used Fantasy and SF books and magazines and getting them in the library. She also collected Kipling's books and Cabell's

Poictesme books. Her other favorite authors in no particular order include Tolkien, Bujold, Kage Baker, Sharon Lee's & Steve Miller's Liaden books, Heinlein's books up through *The Moon is a Harsh Mistress*, and Asimov's books up through *The Gods Themselves*. One day she read Eddisson's *The Worm Ouroboros*, which referred to Njal's Saga, so she bought a modern English translation of it and fell in love with its terse language and bloody plot; she bought a lot of other modern translations of other Norse sagas.

In the mid-1960s Lee and several other wonderful SF readers met at the UCLA Book Store and talked for hours. They founded The Third Foundation science fiction club, which met regularly each month. They attended Westercon XX (1967) and the Los Angeles Science Fantasy Society, where Lee met Barry Gold. They eventually became part of the filking community, writing lyrics about their favorite subject matters and singing the resulting songs at science fiction conventions.

Lee got an M.A. in English Literature from UCLA, but left academia and teaching English 1 (Exposition) for even odder jobs.

Lee Gold started playing Original D&D in 1975 and started Alarums and Excursions, her roleplaying game amateur press association, a few months later. She's written several professional roleplaying games, two about Japan, one generic. In 1990, after getting over three shelf-feet of books on Norse myths, stories, and history, she created the RPG VIKINGS.

Nowadays Lee Gold edits two fanzines:

Alarums & Excursions: https://en.wikipedia.org/wiki/Alarums_and_Excursions: a monthly roleplaying game amateur press association

Xenofilkia: https://conchord.org/xeno/: a filk fanzine

If You Enjoyed This Book Visit

PENMORE PRESS

www.penmorepress.com

All Penmore Press books are available directly through our website.

SON OF THUNDER
BY
STEVE MOORE

Esther Brookstone is at it again, this time obsessing about the life and times of St. John the Divine, all triggered by the discovery of a parchment hidden in the frame of a Botticelli painting that she authenticates. As in Rembrandt's Angel, she soon gets into trouble, and her paramour, Interpol agent Bastiann van Coevorden, again comes to her aid. A race to find the saint's tomb results, because Esther has competition. Three centuries of action involving the saint, the Renaissance artist Sandro Botticelli, and Esther and Bastiann, make this sequel a book of mystery, thrills, and suspense that will keep readers guessing.

A deftly crafted and consistently riveting read from beginning to end. Rembrandt's Angel showcases author Steven Moore's genuine flair for originality and his impressive mastery of the Mystery/Suspense genre.
—Midwest Book Review

PENMORE PRESS
www.penmorepress.com

THE MAN IN THE SPIDER WEB COAT
BY
PHILIP ACKMAN

Titus Buchanan, a professor who runs a think tank at Williams College, believes he's figured out how to stage a successful revolution. When the United Nations adopts a historic vote spelling the end of colonialism, Buchanan seizes the opportunity to test his theory. His laboratory will be the Splendid Islands, a collection of palm-fringed cays scattered across three quarters of a million square miles of the South Pacific. Its inhabitants will be his lab rats.

But complications arise. The Splendids belong to New Zealand, and New Zealand has no intention of giving them up. The United States has its own secret "space age" agenda for the islands. The Queen of England is bound to support New Zealand, but she doesn't want Britain to fall out with the Americans, who favor independence. Meanwhile, the islanders, gripped with revolutionary fever, have ideas about self-rule. Reverend Geoffrey Brown, originally recruited by Buchanan to run the revolution, joins forces with an unlikely crew of locals and sets out to match wits with powerful opponents.

PENMORE PRESS
www.penmorepress.com

Midshipman Graham and the Battle of Abukir

by

James Boschert

It is midsummer of 1799 and the British Navy in the Mediterranean Theater of operations. Napoleon has brought the best soldiers and scientists from France to claim Egypt and replace the Turkish empire with one of his own making, but the debacle at Acre has caused the brilliant general to retreat to Cairo.

Commodore Sir Sidney Smith and the Turkish army land at the strategically critical fortress of Abukir, on the northern coast of Egypt. Here Smith plans to further the reversal of Napoleon's fortunes. Unfortunately, the Turks badly underestimate the speed, strength, and resolve of the French Army, and the ensuing battle becomes one of the worst defeats in Arab history.

Young Midshipman Duncan Graham is anxious to get ahead in the British Navy, but has many hurdles to overcome. Without any familial privileges to smooth his way, he can only advance through merit. The fires of war prove his mettle, but during an expedition to obtain desperately needed fresh water – and an illegal duel – a French patrol drives off the boats, and Graham is left stranded on shore. It now becomes a question of evasion and survival with the help of a British spy. Graham has to become very adaptable in order to avoid detection by the French police, and he must help the spy facilitate a daring escape by sea in order to get back to the British squadron.

"Midshipman Graham and The Battle of Abukir is both a rousing Napoleonic naval yarn and a convincing coming of age story. The battle scenes are riveting and powerful, the exotic Egyptian locales colorfully rendered." – John Danielski, author of *Capital's Punishment*

PENMORE PRESS
www.penmorepress.com

Mistress Suffragette

by

Diana Forbes

A young woman without prospects at a ball in Gilded Age Newport, Rhode Island is a target for a certain kind of "suitor."   At the Memorial Day Ball during the Panic of 1893, impoverished but feisty Penelope Stanton draws the unwanted advances of a villainous millionaire banker who preys on distressed women—the incorrigible Edgar Daggers. Over a series of encounters, he promises Penelope the financial security she craves, but at what cost? Skilled in the art of flirtation, Edgar is not without his charms, and Penelope is attracted to him against her better judgment. Initially, as Penelope grows into her own in the burgeoning early Women's Suffrage Movement, Edgar exerts pressure, promising to use his power and access to help her advance. But can he be trusted, or are his words part of an elaborate mind game played between him and his wife? During a glittering age where a woman's reputation is her most valuable possession, Penelope must decide whether to compromise her principles for love, lust, and the allure of an easier life.

PENMORE PRESS
www.penmorepress.com